Absolutely loved this book. From the b
story and couldn't put it down! Heath
zle as the tale unfolds—a story of a mother's love, God's guidance, and friends'
kindnesses. . . . In Hana, Isaac, and the other characters, we are blessed with the
reminder that God never leaves us nor forsakes us.

Karen Sue Murdy, clinical exercise physiologist and motivational speaker

A tender story of failure, forgiveness, and relationships all wrapped up in a mother's love for her special needs son and a heavenly Father's care for His precious children, both young and old.

Kim Marxhausen, educational psychologist and author

In a gripping, soul-searching style, Kaufman shows deep sensitivity to the life of a special child and his mother. What a gift it can be to develop the trust of an autistic child like Isaac! In scenes that will stick in your memory, the author demonstrates the power of openness and forgiveness. . . . It is amazing how a Christian community can help heal the brokenness within us all.

David Ludwig, psychologist, co-author of *Christian Concepts for Care*

Kaufman does not shy away from difficult topics. She realistically portrays the difficulties of dealing with autism—everything from the misguided advice of strangers to the strain on marital relationships. But in the midst of the stress, she never loses sight of the intense love and joy that can be found. . . . She paints a portrait of hope and love, and by letting us know and understand Isaac and how he sees the world, she gives dignity to those who have this condition.

Cynthia A. Graham, author

Timely and relatable. You will feel the emotions of the characters as it sends a strong message in a gentle way. Kaufman's writing skills capture your attention and create a sense of actually being in the story! This narrative gives insight to real pain, deep hurt, and God's amazing love that turns everything for our good and His glory. . . . A tender reminder of seeking God first and patiently coming alongside one another in love.

Kim E. Bestian, author of *Blueprints for Children's Ministry*

A touching story of resilience and a reminder of God's providence. It will capture the heart of anyone who can identify with a child who is "different" and the challenges that may come along with that. Through rebuilding of faith, instilling of hope, and the love of a special friend, the main character shows that one can rise from the ashes of a broken life to one of newfound joy, happiness, and peace.

Laura Montgomery, Director of Educational Resources,
Lutheran Elementary School Association

Christ's love for His people and His Church is woven throughout this story and each of our stories. . . . Kaufman's characters are real—living, breathing, forgiven, and grace-filled people. She accurately depicts the joys and challenges of parenting a child with special needs—the joy in small victories, the isolation, the stress of worrying if you've done enough, the difficulty in finding a church home to embrace your child—all while reaffirming Christ's love for His hurting children.

Karen Wittmayer, Assistant Director,
Lutheran Association for Special Education

"So now faith, hope and love abide, these three, but the greatest of these is love" (1 Corinthians 13:13). Kaufman artfully portrays these themes in telling the impactful life stories of Hana, Isaac, and Pastor Matt. . . . This inspiring story reminds us of God's presence in everyone, as our faith leads us to hope and the overwhelming power of His love.

Karen Scuito, Director of Development,
Lutheran Association for Special Education

I was hooked by the third paragraph. . . . Hope Lutheran Church is peopled by folks we all know—or wish we did. Kaufman masterfully integrates biblical truths and sprinkles insights about autism and human nature throughout this lovely book.

Lenore Buth, author and blogger

A beautiful story that grabs you at the first page and won't let go until the end. . . . In the story of Hana and Isaac, we see how lives can be changed when we love and care for our neighbor without judgment. . . . A fantastic reminder that our heavenly Father is always with us, no matter how tumultuous life may seem.

Clarion Fritsche, missionary and homeschooler

Loving Isaac will broaden the perspective of readers who seek to reach out and be inclusive faith communities for all people who are hurting. . . . The novel explores relationships and their complexity in the context of real-life challenges—loss, change, abandonment, family turmoil, and the yearning for trusted others to rely upon. It is the story of healing, hope, and new life.

Mary R. Jacob, EdD, co-author of *Christian Concepts for Care*

Kaufman ushers us into the unpredictable and often confusing life of someone on the autism spectrum. . . . You might find yourself in these pages as church members show us what to say, and not say, when interacting with a special needs child and his mom. This is a compassionate, inside look at autism and the challenges and joys of loving someone on the autism spectrum. . . . A must-read.

Ruth N. Koch, MA, NCC, Mental Health Educator

LOVING
ISAAC

A NOVEL

Heather Kaufman

CONCORDIA PUBLISHING HOUSE • SAINT LOUIS

For Isaiah
and my brave family

Copyright © 2018 Concordia Publishing House
3558 S. Jefferson Avenue, St. Louis, MO 63118-3968
1-800-325-3040 · www.cph.org

Scripture quotations are from the ESV® Bible (The Holy Bible, English Standard Version®), copyright © 2001 by Crossway, a publishing ministry of Good News Publishers. Used by permission. All rights reserved.

Library of Congress Cataloging-in-Publication Data

Names: Kaufman, Heather (Heather M.), author.

Title: Loving Isaac / Heather Kaufman.

Description: Saint Louis : Concordia Publishing House, 2018.

Identifiers: LCCN 2017048925 (print) | LCCN 2017052023 (ebook) | ISBN 9780758657909 | ISBN 9780758657893

Subjects: LCSH: Mother and child--Religious aspects--Christianity. | Kaufman, Heather (Heather M.) | Kaufman, Isaac. | Autistic children--United States--Biography. | Autism--Religious aspects--Christianity.

Classification: LCC BV4529.18 (ebook) | LCC BV4529.18 .K38 2018 (print) | DDC 277.3/083092 [B] --dc23

LC record available at https://lccn.loc.gov/2017048925

Manufactured in the United States of America

1 2 3 4 5 6 7 8 9 10   26 25 24 23 22 21 20 19 18 17

So now faith, hope,
and love abide, these
three; but the greatest
of these is love.

1 Corinthians 13:13

Part I

Faith

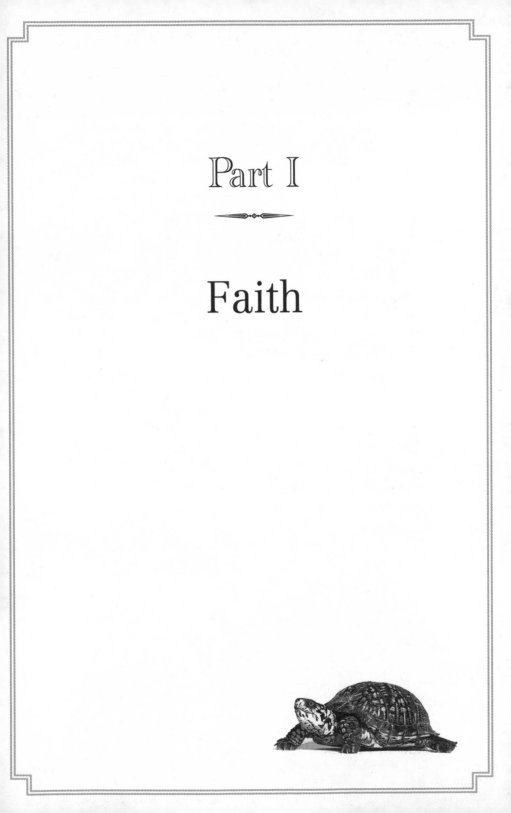

Hello, Sweetie,

We saw you today for the first time, your daddy and I. You were just a little blob on a screen, and it was hard for me to believe that it was really you. How could something so small be making me so sick? But then they pointed out your little stub arms and we heard the thump, thump, thump of your heart, and it all came crashing in on me—the realization that you are here, right now, inside me, alive and growing and waiting to meet me.

Your daddy was holding my hand and staring so hard at you, like you were a puzzle he was trying to figure out. "There's our guy." (Your daddy is convinced you are a boy.) "He's cute as a button!"

So that is what I'm going to call you: Button. We can't wait to meet you, sweetie. You are loved so much already.

XO

Mommy

1

The sun glinted off the water and threw flashes of light into Hana's face, which made it hard to keep an eye on her son. She shifted in the lawn chair and shaded her eyes, finally making out Isaac's squatted form by the water's edge. "Ten more minutes," she called and then slid deeper into her seat and tilted her head back, offering her neck to the sun.

It was nice—this heat, this unthinking heat. Sweat pooled at her lower back, and her thin shirt clung to her body. If she closed her eyes and focused only on the sensation of the sun hitting her skin, she could trick her mind into thinking, for a few minutes, that she was at the beach.

As happened all too often, however, whenever she closed her eyes for too long, the memories came back, shoving into her consciousness like uninvited guests. Screams, pained and piercing, ripped through her propped-up images of the beach, leaving them in shreds. Hana jerked her eyes open and blinked rapidly in the glare of the sun until her breathing slowed. Her eyes sought and found her son, who was still happily huddled by the creek. She leaned back, breathing easily again, her eyes wary slits, sentinels in charge of staving off the memories.

"Aunt Hana, Mom says to tell you dinner is almost ready." Preteen Clementine, whose wild red hair looked like it had just caught fire in the unforgiving Oklahoma sun, stood before Hana, her arms akimbo.

"Okay, thanks, sweetie."

"Isaac, dinner is ready!" Clem shouted in her cousin's direction.

"It's okay, I'll get him. You go inside and help your mom." Hana stood up and watched her niece tramp back through the dry, brown grass. "Isaac, it's time to go inside." Hana approached her son, watching as he settled deeper into his squat. His sandy brown hair was shaggy and spilled over his ears. She'd have to force him into a hair salon soon.

"But there may be turtles." Isaac mumbled his reply and kept his eyes trained on the water. "You said ten more minutes."

"I know, but your aunt Kara made a nice dinner for us, and it's ready for us to eat now. We can come back outside after, and you can look for turtles again."

"But maybe—then—maybe I will miss the turtles." Isaac shook his head, his voice catching in his distress, staring determinedly at the small creek.

It wasn't a scene—not yet. Hana knew she could engage in several more minutes of conversation before it became one, but she didn't have the patience right now and so skipped ahead to what she knew would work, even if it made her feel guilty. "Maybe you will see a turtle inside, Isaac."

That got his attention. He looked up at her briefly, his gray eyes hopeful, meeting hers fleetingly before jerking away. "But turtles don't live inside."

"Rocky does."

"But Rocky is my turtle."

"Yes, and Rocky told me his friends might be coming for a visit." She knew she wasn't really fooling her son, whose knowledge of turtles and their habits far surpassed her own, but she also knew that even the mere suggestion of seeing a turtle indoors was enough to niggle at his mind and prompt him to action. Sure enough, Isaac cocked his head, listening to her intently but still watching the creek.

"You know how we're visiting Aunt Kara? Well, maybe Rocky has family who will come visit him too."

Isaac stood and half turned toward her, his lanky frame swaying slightly with his hesitation. "Rocky's family is probably all over the place. How will they come here? What if they don't?"

"Then you can come right back outside after you eat, okay?"

"Okay, and maybe there will be turtles inside." She heard the wistful tone in his voice and could tell he didn't really believe her but wanted to badly enough that he was willing to come inside—just in case. "Maybe they will be there. Can that happen?"

"Yes."

"It *can* happen?"

"Yes, maybe it will happen."

"We *will* see turtles inside?"

"Yes, it's possible that we will see turtles inside."

Isaac nodded and finally walked up to her. Hana was taken aback again at his recent growth spurt. He could almost look her in the eye and he was only seven—*seven!* When did that happen? Granted, Hana wasn't very tall, but still it was unnerving how quickly Isaac was shooting up.

She walked quietly beside him toward the squat ranch-style house, her feet crunching through the brittle grass. It was going to take a while to get used to all the brown. This corner of the world could be summed up in three words: brown, dry, and flat. She would never have chosen to be here if she'd had any other option. They reached the back door, and Hana let Isaac go through first. The quietness of the backyard was quickly broken.

"Aunt Hana, Mom says you should get the drink orders." Alex entered the dining room carrying a platter of burgers. At fourteen, he was already taller than Hana.

"Okay, hon, I'll start with you. What do you want to drink?" Hana ruffled his bright red hair.

"I've got mine already, thanks." Alex grinned at her. *Such a sweetheart.*

"Can you take me to see Rocky?" Five-year-old Charlie came bounding into the room and tugged on Isaac's arm. His hair was a duller red than his siblings', but still shone in the evening light streaming through the window.

"Okay, but don't be long," Clem ordered as she entered the room behind her younger brother. Seven years separated the two, and Clem had embraced her role as big sister with both arms, adopting an authoritative tone and posture that communicated in no uncertain terms that even though they shared a mother, she, Clementine McCauley, was Charlie's "other mother," and he'd better listen.

"He's just in the other room. We'll be *right* back." Charlie rolled his eyes as he dragged Isaac away.

"What do you want to drink, Clem?" Hana asked her niece.

"Apple juice, please." Clem plopped down into her seat and whipped out her phone. "And Charlie will take milk—the vitamin D kind because he needs to add weight. The doctor says he's too skinny," she informed Hana in a matter-of-fact voice.

Hana chuckled as she entered the kitchen. "I have one apple juice and one vitamin D milk," she called to her sister, who was bent over checking the corn on the cob in the oven.

"Glasses are in the cabinet above the dishwasher." Kara nodded in the right direction.

As Hana retrieved the glasses and began rummaging in the fridge for the correct beverages, she glanced at her sister out of the corner of her eye. Ever since Hana and Isaac had arrived yesterday, Kara had kept a busy distance. She'd been kind and effusive over the phone, offering up her home to Hana quickly and assuring her repeatedly that they could stay until the new home in Richmond was ready for them, but Hana knew how easy it was to communicate sisterly solidarity from long distance. Up close and personal was another matter entirely. Was it concern over Hana's feelings that kept Kara distant or regret for opening up her home? Whatever the reason, the silence was unsettling—and annoying.

"That smells great," Hana commented as she poured apple

juice. "Do you have some off the cob for Isaac?"

"No, I didn't remember that he won't eat it on the cob," Kara sighed as she placed the pan of corn on the stove a bit too forcefully, causing some of the foil-wrapped pieces to skid into one another.

"It's not a big deal. I can cut some up for him." Hana finished pouring and moved in her sister's direction. Kara was three years younger, but the two had always been confused as twins growing up, Kara shooting up early and reaching her full height by grade school while Hana lagged behind. They stood side by side now, Hana methodically stripping corn off the cob for Isaac while Kara stirred the baked beans. They both had the same sporty, petite build, barely reaching five foot one. Their hair was the same light brown and currently pulled back in ponytails, Kara's curling at the ends and Hana's shorter locks spiking out like a starburst. Their biggest difference was in the eyes—Hana's were dark brown while Kara's were green. Hana glanced at her sister, noticing how Kara didn't turn toward her but kept her focus fixed on the beans. Talking hadn't come easily for them in years, so why was she so surprised by this strained silence?

"Hey, honey." Hana felt a hand on her back and turned around with a grin.

"Oops, sorry!" Troy laughed and ducked his head, moving to his wife and wrapping an arm around her waist. "You two are impossible to tell apart sometimes!"

Hana laughed, thankful for the levity that broke the tension between her and her sister and happy to see Kara finally smiling, even if the smile was not directed at Hana.

"Can you round up the kids?" Kara asked.

"Alex definitely takes after Troy," Hana observed as Troy left to do his wife's bidding. "Well, they all do, what with all that red hair, but Alex really does. It's sweet to see."

"Yes, I wouldn't be surprised if he surpasses him in height." Kara flicked a smile in Hana's direction. "Isaac's much the same way. He's getting so tall, he must get it from—" She stopped abruptly. "Oh, I'm sorry," she mumbled.

"No, it's okay." Hana smiled and tried to sound casual. "Yes, Isaac gets his height from his dad. Certainly not from me!" She tried a laugh, but it didn't stick.

"Have you heard . . . is he . . . " Kara's eyes lost some of their guardedness as she turned toward Hana and looked her full in the face for the first time since they'd arrived.

"Aunt Hana, Isaac wants to bring Rocky in the dining room." Charlie tugged at Hana's shorts. "No pets at the table, right, Mom?"

"It's okay, sweetie, he can put him on the china cabinet." Kara guided her youngest into the next room while balancing the baked beans. "Hana, can you bring the corn?" she shot over her shoulder, the moment broken.

Silence finally reigned in the McCauley house as they gathered in the dining room and settled into their seats. Rocky presided over the meal, appraising the family through squinty box turtle eyes from his perch in his aquarium on the china cabinet.

"Come, Lord Jesus, be our guest, and let Thy gifts to us be blessed." Troy led them in prayer before they began passing the burgers, corn, and beans.

"Where's my burger?" Isaac shouted.

"I forgot to let Aunt Kara know." Hana turned to her sister. "He doesn't like his burger on a bun."

"It's okay, we'll just take it off." Kara separated a burger and offered the meat to Isaac.

"No!" Isaac yelled, hitting his aunt's hand, dislodging the patty from her grasp, causing it to hit the table. "I want my burger!"

"I'm so sorry, he doesn't like any cheese on it." Hana grabbed the burger from the table and wiped up the greasy smear it'd left behind. "Isaac, you do *not* hit your aunt, do you hear me? Apologize to her."

Isaac grunted, frowned, and shook his head.

"It's okay, really," Kara quickly jumped in.

It wasn't okay, but Hana didn't feel up to forcing the issue. "I'm going to go fix it, Isaac. Calm down. I'll go fix it, and you can have your burger." She tried to keep her tone even in front of the rest of the family, but her words came out snippy anyway.

Hana left the table without looking anyone in the eye and made her way to the kitchen, where she ran the faucet and began scraping the melted cheese off the burger. Inexplicably, she felt her chest seize up and her breathing shorten, the signs of a panic attack that had become all too familiar in the past year. Silly, really, this was an easily fixed hiccup, one that Isaac would quickly recover from. He'd eat his clean burger, go back outside to the creek, and be happy. Still, she curved her body over the sink and turned the faucet on high to muffle her sharp gasps for breath. Her sister understood. Troy understood. She hadn't seen a lot of them, with Troy being in the Air Force and them moving every two to three years, but they'd visited one another enough for them to be familiar with Isaac. She needed to get control of herself. Hana willed herself to breathe evenly as she placed the newly washed burger back on Isaac's plate. She paced the kitchen, hands on hips, focusing on her breath until she calmed down enough to rejoin the family in the dining room. Her heart was still pounding uncomfortably, but it wasn't anything she couldn't manage in front of the others.

The family was all talking happily, and Isaac accepted the burger, as she knew he would, yet Hana couldn't suppress a mounting sense of dread. It was one thing to be understanding, but it was another to have Isaac in one's home. How long before they outstayed their welcome?

Isaac spotted one turtle after dinner and so submitted himself to bedtime preparations without complaint. It had taken a lengthy walk along the creek to find one, but it'd been worth it. Kara had given the two of them complete rein of the finished basement—a bedroom, bathroom, and family room all to themselves. Hana was overwhelmed by the generosity, but it also added to the feeling that she was intruding. She tucked Isaac into the air mattress on the floor in the bedroom, turned on his sound machine, and turned off the light.

"Rocky wants to be next to me." Isaac's voice sounded small in the darkness.

"Okay, sweetie, I'll move him."

"I'm not sweetie; I'm Isaac."

"Yes, you're Isaac. I'll move Rocky next to you." Hana placed the small aquarium on the floor next to the air mattress. "Goodnight, Isaac. I love you."

There was no response. Isaac was curled on his side, staring at Rocky. Hana left the door open a crack so the nightlight in the hall would shine through, then crept through the family room and back up the stairs to the main floor.

Troy was playing video games with Alex in the living room. They'd had to move the PlayStation up from the basement, and even though the basement television was twice as big as the one in the upstairs living room, neither had complained. Hana watched their avatars go on a dangerous mission for a couple of minutes, then moved to the smaller family room at the front of the home. Clem was curled up on the love seat with her phone. "Where's your mom?"

"Giving Charlie a bath."

Hana sat next to Clem and propped her feet on the coffee table. A surreptitious glance told her Clem was on Instagram. She felt like she should engage her niece somehow, but the words failed her. Instead she leaned back and stared at the ceiling, wishing she'd remembered to grab her book from her bedroom before tucking Isaac in.

"Do you miss Cincinnati? Do you ever miss *him*?" Clem asked abruptly. Her fingers still scrolled through the photos on her screen, her eyes flicking to keep up, but she'd shifted slightly in Hana's direction.

Hana looked uneasily at her niece. "You mean Zeke?" Saying his name aloud was harder than she thought it'd be. Fear rose in her chest as she thought of his face the last time she'd seen him—closed, furious, hard, his eyes boring into her as if truly seeing her for the first time and despising what he saw. It was a face that had become all too familiar. But then there was before. Hana let herself remember the before face with the winning smile, bright eyes, engaging laugh, and she swallowed hard before replying, "Well, it's complicated, sweetie. Yes, I do . . . sometimes."

"You're staying for the whole summer, right?"

"Yup. We're moving into our new home in August."

"Oh, good; I like having you here." Clem finally looked up from her screen, her wide green eyes meeting Hana's with uncomplicated honesty.

Hana found herself fighting tears. "Thank you, honey, that's so nice of you." She put an arm around Clem and drew her close.

"I guess Uncle Zeke was a jerk? At least, that's what Mom says. Is that true?"

Clem's question was like a stone tossed into the water, the ripples expanding in lazy circles, eventually knocking against the wall Hana guarded inside, the wall that contained the giant that was her past. She stared at her young niece and debated how to answer. She wasn't sure what Kara had told her children, what explanation for Hana and Isaac's sudden stay, but she didn't think she should be the one to discuss it with them. "Yeah, you could say that."

"I'm sorry." Clem turned back to her phone.

"Yeah, me too, sweetie, me too." Hana kissed the top of Clem's head and didn't say another word.

※

Kara poured them glasses of red wine, and the sisters took their drinks out to the back patio. The fireflies were out in abundance, their shiny bottoms reference points in the surrounding darkness, the drone of crickets their accompaniment. Hana decided to start talking first, to just jump in and break the tension suspended between them. "The kids seem well adjusted. How long have you all been in Altus? Has it been a year yet? Are they missing Michigan?"

"Almost a year." Kara leaned back and swatted at a bug. "It's okay; we're all adjusting fine. I much prefer the West Coast, though. Even while we were in Michigan, I missed the West Coast."

"The climate here seems like an acquired taste." Hana glanced around the dry backyard. "Not to mention the nearest town with anything interesting in it is forty-five minutes away." She'd meant it as a joke, but Kara wasn't laughing. Hana couldn't make out her face in the dark. Nervously, she sipped her wine. "I imagine that even though you're not on base, you can still hear the planes? Charlie must like that."

"Hana, how are you doing?" Kara cut through the small talk, her disembodied voice reaching out swiftly and softly through the dark. Hana could feel her sister's eyes on her.

"I'm—I'm okay," she lied. "I just hate feeling like I'm putting you out."

There was a pause. "No, don't feel like that. We're family. We're going to be there for each other no matter what. You're doing the right thing, you know—starting over somewhere else."

"I probably should have done this a year ago," Hana sighed. "I never should have let it go on as long as it did. I just didn't want to shake Isaac up any more than necessary."

"You didn't know Zeke would react the way he did. You couldn't have known. You were just taking things one step at a time."

"I suppose so . . . " Hana leaned back in her seat and stared at the dark silhouette of a nearby tree. She didn't really want to keep talking about Zeke. The twin images of him from her earlier conversation with Clem still crowded her mind, and she felt like she was being watched all over again, his presence palpable, even from so far a distance.

"So this job in Virginia . . . you're teaching freshman Algebra. Right up your alley, I'd say."

"Uh-huh."

"I think that's great!" Kara said a little too enthusiastically. "I'm so proud of you for getting that job back in Cincinnati, after . . . just, you know, getting back on your feet the way you did. And now with this new job in Richmond."

The compliment was clumsy and haltered. Hana knew what Kara was trying to do. She'd always been a glass-half-full kind of person, but her words sounded forced. Hana told herself to take it as a compliment and move on.

She had stayed home with Isaac before circumstances had landed her back in teaching a year ago. Kara had also stayed at home after her kids were born, but she'd always done it better than Hana. Her children were constantly being appropriately enriched through carefully crafted activities that were then photographed and shared. Hana's efforts had paled in comparison, and she'd lived with a guilty sense that she was never quite doing enough for Isaac as a result. Kara was built for motherhood, plain and simple.

The tension between them, however, had begun well before they'd entered motherhood. It'd begun back in college when Hana had called her sister and said, "So I met this guy . . . " It'd been downhill from there, Zeke remaining a sore spot between them. Kara disapproved of his demeanor, his interests, the way he talked. And then Kara had met Troy, a tall, red-haired cadet with freckles and an engaging laugh. He was the sun and the moon and the very definition of manhood. Kara's dislike of Zeke had amped up as she insisted Hana find someone like Troy. The first bitter seeds of comparison had been sown, and there they were left to germinate over the years.

"In Richmond, I can be close to Dad and still be as far away from Cincinnati as possible," Hana commented. She hadn't really wanted to go back to Richmond. She hadn't lived there since high school, and any roots or connections she'd once had would have to be reformed. But with their mother gone and their father in an assisted-living facility there, it was the logical place to go once it'd been obvious they couldn't stay where they were.

When she'd left Zeke a year ago, she'd let him have the house. She didn't want any part of the place that contained their old life together. She'd found an apartment for her and Isaac and left everything else behind. And now she was doing it again. She could hope that Richmond would feel like home after all, but really it'd been so long since she'd been back that it would be just like starting over. From scratch. Again.

"I'm sure Dad will enjoy that—having you close. I just wish Zeke hadn't made Cincinnati impossible for you all."

"Just as well," Hana said, a little more sharply than she'd intended. Zeke had been the one to receive a job promotion that took them to Ohio in the first place, and now any connections she had there also connected her to Zeke. She turned her head away from her sister and took a large gulp of wine. "It's just as well." She wished they could talk about the future without mentioning the past, but the past was dictating Hana's present and future plans, no matter how badly she wanted to wall it off, to keep the giant at bay, to pretend that part of her was done and over. Still, she pretended; if only for her own sake, she pretended.

"And the new house—do you have any pictures?"

Hana pulled out her phone and opened her photo album, handing it to Kara. "It's a small ranch. We'll be renting. I didn't want to deal with buying—at least not right now."

Kara swiped through the pictures, making the appropriate ooing and ahhing sounds as she did so, even though Hana well knew there was nothing spectacular about the house.

"It's an answer to prayer, isn't it?" Kara looked up, her face awash with light from the phone. "You finding this house and your new job."

Was she trying to evangelize her? They'd grown up in church together, but Hana's attendance had trickled down to nothing over the years while Kara's commitment had remained steady. At the mention of answers to prayers, Hana felt a mixture of guilt and sadness fill her. She'd tried praying again, when she was at her lowest, and look where it'd gotten her. "Yeah," she managed around the lump in her throat. "It wasn't easy taking Isaac out of a school he was just getting used to, but I'm hopeful he'll make strong connections in his new school."

"Yes, absolutely, I understand what it's like to be in transition—to have your kids hop from school to school. It's not easy."

No, you don't understand. It's not the same. You can't possibly understand. You have a wonderful husband and marriage, and three perfectly normal, healthy children. How can you possibly understand? Hana tried to uproot the ungracious reaction, but once there it held fast and festered. Kara had her life put together just right, and it'd happened effortlessly and without her even searching for it. She'd had Alex right away, while Hana had tried for years before finally getting pregnant. She never had to worry about money, while Hana had gone through many a lean year. Kara's was a prettily packaged life, the kind with ribbons and a bow that catches your eye. Hana's was a banged and dented UPS box left on the wrong doorstep.

In her darkest moments, Hana wondered if Kara was glad for the current situation, since it proved her belief all along that Zeke was no good. *She's giving us a home.* Hana tried to breathe through her angry thoughts. Her sister hadn't actually done anything to warrant this reaction. But that was always the way with Kara. She'd never come right out and *say* anything hurtful—but somehow what was left unsaid just piled up and up, a compost heap, enriching those bitter seeds planted long ago.

The sisters finished their drinks in silence. Hana's eyes followed a lightning bug across the yard, watching the progression of light and realizing it was a beat out of sync with the crickets. Blink, chirp, blink, chirp. She smiled at the observation and turned to make a comment to Kara but found that her sister was no longer there.

―――――

Hana entered the bedroom quietly. She'd gotten ready for bed in the bathroom next door and only needed to slip silently between the sheets. The sound machine was set to rain, its soothing shushing noise filling the small room. In the dim light from the hall, Hana could see Isaac spread-eagled on the air mattress, one hand resting on Rocky's aquarium, his mouth agape. He hadn't asked once for Zeke, although that didn't really surprise Hana. She doubted if he'd ask for her should the roles have been reversed. Gently, she knelt by Isaac and watched him for several moments. She grew braver and reached out a hand to slowly stroke his shaggy bangs. Her throat caught as she reached the small bald patch at the temple, where Isaac had pulled out his hair. He didn't let her touch him like this when he was awake. She couldn't remember the last time she'd gotten a hug out of him. A hug would wake him, so she contented herself with softly stroking his hair, his cheek, tracing his eyebrows.

The comfortable full bed stood ready only feet away, but Hana lingered. She stretched herself out on the floor, parallel to her son, staring at his peaceful face. He was so anxious all the time. So anxious. No hugs, no endearments, no touching. But in sleep—she loved how peaceful he looked. Hana lay next to her son, softly tracing his features and murmuring to him, "I love you, Button."

Hello, Button,

Well, it's official—you are a boy! And how your daddy is gloating, saying he knew all along. I would have been happy either way, but now knowing that you are a boy, I couldn't be any happier.

Your nursery is almost ready. Daddy wants to decorate it with Phillies memorabilia. He is determined that you will be a bigger fan than even he is. I finally convinced him to change it to a general sports theme. The Phillies decor is too big boy for me. Your father thinks the sports theme I chose is too cartoonish, too babyish. I tried telling him that you ARE a baby, but does he listen to me? Well, anyway, in this case he is. I'm getting my way!

So your nursery is almost done, and it makes me want to meet you even more. Two more months to go. I get so tired, and you kick me so much, young man! People ask me all the time if I'm having twins. Sheesh. You can imagine how that makes me feel. But you're worth the discomfort.

We're trying to find just the right name for you. We've waited a long time for you, sweetie. You are the answer to so many prayers! And you deserve a happy, joyful name. I think we'll probably wait until you come and decide once we see your sweet face.

XO

Mommy

2

Hana had been dreading Sunday ever since they arrived. She knew Kara and Troy attended Hope Lutheran Church regularly. In fact, wherever they were stationed, they always found a church and faithfully attended every Sunday. Church attendance had been sporadic for her and Zeke, and later on, with Isaac, it had dwindled to nonexistent. Even though it had been a while since Hana had tried attending church with Isaac, she knew it was important to her sister, and so she would try.

The morning was touch and go, as if Satan knew something of spiritual import was about to happen and so pulled out all the stops. Alex ate the last banana for breakfast, and since bananas were pretty much the only food Isaac would eat for breakfast, he had a meltdown. Clem woke up hating her hair and making sure everyone in the house knew it, so Kara spent most of the morning locked in the bathroom trying to wrangle Clem into a hairstyle that would get them out the door. Then Isaac had another meltdown as they were leaving since he found out that he couldn't take Rocky with him. Only the promise of Charlie sitting next to him in the car and lunch at McDonald's after church worked in coaxing him out the door. Finally, the McCauley clan was packed in their gray Chevy Traverse, minus Charlie, who was smooshed in the back of Hana's beat-up red Civic with Isaac, who was still loudly protesting both the absence of bananas and Rocky.

This is a test, right? Hana stared at the back of her sister's SUV as they left the subdivision, her heart racing. She'd abandoned her cup of coffee that morning since she already felt jittery and didn't need further stimulation. She'd increasingly felt this way over the past year—a mixture of panic and adrenaline that came in waves—sometimes manageable, sometimes not. But she managed the unmanageable ones anyway. Isaac was panicky enough for the both of them, and she couldn't afford to give in to anxiety herself. She offered up a stilted prayer. Lately, when she did pray, it wasn't with the easy familiarity that she used to have. Instead it was a series of requests—a blind SOS. *Help me breathe. Calm Isaac down. Don't let him make a scene.*

Hope was situated off a rural road, seemingly in the middle of nowhere, even though it was only ten minutes from town. The building sat surrounded by yawning fields. It was early June, and the winter wheat had recently been harvested, so the fields were stubbly and broken, which meant the horizon looked even more expansive. Hana parked in the dusty, unpaved lot next to her sister and opened the back door for Charlie and Isaac.

"This building looks brand new." She gestured to the lofty structure ahead of them. Hope was taller than she'd imagined, or maybe just appeared so due to its surroundings. Its rib-steeled siding made it look more like a barn with a steeple tacked on top than a church. It had a new industrial feel to it.

"A tornado ripped through here three years ago," Kara said as she shepherded her kids toward the building. "They had to rebuild, so it's pretty new."

The fluttery panic returned as Hana approached the front door. Charlie was holding Isaac's hand, and Isaac was calm and happy. Hana tried to slow her breathing, but it felt like someone was sitting on her chest, and she couldn't get past a few shallow breaths at a time.

There was a handful of people mingling outside and two greeters at the door. "Welcome to Hope!" A man in his midforties handed her a bulletin with a smile. He had on dark-washed jeans, boots, and a cowboy hat.

"Hana, this is our good friend Daniel Madison." Kara came up beside Hana. "Daniel, this is my sister, Hana."

"It's good to meet you, ma'am. My wife, Charlotte, is just inside, and I'm sure she'd like to make your acquaintance."

Hana noted the slow drawl as she shook his hand and followed her sister inside.

"The Madisons have about twelve acres of land not too far from here. You'll just love Charlotte and the kids." Hana felt the tension in her easing up a bit. Isaac was still calm, and she allowed herself to hope that the morning would actually be a smooth one. They all entered the narthex, which was vaulted and noisy. "The sanctuary is straight ahead," Kara said, pointing to two sets of double doors with glass panes. "And there's a hallway down each side of the sanctuary with classrooms off of them. Both halls dead-end into the fellowship hall, which is directly behind the sanctuary." Kara gestured with both arms, like a marshaler. "Also, there's a cry room—you know—should you need it." She glanced in Isaac's direction before quickly looking away. Hana felt a surge of irritation, which made no sense because she, in fact, wanted to know where the cry room was and would have asked Kara herself had she not offered the information. "It's the first room down that way." Kara pointed to the right of the sanctuary.

"Thanks. I'm hoping we won't need it." *Please let us not need it.*

"Oh, Charlotte, come meet my sister!" Kara skirted past Hana and gave a tall woman a quick side hug. Charlotte was thin and willowy, her bright blond hair long and flowing, adding to her swaying, easygoing vibe.

"You must be Hana. It's so good to meet you." Charlotte grasped Hana's hand in both of her own. A young girl, no more than five, with blond pigtails tugged at Charlotte's crinkle gauze skirt. Charlotte swooped her up in her arms. "This is my youngest, Ruthie."

"It's nice to meet you." Hana found herself smiling and genuinely meaning it. She could sense that Charlotte was an authentic person, which was refreshing. "Hi, Ruthie. I have a son, Isaac." Hana pointed to her son, who was still being led by the hand by Charlie.

"How old is Isaac?" Charlotte asked. "He looks like he could be around the boys' age. Zach is eleven, and Tommy is ten."

"Isaac is seven. Yes, he's tall for his age!" Hana laughed.

"Charlotte's oldest is best friends with Clem," Kara interjected, motioning to a corner where Clem and a girl around her age with a long blond braid were in tight conversation.

"Yes, Sam and Clem are inseparable," Charlotte laughed. "It's so nice to meet you, Hana. Maybe we can talk more after the service." People were beginning to slowly trickle into the sanctuary, the narthex was quickly emptying, and Hana's anxiety came crashing back.

"Yes, I hope so." She moved quickly to locate Isaac. She should have spent more time that morning prepping him. "It's time to go sit down, Isaac." Kara, Troy, and the kids appeared to be waiting on them. "You go on in without us," she told Kara. "We'll want to sit in the back anyway."

"We can sit with you," Kara offered hesitantly.

"Oh no, don't worry about it. Just sit wherever you normally sit. I think it'd be better for Isaac to be nearer the back in case we need to leave."

Kara nodded. "Come on, Charlie."

"No, I want to sit with Charlie!" Isaac shouted, his voice echoing off the vaulted ceiling. He held tightly to his young cousin's hand.

Hana looked beseechingly at her sister. "Can Charlie just sit with us, please? I think it'd help so much."

"Okay, that's fine." Kara's tone was flat and hard to read. She gave her youngest a peck on the head and entered the sanctuary with the rest of her family.

The narthex was now completely empty. Hana stood in the middle with the two boys, who were still holding hands. Charlie looked up at her in confusion. "Are we going to go sit down, Aunt Hana?"

Hana forced a deep breath into her lungs. It sounded like a gasp. "Yes, sweetie. Let's go sit down." She led the boys to the double doors on the right to be nearer the cry room. They entered just as the pastor led the Invocation. Hana ushered the boys into the very last pew, only surveying her surroundings once everyone was seated. There were two aisles leading to the front, which meant the pews were arranged into three sections. Hana and the boys were in the far right. It was a large sanctuary by any standard, which dwarfed the number of attendees. Hana imagined that if the current smattering of people in the pews were all sitting together, the number would actually appear rather large. The closest people to them were an elderly couple a few pews ahead. Hana turned her attention to the pastor. He was stocky and not much taller than she. His hair was a deep black, but his beard was streaked with gray, giving him a distinguished look. She glanced at her bulletin. Pastor Matthew Schofield.

Isaac was standing between her and Charlie, swaying from side to side and still holding Charlie's hand. Charlie stumbled and caught himself. He was such a patient boy. They'd moved on to Confession and Absolution, the congregation responding after the pastor. The words were familiar, and Hana tried to pay attention to them, but her mind was torn. She felt bad for Charlie, whose arm was being jerked around as Isaac began to rhythmically beat his chest with the hand that held Charlie's. She bent down. "Can you let go of Charlie's hand, Isaac?" she whispered. Charlie looked at her gratefully.

"No!" One word, uttered sharply and loudly. It punctuated the service, and several people glanced in their direction.

Hana instantly regretted addressing her son. He wasn't banging that hard yet, and he wasn't hurting Charlie. She should have left well enough alone. "Okay. Remember what we said? Inside voices. We need to be quiet." She shot Charlie an apologetic look.

Isaac settled once the first hymn began. He loved music, and although he never tried singing himself, he swayed harder whenever music played, a look of concentration on his face. His eyes were fixed on the organist. Once they sat down for the sermon, however, things turned south. Isaac had a hard time sitting still. Hana had brought crayons and paper and even a snack. She'd hoped to last longer before breaking out the food, but Isaac began moaning soon after everyone was seated. Hana offered him a box of animal crackers.

"No!" Isaac shouted and turned from her. A few more people turned to look in their direction. Isaac jumped to his feet and swayed in the pew. Since they were in the back, Hana didn't mind him standing, but Isaac still had poor Charlie's hand firmly grasped in his own, which meant that when he stood, he took Charlie with him. Hana's breathing became more labored, and her face burned with embarrassment. It was one thing to be surrounded by people who knew you and knew your son and hopefully were understanding. It was different when you were in a new place surrounded by people who didn't know you or your son and who were judging you based on first impressions. Why had she agreed to come?

Hana offered the crayons and paper to Isaac next. Charlie tried to help by taking the coloring materials from her and quietly coaxing, "Let's color, Isaac." Isaac looked at his cousin and sat down as Hana took a hymnal and placed it on Charlie's lap so they had a hard surface to use. Hana let out a sigh of relief as Isaac watched Charlie draw. She turned her attention back toward the front.

Pastor Schofield was in the middle of his message, and Hana hadn't heard a word. As Isaac quieted, Hana's sense of failure only increased. She wanted to pay attention, but she found herself feeling on edge, waiting for the next bout of discontent from Isaac. She couldn't remember the last time she'd sat through an entire message and actually listened. For a while, she'd tried listening to recorded sermons in the car, but she hadn't kept up with that. *I'm a failure, aren't I?*

she half thought, half prayed. *I wish for once I could be a good Christian like Kara, but I'm not. I'm not.*

Hana found herself observing Pastor Schofield and his idiosyncrasies rather than paying attention to what he was saying. He was a self-contained speaker, never straying from the pulpit and never using his hands for emphasis. Rather he stood in one place and gripped the sides of the pulpit as if it were a bucking bronco and he dare not let go. His voice altered between soft and pronounced. Whenever he got to a point, he leaned hard into the pulpit as his voice slowly mounted. The increase was so slow that she didn't realize he was shouting until the point was over and he was back to a soft cadence. It was mesmerizing, really.

"Aunt Hana, Isaac's *hurting* me." Charlie's voice was soft and whiny. Hana's head whipped around to check on the two boys. The hymnal had slid to the floor, where it lay sprawled spine up. "He won't let go," Charlie continued. "I've asked him, and he won't let go." Charlie's patience was astronomical, but he was, after all, only five, and Hana felt a wave of guilt sweep over her as she saw the way Isaac was gripping and twisting his cousin's hand.

"I'm so sorry, sweetie. Thank you for being such a good friend to Isaac. He doesn't mean to hurt you."

"I know, but it *huuuurts*." Charlie's voice caught on the last word as he began to kick his little legs back and forth in agitation.

"Isaac, you need to let go of Charlie's hand," Hana whispered to her son. "Do you see how Charlie is getting upset? You're hurting his hand, so you need to let go."

"No!" Isaac shouted and swung his head in a low arc back and forth. Hana felt pity for him. She knew how he hated to sit still. It triggered his anxiety, and holding Charlie's hand was the only thing that tethered him to calm, and now here she was tearing it away from him. Hana knew her sister would have a fit if she could see how far Hana had let this go. She could just hear her voice now. "You can't expect Charlie to babysit Isaac! He's only five, Hana."

Hana grasped her son's hand and tried to pry his fingers open. It was time to make use of that cry room, but she'd rather not take Isaac out while dragging Charlie by the hand. She could tell that her little nephew was at the breaking point, and pretty soon she'd have two meltdowns to deal with. Gritting her teeth, Hana pried Charlie's hand from Isaac's.

"No, no, no, no!" Isaac began shrieking. "I want Charlie! I want Charlie!" He leapt to his feet and began beating himself on the chest, hard this time. As he so often did when self-soothing, he began a full-throated moan that rose in pitch the more agitated he got. "Eeeeeeeeeee," he moaned, his voice filling the lofty sanctuary, the dull sounds of his fist connecting with his small chest a sickening accompaniment.

For a split second, the congregation held its breath, suspended, still looking forward to Pastor Schofield, who was still standing firmly planted, hands on pulpit. And then the reaction set in, and heads began to turn. Pastor Schofield paused midsentence, his eyes flicking to the back, and then he quickly cleared his throat and continued. Hana looked in horror at the dozens of faces all staring at her. She caught sight of a few disgusted expressions as she quickly stood and grabbed Isaac's hand and dragged him from the sanctuary. Isaac's moaning turned to shrieking again as she pulled him behind her. Finally, she was on the other side, in the narthex, where his shrieks still sounded loud, thanks to the vaulted ceiling. Why did they have to make this church like one big metal megaphone? Hana knew everyone inside the sanctuary could still hear Isaac. Her breath caught in her throat as she dragged him, still shrieking, to the cry room. Hana hadn't realized how much she'd been relying on this mysterious cry room. In the back of her mind, she'd thought, *At least I can take him someplace out of the way and quiet*. But as she entered now, three surprised faces met her. Hana stood in the doorway of a small, tight room with only a few armchairs. Isaac had stopped wailing to begin thumping again, his moaning filling the small room. Two of the women were nursing small children. The third was holding a squirming toddler. All three stared at Isaac in silence as he continued to alternately moan and shriek. *We can't stay here.* The thought flooded Hana with certainty. She couldn't stay in this room and try to console her seven-year-old son in front of these women with small children who would not understand. Quickly, she turned back around and, without a word, left the room, dragging Isaac back to the hall.

Kara stood in the middle of the narthex, a wild expression on her face. *"There* you are!" she hissed, striding toward them. "What on earth were you thinking, Hana? I went to go get Charlie, and he has *bruises* on his wrist!"

Hana stared at her sister, tears finally streaming down her cheeks. "I'm sorry, Kara. I'm sorry. I didn't realize how tightly Isaac was holding his hand. If I had known—"

"It's your *job* to know, Hana. Honestly, sometimes I feel like you think Isaac is the only kid who needs to be looked after. When I leave my son in your care, I don't expect him to get injured."

"I—I realize that. It's inexcusable, I know. I should have been paying better attention to him. I'm sorry." Hana's voice caught; the effort of keeping her sobs quiet had given her the hiccups. She stood hiccuping, trying to keep it all together. "I'm taking Isaac home now. Please tell Charlie I'm sorry." She turned quickly and brushed past her sister. Isaac's moans slowly tapered off as they left the building.

Hana paused for a second to get her bearings, blinking past her tears to try to find her car. Quickly, she dragged Isaac to the car, finally letting her sobs out now that there was no one around. She flung open the back door. "Get inside, Isaac." All the pent-up emotion found release in the phrase, which ended in a half hiss, half growl, "We're going home."

Isaac stared at the back seat as if it contained live snakes, and she knew the idea of sitting once again in a constrained area—and this time by himself—triggered panic in him. He began shrieking again, and Hana felt her anger and frustration turn toward her son as he continued to shriek into the abyss of the back seat. Why couldn't he give her this one hour? Was it too much to ask? "Knock it off, Isaac. I mean it!" Now that they were out of earshot of the others, Hana felt her anger kindle, unwanted and hot in her stomach. "Just knock it off, please, please, I'm begging you!" A row behind them, a young father was finishing up disciplining his daughter, who was shedding some tears of her own. Hana caught them staring and felt her face heat up. They'd probably heard the unchristian tone she'd just used. Her anger sizzled and leapt from Isaac to them. She realized belatedly that she was glaring at them.

"Daddy, he's being bad!" The little girl pointed at Isaac, as if to prove to her father that there were worse children out there than her.

That did it. It was one thing to berate her own son, and something else entirely to hear someone else do it, even if it was only a little girl. Hana stopped and snapped, "He has autism, okay? Are you satisfied? He's doing his absolute best, but you horrible people don't care!" With a half hiccup, half sob, Hana forced Isaac into the back seat, flung herself into the car, and peeled out of the parking lot. She'd just yelled, not only at her own child, but also at a random child and her father in the parking lot. She'd disrupted an entire worship service, bruised her nephew, and shouted at a little girl.

"I am a failure. I am a complete failure." She joined her sobs to those of her son and fled as fast as she could from Hope.

Hello, Button,

You're here, all nine pounds of you, and you are loud and challenging and beautiful. We've decided to give you a name that means "laughter" because we've waited for you for such a long time, and you are the bringer of such joy!

Your daddy likes to strip you down to just your diaper and carry you around shirtless. The nurse said something about skin-to-skin contact creating a bond, and he's taking it very seriously! I love seeing you in his arms.

You are hungry all the time, and I can tell that you are going to be a big boy. Maybe you will even be taller than your daddy! I wonder all sorts of things about you—the kind of boy you will become, what interests you will have, what talents and dislikes. And I wonder about the kind of man you will become. What kind of profession will you choose? Whom will you marry? Will you give me grandkids someday? Funny thoughts, but I like thinking them. It's like you are a mystery gift that will slowly open over the years—new surprises every day!

I hope you are passionate and funny like your daddy. I guess if you got my dimples, that'd be okay too. Oh, I wonder who you will be!

XO

Mommy

3

Troy found Hana in the basement packing. Isaac sat calmly eating McDonald's and watching a television show in the next room. Troy stood silently in the doorway, hands in pockets, not saying anything. Finally, he cleared his throat. "You don't have to leave. We don't want you to leave."

"Yes, I do. Kara doesn't trust me with the kids. How can I stay here when Kara doesn't trust me?" Hana moved quickly, her body still shaking with adrenaline. At some point during the horrible car ride home, her anger had shifted to shame and sadness, which, in turn, had morphed back into anger. She didn't know where she'd go, but anywhere other than here was an improvement.

"Kara is protective, especially of Charlie." Troy moved into the room.

"And I'm protective of Isaac," Hana snapped.

"Hey, hey, I'm here in peace." Troy raised his hands.

Hana sighed and paused her frenzied packing. "I know, and I'm sorry. It's just—you should have seen her, Troy. She was so . . . livid."

"Trust me, I know what she looks like angry," Troy chuckled.

Hana smiled shakily. She appreciated her brother-in-law; she really did. He'd always been much more levelheaded and understanding than her sister.

"This will blow over, I promise," Troy sighed.

"I love your kids, Troy. I would never ever put them in danger or intentionally harm them."

Troy looked at her earnestly. "I know, Hana. Absolutely, I know."

"But, I—I really need you all to understand that, especially since . . . " She broke off, unable to say the words, but Troy seemed to immediately pick up on her meaning. He observed her soberly.

"It's okay, Hana. Charlie wasn't seriously hurt, and he's already forgotten about it. I know—we both know—that you love our kids and love your son and want what's best for all of them. We know that. I promise."

Hana looked down, her anger giving way to sorrow once more. Troy put an arm around her, and she leaned sideways into him, crying.

"Look, I don't know everything that passed between you two, but I do know that Kara cried all the way home, and it wasn't out of anger. I think the two of you need to talk and sort this all out. She wants you to stay."

"I feel like such a failure. There's no way I can ever go back to church, even if I do stay here."

"Well . . . " Troy paused as if unable to find an appropriate response. "People should be understanding, especially in church. And if they're not, well, then shame on them."

Hana took deep, calming breaths. They stood in silence for a moment before she finally stood upright and swiped at her face. Her nose was running. "You're right; I need to talk to Kara."

Troy handed her a handkerchief. "She's in our bedroom."

Hana blew her nose and tried to collect herself. "Thanks, Troy." She squeezed his hand and left the bedroom, making her way past Isaac and up the stairs. The McCauley children were all in the dining room eating a late lunch of mac 'n' cheese and chicken nuggets. Hana snuck past them and down the hall to the master bedroom. She paused outside, trying to figure out what to say when she went in. Finally, she raised her hand and knocked.

A muffled "Come in" greeted her. Hana slowly opened the door to find her sister sitting on her big king bed. Her once immaculate makeup was a sorry mess—mascara streamed down her cheeks, and her lipstick was smudged. Hana opened her mouth, but nothing came out.

"I'm so sorry!" Kara opened her arms. Hana went to her, crying once more.

The sisters sat perched on the bed, both crying, their arms about each other. "I'm the one who should be apologizing. Is Charlie okay?"

"Yes, yes, he's fine. And he adores Isaac. I don't want you thinking that I don't want them together."

"I don't think that. I just feel so bad. I was only focused on Charlie helping Isaac. You were right; I need to look after him too. Sometimes I forget about that."

"That may be, but I had no right to accuse you of being negligent. Especially not after everything you've been through. If I was any kind of sister, I would have sat back there myself with you and helped instead of just leaving you by yourself with two kids to take care of." Kara leaned back and wiped her puffy eyes. "Please stay. We all want you to stay."

"I will if you're sure." Hana sat back, too, and then caught sight of the two of them in the dresser mirror. "Look at us! Quite the pair!" She laughed shakily.

Kara laughed, too, and squeezed Hana's hand. "And please don't feel embarrassed. We explained about Isaac to people who asked."

Hana felt a twinge of irritation at the idea of her son being openly passed around as a curiosity after church but quickly tried to squelch the feeling. In a way, it was nice that Kara had offered up an explanation, so Hana didn't have to. "There's no way I am going back."

"Oh, please don't say that! Church is a place for everyone."

"Maybe so. Well, it should be, I guess, in theory. But it's a lot harder when dealing with someone like Isaac. People may want to be accommodating, but the desire doesn't always mean results. And half the time the desire isn't even there!"

"Just so you know, Pastor came over to us immediately after the service and asked after you. He was very concerned that you feel welcomed back."

Hana flushed deeply. "That's kind, but I just don't see us going back."

"Well, he's coming here tomorrow to visit."

"What?" Hana looked up abruptly. "No, he doesn't need to do that!"

"It's what he usually does, Hana. He always follows up with visitors."

"But an in-home visit? That seems too much and too awkward."

"He visited us in our home when we first attended. Really, don't read too much into this. He isn't singling you out or anything, so don't feel embarrassed."

"But it's not like I'm going to live here forever or become a member or anything!"

"Still, it's a nice gesture. Would you rather a pastor not care about visitors?" Kara asked with a grin.

"No, I know, it's just . . . humiliating."

"It doesn't have to be. Pastor is very down-to-earth. Kind of introverted, but really nice once you get to know him."

"But what if he asks me personal questions? I don't really want to . . . get into anything."

"Then don't," Kara answered. "He's not going to pry, and you don't have to give any information that you don't want to."

Hana stared at a hanging spider plant in the corner of the room. A meeting with the pastor who had witnessed her son's meltdown was the last thing she wanted to endure, but Kara was right—it was a nice gesture, and it would probably seem rude if she didn't accept it. "Well, alright," she relented, "but it's going to be a very short conversation."

The children were awash in the glow of summer break, the time off still a novelty, still living up to all the hype and anticipation, the inevitable boredom yet to arrive. Kara had enrolled them in a summer camp, but that didn't start for another week. In the meantime, they spent their days at the community pool or vegging in front of the television. On Monday, they were all down in the basement, enjoying a snack after having spent the morning outside, when the doorbell rang.

Hana tried not to look nervous as she and Kara made their way upstairs. She'd dressed up for the occasion, as if the presence of a man of God demanded a certain level of decorum. As Kara led Pastor Schofield into the living room, Hana instantly regretted her dress. He was wearing a pair of jeans, boots, and a polo. In fact, he looked so completely approachable that he might have just been a friend stopping by.

"Hana, it's so good to meet you. I'm sorry we didn't get a chance to meet yesterday." He offered her his hand.

As Hana took it, she noted that he couldn't be taller than five foot six. His hand was large and warm. She swallowed her nervousness and squeaked out, "Good to meet you too." Could he tell that she was a bad Christian? Did pastors have a sixth sense about these things?

"Cookies, anyone?" Kara asked briskly, leaving the room before either of them could answer.

"Where's your son? I was hoping to meet him as well," Pastor Schofield asked. His eyes were a bright and inquisitive hazel.

"He's in the basement. I'll go get him." Hana was surprised that he'd asked after Isaac and not a little pleased. Quickly, she left and, once out of sight, jogged down the basement steps, her dress flaring. "Isaac, Pastor Schofield is here to meet you."

Isaac was sitting on the couch with Rocky next to him, watching Alex play a video game. "I'm busy."

"But he's come all the way here to meet you. And your aunt Kara has cookies."

Isaac looked up at the mention of cookies. "Okay, but I'm bringing Rocky."

"That's fine." Hana led her son upstairs and into the living room, where Kara was offering Pastor Schofield a platter of cookies.

"So this is Isaac!" Pastor Schofield put his cookie down and extended his hand.

Hana had never seen her son so dumbstruck. He stood silently, as if in awe, staring at the big-boned man before him. She laughed at the expression on his face. "Isaac, are you okay?"

He was staring straight at Pastor Schofield's face, which was unusual behavior for him. Typically, Hana had to work hard to get him to maintain eye contact for more than a few seconds. His mouth was slightly agape but now began working up and down. Finally, he blurted, "Do you have hair on your face?"

Hana flushed. "Oh, I'm sorry; he just says things—"

Pastor Schofield let out a huge laugh, tipping his head back as he did so. "Why yes. Yes I do, young man."

Hana waited for Isaac to correct him. He wasn't "young man"; he was Isaac. But the correction never came. Instead he set down Rocky and reached for the man's face. Pastor Schofield was short enough and Isaac tall enough that Isaac was able to get as high as the pastor's chin, where he commenced stroking his beard.

"Oh, Isaac, you can't just . . . " She shot Kara a look that said, *I told you this visit was a bad idea.*

But Pastor Schofield was bending over, his eyes twinkling in amusement. "It's okay, but I have to warn you, Isaac . . . " he paused as if telling a secret. "There may be leftover lunch in there."

"Ewwww," Isaac said softly, reverently, as he stroked Pastor Schofield's beard. "Does it hurt?"

"No, it doesn't. Maybe if you pulled it, it would hurt though."

Isaac nodded. "Sometimes it can hurt when you pull hair."

Hana could see that Pastor Schofield had noted the bald

spot at Isaac's temple but wasn't mentioning it. She swallowed past a lump in her throat. It was so good to see Isaac with a male figure again.

"I like your turtle, Isaac." Pastor Schofield was still bending over, somewhat awkwardly, at the waist, looking past Isaac to Rocky.

"Yes, he's my turtle. His name is Rocky." Isaac continued stroking Pastor Schofield's face with one hand and bent slowly to retrieve Rocky's cage with the other.

"He's a box turtle, isn't he?"

"Yes, he is an Eastern box turtle, or at least, at least that's what I read about. He looks like the pictures of an Eastern box turtle in my books."

"Ah yes, I think that's also called the common box turtle." Pastor Schofield glanced up at Hana and Kara's surprised expressions. "What? I'm a bit of a nature buff." Isaac's eyes were shining.

Hana had never seen her son talk this long with anyone before. His attention span was short, but it was as if the facial hair held sway over him, tethering him to the pastor and everything he was saying. "Isaac, can you let Pastor Schofield sit down?" Hana put a hand on her son's shoulder.

"But I want to touch it."

"How about you sit next to me, and then before I leave, you can touch my beard again?" Pastor Schofield suggested.

Hana looked at him in surprise, happy to have someone else offer a compromise for a change. Isaac seemed satisfied with this solution and sat next to Pastor Schofield on the sofa with Rocky on his lap. Kara offered the cookies again, and both pastor and boy dug in. Hana was too entranced at what she was observing to eat.

"Kara mentioned that you've come to stay for the summer. We hope you'll consider our church your home while you're in the area."

"Oh, um, I mean . . . " Hana was never sure just how much Isaac picked up on and didn't want to embarrass him in front of a guest.

"I think Hana was wondering if that was such a good idea, considering yesterday." Kara came to her rescue. "I told her that they are very welcome."

"Yes, absolutely." Pastor Schofield sat forward earnestly, turning to Isaac. "What do you think, young man? Do you want to go back to church next week?"

"No!" Isaac yelped, his brow furrowed.

"What if I told you that you could sit in the special pew right up front?" Pastor Schofield didn't miss a beat. "No one ever sits in that pew, but you could."

"Is it near you?" Isaac asked, staring hard at Rocky.

"Yes, it's the closest seat in the house."

"He doesn't like sitting still for long," Hana offered.

"But I need to take Rocky," Isaac said, as if outlining the stipulations of a tricky contract. "I can't leave him alone."

"Isaac, no, you can't—"

"Okay, it's a deal." Pastor Schofield extended his hand, not waiting for Isaac to offer a hand back but instead grabbing and pumping it enthusiastically. "You can have Rocky with you, and you can sit in the special pew right up front where you can see me, and then maybe afterward you can give my beard a pet. How does that sound?"

Isaac looked at a loss for words. He stared down at Rocky and mumbled, "Okay."

"Good, so that's settled." Pastor Schofield turned toward her. "So, Hana, now that your son and I have an agreement, what do you say? Will you come join us in the special pew next Sunday?"

Now it was Hana who was having a hard time maintaining eye contact. She looked from Pastor Schofield's intent eyes to her son's pleased expression, finally managing a mumbled, "Um, yes."

"Oh, I'm so glad!" Kara exclaimed, smiling so broadly that her dimples popped.

"And Hana, did I hear correctly that you're a math teacher?"

Hana shot a glance at her sister. *How much did you tell this man?* "Yes."

"Well, I don't know if you're interested or not, but if you're looking for work, the Madisons mentioned just the other day that they need a math tutor for their children."

"You met Charlotte yesterday. Remember, Hana?" Kara looked at her eagerly. "She homeschools their four children."

"They're so kind as to let me fish on their property," Pastor Schofield continued. "Last week when I was out there, Charlotte mentioned that she was interested in a math tutor for her kids over the summer. Would something like that interest you?"

Hana didn't know what to say. Pastor Schofield was observing her expression and quickly jumped in, "Of course, you don't need to decide on that now. Just wanted to throw that out there."

"Thank you; that's good to know." Hana was overwhelmed by the generosity of the man sitting in front of her. The question of how much he actually knew about her and her past gnawed at the back of her mind, though. Hana knew that Kara wouldn't go blabbing her story around, but a minister was different. People told ministers things in confidence all the time, embarrassing, horrifying things. How much had Kara told this man? And what must he think of her?

So as not to appear uninterested, Hana mustered up a few questions of her own. How long had he been at Hope? Ten years. How big was the congregation? Two hundred, although it constantly shifted since many of the members were Air Force, causing the congregation to change often. Was he from here? No, he was originally from Idaho. Hana didn't feel like it was appropriate to ask personal questions about hobbies and family, although it seemed, from the lack of a ring, that he was single. Pastor Schofield appeared to be an open book, but if she didn't want him prying into her personal life, then the least she could do was respect the same boundary with him.

The visit drew to a close, and Pastor Schofield let Isaac stroke his beard again as promised. "Now, I expect to see you and Rocky in the special pew first thing Sunday morning, okay? We've never had a turtle in church before, so it will be very exciting."

This made a world of sense to Isaac, and he nodded seriously before leaving the room. Kara lagged behind as they walked Pastor Schofield to the front door. "Thank you so much," Hana's voice caught. "Especially for allowing Rocky to come to church. It's been so long since I've been able to sit through a service. I—I'm looking forward to hearing a full message for once." Something fluttered in her chest—not the usual panic, but a breathless combination of anticipation and confidence that left her feeling simultaneously energized and weak in the knees.

"Absolutely. My pleasure. The way I see it, if Isaac needs that turtle in order to be in the house of God, then the turtle needs to be there. We wouldn't deny a person entrance just because he needed a service dog, would we? I don't see this as any different."

"How did you get to be so . . . good with . . . "

"I don't know that I'm especially good with people with different needs." Pastor looked away thoughtfully. "I suppose the pastoral office does train us to meet many different people with many different needs, but I think my training started in childhood." He paused, and a haunted expression flitted across his face. "When I was young . . . I knew a child who had autism, back before autism was even really understood to be a diagnosis. He wasn't—he wasn't treated well, and I think my training started there."

"Thank you," Hana choked. "I wasn't expecting you to be so understanding."

Pastor Schofield looked at her sadly. "That's a problem, right there. Not your problem," he was quick to add. "More of a larger church issue. Compassion, accommodation, inclusion—these things should never come as a surprise." He rubbed a large hand over his face. "God bless you, Hana.

I look forward to seeing you and Isaac on Sunday." He turned and nodded to Kara before leaving.

The door closed quietly behind him, and Hana turned around in a daze.

"Nice man, isn't he?" Kara smiled.

"Very nice," Hana said absently. "Very nice."

Matt's hands trembled and his heart thudded uncomfortably, pulsing straight through his hands and into the steering wheel, a booming bass to the radio's music. He'd thought of Elliott daily, constantly, until it'd become unbearable, and as a result he'd transitioned to keeping the thought of Elliott at bay, secreted away. Meeting Isaac today, however, had brought it all back, and he'd been helpless as it crashed over him, wave after wave.

Isaac's averted face had reminded him sharply of his childhood. Matt had lost himself in memories as Isaac's small hands found his face and sank into his beard. How precious in the sight of God were these, His children, no less made in His image for the physical and mental difficulties they endured while on earth. Matt swallowed hard, his chest constricting as he prayed fervently for Isaac and for his own heart.

Hello, Button,

You are such a wide-eyed, big boy. Eleven months old already! We are waiting for you to crawl, but you are perfectly content to just sit and stare at us. You seem to take everything in with those big eyes, just observing everything and everyone. You like to kick off of things, and you will bounce on our laps or shove yourself around the floor. You don't seem to know how or what you're doing, though, and always seem confused when you end up in random places.

You like the vacuum cleaner—A LOT—and will smile and coo when I clean. Our floors have seen more vacuuming in the past five months than in the past five years! You don't care much for toys; you're too busy observing your world and would much rather be carried around, so you can see all there is to see.

Your daddy and I love to debate which name you will say first. He works with you every single day, saying "Dada" over and over. You just look at him like he's lost his mind. I don't blame you, silly boy!

XO

Mommy

4

Only God was awake at five in the morning. With the sky still dark and light only a faint rumor, the earth stretched sleepy and silent before him. Pastor Matthew Schofield enjoyed these early hours, when the birds were just beginning to call to one another in anticipation of a new day, and a man could stand silent and still in the midst of God's creation. He stood along the bank of the Madisons' three-acre lake, fishing rod in hand, his feet firmly planted in the mud along the water's edge. He faced east and waited for a bite and for the light just beyond the horizon.

Matt tried to come out here once a week. The time outdoors spent in silence and prayer was just what he needed to stay fueled. It was easy to follow the direction to "be still, and know that I am God" from the bank of a quiet lake. Ironically, some found Oklahoma's wide-open landscape confining, as if the absence of buildings and the typical hustle and bustle of larger cities was isolating. Matt had always found the opposite to be true. The less cluttered his surroundings, the freer he became. Boise had also been open, but not like here in the South. Wherever you went in Idaho, you were always at the foot of a mountain, the suggestion of height always in the periphery, but here it was just flat, unhindered horizon, as if the space between man and God had suddenly shrunk.

A ripple sounded loudly through the silence. Matt tugged on his rod, dancing his line through the water, flirting with the fish. He hoped Hana would follow through with his suggestion to tutor the Madison children. He planned to also plant a bug in Charlotte's ear. It would do Hana good to be surrounded by loving people, and there were few people who were as welcoming as the Madisons.

He would need to bring Isaac out here. He often saw turtles perched on floating, rotting wood, their long necks arched, shells baking in the sun. Isaac would love it out here. Or maybe not. Maybe he'd be upset that he couldn't hold the turtles. Matt made a mental note to ask Hana about it.

After leaving the McCauleys', Matt had phoned Ron Edwards, Hope's head elder. "Ron, we're going to have a turtle in church this Sunday."

"Okay . . . "

"Can you let the rest of the board know?"

"Okay . . . "

Matt was jittery and excited about seeing Isaac and Rocky next Sunday. *"As you did it to one of the least of these My brothers, you did it to Me." The least of these. Lord, may Hope be a place where we minister to all of Your children. Give us open arms and open hearts.*

The people of Hope were welcoming overall, but as Matt knew all too well, people, even Christians, could be cruel even without meaning to be. *Soften the hearts of our congregation that they might receive this little one with love.*

He thought with a pang of Hana's words, "I wasn't expecting you to be so understanding." What had she experienced in the past that made her think otherwise? "I'm looking forward to hearing a full message for once." It was important for every person to be fed, no matter his or her circumstances. Matt recalled Hana's horrified expression as she'd dragged Isaac from the service and contrasted that with her bright face at the end of his in-home visit. *Feed the hungry, Lord. May Hope be the conduit of Your very self to those who are thirsty and hungry.*

Usually when he fished, his mind was a calm surface, the only activity that of praise and supplication to God; however, this morning Matt's thoughts were jumpy, his mind latching on to one thing and then another, his prayers all centered on a particular woman and her son. He thought of Isaac's hand in his beard and smiled. The wonder in the boy's face had been priceless.

"Freak! If you're going to play with idiots, then you're an idiot too!"

Matt's smile froze, his heart pounding. A small, broken face rose to the surface of his mind. Elliott. Elliott the idiot. Cruel taunts were sadly often the result of children observing and mimicking the cruelty of adults charged with their care. Hatred often started young and grew from there if left unchecked. Matt swallowed hard. The memories had continued to stalk him after the visit. It helped seeing that Hana clearly loved her son and took good care of him. He was glad to see Isaac so well loved, and Hope would love him too. *May we love him too, Lord, and teach him Your love through Christ Jesus . . .*

The sun was rising, its beams reflecting off the water and bouncing into his face. He let himself relax and enjoy his favorite part of the day, that moment between night and day, dark and light, before people had a chance to mess anything up—when everything was still pristine and brand new. Matt closed his eyes. This was grace—this moment when God made everything new.

Hana drove up the long dirt driveway. The Madisons lived only a few miles past the church, their property marked by a large wooden arch at the start of their driveway, the word "Welcome" bookended by rearing horses at the top. Charlotte had called on Tuesday, asking if Hana would come out that week and meet with her about tutoring. Pastor Schofield must have said something to her. Hana was a little taken aback by how much he, and now Charlotte, wanted her to feel welcome. It was Thursday, and Kara had offered to watch Isaac while Hana made the trip out to the Madisons.

The lane leading up to the property was long and winding. Hana could see a two-story white clapboard house in the distance. She passed a small grove of apple trees on the left. The trees were followed by an impressive vegetable garden, surrounded by tall chicken wire staked to the ground. To her right was a large barn and chicken coop. The drive ended in a wide gravel circle in front of the house. A carport straight ahead was already full of vehicles, so Hana pulled up behind it and parked. As she stepped out, two boys came running from the barn.

"Hey, are you our new teacher?" The taller of the two came to a stop by her car, his brown hair sweaty and matted to his forehead.

"Oh, um, maybe."

"Mom says I'm not catching on with my numbers and need 'extra help.'" The boy rolled his eyes as his brother joined him.

Hana laughed and offered her hand. "Well, maybe I can help you. I'm Hana."

"I'm Zachary, but everyone calls me Zach." The boy grinned, exposing two missing front teeth.

Hana shook his hand and moved on to the brother, who was staring at her shyly. He was a lot shorter than his brother and, apparently, less outgoing. "This is Tommy," Zach offered, shoving his brother in front of him. Tommy smiled at her, his curly brown hair adding to his cuteness. He grinned and ducked back behind his brother.

"Boys, quit talking Miss Hana's ear off and come inside!" Charlotte appeared on the wide front porch. "Hi, Hana!" She waved with a smile as her two boys sprinted toward the house. Hana waved back and followed them up the porch steps. "We weren't too hard to find, were we?" Charlotte pulled her into a hug.

"Not at all," Hana mumbled into Charlotte's shirt. The woman was so much taller than her that Hana felt like one of her errant kids, tumbling back home when called. "You have quite the place here. So much space!"

"Yes, we moved here about five years ago. There's twelve acres total."

"That's amazing!" Hana followed her inside, where the smell of sweets greeted her. "Do you all farm?"

"No, just outdoor enthusiasts," Charlotte laughed. "Daniel actually works as a grant writer for Western Oklahoma State College."

Hana tried not to laugh. She pictured the tall cowboy who'd greeted her on Sunday and couldn't imagine him writing grants. She just raised her eyebrows and nodded politely.

"We've always dreamed of having land. Now we raise chickens, grow a ton of produce, and love every second of it. We sell quite a bit, too, at the farmer's market. Would you like a quick tour of the place?"

"I'd love that."

"Boys, go keep an eye on your sister while I take Miss Hana outside." Zach and Tommy scurried off as the two women went out the back door. For the next half hour, Charlotte took Hana around the property, showing her the garden, apple trees, barn, chicken coop, and pasture. "We have one horse, Sublime. She's really more Samantha's horse than anything. Sam rides her in the pasture and gives riding lessons to kids. We also have a three-acre lake in the back of the property." Charlotte gestured past the apple trees.

"That's where Pastor Schofield fishes, right?"

"Yes, he's out early and often has come and gone before Daniel even leaves for work."

"He's very nice, your pastor," Hana said quietly.

"Yes, he is. He's kind of a private individual, very smart. You should try one of his Bible studies. It's almost like being in Bible college," Charlotte laughed. "I was so glad when he mentioned you to me. I had just decided to look for a math tutor when poof! God plops a math teacher right in my lap!"

Hana smiled but felt a little uneasy. She used to believe in God's providence, once upon a time.

Charlotte guided them back to the house. "I would greatly appreciate the help with my oldest three. Zach and Tommy are both in fifth grade; I held Zach back a year. Sam is in eighth and very advanced. Actually, that's my problem with her. I'm beginning to feel out of my depth. I'm not exactly gifted in the field of mathematics." She offered Hana a rueful smile. "The other two are just struggling, especially Zach, so I could really use the extra help."

Hana relaxed as Charlotte continued talking about her kids and their various strengths and struggles. Kara had assured her the other day that she hadn't told Pastor Schofield any specifics of Hana's situation, which meant Charlotte wouldn't know either. And, thankfully, no one had been nosy enough to ask, so Hana entertained hopes of spending the rest of her summer with her past a continued anonymity. The last thing she wanted was to appear as a tragic figure in the eyes of these church folks.

"I also wanted to mention that you're welcome to bring Isaac out with you," Charlotte said as they approached the back door. "And any of the McCauley children, really. Sam and Clem are best friends, and Ruthie has a bit of a crush on Charlie," Charlotte laughed.

"Thanks, I may do that!" They entered to find Ruthie sitting at the dining room table in tears. She looked up as the women entered and let out a wail.

"Mommy, Zach and Tommy won't fiiiiiind meeeeee!" Her chubby chin trembled, and her brown eyes spilled tears as Charlotte scooped up her youngest.

"What do you mean, honey?"

"They said we would play hide-and-seek, and then they didn't find me! I waited and waited and they wouldn't find me! And now I can't find them!"

"Why am I not surprised?" Charlotte sighed. "Would you mind waiting here, Hana, while I hunt down those two? Help yourself to the brownies on the counter. There's milk in the fridge."

Hana nodded as Charlotte left with a still-wailing Ruthie.

As the kitchen quieted, Hana looked around, observing the tasteful, rustic decor. The house was old and charming with tall ceilings and beautiful wooden trim. Charlotte had a rooster theme in the kitchen. There was an island between the kitchen and dining room and above it a beautiful hanging rack of copper pots and pans. Charlotte clearly had a love of ceramic pots, for they were everywhere—on the island, in the kitchen, on the table—and they all housed varying-sized bouquets of wildflowers. It was such a lovely, cozy atmosphere, and it filled Hana with a sharp longing. She and Zeke had never desired to live on land, but this cozy family atmosphere . . . they'd wanted that. They'd had that, for a while.

Hana swallowed the sadness filling her chest. Why was it that she couldn't just enjoy good things without sadness coming along and ruining everything? Or worse, envy rearing its ugly head? She felt like she was always mooching off of other people's happiness, picking up scraps wherever they could be found, grasping at the crumbs in a scraped-clean dish with only a hint of the flavor to satisfy.

She stared at the full pan of brownies cooling on the island, knife and plates at the ready, and willed her sad thoughts away. In an effort to busy her hands and mind, Hana began cutting the brownies into generous squares. She'd just finished when Charlotte entered, holding a boy by the arm with each hand. Ruthie had calmed down, probably after witnessing her brothers receiving their just deserts. Charlotte deposited her boys into chairs at the table and joined Hana in the kitchen. Ruthie sat smugly across from her brothers.

"My apologies; my boys seem determined to show their true selves to you today."

"I wouldn't have it any other way," Hana laughed. "Will I be meeting Sam?"

"Not this morning, she's at 4-H. But hopefully soon." Charlotte took the pan of brownies from Hana and headed to the table. "Would you bring the plates?"

Once they were settled and everyone had been served, Charlotte brought in their current curriculum to show Hana, along with some of the boys' completed homework. After nearly an hour of chatting with the family and looking through the books, Hana could tell that a large problem was simply that the boys' minds were prone to wander. They were two rowdy, active boys, mere feet from a great outdoors, and they didn't have time for sitting inside and staring at books. Hana again felt a horrible stab of envy. Did Charlotte know what treasures she had? Were the boys loud and rambunctious and sometimes irritating? Most likely. But how precious to see two strong boys becoming men, eager to help their dad on the land, aching to be a part of the wild. Isaac, too, loved the outdoors, but it wasn't the typical way a boy loved the outdoors. There was no shouting and running and building forts and playing hide-and-seek. There was no helping with chores and mimicking Dad and pretending to be a man. Instead, Isaac was content to pace by the water for hours, looking for turtles. Guilt, sharp and quick, ripped through her heart. No, she had a beautiful son. He was her unique boy. She wouldn't compare him to others. Comparison was never a fair game—not for Isaac, not for anyone. She knew this, and yet she played the game anyway—constantly.

As the meeting drew to a close, Charlotte gave the okay for her boys to return outside. With great whoops, they dashed from the table, the screen door crashing behind them. Ruthie paused her coloring and gave Hana a world-weary look. "Boys," she sighed.

Charlotte pecked Ruthie on the head and escorted Hana outside. "Poor Ruthie. She's my girly girl. Sam is so much older than her and is a hard-core tomboy, and you've seen how Zach and Tommy are with her. I intentionally try to carve out 'princess time' each day for Ruthie, just the two of us."

Hana watched with curiosity as a cloud passed over Charlotte's face. It was the first hint Hana had seen of something dark in her new friend's expression, and for the first time Hana wondered if perhaps Charlotte was hiding something painful too. She did this all the time, Hana realized; she let herself think that she was the only one hurting, the only one with something so big it couldn't be talked about. Silly, really, and selfish, to think that she had a special claim on what it meant to grieve, to hurt. And how foolish to let herself be so easily baited into jealousy, as if someone else's life was somehow charmed and pain free, just because there wasn't something glaringly obvious to the contrary. It was a gross oversimplification, come to think of it. Hana felt a fresh affinity for the woman before her. "Charlotte, thank you for the introduction to your family, for being so welcoming. I'd love to tutor your children."

"Oh, I'm so glad!" The cloud broke and Charlotte's usual sunny expression resurfaced. "Would once a week work for you?"

"Yes, absolutely. Perhaps Wednesdays?"

"Wednesdays it is." Charlotte drew her into another big hug, and Hana returned it this time.

As she drove back down the long gravel lane, with Charlotte waving in the rearview mirror, she heard shouting and glanced to the left to see Zach and Tommy racing from behind the chicken coop just ahead of her. She slowed as she approached them. They ran parallel to the lane, yelping and howling like wolves, grinning and waving, escorting her in a boisterous, prolonged farewell.

Hello, Button,

You are nearly two now, sweetie, and as adorable as ever. You are only saying a few words. You like to keep your thoughts to yourself, and sometimes I just wonder what's going on behind those big, bright eyes of yours. You have just started to walk, and it's a whole new world for you. You move your chubby hands along the couch for support, making your way to the nearest appliance so you can unplug it from the wall. Seriously, I wonder if you will be an electrician! You just love out-lets and cords and anything that has a button and will make noise when turned on. Such a curious boy.

Your daddy is worried that you aren't saying more words, but I try to tell him that you'll talk in your own time. I'm sure once you do, there will be no stopping you!

You are my big, bouncy, curious, wide-eyed boy, and I think you're perfect just the way you are.

XO

Mommy

5

Hana approached Sunday with much more excitement this time. She'd been talking Pastor Schofield up all week to Isaac, with the hope that it'd calm him and stave off the anxiety that had filled him last Sunday. "Remember Pastor Schofield? The man with the beard who came and talked to you about turtles? We're going to go see him today." Hana was in the downstairs bathroom, washing Isaac's face with a soapy washcloth.

"He wants me to bring Rocky."

"Yes, he does. And we're going to go sit right up front to hear him speak. Since we'll be right up front, you won't be able to stand because then you'll be blocking other people. But that'll be okay because as soon as the service is over, you can talk with Pastor Schofield again, okay?" Hana felt like an Olympic coach prepping her athlete for the performance of his life. And, surprise of all surprises, Isaac appeared to actually be listening to her.

On the ride to church, Isaac sat in the back seat, holding Rocky and looking out the window. Hana trailed her sister's SUV and parked next to her in the dusty lot. As she stepped out of the car, she wondered anxiously about people's reactions. Pastor Schofield had been understanding, but would anyone else be?

Kara stayed by her side as they entered the church. Hana hoped to see Charlotte and was looking around for her, when she was pulled into a ferocious hug.

"You must be Hana. I'm Lynn Clay, DCE here at Hope."

Hana tried to catch her breath and wiggled her way out of the overbearing hug to see who was speaking to her. A smiling young woman with bright brown eyes and curly brown hair stood staring at her. She wasn't much taller than Hana and was still holding Hana by both arms, as if she just couldn't get enough of her. DCE. Hana didn't know what that stood for and felt silly asking.

"Lynn is our Director of Christian Education," Kara interjected, as if reading her sister's mind.

"Oh, I'm just so glad to meet you! I apologize for not greeting you last week. I strive to meet all our new families and make them feel welcome." She moved to Hana's side and linked arms with her, walking her to the visitor's center at the left of the narthex. "Let me give you a welcome packet." She kept her grip on Hana's arm as she grabbed a folder from a stack nestled among numerous notices and sign-up sheets. "It's chock-full of information about our children's programs. There's also a visitor's card in there if you wouldn't mind filling it out and putting it in the offering plate during the service."

Lynn was talking briskly and professionally, her tone collected and friendly and her demeanor engaging, but Hana felt on edge, partly because Lynn was still holding her arm.

"Now where is that handsome young man of yours?" Lynn looked around and caught sight of Isaac with Charlie and Alex. Hana was about to call Isaac over, but Lynn was already dragging her over to the children. "There you are!" She dropped Hana's arm and squatted in front of Isaac, both hands on her thighs as she grinned at Isaac's averted face. "It's so nice to meet you, Isaac. I'm Miss Lynn."

Hana noted the singsong voice Lynn adopted as soon as she addressed Isaac. It was the over-the-top, cartoonish voice usually reserved for infants or especially cute pets.

Isaac looked at Lynn briefly before turning back to his cousins. Lynn caught sight of Rocky, and a look of surprise passed over her face. "What do we have here?"

"Isaac's pet turtle is very important to him, so Pastor Schofield said—" Hana began to explain.

"Pastor said the church has never had a turtle here before," Isaac jumped in, engaged now that his turtle was being discussed. "And he said I can bring Rocky and sit in the special pew."

"Oh, how nice," Lynn said, straightening. "I'm surprised he didn't mention it to me."

"I see you met Lynn." Pastor Schofield came up behind them and put a hand on Lynn's shoulder. "Hi, Isaac. I'm so glad you and your mother came today." He moved toward Isaac and knelt to get a better look at Rocky. "And you brought Rocky, just like I hoped you would."

Isaac took advantage of Pastor Schofield kneeling to stick his hand in the man's beard, causing him to laugh.

Hana couldn't help smiling. The nervousness she'd felt ever since Lynn had grabbed her dissipated at the sight of this man interacting with Isaac. He looked so different here in the context of church. Even though most of the congregation dressed casually in jeans and sundresses, Pastor took it a step up and wore dress pants, a checkered shirt, and a sports jacket. A clerical collar finished off his polished look.

Pastor Schofield stood and turned to greet her, folding her hand in both his own, his body momentarily separating her from everyone else. "Thank you for coming," he whispered, his eyes serious and bright. She flushed beneath their intensity. "Now, how about I show you to that special pew?" He turned and they were once again a part of the group.

Isaac and Hana began to follow Pastor, but Lynn put a restraining hand on Hana's arm. "I insist you let us take you out for lunch after service."

"Oh no, Lynn. You don't have to—"

"I want to. It's a chance to get to know you and Isaac better. We'll talk after." She gave Hana a knowing smile and released her so that Hana could follow Pastor Schofield and Isaac into the sanctuary.

The service was a completely different experience for Hana this time. She initially felt self-conscious following Pastor Schofield up to the front, as if everyone's eyes were on her, judging her every move, but then she snuck a peek behind her and saw that it was just all in her head. No one was staring, no one was pointing, no one was whispering. *Calm down, Hana,* she counseled herself. She'd thought that Isaac would be nervous sitting up front, but having Rocky calmed him enough that the need for standing and swaying was gone. He sat where he was told, keeping Rocky on his lap. Pastor Schofield made a point of sitting right next to him during the opening hymn. His deep baritone enthralled Isaac, who stood next to him and stared at him openmouthed. Hana felt slightly embarrassed since it was only the three of them sitting in the front pew, and they almost looked like a family, but she was too thrilled to see Isaac so engaged to be embarrassed for long.

The sermon was touch and go, requiring the greatest effort out of Isaac. For the most part, however, Isaac sat contentedly with Rocky on his lap, staring at him. A few times he got fidgety and began to rock in the seat and moan to go outside, but Hana was able to calm him by telling him he could go talk to Pastor Schofield as soon as the service was over. She'd redirected his attention each time to Pastor Schofield, who had been looking straight at Isaac each time and gave him a big grin and a wink when Isaac calmed down.

And then came the Benediction, signaling the close of the service. Hana's heart was full by this time. She'd actually been able to listen to the message, which had been a continuation on the congregation's study of Colossians. The service drew to a close, and Isaac leapt to his feet with a hearty "Amen!" Hana shushed him quickly but not before a smattering of laughter greeted them. But it was friendly laughter, and Hana found herself joining in. "Amen" signaled the end of waiting and the beginning of something else. It was time to eat, time to go to bed, time to get up from the pew. "Amen" was the starter pistol, and without stopping to ask for permission, Isaac was off, running to meet Pastor as he descended the steps.

Pastor laughed and drew Isaac into a quick side hug. "You did it, young man. I knew you could, and I think Rocky enjoyed himself. What do you think?"

"Can we show Rocky around?"

"Absolutely. I usually stand in the back to greet everyone as they leave. Do you and Rocky want to stand with me? That way everyone can meet him. Then afterward you can show Rocky around the church." He turned to give Hana a smile, and her heart leapt with happiness.

"Thank you," she mouthed.

"Your son is adorable." Hana turned to find Lynn at her side, watching Pastor Schofield and Isaac moving to the narthex.

"I don't know about adorable." Hana forced a smile. What was it about this nice woman that set her on edge?

"He did so well today."

"That's in large part due to the kindness of your pastor."

"Yes, he is kind, isn't he? Listen, if there's anything you need help with regarding Isaac, please do let me know. It's part of my job, and I'm happy to assist."

"Thank you . . . " Hana answered hesitantly. She wasn't sure exactly what help this overenthusiastic woman could be, but she appreciated the sentiment. She watched as a man carrying a toddler approached them.

"This is my husband, Nick, and our daughter, Amelia." Lynn turned to her family and took Amelia into her arms. "We'd love to take you and Isaac out to Buena Vista. It's a Mexican place that you all will just love."

Hana really didn't want to accept. Isaac was choosy with his food, and Mexican wasn't on his list of approved fare. She could just imagine the potential meltdown.

Lynn must have sensed Hana's hesitation, for she took hold of her arm again and moved her in the direction of the narthex, Amelia on her left hip, and Hana joined to her right. "Just say yes, girl."

They entered the narthex, where Pastor Schofield stood by the doors with Isaac and Rocky, introducing the pair to all who filed by. Surely Isaac had been tested enough today, and she hated to impose on his good behavior even more, but the woman at her side was relentless, and Hana was worried that she'd offend her if she refused. "Well, okay then." She smiled at Lynn.

"Wonderful! Let us know when you're ready to leave, and you can follow us there." Lynn released Hana, who turned to see Kara waiting for her.

"Lynn makes friends fast," Kara laughed as Hana approached.

"You can say that again." Hana rolled her shoulder, which was a little tense after being in Lynn's possession. "We're going out to lunch with them. It'd be great if you all could come too." The thought perked her up. It'd be so much easier with her sister there.

"That's okay, you all have fun." Kara scanned the narthex for her brood. "Well, I think we're off. Looks like you might be staying a while longer though." She nodded toward Isaac, who was proudly holding Rocky aloft and explaining to all who would listen that he was an Eastern box turtle.

"See you back at home." Hana hugged her sister and then stood near the visitor center, watching Isaac and Pastor Schofield and keeping an eye out for Charlotte. Finding her, Hana waved and smiled, crossing the space to greet her.

"I'm glad to see you back this week," Charlotte greeted her.

"I'm glad we came back. Isaac is besotted with your pastor." Hana pointed to her son.

Charlotte laughed. "Honestly, I didn't realize how good he is with kids until Isaac. Not that he hasn't always been loving, but Isaac seems to bring out the paternal side in him."

"Does he not have a family of his own then?" Hana asked slowly. "I mean, I assumed not since I didn't see one here."

"No, he's never been married. I don't think he really has

the desire either. Sorry, that's just speculation; ignore me."
Charlotte waved her hand as if to clear the air of her comment. "It's just that he seems very content by himself. He's a
great pastor and very knowledgeable. He has his PhD, and I
know he writes for various publications. I keep telling him he
should write a book someday."

"Wow!" Hana looked at Pastor Schofield in surprise, appraising him in a new light. "He's so humble. I didn't realize
he was so . . . intelligent? That sounds bad." Hana laughed.

Charlotte smiled. "No, not at all." She turned to watch
Pastor Schofield and Isaac. "It's nice to see this side of him.
It's definitely a softer side." Charlotte turned back around. "I
have to go, but I'll see you Wednesday?"

Hana nodded and watched her new friend leave. The
crowd in the narthex eventually thinned, and Pastor Schofield finally left his post to bring Isaac to her.

"Ready for that tour?" Pastor Schofield asked brightly.
"Now that Rocky has met everyone, I'm sure he'd like to be
shown around, right, Isaac?"

"Hana, you about ready?" Lynn approached them. Her
face brightened as she saw Pastor Schofield. "Wonderful
message today, Pastor, as always! We're taking Hana and
Isaac to lunch."

"That's nice of you, Lynn. I promised Rocky a quick tour
though. Can we impose on your patience a bit longer?"

It was asked so nicely and seemed so reasonable that
Hana was surprised at Lynn's quick frown. "Oh, I would, but
you know it's already getting so late, and Amelia really needs
to go down for her nap at her usual time; otherwise she'll be
a bear." She grinned comradely at Hana as if to say, "Kids,
what you gonna do?"

"It's just . . . I don't like to not deliver on my word, Lynn."
It was the first time Hana had sensed displeasure or disap-
proval from him. Despite the awkward moment, the fact that
it was in defense of her son filled her with warmth. "Five
minutes, tops, just to walk them to the fellowship hall and
back," he said.

"It's just a turtle, right? I'm sure he can 'see' the church another day." Lynn bounced a perfectly content Amelia on one hip and smiled brightly at Isaac, her voice jumping up to singsong again as she said, "Wouldn't you like to go out to lunch, Isaac?"

"Is Pastor coming?" Isaac frowned.

"Not this time, sweetheart, but you'll get to meet my family. Wouldn't that be nice?"

"I'm not sweetheart; I'm Isaac!"

Lynn backtracked quickly. "Oh, I'm sorry." Her voice fell to her normal tone. "He doesn't like nicknames? I didn't realize that."

"It's okay." Hana was barely checking her irritation. Why had Lynn been so quick to leave out the pastor? It would have been nice to ask him to join them. For some reason, a perfectly nice atmosphere had been shattered, and now she needed to act quickly to diffuse the situation. "Isaac, these people have asked us out to lunch. Maybe next week Rocky can have a tour of the church." Honestly, it was easier at the moment to bend Isaac to her will than Lynn, so she took the path of least resistance. Pastor Schofield was quick to back her up.

"Yes, next week will be great, Isaac." He bent to look the boy in the eye. Instead of replying, Isaac instantly reached out a hand to stroke Pastor Schofield's beard, the default response, it would seem, to the man crouching.

Lynn laughed at the sight of Isaac's hand in Pastor Schofield's beard. She leaned toward Hana confidentially. "Is that one of his sensory things? He likes the feel of hair?"

Hana bristled. "Not exactly."

Pastor Schofield continued to look intently into Isaac's face. "Next week, Isaac. Do we have a deal?"

"No! You promised today!"

"I'm going to get Amelia in the car," Lynn spoke up. "We'll pull up to the front—we're in a gray Impala—so you can follow us when you're ready." Lynn exited, leaving Hana and Pastor Schofield to deal with the aftermath.

"Instead of a tour inside, how about I give Rocky a tour of the parking lot?" Pastor Schofield was already offering a solution, while Hana's mind was still whirring with irritation and regret at agreeing to the lunch. "We don't want to tire Rocky out with too much new stuff in one day. An indoor tour next week will give both Rocky and me something to look forward to."

"Outside tour today and inside tour next time."

"Exactly."

"Okay, we can do an outside tour," Isaac relented.

"Deal." Pastor Schofield stood and led them outside. While Lynn strapped Amelia into her car seat, Pastor Schofield led Rocky, Isaac, and Hana on a tour of the parking lot that included an examination of the trees, front walkway, and sign. They ended their brief tour at Hana's car, Pastor Schofield holding open the door for Isaac.

Hana gave him a tired smile. "Thank you. This was the perfect compromise. As you can tell, Isaac does well when he has concrete explanations and things to look forward to."

"As do we all." Pastor Schofield returned her smile and held her door open as well.

Hana slid into the car, aware of her skirt bunching around her thighs and self-consciously smoothing it back over her knees. "Until next week."

"Until then." Pastor Schofield closed the door and thumped the top of the car in a friendly good-bye as Hana pulled out of the parking spot to meet the Impala out front.

Buena Vista was a small establishment on a quiet stretch of road a few blocks from downtown. The inside was noisy, as Mexican restaurants tend to be, with a smoky bar and blaring televisions overpowering the booth area. They were guided to a corner booth, and Hana could tell that Isaac was already getting jittery. "Rocky will be just fine in the car, Isaac," she assured him. "We rolled down the window and gave him plenty of water. You can feed him when we get home."

"But what if somebody *takes* him?" Isaac wailed.

"Oh, nobody will take him," Lynn jumped in. "Very few people would steal a turtle."

"But he's a special turtle."

"I'm sure he is," Lynn continued. Hana could tell that she was trying hard to avoid nicknames, the "sweeties" and "honeys" and "dears" backlogging in her throat. "He's a very special turtle to *you*, but I doubt that anyone else will want to take him."

Hana sighed. It was clear that Lynn was trying to be helpful, but she was failing to see things from Isaac's point of view. In his mind, they'd just left a million-dollar prize lying around for anybody to snatch up. "Isaac, how about we go check on Rocky throughout the meal. You're right, he's a very special turtle, and we'll go check on him in a little bit to make sure that he's okay."

"Okay, can we check in five minutes?"

"Yes, we'll check in five minutes." They settled into their booth, and Hana ordered a plain cheese enchilada for Isaac and the taco salad for herself before taking Isaac back outside to check on Rocky as promised.

"So, Hana, tell us about yourself," Lynn said when they'd returned. She dunked a chip in salsa while Nick entertained Amelia with crayons. "How did you end up in Altus?"

Hana took a big swallow of her soda, the sudden iciness hitting her chest hard and causing her to cough. "Well, we recently moved from our home in Cincinnati and are in-between homes right now. Kara and Troy were kind enough to let us stay for the summer."

"So you're from Cincinnati?"

"Richmond, Virginia, originally, and then went to college in Philadelphia . . . and then ended up in Cincinnati."

"Is that where you met Isaac's father? In college?"

The question deftly penetrated straight to the walled-off part of Hana, unexpected and sudden. She found herself gasping at the sharpness of it—this question that accosted like a battering ram. "Uh, yes, yes, I met Ezekiel in college."

She was whispering, as if by keeping her voice quiet, she could undo the damage Lynn had done, could lull the giant behind the wall back to sleep.

"What an unusual name—Ezekiel." Lynn turned to her husband. "We were considering some unusual biblical names for Amelia, remember, dear? It was Michal at first and then Naomi for a while, but in the end we just loved Amelia." She nuzzled her daughter's nose, causing her to giggle.

Hana smiled woodenly at the little girl, looking at her but only seeing the giant who, yes, was awake and seething behind the wall. It was infuriating how a simple question could undo all of Hana's best efforts, even more upsetting how oblivious Lynn was to Hana's discomfort. "Unusual, yes, I suppose so. He always went by Zeke, though."

"Has it been hard for Isaac?" Lynn leaned forward, casting a cautious eye in Isaac's direction. "To be away from his father?" she whispered.

Hana tightened her jaw. The suspicious part of her thought the question was less out of concern for Isaac and more about Lynn's desire to get the scoop on what, exactly, was going on in Hana's life. She tried to set her suspicions aside and give the shortest answer possible. "Isaac has been doing just fine. He's been very happy to stay with his cousins. They're so good with him, and he has enjoyed getting to spend time with them. He's also looking forward to Richmond, to reconnecting with his papa. We both are." She said it louder and more forcefully than was probably warranted, but now that the giant was awake, speaking positive words about her and Isaac made her feel like she was regaining ground, retaining some control. There was a past, yes, but there was also this bright future, and she'd speak as long and loudly as possible about that future. Before Lynn could ask another probing question, Hana jumped in with questions of her own.

"How about you two? How did you meet?"

"College as well. Love at first sight and all that," Lynn laughed. "Nick's a lieutenant. We've been stationed here two years. I was very fortunate to receive a call to Hope. I just love my position and the people I get to meet and impact." She shook her head, apparently overwhelmed at her blessings. "I hear you're going to tutor the Madison children. That's wonderful!"

Word certainly traveled fast. "Yes, they seem like a lovely family."

"They're the best, yes. Hey, listen, I hope you don't mind, but I'd like to ask some questions about Isaac, just so I can get to know you all better and, hopefully, better meet your needs while you're at Hope."

"Really, that's not necessary. We're going to be here for such a short time."

"It's no trouble! We want you to feel welcome no matter the length of stay." Lynn whipped out a form from her oversized purse. "Here, this is something you can take home with you and fill out at your leisure. Just some questions about personality, preferences, things like that."

Hana swallowed past the lump in her throat. "I don't know how applicable this will be to Isaac, seeing as he's—"

"Special needs?" Lynn filled in. "Totally okay. Just fill in whatever makes sense on the form. We want to include and love on absolutely every child who walks through our doors." She beamed in Isaac's direction. He was busy eating chips and sipping soda. "So like I said, you can just fill that out at your leisure, but in the meantime, I have some other questions. Like are there any additional needs he may have that we can accommodate?"

"Um . . . " Hana stared at the form. It was a compilation of multiple choice and fill in the blank. "I guess, I mean, you kind of saw how it went this morning. Pastor Schofield met with us last Monday and agreed to let Isaac bring Rocky into the service. That's probably the biggest help you can give us."

Lynn smiled tightly in Isaac's direction. "Yes, absolutely, I'm so glad that was helpful. Moving forward, though, if you have any other concerns or needs, you can absolutely come to me directly."

"Okay . . . thanks. I guess a separate cry room would be nice."

Lynn frowned. "What do you mean separate?"

"Well, it's just that your current one seems to be intended for small children. Last week there were nursing mothers in there, and I don't want to make them feel uncomfortable bringing my seven-year-old son in there."

"It's geared toward small children because that's usually who needs a cry room," Lynn stated, as if in defense of the current arrangement. "But I see what you mean about possibly needing a different space. I will certainly see what I can do." She pulled out her phone and input a note to herself.

"Thanks." Hana folded the form Lynn had given her. She felt awkward. Had Lynn only brought them out here to quiz them? Was this just "part of the job"?

Thankfully the food arrived, and the next half hour was spent eating with only a few more questions from Lynn. They fed Amelia food they had brought, explaining that they fed her only organic food, and it was just too hard and unreliable to count on finding items in restaurants that fit the bill.

Hana took Isaac to check on Rocky every ten minutes, thus assuring him that everything was okay. Isaac picked at his enchilada but mainly ate the chips. When the check arrived, Lynn insisted on paying. Amelia, who had been adorable and well behaved all meal, began to get fussy as they all left the restaurant.

"She's just tired," Lynn said as Nick strapped Amelia into her car seat. "I'm surprised she was so well behaved during the meal. We're currently going through the 'terrible twos.'" Lynn rolled her eyes and sighed. "You know what I mean. They have a mind of their own and realize they have their own opinions and want to assert them. She just wants to do everything herself too. She's so independent."

Hana just smiled tightly and didn't reply. Isaac was finally walking without support at two and had finally acquired a ten-word vocabulary. She looked at the pretty, eager woman before her and felt an unexpected wave of compassion. Lynn was just trying to help. She didn't know what it was like to hold your son tightly as he screamed through a panic attack, to go through rounds and rounds of medications to figure out the exact cocktail that would help him, to watch him like a hawk because you're scared he's going to hurt himself—to tear out his hair until his scalp bled or bruise his chest from incessant pounding. Lynn didn't know. How could she possibly know? And so how could Hana hold it against her?

"Thanks, Lynn." Hana opened her arms to offer a hug and watched as Lynn's face lit up.

"Oh, you're so welcome, Hana!" Lynn squeezed her tightly. "I'm glad we got a chance to get to know one another better." She walked to her car. "You call me if you need anything." She jiggled a hand near her face, mimicking a telephone.

Hana nodded and waved then turned to her own car and the tedious task of convincing Isaac to get in the back seat.

She pulled mindlessly out of the parking lot and then pulled over to the side of the road, realizing she didn't know how to get home from the restaurant. She took out her phone and plugged in Kara's address in the maps app. As she waited for it to load, she glanced at Isaac in the back seat. "What did you think of that lady, Isaac?"

Without looking at her, he replied, "She's loud."

Hana turned back to the front with a grin. She couldn't agree more. She glanced down at her phone, which now displayed the quick route back to Kara's. She was just getting ready to pull back into the street when a delayed ding of voicemail greeted her. A quick look showed it to be her cousin Vicky's number. Hana hit play and put it on speaker as she pulled into the street.

"Hi, Hana, it's Vicky." The nasal tone of her cousin's voice filled the car. "I thought I should tell you . . . Brian and I came home the other day, and there was a car, like, staked out in the front. I didn't think nothing of it, but it stayed there all night, you know? And there was someone in it, we couldn't see who, but just someone sitting in the car all night. We finally called the police."

Hana's heart began thudding uncomfortably.

"When the police showed up, the car pulled away real fast, went right by the house, and I saw it was Zeke."

Hana dropped the phone then scrambled to pick it up, to switch off speaker, close out of the voicemail, to stop Isaac from hearing anything further. The car swerved, and Hana's hands trembled. She glanced in the back seat, but Isaac hadn't noticed anything. Shaking, Hana opened her voicemail and put the phone to her ear, listening to the message again, this time to the end.

"So he was, like, staking our house out, Hana. He never came to the door or nothing. He just sat in the car for hours. Weird and creepy, you know? I just . . . thought you should know."

Hana dropped the phone again, not like the first time, as if it were hot and untouchable, but as if it were inconsequential—not there. As if she were holding her hand to her face for no reason whatsoever and in her hand—nothing.

She was driving in circles, finding streets and turning, always right, and so she was circling. She didn't know where she was or where she was going. Her phone that wasn't there, in her hand, was instead lodged between the seat and the center console. The maps app was still open, the automated GPS voice desperately calling out, "Make a U-turn in point one miles."

Hello, Button,

You are Mommy's curious, adventurous boy. Now that you're moving, you want to get into everything, see everything, be everywhere. We just celebrated your second birthday. You loved the cake but didn't understand the presents. You looked from them to us, as if you were saying, "What do you expect me to do with these?" I imagine by Christmas you'll get the idea and be tearing right into your gifts.

We have a doctor's appointment next week for your two-year check-up. The doctor agrees with your daddy about you not speaking—that it's something we should worry about. I disagree. You will tell us what's on your mind when you're ready!

So much energy bundled up in one little body! I can rarely get you to sit still in my lap long enough for a hug. You want down; you want out; you want to explore! You got a bat and ball from your daddy for your birthday, and he's been spending each evening tossing the ball to you, trying to show you how to swing. Most of the time the ball just bounces off you and you look at him as if to say, "Well, why'd you do that, silly man?" Then you throw the bat and off you toddle, lost in your own little world. I just know that when you invite us into that world, it'll be the sweetest moment. I can't wait.

XO

Mommy

6

The phone call came after dinner Tuesday night. "It's for you." Kara entered the dining room, where Hana was clearing the table.

"Is it . . . ? How did he . . .?" Hana jerked her head up, panicked, eyes latching onto Kara's.

"No, no, not . . . him. It's Pastor."

Hana let out a shaky breath and took the phone in trembling hands, turning to collect herself before bringing the phone to her ear. "Pastor Schofield?"

"Hi, Hana." His voice was warm, kind, open. "I wondered if . . . you're going to be out at the Madison home tomorrow, right?"

"Yes, I begin tutoring tomorrow, why?"

"Well, I was wondering . . . if you'd like, I don't know if it's of any interest to him, but would Isaac want to go fishing with me while you're tutoring?"

Hana sat down and stared out the sliding glass door into the backyard, surprised. "Don't you normally fish early?"

"Yes, but I can go out later, so Isaac can join me. Is that something you think he'd enjoy?"

Hana placed a hand against her mouth to keep from crying. This man was being so kind to her and her son. On the heels of that thought came another. He was being *too* friendly. If there was one thing Hana had learned, it was that you couldn't really trust anyone—not really, not fully. "That's so kind of you, but . . . " How to let him down without making it awkward? "Isaac loves the water, but I don't know about his being out there, alone, with someone he doesn't really know." She hoped it sounded like she was worried about Isaac's reaction and not about Pastor Schofield personally.

"Oh, of course," he was quick to respond. "If it would make him feel better, make you feel better, his cousins could join."

Hana paused to consider. That could work. Isaac wouldn't be alone with someone they didn't really know, and Charlotte had said that the McCauley kids were welcome anytime. "Okay, that sounds nice. I'll run it by everyone here, but I think that'll work out well."

"Wonderful! I'll bring a handful of rods and meet you all there tomorrow."

Hana replaced the receiver, not sure whether to be happy about this pastor's interest in Isaac—or wary. She didn't want to be suspicious, but suspicion was now second nature. It had been cultivated in her over the years, something she had learned to adopt—unwanted yet so necessary.

Matt cast his line and looked out over the water. Everything looked louder during the day. The sun full on the pond seemed to shout its presence. The brush along the water's edge had lost its sleepiness and was alive with creatures. The air itself hummed with alertness. Gone were the quiet, dark early hours, when peace lay thick and close, and the pond lay before him hushed and waiting. He glanced over at Isaac, whose face was engaged and happy as he crouched at the water's edge and looked hard for turtles. It was worth it.

Alex stood by his side, holding the extra rod Matt had brought. Clem and Sam had run off to the barn, and Ruthie had pounced on Charlie as soon as he'd entered the house, so it was only Matt, Alex, and Isaac here at the pond. Matt had shown Alex how to tie his line, bait his hook, and cast the line. Isaac hadn't been interested, which Matt had expected, and had instead opted to keep watch for turtles. Alex was proving to be a natural, jerking the line to tempt the fish, mimicking Matt's every move.

"Do you catch one often?"

"Sometimes." Matt smiled. "It's not really about the catch, it's about the possibility of the catch."

Alex nodded his head seriously. Isaac jerked to his feet and pointed. "There, I see one!" Sure enough, there was a turtle sunning itself on a log, its neck stretched out long and eager for the sun.

"Great eye, Isaac!" Matt was glad they'd spotted one, glad he could help bring such joy to the young boy. Isaac was skirting the pond, trying to find the closest point to the turtle. "Don't go too far," Matt cautioned. Isaac finally stopped, partway around the pond, but still in sight of the two fishermen. He crouched again and studied the turtle.

Matt didn't know what it was like to be a father. He'd never really wondered until recently, but Isaac elicited a sense of overwhelming protectiveness that Matt assumed was part and parcel to being a father. Such thoughts had naturally led him to the question of where Isaac's actual father was. When Kara had told him that her sister and nephew were coming to stay, she'd alluded to "personal problems back home." Did those personal problems involve Isaac's father? Or perhaps the father had never been in the picture in the first place. There was no ring on Hana's finger. Had she ever been married to Isaac's father? Usually, Matt didn't indulge such musings, as they were a temptation to judge, but he couldn't seem to shake the gnawing curiosity over Hana and Isaac's past. It'd grabbed hold of him and wouldn't let go. He glanced again at Alex, who was perfecting the fisherman's art of silence. Such a strong and loving young man. Growing up quickly. He probably knew about Hana and Isaac's past, but Matt wouldn't ask. That would be prying. He wouldn't ask, even though every part of him ached to know.

"I'm glad you invited us out today," Alex said, keeping his eyes on the water. "I know Aunt Hana is glad too."

"My pleasure." Matt hoped that was the case. He'd sensed worry in her voice over the phone, and he'd kicked himself for suggesting that he spend time alone with her son. He'd unintentionally invited himself into a trusted inner circle, a place he hadn't earned yet. She'd been right to hesitate.

"Even though he won't say it, I know Isaac is happy too," Alex continued. "My mom says he needs a 'solid male role model.'"

Matt swallowed hard, a lump in his throat. If he could be that for Isaac, even for a short time, he was glad. Here was a prime time to ask after the most obvious male role model in Isaac's life, but he resisted.

"Mom won't tell me what happened with Uncle Zeke, but it must be something bad. I mean, they haven't been together for like a year, but something must have happened because suddenly they're moving in with us, you know?" Alex's face showed frustration. "I wish they wouldn't treat me like a little kid. Clem and Charlie, I understand. I mean, they *are* little kids, but I'm old enough to know what's going on, right?" He turned to Matt. "I really hate it when they lump me in with the other two, like we're all the same. Sometimes they spell things out and Charlie isn't even there. Hello, I can spell," he snorted. "I don't like not knowing what's going on."

Matt felt torn. He was at a crossroads here, stuck between counseling a young man and satisfying his own fleshly curiosity. He breathed a prayer and proceeded cautiously. "Yes, you're at a challenging age, Alex. I remember when I was fourteen. You're becoming your own person but still under your parents' roof and their rules. But God places us in families for a reason. Your parents are there to guide and protect you, to nurture you to a place where you can build on the foundation they've laid. If they're not telling you certain things, they have good reasons not to, and I bet you it has to do with your welfare." Matt hesitated. "Uncle Zeke, so that's Hana's . . . ex-husband?"

"Yeah."

He thought he'd heard that right. Divorced—okay, that was one piece of information, innocently gained. "Well, if it's really upsetting you, and you want to know what's going on, you can always talk to your parents and express your feelings. There's nothing wrong with letting your feelings be known. You have two great parents who love you. They'll listen to you."

"Yeah . . . " Alex's voice trailed off. "Sometimes, though, you want things given to you without having to ask for them. Like, I want to be trusted without having to ask for it."

Matt shot a surprised glance at the young man beside him. Such an astute boy. Easy to forget he was just fourteen. "You're right. It's nice to have things given to you without asking for them. I do think your parents trust you, though. Withholding information doesn't mean they don't trust you."

Alex pondered this for a moment and then sighed heavily. "Yeah, I guess you're right." The fishermen's silence fell on them again, and Matt welcomed it so he could sort through his thoughts. He'd always been like this—an overthinker. Someone slow to speak, taking his time to process. He was a gatherer of information. Someone who was loathe to move until he'd weighed all the options and possible outcomes. Hana had been separated from this Zeke for a year, so were the "personal problems back home" tied to Isaac's father or to something else? He sensed that Hana was hurting. It was the pastor's dilemma. You see someone who is struggling and in need of pastoral care, but how do you minister to the hurt without an invitation? Matt felt the responsibility of the Office heavy on his shoulders. He felt certain that God had brought Hana and Isaac to him for a reason, but how to help without prying? *Lord, show me how.*

Matt looked up to see Isaac dropping stones in the water, ripples radiating lazily from the point of contact. His eyes still on the turtle, Isaac methodically grabbed the rocks at the water's edge and dropped them, plink, plink, plink, one by one into the water.

Elliott had loved water too.

Matt's eyes glazed as he continued watching Isaac, this time seeing another small boy instead. Plink, plink, plink. How many hours had he spent by the water's edge as Elliott dropped in one rock after another? Maybe that was what made Matt take up fishing. There was peace to be found by standing silent next to a body of water. Plink, plink, bloop. Occasionally, Elliott would let loose a larger rock, and it would enter the water with a heavier sound as the ripples accepted it quickly, enfolding and carrying it down. Matt had tried to teach him how to skip rocks once, thinking it'd be a more interesting activity. But no, Elliott preferred dropping them in, squatting and leaning over the water . . . an easy target for anyone passing by. Matt swallowed quickly, dismissing the memory, asking it politely to leave before it got too comfortable and decided to stay.

He looked again at Isaac's hunched form. Perhaps help came in the form of his physical presence. Just being there, being available should Hana and Isaac need someone. Zeke— an uncommon name. Had he done something to cause Hana and Isaac to come to this corner of the world?

The dusty air above the loop of road in front of the Madison home was filled with the shouts of children. Zach and Tommy, alive with the relief of being released from their math homework, were playing tag with Charlie. Ruthie was pouting behind her mother's skirt, her fingers in her mouth. She wasn't taking too kindly to being deserted by her sweetheart. Hana stooped to her level and gave her a grin. "I'm sure the boys won't mind if you go play with them, sweetie."

Ruthie grunted and turned her head into the folds of Charlotte's skirt. "No, they're too fast."

Charlotte patted her youngest's head. "Someone is overemotional today."

Ruthie had cornered Charlie into playing house with her while Hana tutored. Charlie had tried to turn it into a game of cops and robbers, had tried to convince Ruthie that they were robbers hiding out. Ruthie had acquiesced as long as Charlie agreed to be her robber husband and as long as they had a robber baby. Now he ran and whooped with the older boys, and Hana couldn't blame him for rejoicing in his freedom.

Sam and Clem joined them outside, and Hana was delighted to see how close the two were, even as she worried for Clem. The McCauleys would be moving again, and she'd be separated from her best friend. Clem was at the age when friends were becoming a formative part of her life, and Hana was sad to think of the two separated. Clem didn't have a built-in friend in the form of a sister, as Hana had growing up. Sure, she was close to her brothers, but seeing her giggling enthusiasm around Sam, Hana realized how good the friendship was for Clem and how fortunate Hana herself had been to have a close sister—even if that closeness had become strained over the years.

"There's Alex!" Sam shouted and waved to the three figures in the distance, bounding away from her best friend to meet them. Clem frowned and then followed suit.

Pastor Schofield carried several rods over his shoulder. Alex carried one as well, and Isaac followed closely behind them. "Looks like they had a good time," Charlotte commented. "Thanks again for this morning. I hope my brood wasn't too unmanageable."

"Not at all." Hana shielded her eyes from the sun to watch the fishermen arrive. "They were a pleasure to teach." Sam had caught up to the trio and was happily chatting up Alex as they approached the two women. Hana observed Sam's flushed cheeks and bright eyes, the way they never left Alex. Sam, who was seemingly oblivious to anything "girly," was now tucking her hair behind her ears, smoothing it out, grinning madly at Alex. Clem noticed the transformation too and was pouting in the back, casting a suspicious eye between her brother and best friend.

"How'd the fishing go?" Hana approached Pastor Schofield with a smile.

"We saw two turtles!" Isaac held out two fingers to her. "This is the *best* turtle place."

"That's awesome, Isaac!" Hana felt gratitude course through her. It'd been awhile since Isaac had had this much fun with other people.

"As you can see, it was a success." Pastor grinned at her.

"He wasn't any trouble, was he?"

"Not at all. Don't worry about it," Pastor was quick to assure her.

All three had gotten some sun, even in the brief time spent outdoors. Alex and Isaac both looked more cherry than tan. Pastor's full beard hid much of his face, but his brawny arms looked tan from the sun. He was such a conundrum. In the context of church service, he appeared polished, solemn, and studious—the published PhD. But outside church, he came across as a stocky landsman, at home in the outdoors.

"Thanks again for inviting Isaac along."

"We can make it a weekly thing if you want," Pastor offered. "That way, Isaac has some place to be while you're working."

Hana felt safe and happy with his eyes on her. She imagined it was part of being a pastor—this ability to make people feel safe and welcome. Did pastors learn this quality, or was it something innate? "Yes, I'd like that. Would you like to come back with Pastor?" Hana asked Isaac.

"To the turtle place? Yes!"

"Can you say thank you?" Hana placed a gentle hand on Isaac's shoulder and turned him to face Pastor. "Can you look him in the eye and tell him thank you?"

Isaac faltered but finally turned his face to Pastor. "Thank you."

"You're very welcome, young man." Pastor ruffled Isaac's hair, and Hana expected him to protest, surprised when he didn't. Inexplicably, Pastor had a free pass when it came to Isaac's pet peeves.

Sam was still talking with Alex, Clem a disgruntled third wheel. Charlotte had placed a pouting Ruthie on her hip and had joined Hana and Pastor, and the boys were still running wild.

"Why don't you come to Bible study tomorrow night?" Pastor asked Hana. "We begin with everyone gathered in the fellowship hall for a time of prayer, and then the men and women separate into their own studies. We just started new studies this summer, so you wouldn't have missed much. What do you say?"

Hana turned to Charlotte. "Do you and Daniel go?"

"We'd love to but just don't have the time this summer." Charlotte looked apologetically at Pastor. "But you should go. It'd be a great way for you to meet more people."

"I suppose I could go tomorrow, try it out." Hana turned back to Pastor.

"Wonderful!" Pastor smiled at her encouragingly. She bet there were dimples hidden beneath that beard. "We're glad to have you."

"Well, I'll plan to see you tomorrow then." Hana turned to Charlotte. "I better get these guys home, and thanks again. This morning was great."

"Thank *you*." Charlotte pulled her into a hug then reached into her pocket for an envelope that she tucked into Hana's hand. "Before you leave, I wanted to put the bug in your ear. Each summer we host a churchwide picnic on our property, and we'd love to see you and Isaac there."

Hana opened the envelope to find a cheery card listing all the details.

"As you know, Pastor, we already have the date approved by the elders." Charlotte pulled out another envelope and handed it to him. "If you could announce this next Sunday, that'd be great. We'll have a sign-up sheet for people to bring food. It's about a month from now, the weekend before VBS starts, but I'm hoping people still sign up and come."

Pastor took the envelope from her with a smile. "Certainly! I always look forward to these picnics. I'm sure everyone who is able will come."

"Well, you can definitely count me and Isaac in." Hana waved the card cheerfully at Charlotte. "And for the record, I'm happy to help in any way I can. Maybe I could come over and help you. How do you all normally set up?"

"Oh, really? That'd be so great. We have a handful of picnic benches that we set out along with crates and barrels for more seating. We have a hayride, horseback riding, and a bunch of outdoor games like horseshoes. Daniel can manage a lot of the heavy lifting, but it'd be nice to have help with some of the aesthetic stuff, like hanging up lights, and help with the baking, stuff like that."

"You name it, and I'll help you with it."

"You're a gem. I'll be in touch." Charlotte gave her another squeeze before turning to call the boys to the car. Zach and Tommy came racing from the barn, Charlie trying his best to keep up. Good-byes were said, hugs given, and soon Hana had everyone loaded into the McCauleys' vehicle.

Pastor led the way down the gravel lane in his car. When they parted ways at the road, he gave her a friendly honk. Hana smiled and waved to him, hoping he could see her in his rearview mirror.

<hr />

Matt saw her friendly wave as he drove away. For the first time in a long time, he found himself looking forward to seeing someone. Not that he didn't enjoy the company of his congregation, who were both friend and family to him. Over the past ten years, he'd spent many happy hours visiting with his congregants. His family was back in Boise, and he'd visit them on holidays on and off. They hadn't come to him since his installation, and that was okay. His parents were older, and he didn't expect them to make the long trip south to see him. Likewise, his sister was busy with her two children, and he was happy to come to them rather than vice versa. He visited them whenever he could, but he was happy at Hope.

Yes, Hope was both friend and family to him, but Hana was something different. What, exactly, he wasn't sure, but he didn't question it. Maybe through her involvement with the Bible study, which was a more intimate setting than Sunday morning worship, Matt, or someone else, could minister to her better. Even if she didn't confide in him, maybe she would find a listening ear in one of the women at the church. He knew he should be content if that was the case, but he found, surprisingly, that he wasn't. He wanted to be that listening ear himself.

Hello, Button,

I haven't written in a while. A whole year, in fact. And I'm sorry. It's just that . . . I don't know that you will ever read these letters. Or if you do, if you will really understand them. I feel like this is me writing to myself, or to an idea of who you are or will be—an illusion. Or a diary. I just don't know what this is anymore, but I'm going to try to write to you—for me. Just to keep alive the idea that you will read them and know me better, somehow, sometime.

This past year has been one of questions. It's been just one big question after another. The doctor has thrown a lot of words and information at us. You have been identified as being on the "autism spectrum." We didn't know what that meant. We had heard of it, but neither of us knew anyone with this diagnosis. We learned quickly, though, and are still learning, and it frightens me so much. To me you are just my sweet, busy boy. But you're not like other kids your age.

Therapies, medications, they're all being thrown our way. I've been reading too many books and websites about this, and I know I need to stop but I can't seem to do it. I feel like I've failed you somehow. I wish I could talk to your daddy about this, but he refuses to talk to me. It's as if he wants us to process this separately. I guess people have their own way of coping, but I wanted to do it together.

But we still love you, Button. We both love you so, so much—all the time and forever. If there's one thing I want you to know it is this: you are loved and wanted. We don't know what we're doing, but we're your parents, and we will do our best to help you, and we will love you furiously all the way.

XO

Mommy

7

Hana pulled into Hope's parking lot Thursday evening full of questions. What was she doing here exactly? She felt like she was playing church and at some point she'd be called out on it, exposed for the bad Christian that she was. Faith was something Hana had held onto in the back of her heart like a spare tire, something you haul around with you on the off chance that you need it. But here she was, frequenting this church and accepting the kindness of this pastor and all the while knowing she wasn't worthy. She didn't belong in church, not anymore. It'd been too long, and she was too broken. But Pastor's kindness drew her. She kept finding herself saying yes to him. He made her feel like God was smiling at her. She wished she could believe that, but her prayers felt blocked. How many nights had she stared at the ceiling, asking God to intervene, to come to her rescue, to show her what to do? She wasn't sure if God was listening anymore. And then when she'd tried to do what was right, tried to read His Word and teach Isaac about Him—well, that had blown up in her face.

This night would have been easier with Kara and Troy in attendance, but they'd taken a break from the Bible study for the summer, so Hana approached the church alone. As she neared the entrance, she noticed other attendees all holding

Bibles, and suddenly her bare hands felt conspicuous. She wasn't as familiar with the Bible as she knew she should be. She didn't even own one! Well, at least she *used* to own one before it'd been taken from her. That counted for something, right? Still, her empty hands solidified that she just didn't fit in at a Bible study. She loitered by the front door, feeling awkward and letting people pass her, before taking out her phone and quickly downloading a Bible app. There. If anyone asked, she could truthfully say she had the Bible on her phone.

"Hana, it's so good to see you!" Lynn came up behind her and linked an arm through hers.

Hana turned, her heart sinking. She didn't feel up to Lynn's incessant cheerfulness tonight. Nevertheless, she put on a smile. "Good to see you too."

"Well, come on in. You can sit by me." Lynn led her inside, and together they made their way to the fellowship hall in the back of the church.

"Where's Nick?"

"At home with Amelia. He's such a sweetheart to stay home so I can come. We're doing a study on women of faith in the Bible. It's been so great. I'm sure you'll love it."

Hana stifled a sigh. She didn't feel cut out for such a study. She hoped she wouldn't be expected to say or contribute anything. Hopefully she could just sit and listen, and no one would call on her.

The fellowship hall felt more like a gymnasium. The floors were hard and lined with colorful tape, as if ready for children's games. Hana wouldn't have been surprised to see some basketball hoops and bleachers nearby. Instead a handful of foldout tables and metal folding chairs were set up. A cluster of about twenty people were seated, Pastor Schofield standing nearby. Past him was the kitchen, stretching clear across the back wall with several large windows exposing industrial appliances and a long kitchen island.

Lynn directed Hana to a seat at the first table. Hana wanted to say hi to Pastor, but Lynn was already introducing her to several other women. Dorothy, a retired teacher, who was there with her husband, Harold. Nicole, a young mother of three children. Tim and Clara, a newly engaged couple. Hana smiled and nodded and tried to fit in, but she was thankful when Pastor cleared his throat and called for everyone's attention.

"Thanks for coming out tonight, everyone. Before we get this evening started, I'd like to welcome Hana Howard." He turned to her with a big smile. Hana tried to smile back but was too worried he'd ask her to say something in front of everyone. Instead she froze with a half smile, half grimace on her face. But Pastor simply said, "We're glad to have you with us tonight," and then turned to the rest of the room. Hana let out a sigh and tried to relax. "Does anyone have any updates or prayer requests?"

A couple of heads turned in her direction, and she wondered if people expected her to immediately raise her hand and unload her woes. Hana tried to ignore them and instead stared at the shiny clerical collar at Pastor's neck. It was very white and stiff. Did he iron it himself? Why did pastors wear those things anyway? A man across the room began speaking, and Pastor listened and wrote notes as he spoke. She used to be the kind of person who kept up with prayer requests. She remembered when she used to pray, and God used to listen. She remembered.

"Any others?" Pastor scanned the room, his eyes finding hers but leaving just as quickly as they arrived, not singling any one person out. She should have been listening. Not only had she not written the requests down, she hadn't even been listening to them. Hana flushed and stared down at the table. "Okay, then, let's open with prayer." Pastor nodded to the group and bowed his head. Hana clasped her hands tightly in her lap and followed along as he addressed all of the requests. Hana listened this time and murmured "Amen" at the end, along with several other people.

Everyone rose to their feet and began to part ways. "Our class meets just over here." Lynn led her to a classroom off the hall they'd just left. Hana noticed the group was uneven, with only six men in attendance. The rest of the women followed Lynn into Room 108, where a television was set up in front of several rows of chairs. "So the way this works is that we start with a twenty-minute video and then end with questions and discussion from the study guide." Lynn held up a book with bright flowers on the cover. "Don't worry, you can share with me. Although, I'm sure Pastor has an extra in his office that you can get afterwards."

Hana gulped. So there would be a "discussion." Hopefully she could just listen. She didn't have much to "discuss." The focus of this week's lesson was "Ruth: Faithfulness during Life's Challenges." The video was brief and featured a perfectly manicured woman gesticulating passionately about what it meant to be faithful. Hana tried to listen but felt guilty. She wasn't faithful. So what if she was in church right now? It hardly spoke well of her if it took the absolute worst thing happening to drive her into a church. That wasn't faithfulness. That was seeking an escape; that was coming to God on your own terms—treating Him like some sort of divine Pez dispenser. The video ended, and the other women began turning their chairs to form a circle. Hana followed suit, her heart in her throat. Here was the dreaded discussion time. She suddenly found herself grateful to be next to Lynn, who did enough talking for a multitude of people. Lynn, however, had other ideas.

"Before we begin discussion, how about we go around the room and introduce ourselves to our newcomer? And then, Hana, you can introduce yourself at the end."

There were affirmative nods and smiles all around, but all Hana could think of was, *I have to introduce myself. I have to say something about myself. What is there to say?* She listened as one by one the women gave their names, some of them adding additional things about themselves, but Hana could only struggle with her panic about what to say. Finally, it was her turn, and all eyes were on her.

"Um, my name is Hana. I'm Kara McCauley's sister. I have

one son, Isaac, whom most of you probably met last Sunday leaving church." She laughed, and others laughed with her. Maybe this wasn't so bad. "He has a pet turtle called Rocky, who I think you also met." More laughter. "We're in Altus for the summer with my sister and her family. We'll be moving to Richmond in August, where I'll start a teaching job. Thank you for opening your doors to us during the time that we're here." Short, sweet, and simple.

"If you don't mind my asking, is Isaac's father in the picture?" An older woman spoke. She'd identified herself as Regina Chance, a longstanding Sunday School teacher at Hope.

Why did people keep asking about her past? Why did they insist on prodding the giant when she was working so very hard to keep him quiet? She wished people would let her share what she wanted without feeling the need to follow-up with questions. In the back of her mind, she knew it was natural to ask people about themselves in an effort to get to know them better, but at the moment she didn't care. She wanted to be done talking. "Uh, no, no he is not." It was a brief reply and one that maybe came across as rude, but the question had rankled her, and she couldn't bring herself to feel badly for her abrupt response.

Sympathetic murmurs spread throughout the group. "It's hard for a young boy to be apart from his father," Regina said, as if she even knew the first thing about Hana's situation.

"Well, Isaac is actually doing quite well. He loves his cousins, and we're doing fine, both looking forward to our new home." As usual, Hana redirected focus to the future and the possibilities it held, much like a magician employing sleight of hand—look this way, this way! Ta-da! The past has disappeared!

"If there's any way we can pray for you, please let us know," a lady named Elizabeth offered.

"Thank you," Hana managed, feeling weak and exposed, even though she hadn't really disclosed anything.

"I hope to see Isaac in my classroom. He'll be in . . . first grade?" Regina continued.

"Yes." Hana didn't offer that she used to homeschool Isaac, before everything fell apart, and that this past year in a public school for the first time had been a trying adventure and that she didn't like the idea of thrusting yet another new classroom on him.

"Did you fill out that form I gave you?" Lynn asked brightly.

Hana shook her head no. She'd barely even looked at it. Had actually forgotten about it until now.

"Be sure to give me a copy when you have it, Lynn," Regina requested.

Hana felt like she was being paraded around the room. "It might be best if I keep Isaac with me. I don't know how he'd do in a Sunday School setting."

"Well, we can revisit it later, dear." Regina shook her head knowingly and patted Hana's arm. "I've had many special needs children in my class over the years."

Hana bit her tongue. That didn't mean anything. Isaac was his own unique person.

"Let's open to page 51." Dorothy refocused everyone's attention to the study. Lynn held her book open between them, pulling it back only to jot notes under the various questions as the discussion unfolded.

Hana squirmed in her seat. She was wearing shorts, and the metal folding chair was sticking to her thighs. She just knew she'd have huge red marks on the back of her legs when she stood up. Everyone else was wearing skirts or pants. Was this one of those churches that didn't believe in shorts? But Kara wore shorts. Unless no one in the church knew that Kara wore shorts. Great, another thing Hana was doing wrong.

She vaguely remembered the story of Ruth—that and Esther had always stood out to her as the two romances in the Bible and, therefore, two of the more interesting stories. But before Ruth met Boaz, before the happy ending, there was death, there was isolation, there was fear of the future. Before she quite realized it, Hana found herself drawn into the discussion. She knew what loss was like; she knew what it meant to be a stranger; she knew what it was like to have your family ripped apart. The application portion was a little harder to take in, though. How to be faithful like Ruth? Hana listened as the women shared what "life's challenges" meant to them. Several of them shot Hana pointed looks during this time, but she remained steadfastly silent. Finally, someone said something that stuck out: "It's not really about our faithfulness; it's more about God being faithful. He's the only one who is truly faithful, and we can find hope in that." Hana stared hard at the woman who had said this. What was her name? Clara, maybe. The young woman who was engaged.

The study drew to an end, and someone led them in prayer. Hana peeled herself off the chair and stretched. "I hope you didn't take offense at what I said earlier." Hana turned to find Regina by her side. "About working with people with special needs."

"No, it's fine." Hana tried to smile.

"It's just important for your son to be taught God's Word, and being with other kids his age is a good thing and will help with his social skills."

Hana bristled. "I'm well aware of his social skills." She tried to keep her tone even. "He's been in behavioral therapy for a long time, and I work hard with him."

"Oh, that's good, that's good. And I didn't mean to suggest otherwise." Regina patted her arm again. "I think being in my class will help with all of that."

Hana regarded the woman before her. Just because she had taught a lot of children over the years didn't mean she knew what was best for Isaac. Then again, maybe Hana was too quick to dismiss anything that felt too hard with her son. "I will consider it, Regina. Thank you."

The older woman must have heard the tenseness in Hana's voice, for she grabbed hold of Hana's hand and stared intently into her eyes. "It's hard, I know, but complacency doesn't do anyone any good. We must always push, push them outside their comfort zone. We cannot let them or ourselves just wallow in it. We must always strive to integrate them as much as possible into everyday life. I *do* know what it's like, Hana," she concluded gently. "I have a granddaughter with Down syndrome." Her voice caught. She brushed at her cheek.

Hana just stared at her, unsure how she should respond or what, exactly, the woman meant or intended by her words. Did Regina think that because she had a relative with a disability, she knew what Hana was going through and could therefore give advice to her without even knowing her or her son? And what advice was it anyway? Some garbled words about pushing forward, whatever that meant. And now Hana was supposed to what? Feel sorry for her?

Regina was still swiping at her wet cheeks, too preoccupied with her own words to notice their impact. In the back of Hana's mind, she knew that Regina was just trying to relate, but it didn't feel right, and it most certainly didn't feel helpful. Hana murmured something in reply and turned to leave, pushing past Lynn, who was busy talking with Clara. She'd push forward all right—right out of this place.

Matt stood outside his office in conversation with Ron. The men's study always ended earlier than the women's, which meant there was a lot of standing around and waiting as the wives finished up. Matt's back was toward the fellowship hall, so he didn't see Hana come barreling out of Room 108 until she brushed up against him. He turned and a happy jolt ripped through him as he realized who it was.

She was turning to apologize for bumping into him, and he felt taken aback by her tight expression. "Hana, is everything okay?"

"Oh, um, yes." He watched her compose herself, watched her draw herself together, as if pulling some invisible string that brought all her various pieces together. She cleared her throat. "I'm . . . uh . . . supposed to ask you for a copy of the women's study guide."

"Oh. Yes. I have a few extra in my office." Matt turned. "I'll catch you later, Ron." He entered the office, expecting Hana to follow. He turned to find her standing in the doorway. Her features were composed now, but he knew he hadn't misread that distraught look earlier. "You can come in, sit down." He gestured to a couple of chairs in front of his desk.

"It's okay, I've been sitting for a while. I'll stand." She took two steps into his office and stopped.

He hoped he hadn't made her feel uncomfortable by the invitation. She was glancing around his office. He looked around too, wondering how it looked to her. Built-in bookcases lined the walls, filled with his extensive library. The room was windowless, which made it seem smaller. The wall-to-wall books certainly added to the cramped feel. His desk, likewise, was scattered with books. His laptop was in there . . . somewhere.

"Charlotte mentioned that you write?" She turned her eyes from his shelves to him.

"Yes, I contribute on and off to several journals; I've written several chapters for various books, stuff like that."

"That's impressive." She looked intimidated, and he hated that she felt that way.

"Not really, just something I like to do." He tried to make light of it, tried to put her at ease. She rattled him. It'd been a while since someone had done that. He found himself constantly wondering what she was thinking. "How about you? What do you like to do?"

He watched her hug herself, her arms resting on opposite arms, as if shielding herself from the cold. "Oh, I don't know." She shrugged. "I guess I don't have much time for myself these days. I used to enjoy Zumba."

"That thing where you prance around to music?"

She looked up at him sharply, a worried expression on her face. He laughed. "Don't worry, we don't have a 'no Zumba' clause in the church constitution. At least none that I'm aware of!" She laughed with him, which made him beam. "So you like Zumba. What else?"

"Hot wings."

"Hmm. Zumba and hot wings."

"I didn't say I like them together."

"I should hope not." He chuckled, and she laughed with him. She was pretty all the time, but *really* pretty when she laughed. The thought came quickly, passing in and out of his mind before he had a chance to completely register it. Pretty. Yes, Hana Howard was pretty.

"And you like writing and fishing and . . . "

"And I would agree with you on the hot wings." They stood smiling at each other. He felt like he was going to jump from his skin. It was a new sensation for him.

"So that book . . . "

"Oh yes." He turned to the shelf behind his desk. Since when did he stand around smiling at women and talking about hot wings? "Here you go." He handed her the slim volume.

"How much do I owe you?"

He raised a hand in protest. "Nothing."

"Oh, well, thank you. That's kind of you." She turned as if to leave, then hesitated and turned back. "And thank you for your kindness to my son. It means a lot to me for him to have that kind of example."

He was barely breathing. He was staring straight into her brown eyes and found he couldn't say anything for the tight-ness in his chest.

"His father, Zeke . . . he isn't . . . kind, and so it means a lot for Isaac to have someone like you being so nice to him."

"I'm sorry to hear that, about his father." Matt felt his heart constrict beneath this fresh knowledge—that whatever else Zeke Howard was or had done, he was an *unkind* man. He wanted to ask her more, but wanted even more to respect her—to respect her privacy, her feelings. And so he remained standing stock-still, barely breathing.

"Thank you." She gave him a half smile. "I'm sorry too."

She turned to leave, but he stopped her, finally finding his tongue. "Hana, wait." He gulped and prayed for the right words. "If you, if you need a listening ear, someone to pray with you, or to just be there for you, I'm here." She turned to him, her eyes full of tears. "Whatever you need." His voice wavered.

"Thank you," she whispered and ducked out of his office.

He sat down hard in the nearest chair and gasped. Air, he needed air. How long had he been holding his breath? His heart thudded loudly in his chest. He couldn't get her tear-filled face out of his head. He felt a deep and burning anger toward Zeke, this man he'd never met, whose actions he didn't even know. He closed his eyes and prayed for forgiveness. To feel such blind rage—it wasn't right. And it wasn't normal for him. He sat, breathing hard, in the middle of his office, in the midst of hundreds of books, which stood silent witness to the chaos Hana had left behind.

Hello, Button,

You are an impatient little fellow. If you can't figure something out the first time you try it, you shriek at the top of your lungs. Your daddy will just yell for you to be quiet, which bothers me a lot. Either that, or he'll just take away whatever it is you're frustrated over. Anything to get you to be quiet. Even if you didn't have the unique challenges that you do, kids are noisy in general, and I often wonder if he'd be yelling at you regardless, which depresses me, so generally I just try not to think of it and just get to you first before he has a chance to blow up.

You're a smart little guy, you really are, and I see you trying hard every day at things that other kids don't even think about. It makes me so proud to see you try so hard.

We have you in physical, behavioral, and speech therapy—so many therapies for such a small boy! Your favorite thing in the world is to sit outside and look for bugs, turtles, and frogs. You love the outdoors, but not in the way your daddy does. I think that's hard for him to understand and accept sometimes. He wants to play ball with you, but you just want to sit in the dirt and trap bugs or stand by the water and drop rocks in it.

And the vacuum—oh how you love any household item that makes noise! Sometimes I'll just get out the vacuum and run it over the same stretch of carpet over and over to see the look of joy on your face. I don't care how that joy comes; I just want to see it in your face—to know you're happy, even if it's for reasons that I don't understand. I just want you to be happy.

XO

Mommy

8

It felt real. So real. At first, the kiss was soft and gentle, just the way she remembered it. How she missed these kisses! How she missed her husband, her best friend! Her mind was awash in unthinking happiness at the feel of his lips, his arms—that sense of belonging and comfort.

At first, the kiss was subtle and sweet, and then, like a switch, it turned sharp. His lips became a vise, and she couldn't break free. She tugged and tugged, but he only bit down harder. Bleeding—her lips were shredded and bleeding, the taste of metal pooling in her mouth. His arms were too tight, like bondage rather than shelter. She felt her neck snap back under the pressure of his mouth. Her arms were pinned to her sides, and she wondered when it would be over, wondered when she would finally die.

Hana woke up screaming, the taste of blood still in her mouth. The bedsheets were twisted around her, and she kicked them off frantically. Isaac was standing in the corner, startled and moaning, hitting his chest, looking at her wildly. She wanted to reach out to him to comfort him, but she had no comfort, none for herself and none to give. Hana curled into a ball on the bed and sobbed until someone flipped on the light and crawled into bed with her and put her arms around her. Hana turned and grabbed her sister's arm as she shushed and crooned and held her. Troy was close behind and led Isaac out of the room as Hana continued to sob and Kara continued to shush.

She'd had nightmares before—many, in fact, over the past year, but none that had felt so real. "I hate him!" Hana spit the words out into the folds of Kara's nightshirt. Everything came rushing back, like bile in her mouth. "I hate him, Kara! I hate him so much!"

"I know; I know."

She could hear Isaac wailing in the other room, and the mother guilt came pouring in. How could she be strong for her son when she felt so weak? *God, help me,* she prayed and felt the words beat against the bedroom ceiling, frantic as a caged animal.

Everyone was gracious and didn't mention the nightmare the next morning. Troy had quieted and comforted Isaac, and Kara had spent the rest of the night with Hana. Even though no one made a big deal out of it, something had shifted for Hana. She stood in the backyard in the unforgiving sun and said, "Something has to change," out loud to the air and the prickly, burr-riddled grass, to the bugs and stream where Isaac patrolled for turtles. "Something has to change," she said out loud to herself and to a God she wasn't sure was listening. She was tired of feeling out of control, powerless. She was tired of reacting, of waiting for things to happen to her, waiting for the hammer to fall. She was tired of looking over her shoulder and wondering, waiting, always waiting for something bad. "Something has to change."

"He was here again yesterday, Hana." Vicky's voice was quiet and strained on the line, three days after the first phone call. "No stakeout this time. Just a drive-by—several times. Like he was circling the block, you know? I just happened to be outside working in the garden and saw him. I called the police, but by the time they got here, he'd left."

Hana's voice, tight and controlled. "Thanks for letting me know, Vicky. I'm sorry." She and Vicky had always been close, and Zeke knew this. Did he think she was staying with her cousin? She wished Vicky didn't have to deal with this.

"You don't have to apologize. I'm so sorry . . . "

Yes, poor Hana. Poor, broken Hana. She stood under the brilliant sun and clenched her fists until her fingers cramped.

Later, while Isaac watched television with Charlie, Hana located the study guide Pastor had given her and sat by the stream in the blinding heat with the study guide and the Bible app on her phone. She read about women she had nothing in common with. She read about a Jewish girl who became queen and stood up to a king. She read about a devout girl who carried in her womb the very Son of God. She read again about the foreigner who followed her mother-in-law to a new land. She read about the righteous wife of an evil man—a woman who later impressed a king. Hana looked up passages on her phone and followed along in the study guide and read account after account of women who were stronger than she, more powerful than she, and who made right choices in the midst of chaos and upheaval. She had the chaos and upheaval part down pat. She wasn't so sure about the rest.

She was here in this dry, flat land for a whole summer. Maybe if she poured herself into church she would begin to feel closer to God. She looked at the Bible study in her hands. *Women of Faith.* What did it mean to be a woman of faith? Maybe if she got as close as she could to the church and its people, faith would rub off on her, and God would start listening again. Maybe if she stopped mumbling her prayers and screamed them, straight into His face, loud and long, maybe He would hear her then.

Matt could sense a growing trust between Hana and himself, which made him look forward to Wednesday all the more. But when the day arrived and he met Hana and Isaac at the Madisons, he found a very different woman from the week before. She was guarded and jumpy and wouldn't look him in the eye.

"Where's Alex?" Matt questioned.

"All three are at summer camp this week, so it's just Isaac today. I hope that's okay."

That was promising, at least—that she trusted him with her son. But why wouldn't she look him in the eye? Before he could ask, she was kissing Isaac on the head and turning to enter the Madisons' home. Charlotte waved to him from the porch, and he waved back with a furrowed brow.

Isaac was talkative this time. "Do you think we will see two turtles today?" He carried Matt's tackle box in both hands. "We saw two turtles here before. Do you think we will see two turtles again today?"

"It's possible." Matt looked down at the excited boy. "But we may *not* see turtles today either. That's a possibility too."

"No! Say we will see turtles today!"

"I don't want to promise you something that may not happen."

Isaac abruptly stopped, dropped Matt's tackle box, and began flapping his hands so hard they made sharp cracking sounds, like a flag in a stiff breeze.

"No! No! Say it! Say it! We *will* see them today!"

"We probably will see turtles since there's so many out here."

"Probably or will? We probably will see turtles, or we will see turtles?"

The flapping was becoming so pronounced that Matt was afraid Isaac would hurt himself. He winced at the sound of Isaac's hands, watching him with worried eyes. There had been no verbal sparring with Elliott, who had been mostly nonverbal, and he had no frame of reference for what was appropriate. Was he supposed to lie to the boy? He was look-ing so distressed and the flapping was getting so pronounced that Matt found himself saying, "We *will* see turtles. We will,

Isaac, we will see them." Isaac stopped flapping and ran ahead to the pond, which was just in sight.

Matt picked up the tackle box from where Isaac had dropped it and followed. What did Hana do in these types of situations? Lie to keep the peace? What must it be like to have to constantly deal with that decision over and over again? It would be exhausting—mentally and emotionally—the constant wear and tear of it. Matt reached the pond and set up his fishing spot near Isaac.

He longed to ask Isaac about his mother but wasn't sure how the boy would feel about that. Isaac took up his station at the edge, clenching the handful of rocks he'd scraped from the water's bank. Matt stood a few yards down, knowing Isaac's rocks would scare any fish off, but also not wanting to tell Isaac to stop since he knew how much he enjoyed their time outdoors. So instead he cast his line and silently observed the young boy at his side. "How is your mom, Isaac? Is she doing okay?"

Isaac didn't look at him, and for a moment Matt thought he wouldn't answer, but then he swung his head low and said, "Mom is fine. Mom is sad and fine."

Sad and fine. Truer words were never spoken. Isn't that the veneer most sad people put on? I'm fine. Just fine. "And how about you, Isaac? Are you doing okay?"

"Yes, I'm fine. I don't want to talk. I want to look for turtles."

"Fair enough. Thanks for telling me." Isaac spent most days locked in his head. Matt could identify with that. Isaac preferred things a certain way, and Matt could relate to that too. Silence it was. Matt turned back to his fishing rod.

Isaac was much more verbal than Elliott had been. Matt observed Isaac's profile, hoping he was indeed fine. That was the hardest part—needing to understand the other person but being unable to because they couldn't communicate with you.

It'd been a day much like today when he'd come across Elliott at his normal spot by the lake. He'd instantly known that something wasn't right. Before he saw him, he'd heard him—guttural sobs that'd made Matt's heart sink. He'd found him sitting by the water, soaking wet and alternately sobbing and gagging on water. Matt had knelt by his side, knowing he didn't like to be touched but touching him anyway, asking him what had happened, what was wrong. Tears, snot, and mud streaked Elliott's face. His hands were raised, fingers splayed in various directions, reaching to their farthest points, some twisted at unnatural angles as he rocked himself back and forth—his usual display of distress, except there was nothing usual about the circumstances. "What happened? Are you hurt?" All the while knowing that Elliott didn't have the words to communicate with him. Matt's heart breaking with that knowledge. It was a deep and wordless pain—loving someone but having no ability to help him.

Matt swallowed the lump in his throat and contented himself with the silence Isaac wanted. When their time drew to a close and only one turtle had been spotted, Matt knew Isaac would take it hard. "We have to go back to the house now, Isaac. Your mom will be waiting for you."

Matt could tell Isaac was in genuine distress, his features twisted in pain. "But we only saw one turtle. Last time we saw two turtles."

"But that's sometimes how it goes. We can't control the turtles, Isaac. And maybe you will see more next time."

"But if we stay, we will see the other turtle."

"Maybe, but maybe not. Your mom is waiting for you, so we have to go now."

Matt looked in concern from Isaac to the direction of the house. He didn't want to leave the boy to go get help because that felt irresponsible. He didn't know Isaac well enough to know if he would go wandering off. But he also wasn't comfortable getting physical with the boy and dragging him by the arm to the house. That didn't seem appropriate at all. "Isaac, listen to me. You can come back out with me again to look for turtles, but if you misbehave, I will have to tell your mom about it. Do you understand? I want you to still be able to come out fishing with me, but if you misbehave, then we can't do these trips anymore, and that would make me sad."

That got his attention. Isaac listened attentively but still made no move to follow Matt to the house. Matt walked a few paces toward the house, hoping this would prompt the boy to follow. When it didn't, Matt came close and tried to take Isaac's hand, but Isaac jerked his arm around, preventing physical contact. Matt ended up snagging him by the elbow instead of taking his hand. He tugged gently on Isaac's arm, hoping it would prompt him to action. Instead, Isaac seized up and dropped to the ground. "Don't touch me! Don't touch me!"

Matt instantly let go and raised both hands in the air instinctively, to show he meant no harm. This only escalated the problem, however, for at the sight of Matt's raised hands, Isaac screamed louder, a piercing, frightened wail that filled Matt with fear. He looked in confusion at the cowering boy at his feet. Isaac was now covering his head with his arms, occasionally twisting upward to throw Matt panicked looks.

"Oh, Isaac, Isaac, shhh, shhh. It's okay. I'm sorry if I scared you. I'm not going to hurt you." Matt's voice caught in his throat. He knelt and placed a hand on Isaac's rounded back. Isaac jerked away and continued to wail and cry. "Oh, sweet boy, I'm so sorry." Matt felt the tears gathering in his eyes. Isaac's shuddering form morphed with Elliott's until Matt was forced to shut his eyes and breathe deeply to dispel the image. How had he brought so much pain so suddenly upon Isaac? What had he done? What had he triggered? He stood to his feet, pulled his phone from his pocket, and dialed the Madisons' landline. "Charlotte? Yes, it's me. Listen, I'm out here with Isaac, and he's upset. He needs . . . he needs his mom right now." Matt hung up and waited. He stood at a distance, not wanting to make things worse. "Isaac, your mom is coming out here." No reply. "It'll be okay, Isaac. Your mom is coming. It'll be okay." Matt continued to talk in soothing tones until he saw Hana arriving from a distance, her petite, compact frame a powerhouse of energy as she strode across the field, arms pumping. Matt almost felt like sprinting for cover.

"What did you *do*?" Hana's eyes were wild as she took in the sight of her son huddled on the ground.

Matt blinked in confusion as he realized she'd directed this question at him. "Nothing. He didn't want to come back to the house, so I tried taking him by the hand to lead him, and it just went south from there."

Hana strode past him and cast herself on the ground next to her son. "I'm here, Isaac; Mommy is here." He watched as she opened her arms, and for the first time he saw Isaac initiate the embrace. He moaned and leaned toward his mother, burying his head in her chest as she enveloped him in a protective hug.

Matt stepped back to give them privacy. Hana was murmuring something into Isaac's ear until he quieted. They were one unit—mother-and-son—together on the ground, in each other's arms, and Matt felt like a completely unnecessary cog to their machine. He shifted uneasily from one foot to the other. He hadn't seen this type of closeness in a long time. This was a closeness that shut out the world, that allowed no others, that demanded to be left alone. Matt swallowed past the lump in his throat. It was him and Elliott sitting together in shared and silent grief. He shouldn't be here. Matt shuffled backward a few steps. He knelt and gathered his things. He turned and walked a few paces to the house.

"Pastor."

One word—soft, arresting. He turned.

Her face was lifted to his, acknowledging his presence, asking for him back. In her gaze, he saw hurt, deep and ongoing. He'd seen that type of chronic emotional pain before. He'd lived it.

"I'm sorry. I know you didn't do anything wrong." She looked like she wanted to say more but didn't know what or how.

"You have every right to defend your son." It was hard to look at her directly. Hard to connect with her pain, for once connected, it opened other doors, other levels of pain. "Please don't apologize for being a loving mother." Matt gave up and looked away. "I'm just saddened that I inadvertently caused so much pain. I'm so sorry."

Hana had turned back to Isaac and was encouraging him to stand with her and come back to the house. He'd cried himself out and was silent and compliant, letting Hana take him by the hand, letting her put an arm around him to lead him away. She looked once again at Matt. "I know you're probably confused. I'm sure you didn't do anything wrong. Isaac just has been . . . he's just so sensitive sometimes. He has a hard time reading physical cues, and it just takes one small misinterpretation to set him off."

"Yes, I can see that now. I hope I haven't ruined our relationship." *Between me and Isaac. Between me and you.*

Hana gave him a sad smile. "No, I'm sure you haven't. Everything will be fine. We'll be fine. I'll talk it through with him. It'll be fine; you'll see." Was she trying to convince him or herself?

It was a somber procession back to the house, Matt following meekly behind Hana and Isaac. He stood by as Hana said her good-byes to the Madisons, who had come out to see them off. He offered a wave to the group and then walked to his car, which was parked near Hana's. He watched as she gently helped Isaac into his seat, murmuring something to him before closing the door and turning to Matt.

"May I talk to you privately for a moment?" Hana's face was endless, deep, unsettling. He nodded an affirmative, not trusting his voice, and watched as she threw a glance at the Madisons' front porch, where the last of the family was lingering, out of earshot. "Please don't worry about today. Isaac has trust issues . . . especially with men."

Here it was, then, the revelation he'd been awaiting. She seemed about to spill her heart out to him, and all it'd taken was a harrowing experience involving him and her son to unlock it. But no, she reined herself in before continuing.

"I suppose we all have trust issues to some degree, right?"

She cracked a smile, but it was misplaced, and it stuck in the air between them like a sore spot. He tried to smile back and failed. "That's part of why I would like more people in his life like you." She'd turned serious again. "He needs to be around positive male role models."

Matt cleared his throat, finally thinking of something to say and jumping to say it before it was forgotten. "Well, one can also be *too* trusting. There's a healthy balance, as in all of life."

"Yes, yes, that's true. And it's my job as his parent to help him strike that balance. To learn how to trust the right people. A hard lesson, even for a child without Isaac's challenges."

"And a hard lesson for adults too." Matt said carefully, watching her eyes. They flickered before she continued.

"Yes, a hard lesson for us all." She stood there, wavering by the car, so much unspoken.

He found himself reaching out to her, taking her hands in both of his own, rubbing his thumbs over her knuckles, still struggling to keep his eyes on hers. "Hana, whatever pain is in your past, whatever you are carrying, it's not too big for God. It's not too horrible and scary for Him. He doesn't want you to be alone with a burden. He came to carry it for you." He was preaching to himself; he could sense it—that horrible feeling he got sometimes when the words of counsel coming out of his mouth came straight from head knowledge because he was still struggling himself to translate it to heart knowledge. It used to eat him alive, this feeling that he was a hypocrite. Until he finally realized and accepted that he was in the process of sanctification, too, and that God used the broken to show that there was no question of who got the glory.

She was crying; she was arching over their joined hands, and he could feel her tears, wet on his fingers. "But what if I've been gone too long?"

"Gone? What do you mean?"

"It's been so long since I've been in church, since I've

really prayed with any confidence. Why would God listen to me? Why would He even care?"

Matt closed his eyes for a moment and squeezed her hands reassuringly. "Dear sister, because faith once given is never lost, and the hope we have in Christ once kindled is never extinguished. Because His great and deep and abiding love for us is unconditional and never dies. Our confidence is in *Him* and not in us, and He promises to never cast out those who come to Him—at any time, under any circumstance." The tears were streaming down his cheeks unchecked. Even if he'd wanted to wipe them away, he couldn't have, for she gripped his hands furiously in her own.

She finally looked up at him and released his hands, so she could swipe at her face. "I feel like I'm learning to walk again. Like I've had my legs knocked out from under me, maybe even some broken bones in there, and I have to learn how to walk again."

He smiled at her. "And that's okay."

"I feel like I met you—we met you—for a reason." She turned to Isaac in the car. "I feel like maybe Hope is my training wheels."

Matt laughed at this. "I like that analogy. I do believe that God places people in our lives at certain times to accomplish His purposes."

"I want to be involved at Hope, for us both to be involved. To establish some ground rules now that it's just me and Isaac, church being one of them."

Hmm, church as a ground rule, not exactly the direction he'd go with this. Matt tried to gently steer her in a different direction. "It's definitely a good thing to be involved in a church body, to be around fellow believers, but don't feel like you have to compensate for anything. That's not how God works. We can't *do* more to be *loved* more by Him."

She appeared to be weighing his words. "So don't try harder is what you're saying."

"Right. You couldn't be good enough to receive God's love, so you can't be bad enough to lose it. Does that make sense?

You, me, none of us did anything to receive God's grace, so there's nothing we can do to 'keep' it. It is a gift, one hundred percent."

"So God doesn't pick and choose—like some religious buffet?" She was smiling, and he could sense that her heart was beginning to hear what he was saying.

"A buffet? What do you mean?" He found himself smiling back.

"So, like, God doesn't go down the line of Christians and say, 'Hmmm, this one looks particularly good. Think I'll get me some of that. Ugh, this one's been left out too long and is rancid. Pass!'"

Matt looked at her in surprise, then tilted his head back and laughed, a prolonged guffaw that he couldn't stop. Hana joined him, and together they laughed until his sides hurt. "I haven't laughed this hard in a long time." Matt swiped at his eyes. "A very apt description of what I'm certain many people feel, but no, absolutely not!"

"Well, that's a relief," Hana giggled.

"You have to understand—we're not dishes of food in God's eyes, more or less appealing to Him depending on our . . . uh . . . freshness. We're made in His image. We're His creation. He paid for us by His very blood! You don't need to become more appealing to Him, so He chooses you. You're already chosen! You're . . . on His plate, so to speak . . . and He's not putting you back!" He was grinning madly at her, and she was returning his smile. The agitation he'd sensed from her earlier had dissipated.

"That's strangely helpful, thank you."

"And look, that's not to say you can't get involved at Hope because we'd love to have you around." *I would love to have you around.* "There's an informational meeting about our Vacation Bible School next Monday night if you're interested. Isaac would be welcome to attend our program this summer, and we could work together to ensure it's a positive experience for him."

"I'd like that."

Matt was aware, dimly, that the openness between them in that moment was unusual. Typically when mutual crying had occurred between congregant and pastor, there was an unspoken embarrassment afterward. As if both parties involved had caught the other in some compromising position and were bound to secrecy. There might even be some slight avoidance on the congregant's part for several weeks to come. As if he, Pastor Matt Schofield, was a visual reminder of a momentary weakness. It was hard to visit a place of vulnerability and then bounce back to real life, hard to look the person in the face who saw you stripped of all veneer. At least that'd been Matt's experience. But he and Hana seemed to be connected by a mutual understanding. She didn't appear to feel shame or embarrassment, and he found, with a mounting happiness, that neither did he. There was no scuttling back to dignified positions, clambering back to real life. They stood there raw, bleeding, and yes, even laughing, and okay with it.

Hana felt hope—that was the strange, fluttering sensation in her chest, she was sure of it. It'd been a while since she'd experienced it, so she hadn't recognized it right away. It wasn't until later that night when everyone was in bed that she'd been able to finally identify it.

Hopelessness was a funny thing; Hana should know. Easily shrouded and undetectable until one day, or maybe over a series of many, many days, it becomes detectable for the sheer absence of it. As hope moves in, and hopelessness moves out, it changes a person, and then you notice. And you wonder how you were ever living before.

Part II

——◆◆◆——

Hope

Hello, Button,

Your behavioral therapist tells me it's like you're in a big room—a big, echoey room where everything is loud and vying for your attention. She explained it this way: for most of us, things have different values. The bird chirping outside has less value than the person talking to us. The feel of our clothes has even less value than that. Our brains just automatically rank things that we need to pay attention to, but for you, Button, everything has the same value. Everything you take in is equally urgent to your senses, which explains why you shut down so easily, why it's so hard for you to focus and process. You are facing unseen challenges that most of us don't even have to think about.

I wish that I could take this from you, that I could struggle with it for you. I would give anything to make that happen. But because I can't, instead I'll work through it with you. I hope you know that you're not alone. Sometimes it's hard to tell. You are like a beautiful house with the shutters all closed, and I'm unable to see inside. But I hope you know, sweetie, that you're not alone.

XO

Mommy

9

Matt had always been the "good boy." From an early age, his mother had identified him as "sweet" and "sensitive," and it was a label he'd adopted and grown into. Yes, he was the good boy. He was the one who helped and listened and didn't get into trouble. The one person his mother didn't have to worry over. This trait, so universally loved in a young boy, was quickly scoffed at in high school when he became the "goody two-shoes," the stocky kid with the bad haircut who never had a date. His weight issues coupled with his shyness didn't help in the romance department. He didn't even try when it came to girls, and he told himself that it was because he didn't care, wasn't interested, didn't need it. Easier to deny the desire for something than to confront one's own inability to attain it. But others said it was because he liked boys. The rumors were vicious and coupled with name-calling, which made Matt draw even further into himself. In college, the names turned less vicious, but he was still known as Matt the Monk. He laughed it off every time, laughed it off and pretended he didn't care and didn't need anything as unpredictable and messy as a relationship. He told himself this for so long that it became truth to him. Why complicate and muddy one's life when being alone was so much easier?

He was Matt the good, kind, sensitive boy; the goody two-shoes; Matt the Monk. The world had him all figured out, it seemed. It'd taken years for him to realize that he wasn't good, that there was none good, that his mother's idea of goodness was rooted in a morality that ultimately had no base. It took a college buddy, Mike, inviting him to a Bible study for him to begin seeing himself in a different light. He'd adopted his "goodness" as a badge of honor, ironically finding pride in his perceived humility. He began to understand that perhaps the world wasn't divided by a murky, nebulous sense of "good" and "bad," but rather lost and redeemed.

When Matt went to seminary, it was a surprise to no one but him. It was just one more proof of his goodness. His mother thought it a feather in her cap to have a clergyman as a son and told anyone who cared to listen that her good boy was showing others the way. Matt tried to talk to her about *the* Way, but it never quite sunk in with her, never broke through her secular sense of morality to a deeper, personal place. His father and sister were less thrilled about his career choice but respected it as if he'd chosen a different political party, and they need only be careful with what they said around the holiday table. There were many days when Matt felt inadequate to be a pastor. How could he minister to others when he seemed to fail so gloriously with his own family?

During Matt's doctoral program, he began thinking of his celibacy along the lines of the apostle Paul, that he just wasn't someone who "burned with passion" and, therefore, he would adhere to the apostle's desire that all were as he was, single and focused on the Lord. Just as marriage was a calling, singleness was too, and perhaps that was his own calling. He found other pastors' marriages compelling and saw the real benefit of having a joint ministry with one's wife, but if God never blessed him in that way, then he would accept it. He wasn't sure if this belief was an acceptance of a calling or more of an explanation for how his life was playing out. And he wasn't sure if that mattered or not. All he knew was that he was content—had been content—until now.

In all his years of study and ministry, no one had shaken him as much as Hana Howard. In all his interactions with female parishioners, even single and attractive ones, he'd never been as bothered or as beside himself as he was now. His desire to spend time with her was a confusing mixture of pastoral concern and personal interest, leaving him paralyzed as to how to proceed. But after their heart-to-heart last Wednesday, he felt convinced that he needed to go deeper with her. He'd be amiss not to; she so clearly had baggage and things she was dealing with or needed to deal with. But he hesitated, perhaps because if he went there—opened the pastoral door even wider—then he was afraid that was all he'd ever be to her. A confidant. A pastor. But not a man. That should be okay. But somehow it wasn't.

Matt sat in his office and stared at his sermon notes, unable to concentrate but unable to admit to himself why. He turned his gaze to the phone and thought of calling Hana and—what? Ask her to come in for a counseling session? That seemed inappropriate. A date seemed even more inappropriate. And did he even want that? He wasn't sure. He probably shouldn't want it until he knew more about her situation. He turned back to the sermon notes and tried to make sense of them, to turn his thoughts from confused ambiguity to the concrete reality that he had a sermon to preach on Sunday and he needed to prepare.

It'd been startling, to see him standing over her sobbing son. For a split second, she'd believed it'd happened—her son had been mistreated on her watch by someone they both should have been able to trust. But once the panic had ebbed, once she'd held Isaac in her arms and spoken words of calm to them both, she'd seen it more clearly. Pastor's shattered face had been one of genuine pain—not guilt or anger or any other volatile emotion—deep pain over Isaac's distress. And then she'd known that nothing had happened, that Pastor Matthew Schofield was the last person on earth who would ever dream of harming her son. Pure relief followed—that and a deep, abiding thankfulness to have this kind man in their lives.

And then they'd talked . . . and cried . . . and laughed hysterically . . . and he had categorized them as a team, a unit, a combined force that was fundamentally pro-Isaac. "We could work together to ensure it's a positive experience for him," Pastor had said, speaking of VBS. *We.* She found that she liked being lumped together with him. *We* will make it happen for Isaac. *We will.*

Talking with Pastor, Hana felt God smiling at her, felt for the first time in a long time that there was strength in her corner. It was invigorating. It was liberating. It made her want to tackle the world, starting with Bible study that very next night.

Hana left early for the study so she could stop by a store for a Bible. Her other Bible had been ripped from her. Her desire to even open the Bible had been mocked and thrown into her face, and she'd let the pain and fear of that event prevent her from getting another, from trying again. But no longer.

The shopping in Altus was limited, so she ended up in Wal-Mart in the meager book aisle. There were few books, but, surprisingly, there were multiple Bibles to choose from. She hadn't remembered there being so many options. It seemed one could pick a "version" of the Bible as one might choose an outfit. She'd grown up with the King James Version, but opening that now, she felt overwhelmed by the language. She turned instead to something marked New King James Version. That seemed suitable, right? Something new to start this next part of her life? She grabbed the slim, faux leather volume and headed to the checkout.

"Excuse me, but are you Hana?"

Hana turned to the woman behind her in line. She was slim and beautiful—one of those perfectly proportionate women, not too tall and not too short. Her hair was a beautiful auburn with dark lowlights, and it fell in waves around her shoulders, her trendy bangs framing big, deep brown eyes with long lashes. She was impeccably groomed but without the impression of having tried too hard. A stunning smile shone brightly from her face, but didn't quite reach her eyes. Instead it lingered like a bright accessory, detached and hovering. Hana instantly disliked her and then instantly disliked herself for disliking her. "I'm sorry, do I know you?"

"Oh, goodness, no." The woman laughed, her voice soft and musical. "I'm sorry, I just recognized you because you look so like your sister, Kara." She extended a manicured hand. "I'm Julie Jackson. I attend Hope. I'd heard Kara's sister was coming to stay, and I assume you must be her."

Julie Jackson—even her name flowed off the tongue in a pleasing manner. Hana took her hand, hoping it was one of those flaky, dead-fish handshakes that would give her something legitimate to hold against her. But no, it was an annoyingly nice, firm handshake. "Yes, I'm Hana. I'm surprised I haven't seen you before now."

"Oh, I've been out of town for the last few weeks. My aunt recently passed away, and I went to her funeral and to help my cousins sort through her things."

"I'm sorry to hear that."

"Thank you. She's home with the Lord now." Julie seemed to be getting teary but cleared her throat and looked at what Hana was holding. "Getting a new Bible?"

Hana looked down at the incriminating evidence in her hands in dismay, trying to think quickly. "Oh, um, yes. I'm transitioning between homes right now. My son and I are moving to Richmond in August, and I must have boxed up my Bible with the rest of my books." She tried to laugh in an offhand manner, not wanting to admit that it'd been a while since she'd touched a Bible.

"Ah yes." Julie joined in her laughter and held up her basket filled with a few food items. "Just restocking some essentials myself. I hope you're on your way to Bible study? We'll have a chance to get to know each other more."

Hana cringed inwardly. She shouldn't feel intimidated

by this woman. That was ridiculous. "Yup, that's where I'm headed."

"Oh good!"

Oh good.

"Well, I'll see you there then!"

Hana disliked the ungracious thoughts filling her head. How could she get closer to God if she kept getting irritated with people in the church? She paid for the Bible and left quickly so as not to get sucked back into conversation with Julie.

When Hana entered the fellowship hall, she was relieved to see that she'd beat Julie there. Quickly, she took a seat next to Lynn. Maybe she could avoid unwanted conversation with Julie by hiding behind Lynn's chattiness. Hana became aware of Pastor's eyes on her and slowly turned to meet them. He smiled, his eyes nearly disappearing in crinkles as he did so. And then Julie arrived.

Hana watched as Julie entered the fellowship hall and raised an enthusiastic hand in greeting. For a moment, she thought the wave was directed at her but then followed Julie's gaze to Pastor, who had turned and was nodding and waving back. Julie had been kind and enthusiastic with Hana, but she was practically radiant with Pastor. *Oh, so that's how it is.* Hana felt the realization come upon her gradually. It started as a suggestion and then swelled into certainty. *He's hers.* She watched as Julie approached Pastor and laid a hand on his arm. Watched as she smiled into his face and said something that made him laugh. Her mannerisms with him were proprietary, intimate, like she was drawing lines in the sand with every word and gesture. "Here, ladies, and no farther." So what if he was hers? It didn't matter to Hana. Why would it matter? But it did.

The previously intoxicating notion of "we" now felt deflated and puny in the light of Julie's presence. Hana didn't realize she'd been clenching her hands until she felt her new Bible buckle under the pressure. She glanced down and quickly released her hands, smoothing the Bible's cover and willing herself to relax. She glanced back up to see Julie sitting down across the room from her. She tried to arrange her features into a pleasant expression as Julie caught her eye and gave her a little wave. Hana waved back and quickly looked away.

The night started, as it had last time, with prayer requests. Julie spoke up right away. "Continued prayers for my aunt's family are greatly appreciated. Some of my cousins are taking it pretty hard, and, of course, Steven is not a believer, so he's especially struggling. Pray that God uses this situation to bring Steven to faith." There were sympathetic murmurs throughout the room. Hana watched Pastor write down the request and before she knew it, she had her hand up in the air. She watched Pastor's eyes light up in surprise as he called on her.

"Yes, Hana?" He pointed his pen at her with an expectant expression.

Hana glanced up at her hand as if it didn't belong to her. *Oh look—my hand. What are you doing there, silly?* She dropped it quickly and sat staring at Pastor with a blank expression. Why had she raised her hand? Was it so as not to be outdone by Julie? But that was ridiculous. This wasn't some prayer competition to see who could garner the most sympathy. Everyone in the room was facing her expectantly, rightly waiting for her to say something. Well, she had committed to becoming more a part of the church, hadn't she? And there was no better way than to ask people to pray for you, right? She cleared her throat. "Well, as most of you know, I'm staying with the McCauleys for the summer until my home in Richmond is ready. I've accepted a teaching job there, and our home will be ready in August. I guess my biggest need for prayer right now is . . . " Is what? *Everything.* "Is for Isaac as he starts at a new school. Transition isn't easy for any child, but especially for Isaac. He was diagnosed with autism at two, and group situations are usually hard for him." She had *not* expected to divulge this much, but the more she talked the more kept pouring out. "If you could pray for his new school situation, that'd be appreciated." *There, beat that, Julie.* Did God honor prayer requests that were done out of spite? Hana felt her cheeks go red.

"Thank you for sharing, Hana. We'll be praying for you and Isaac during this transitional time."

"Thank you." Hana leaned back in her seat and avoided looking in Julie's direction. Instead she stared hard at Pastor. So he and Julie Jackson were an item. Hana tried to wrap her mind around it but couldn't.

There was something about Hana that didn't quite click, but she just couldn't land on what, exactly, it was. All during the video portion of the women's study, Julie had sat and gnawed her lip. When she'd talked to Hana at the store, the woman had seemed jumpy and nervous, which had instantly put Julie on edge. She'd heard her mother's voice, shrill in her ear, "Wipe that smile off your face! You look like you're over-compensating for something. No one likes to be confronted with desperate." So Julie had done a quick mental check. Had she said or done anything off-putting to cause Hana to react that way? Was her overbright smile in response to Hana's reticence indeed overcompensating? Was the more reserved facial expression Julie was displaying now too far in the other direction? Julie played this game often—the doubt and second-guessing game in which she never, not even once, seemed to come out on top.

She'd seen right through Hana's story of not being able to find her Bible because it was in storage. Perhaps that's why she'd seemed jumpy—embarrassed for not owning a Bible? Whether she did or did not own a Bible made no difference to Julie, but why pretend otherwise? That's what was irritating. "Small lies lead to larger untruths," her mother used to say, usually as a way to elicit a confession from Julie for something her brother, Robbie, had done. And it usually worked. Julie had taken the fall for many of her younger brother's transgressions, opting to face their mother's wrath alone rather than to submit her brother to it.

Try as she might to focus, Julie stayed distracted throughout the Bible study and after had made a beeline to Pastor's
office. As the VBS coordinator, there were details she needed to discuss, but Pastor had been cagey with her, looking
past her and toward the door as if he expected someone else
to come in at any moment. An ugly suspicion had risen in
Julie's mind, and to test her theory, she'd thrown out Hana's
name. Yup, Pastor had looked at her sharply, and his cheeks
had gone red. Somehow in the short time that Julie had been
gone, this Hana had swooped in and nabbed Pastor from her.
Her earlier irritation with Hana had morphed into anger.

"You're so pretty, so I have no idea why no boy is interested in you." Julie had heard this often from her mother during
high school. "Are you sure you're trying? Really trying? All
those looks, and they're going to waste." And then after college, "Are you a lesbian? Just tell me now—are you? Okay,
well, then why on earth do you not have a boyfriend by now?
Why?" And after years of successful service as a Contract
Specialist for the Air Force, "You're not going to get any more
attractive than you are right now. You're at the peak years,
and if it's not happened by now, it never will."

Julie was thirty-six, single, and stationed in the small town
of Altus, Oklahoma, where prospects in the romance department were slim. Most of the men she met on base were either
married or much too young. When she'd begun attending
Hope two years ago and met Pastor Matthew Schofield, it
wasn't so much attraction at first sight as much as a stagger-
ing relief to find someone single and somewhat attractive in
around the same age bracket as herself. The more she'd become involved with church life, the more her eye gravitated
toward the quiet, unassuming pastor, who, yes, come to think
of it, was rather handsome when she stopped long enough to
really look at him.

Now Pastor's flushed face at the mention of Hana told
Julie everything she needed to know. She'd only been gone
a week and a half to help sort through her aunt's belongings
and to attend the funeral. But in that time, she'd been under

the same roof as her mother again. Funny how the years had softened the blow of her mother's words and strange how quickly the sting could return, as if no time had passed after all. She'd returned with fresh reminders of her failures, only to find that a jumpy woman from out of town had snagged the man she'd had her eye on for two years.

Julie's curiosity about Hana heated up under the new, personal issues now at stake. What did they really know about her? She was Kara's sister from out of town. Wasn't there some sort of scandal associated with her a while back? Maybe a year ago—or even longer? She remembered Kara talking about it constantly at the time, but since Julie wasn't a close friend of Kara's, she hadn't been privy to any of the details. Maybe someone else would remember the details. She didn't like to pry in other people's business, but the fact that Pastor was falling all over himself at the mere mention of Hana's name seemed to make it Julie's business.

"I've come to realize that you're just not going to get married, and I've stopped counting on you for grandkids." Her mother's final words to her as Julie loaded up the small box of personal items her aunt had left her. "Honestly, I've come to terms with the disappointment."

Julie wouldn't accept this newest development lying down. It was a disappointment she wouldn't live with, couldn't live with. No matter that Hana's stay was temporary; she couldn't risk Pastor pining over Hana once she was gone. Julie would never be able to compete with the sense of a love lost. On the drive home, she couldn't tell if the tears pricking the back of her eyes were due to the possibility of losing Pastor or because she sensed her life was slowly shifting, fitting into her mother's prediction with alarming accuracy.

Hello, Button,

Your father has fallen into long, deep silences. I think he's grieving. You're a bouncy, beautiful four-year-old, but we are still finding new things to grieve.

I try to think of it this way: for every new thing I think of that we can't do with you or that you maybe will never do or that you're struggling with, I think of one great thing that we enjoy about you. Like your love of donuts and how your face lights up when we take you to The Donut Hole. Seriously, it's your favorite place on earth. The other day we bought donuts and went to the park and looked for turtles in the pond. You were so happy.

I try to think about things like that instead of the sad stuff. I imagine you with your cheeks full of donut, and it makes me smile. I have to think about that stuff, Button, or I will cry, and I won't stop. And then where would you be? Stuck with a silent daddy and a crying mommy.

XO

Mommy

10

"He left a note this time." Vicky's voice, heavy in her ear, as if she was scared and trying to mask it.

"Oh no, I'm so sorry." The words automatic, polite, also masking a dull fear slowly filling Hana's chest. "What did it say?"

"No, I'm not . . . I'm not telling you that."

"Vicky, I—"

"No, you don't need to know. I just thought you should know there was a note."

Typical Vicky—giving just enough information to whet the appetite but not enough to truly be in the know. Hana stared at her phone afterward, the busy clamor of Sunday morning preparations filling the McCauley house, warm and bright and cheerful. Why now? Why on Sunday morning, right before church?

"Aunt Hana, Isaac took his shirt off." Clem came thudding down the basement steps, Isaac's plaid dress shirt dangling from one hand.

"What on earth? Why?"

"He spilled water on it. He says it's dirty now. He won't put it back on."

Hana sighed and took the garment from her niece. "I'll get him another shirt. Be right up." She moved about the house, participating in the morning activities, but all the while absent. She finagled Isaac into another shirt and cleaned up Charlie's spilled bowl of cereal, but she was absent. It felt like someone else in her body doing these things.

The McCauley kids had come back from camp late last night and were dragging their feet this morning. Hana had decided to try Sunday School but now hesitated. It felt like too much this morning. Too much hard. Too much new. The McCauleys usually didn't attend Sunday School, so it would just be her and Isaac. Too much. Not after that phone call. Hana stopped herself. No, that would be letting him win, letting him control her long distance. She said she was going to do Sunday School, so she would do it.

"Hana, are you okay?" Kara asked with her pajama bottoms still on; blouse on top, makeup half done.

"I'm fine, fine." She would be fine. She would choose to be fine. With autopilot hands, she got herself and Isaac into the car, leaving the rest of the household to finish preparations as she and Isaac headed out to Sunday School.

Isaac sat in the back seat holding Rocky. "Today Rocky can see the church. Pastor said he can take a tour of the church." Isaac was chatty when he was on his favorite topic, and the idea of Rocky getting his very own tour had Isaac in stitches. He was talking so fast that he was verbally hiccuping, skipping and repeating phrases in his enthusiasm. "Do you think . . . the church? Do you think? Will Rocky . . . will Rocky be able to see all of the church? All . . . of it? Even every part of it? Do you think?" Whereas some kids got jittery when excited, legs kicking, body bouncing, Isaac got still, as if the sheer weight of anticipation was immobilizing, and it was all he could do to keep it together enough to keep the words going.

Hana shot a glance to the back seat. Isaac was sitting with his knees pressed together, leaning forward earnestly, eyes wide. She laughed silently and felt some of the numbness slip away. It was good to see him so happy. Hopefully that enthusiasm would get him through the Sunday School hour.

Regina had been overjoyed when Hana had told her on Thursday after Bible study that Isaac would be in her classroom. Hana had wanted to sit in the first Sunday, but Regina had put her foot down.

"This is time for you to be spiritually fed, too, you know. We'll be fine, and you'll be right down the hall if we need you."

When Hana had found out that Clara was the second teacher in the classroom, she'd felt better. She'd instantly liked the younger woman.

They pulled into the parking lot and were no sooner through the door than Regina was by their side. "This must be Isaac. I'm sorry we haven't met earlier." The older woman put a hand on Isaac's shoulder.

Isaac grunted, shivered, and shook Regina's hand off his shoulder as if it were a spider, all the while informing her, "Rocky is getting a tour today. Did you know that? He is going to see all of the church. All of it."

"Oh, okay." Regina frowned in confusion.

"Remember what I told you, Isaac? This is Regina, and she'll be your Sunday School teacher." Hana scanned the narthex for Clara but didn't see her. "I'll walk you down to your classroom, okay?"

Hana led Isaac down the hallway, following Regina to one of the many classrooms. Hana wished she'd enlisted one of Isaac's cousins to come sit with him. There was already a handful of kids in the classroom, and Clara was present and busy talking to them about their weekends. Hana pulled Regina aside before leaving. "He doesn't like to sit still, so sometimes he'll want to stand. Maybe if you put him in the back, so he's not blocking anyone. And he'll want to keep Rocky with him at all times. If he self-soothes, it's okay, just as long as he doesn't hit himself too hard or is too noisy. If he is, you can just come get me, okay?"

"Yes, dear, it'll be fine." Regina patted her arm. "Really, though, you should fill out that form Lynn gave you. These are all good things you could note on the form."

"The form, oh, right." Everyone was so fixated on this form. Isaac was standing at the back of the room, clutching Rocky's cage. "Well, okay, I'll go, I guess."

"Yes, go, go!" Regina shooed her out and closed the door.

Hana lingered in the hallway. Was this the right thing to do? Or was she throwing too much change at Isaac all at once? It was so hard to know when it was appropriate to test his limits and when it was just too much. He protested so much over every little thing that sometimes Hana found herself not pushing him enough so as to avoid a meltdown or pushing him too much and causing him to overload and shut down. Single parenting Isaac was more challenging than she could have imagined, although, if she were honest, she'd been doing it for much longer than a year.

"Will you be joining us for Sunday School?" Hana looked down the hallway to see Julie hovering outside another classroom.

Great. "Hi, Julie. Yes, we're giving it a try this Sunday."

"You trying out Ron's class? I hear it's phenomenal."

"No, I was going to sit in on Pastor's."

"Oh." Julie's expression slipped. "Well, it's right this way."

Hana followed Julie and then sat next to her because it seemed rude to enter a room with someone and then sit somewhere else. Others trickled in as Julie turned to her. "We should grab a coffee sometime—get to know each other better."

"Oh, sure," Hana answered hesitantly. Julie's tone was a little forced, as if she had extended the invite out of duty rather than desire.

"Will your son be participating in our Vacation Bible School program while you're here this summer?"

"I'm hoping so, yes. Actually I'm planning on attending the meeting tomorrow night."

"Oh, you're planning on volunteering?" Julie said a little too brightly.

"Yes . . . is that okay?"

"Yes, of course. I'm the head of the volunteers and will

be leading the meeting, so I guess I'll see you then." Pastor entered at that moment, and Julie broke off to rise and greet him.

Hana sat with teeth gritted. Why did everything feel like a competition with this woman? What were they competing for?

They were going through God's promises, and this particular lesson was on the promise of the Holy Spirit. Charlotte had been right in saying Pastor's classes were intense. Hana found herself impressed at his depth of knowledge and compassion. He took complicated passages and dissected them, making them manageable and interesting. He was a natural teacher.

Hana quickly regretted sitting next to Julie, though, because every time Pastor told them to open their Bibles to a particular passage, Hana had to turn to the table of contents in order to find the right page number. Julie, however, flipped her pages with zero hesitation. Hana quietly observed others around her. Most paged through their Bibles as easily as Julie did. Some had little tabs marking the different books of the Bible. That's what she needed—tabs. She could remember whether a book was in the Old Testament or the New Testament, but beyond that she felt herself flailing. Her Bible pages, too, were obviously brand spanking new. Their shiny gold edges were unmarked, and the pages stuck together, making loud crinkling noises as she pried them apart. She looked around and saw Bibles tattooed with scribbled notes; some even had small doodles in them. Hers was embarrassingly fresh-faced, unspoiled by study.

Through her embarrassment, Hana still listened, drinking up Pastor's words, surprisingly hungry for what he had to say. She heard things that sounded familiar, but they were pounding into her like she was hearing them for the first time. The Holy Spirit was a seal. She didn't realize that. He was a seal upon her until the Last Day. He was a promise and, therefore, a certain reality, given as a gift to her. It wasn't something she could lose. She was sealed and secure in this promise.

What did that mean exactly? She remembered what Clara had said during that first week of study. What mattered was God's faithfulness to us. And then Pastor had reiterated the sentiment, saying that we could count on God's faithfulness even when we couldn't count on our own. She was sealed and secure, secure even from her own wandering and doubt and fear? That seemed too good to be true. The lesson ended too soon. It was more lecture and less discussion based than the Thursday night Bible study, which Hana was grateful for.

She realized with a jolt that she hadn't been called away to come get Isaac. She'd been so enthralled by what Pastor had to say that she'd forgotten to worry about Isaac—had, in fact, completely forgotten about the phone call that morning and all the accompanying fear. Now at the close of the hour, the anxiety began to creep back in.

Hana gathered her things and turned to tell Pastor how much she'd enjoyed the lesson, but Julie had beaten her to the punch. She stood between Hana and Pastor, entirely blocking her. Hana fought a surge of irritation. She felt so stumpy next to Julie—stumpy, frumpy, and grumpy. She chuckled in spite of herself. Could she get anymore juvenile?

Hana ducked out of the class and made her way toward Isaac's classroom. Clara was in the corner, putting away an old flannelgraph, while Regina sorted through the children's handouts and gave them to the few remaining children. "How did he do?" Hana asked as Regina handed her a packet of papers.

"Oh, just fine; we did just fine, didn't we, Isaac?" Regina answered firmly.

Isaac approached her moaning and swinging at his chest. "Can we go now? I want to see Pastor. Pastor said we can take a tour."

"Yes, we can go." Hana turned Isaac to face Regina. "Can you tell Ms. Regina thank you?"

"I have my kids call me Mrs. Chance," Regina corrected.

"Oh, okay." Hana nodded to acknowledge the correction.

Then, to Isaac, "Can you tell Mrs. Chance thank you?"

"Thank you," Isaac said woodenly, his eyes on Rocky.

"Look me in the eye, Isaac." Regina came over and stood directly in front of them, putting a knobby knuckle under Isaac's chin, nudging his eyes upward.

Hana frowned and moved Isaac back a bit so Regina lost her grip on him. "Please don't touch my son like that." It's what she wanted to say. "Better get going, thanks." What she said instead.

"Okay, but before you go . . . " Regina pulled her aside. "Are you entirely sure it's a good idea to let him have that turtle all of the time?"

Hana looked at her in surprise. "Was there a problem with Rocky being in the classroom? Was it distracting or something?"

"Oh, no, not really. I'm just saying from my experience that sometimes giving into children's whims and idiosyncrasies exacerbates behavioral problems."

Hana frowned, unsure how to respond to such a forcefully stated opinion. "It's not really a 'whim,' Regina—" she tried countering but was interrupted.

"I'm just saying it might be a better tactic to wean Isaac off the turtle, so to speak. It's not like he can drag the creature around with him forever. Sometimes what's immediately easier isn't what's best in the long term." She patted Hana's arm, as if she were doing her a favor by sharing this bit of wisdom.

Hana pulled away and reached for her son. "Time to go, Isaac." She couldn't seem to drag her eyes from Regina's, however hard she tried. The woman appeared to be unswervingly sincere in her advice, and Hana didn't know whether to laugh or to cry. So she chose instead to flee, dragging Isaac behind her.

They were in the hall, and Hana's nerves were still settling over the encounter when a bright voice sounded behind them, "Isaac, wait!" Hana turned to see Clara hurrying from the room. She came up to them, slightly out of breath. "You didn't think you'd get away without saying good-bye, did you?" She grinned at Isaac and held up a fist. "Do you want to show your mom?"

Isaac held up a small fist, and the two hit them together gently, saying, "Bump!" at the same time.

Clara turned to Hana with a smile. "So I learned today that Isaac doesn't prefer handshakes. Can't say I blame him. I mean, who knows what germs people have?" She grimaced at Isaac. "So we decided to give each other fist bumps. I told him it's the kind of greeting Rocky would probably approve of. Who's bumpier than a turtle? I bet they bump shells when they greet each other." She looked at Isaac as if to say, "Am I right or am I right?"

"Actually turtles don't do that," Isaac corrected. "They don't bump shells."

"Hmm," Clara said thoughtfully. "Something else I learned today. Thank you, Isaac! You sure know a lot about turtles. You'll have to tell me more next time, okay?"

"In fact, turtles are very solitary creatures," Isaac continued. "If they see a different species of turtle, they would just fight with each other, probably, and not greet each other at all."

"Oh, really?" Clara said, her eyes widened as if she was discovering a great truth. "Come to think of it, that makes sense! Can't recall ever seeing a bunch of turtles all together. So this would be why."

"Yes, this would be why," Isaac repeated, and Hana could see that he was pleased that Clara was catching on. Normally his pleasure would spark her own, but not today, not right now.

"Isaac, that's enough for now," Hana said tiredly. Was Regina right after all? Was allowing Isaac to bring Rocky with him simply the easy solution and not the best thing for him?

"In general, turtles like their own space."

"Isaac, I said *enough*." Hana fought to keep the exasperation out of her tone but knew she was failing. She knew she was taking out her frustration with Regina on her son but couldn't seem to help herself.

"If you are introducing turtles to each other, it should be in a highly monitored area." Isaac sounded like he was quoting from one of his many nature books.

"Isaac," Hana hissed, drawing him aside. "I said enough. No more turtle talk for today."

"It's okay." Clara was smiling. "I enjoy Isaac's passion. You're very smart, Isaac."

"It's more like obsession than passion." Hana smiled, but the smile didn't match her tone, and she inwardly grimaced, wishing she could check her irritation with Isaac and just accept the compliment. "I'm sorry," she backpedaled. "That's nice of you; thanks, Clara." She wanted to say more, wanted to say, "Thank you for taking the time to try to understand him rather than try to force him to understand you," but found she couldn't.

"No problem; Isaac is a great kid." Clara smiled at them both before turning back to the classroom.

The narthex was bustling when they reached it. The peace Hana had experienced while listening to Pastor teach that morning had already dissipated as she stood to the side with Isaac. So many people, and she felt like she was known to all of them—Kara's poor sister with the special needs son—whereas she knew nothing about any of them. It felt uneven, lopsided, as if she were entering a game with the deck stacked, a half hour too late and with no idea of the rules. It was unnerving, the sense that she was already known before she could truly be known.

They entered the sanctuary and made their way to the front. Hana sighed deeply as she saw who was sitting in the second pew, directly in line with Pastor. "Hi, Julie."

"Oh hi, Hana! This must be Isaac." Julie leaned forward to Isaac, who was settling himself in the pew and sitting Rocky on the seat next to him. "You all are sitting right up front? And he brought a turtle with him?"

"Yes, long story." Hana just smiled and turned to face forward as the opening hymn began playing. She was fine with letting Julie stew in her own juices for a while. The service went nearly as well as last week, with Isaac sitting in anticipation of talking with Pastor and showing Rocky around. She'd had to leave with him once when he wouldn't sit and insisted on standing and swaying. She'd walked quickly, avoiding eye contact as she'd led Isaac, moaning, from the sanctuary. Once they'd reached the narthex, however, Isaac had been more distressed at the idea of being unable to watch Pastor than at the prospect of sitting still.

"You can't have it both ways, Isaac," she'd sighed, the weariness settling in her bones. "Either we go home and you miss seeing Pastor and Rocky misses his tour, or you go back in and sit still."

Pastor and the tour had won out, and Hana had made the long trek back down to the front, again avoiding eye contact, especially with Julie. For the remainder of the service, she found that she was more fidgety than Isaac—restless with the idea that Julie's eyes were boring into her back. She felt like Pastor's eyes were on her the whole time, too, but she didn't know why or what he was thinking. Or maybe he was looking at Julie?

After the service, Hana and Isaac intercepted Pastor. "Can we show Rocky around now?" Isaac shouted.

Pastor smiled and ruffled Isaac's hair. "After we greet everyone, okay?" He turned to Hana. "Everything all right? He did good. Really, he did." Hana thought he was probably misinterpreting her funk with the fact that she'd had to remove Isaac partway through the service.

"Yes, of course; why wouldn't it be?" Was he sensing the residue of leftover panic from Vicky's early morning phone call? Or her jangled nerves from Julie?

Pastor didn't look convinced but left with Isaac to greet everyone at the door. Hana saw Julie move in her direction. In order to avoid talking with her, Hana pretended she didn't see her and made a beeline down the aisle for the narthex and from there the restroom. Move of a coward—hiding out in the bathroom—but Hana didn't care. She was afraid of interaction at the moment, afraid her feelings were running too high and wouldn't stay under the surface where they belonged.

She lingered in the stall, listening as women came and went, chatting happily, exchanging inquiries into one another's lives and stories about their own. These women obviously felt at ease with one another and in the church. For them, church was home, not obligation. It was familiar territory, not an uncertain adventure. Could she reach that point? That level of "fit-in" that earmarked you as inherently "part of" and not "other"? And what would that feel like? She was just about to leave the stall when the door to the restroom opened, and two women entered. Hana recognized Julie's distinct voice immediately. She was talking in hushed tones with the other woman, but their words still echoed throughout the room.

"I asked Trisha, and she remembers hearing about a divorce around a year ago."

"Oh, that's right! And wasn't it because her ex-husband had some sort of problem?"

"Problem, you mean, like, mentally? Like his son?"

"No, maybe an addiction? I don't know for sure. Just that there was something wrong with him that led to the divorce. I remember Kara talking about it whenever it all went down. She seemed sure that he was in the wrong, but then again, of course she'd side with her sister."

Hana stood silently in the stall, one hand on the door. It'd been unclear who they were talking about, until they mentioned Kara. She expected to feel anger—hot, heavy, and blinding in her head—but she didn't. She felt absolutely nothing. It didn't feel real. Just like earlier that morning, she felt detached from her body. It wasn't her hand on the stall door, wasn't her feet slowly inching back, instinctively wanting to hide, to be "unseen." This wasn't her right now, and they weren't talking about her. None of this was real.

"I just feel uneasy about the whole thing. And now I'm finding out that she wants to volunteer with VBS," Julie sighed. "I don't think we should be having people we don't know interacting with our children. Right?"

"Yes, I completely agree. Someone should bring this up to Pastor."

"Oh, I'm planning to."

Their voices faded as they left, but Hana still stood, immobile, in the stall. They hated her; these women so at home with one another in this huge metal church in the middle of nowhere. They hated her and found her suspicious and untrustworthy. Because they didn't know her. Because they thought they did.

Hana swallowed past the lump in her throat and forced her hand to push open the door. There, she was moving. It was her hand, after all, and these were her feet, and she was moving, past the sink, the full-length mirror, the welcoming settee pleasantly arranged in the corner. These were her limbs, and she was making them move her body out the door, down the hallway, into the narthex, and then she stopped and blinked and looked around and wondered how on earth she'd gotten there.

"Hana, there you are!" Kara approached her. "Troy and I are taking the kids home."

Hana returned her sister's side hug and managed a big smile. It was a defense mechanism. Whenever things felt impossibly bad, Hana compensated with a smile. That way there were no questions. "See you at home."

She'd felt success. When Isaac had opted to come back into the service, when Clara had fist bumped him in the hallway, she'd felt success. Those things still counted, were still good, happy things to hold on to, right?

With a sinking heart, she realized that the only reason Isaac was doing so well in church was due to Pastor Schofield. He'd taken the time to know Isaac on his own terms rather than approaching Isaac with an agenda, with a desire to shove him into some precut mold. What if she couldn't find someone like that in Richmond? She and Isaac were a unit, a team, a package deal. To not accept her was to not accept Isaac and vice versa. Pastor had made her feel welcome, but now she felt horrible for coming to this church. She was obviously making people uncomfortable. And Isaac just seemed to be a knotty problem or puzzle that Regina and others were trying to figure out. The Hana-Isaac duo was complicated, messy.

The place was nearly empty when Pastor and Isaac approached her. "Is Rocky ready for his tour?" Pastor asked cheerfully, watching her with concerned eyes.

"Yes!" Isaac shouted. Hana plastered on a smile as she watched Isaac's happy face. She loved seeing him so excited. When was the last time she'd done something fun, just her and Isaac? Besides the long car ride to Kara's, which could hardly be classified as fun, especially since Isaac disliked being in close quarters. She should take him out for donuts. She'd ask Kara where the best donut place was.

"Okay, Rocky has already seen the narthex and sanctuary, so how about we go back to the fellowship hall?" Pastor led the way down a hallway of classrooms to the back. As Pastor talked, Hana warred with herself. She wished she'd met someone like Matthew Schofield earlier in her life. Maybe then she wouldn't be in the position she was in. Why did the right people come into your life at the wrong moments? He was so kind and good with Isaac. Why did he have to be a pastor? She must seem pathetic to him—like someone broken and impossible to fix. He'd been kind and reassuring on the Madison farm, but if others in the church were suspicious of her, then how could he not be too?

From time to time, she felt his bright eyes on her. She needed to get her emotions under control, to stop the fear and panic from peeking through, so he would stop looking at her in that concerned way of his.

They finished with the fellowship hall and made their way to his office. Hana swallowed hard, remembering how easy it'd been to talk to him here the week before. Maybe she could talk to him again that way. Invite someone else into the mess that was her life. She stood in the middle of his office half listening to him talk to Isaac. She stared hard at a photograph on one of his bookshelves. He was standing in full snow gear on a mountain with a beautiful woman, both of them smiling. If he and Julie weren't an item, could this be his girlfriend? Where was she now?

"Hana? Hana?" She whipped around to see Pastor standing in the doorway, Isaac nowhere to be seen.

"Where's Isaac?" Hana felt panic jump in her chest as she bolted to the door.

"It's okay!" Pastor held out a comforting hand. "He's right here." He stepped aside to show Isaac standing behind him. "We were leaving, but you didn't follow. Is everything okay?"

"Who is she? Your wife?" Hana motioned abruptly to the picture.

"Oh, um, no—my sister."

"Oh. Right. Okay." Hana mumbled, suddenly embarrassed and unsure why she'd even asked in the first place.

"Hana, I know you said you're fine, but you aren't convincing me."

"No, I appreciate your concern, I really do." Should she tell him what she'd overheard in the bathroom?

"Are you worried about your upcoming move?"

"Kind of, I mean that's part of it."

"That's good . . . that you found a place," Pastor stuttered. "I'm glad for you, but I'll miss you . . . and Isaac. We'll all miss you here."

From what she'd just overheard, Hana seriously doubted that. "Thanks."

"Are you still planning on coming to the VBS meeting tomorrow?"

"About that . . . " Hana decided to divulge part of the conversation without getting into specifics. "I think there might be some concern over having me be involved when I'm new to the church."

"What? Who said that?"

"Oh, it's just the impression I got," Hana said quickly.

Pastor bit his lip in thought. "Here's the thing. If you want to be involved with VBS, then I think you should be. Please don't worry about it." He paused and then looked at her closely. "Hana, you okay? If you'd like, you can come a little early, and we can talk things through more if you like. If it would make you feel better."

Hana turned her attention back to Pastor. Isaac was getting restless, and she knew she was trying his patience. She needed to get him home and fed. Pastor's face was expectant. What had he said? Something about meeting him early tomorrow. "Yes, sorry, yes, we can talk before the meeting tomorrow."

She watched his face shift before her eyes. She couldn't tell what expression finally settled there. Relief maybe. Or acceptance.

"Sounds good. I'll see you then." He turned to Isaac, squatting so he could talk to Rocky as well. "Good-bye, Isaac. Good-bye, Rocky. I'll see you again soon, okay?"

Isaac nodded enthusiastically as she hurried him through the door, wondering at the tightness in her chest. The longer she was around Pastor, the more she wanted to tell him everything. But then he really *would* look at her as if she was broken, and she didn't think she could take that look—not coming from him.

Matt watched Hana and Isaac leave and felt a dull acceptance fill his chest. She was moving to Richmond, to a new life. He sensed that she was trying to pick up the pieces of her life again and that she was finding where her faith fit into her new life. From speaking with Kara, he knew that she and Hana had grown up with a church home. Had Isaac and his many needs driven her away from church life? Or had it been Zeke? Or a combination of both? And now she'd heard hearsay in the congregation about her volunteering in VBS and she was feeling unwanted. Matt knew with a sinking sense of certainty that when it came to Hana, he needed to put his pastoral robe on and leave it there. She was in a pivotal time in her life and was reaching out to this congregation to find where church fit into her life again. This was a crucial time for her and Isaac, and she needed someone to minister to her—not to romance her. Matt needed to let go of this nervous, jittery, happy feeling she elicited in him. He needed to let that go and not look back.

Hello, Button,

You are over the moon because you finally have what you've been wanting for a long time now—your very own pet turtle. We found him in the middle of the road, sitting there like a present waiting for us to discover him. Your daddy wasn't thrilled about it, but you can be a very insistent little fellow when you want to be. It took some convincing, but now you have your very own turtle!

When I asked you what you wanted to name him, you immediately said "Rocky." I assume this is because he looks like a rock from a distance. A suitable name then. I hope this helps you. I've created a little chore chart for you, listing all the things that Rocky needs. Food, clean cage, all of that. We went to the pet store together and picked out an aquarium, but I think we may also need to get a smaller cage too—one that you can carry around with you. You don't want to be separated from Rocky, not even for a moment.

Your daddy would have preferred a dog, I think, but you want nothing to do with mammals. You've always preferred reptiles. I told your daddy that at least you don't have a fascination with snakes. I don't think I could handle having a snake in the house! But I think he might have even preferred a snake over a turtle. He said at least snakes are elegant, mysterious, and sometimes deadly, whereas turtles just sit and do nothing. I tried telling him that turtles can be deadly too—remember that book on snapping turtles we got from the library!— but I think turtles just aren't "flashy" enough for your daddy.

We've been learning about turtles together, you and I. Like I didn't know that many turtles can live to be over one hundred years old! Can you believe that? I wonder how old Rocky is. Strange to think that he could out-live us all. I told your daddy about their lifespan, and he said maybe with any luck he's ninety-nine and we only have to deal with him for a year. He was trying to be funny, I think, but it upset you so much that you screamed for an hour, worried that Rocky was going to die. I had to convince you that he was the same age as you and had many more years ahead of him. But then that upset you because you were afraid Rocky would have no one to care for him when he got to be one hundred. So I had to tell you that he would live just as long as you and no longer.

Your daddy thinks I shouldn't promise things that I can't deliver on, and in theory that's probably true, but what's the harm, I tried telling him, what's the harm in telling a boy who loves his turtle very, very much that he and his turtle will live a long, happy life together?

XO

Mommy

11

The early morning air was chilly and misty with dew, the moisture settling around Hana like a clammy glove, the droplets mingling with her sweat and creating a sheen that chilled beneath the fingers of the wind. Her feet pounded the pavement, and her breaths wheezed out of her with each footfall as if forced out by the exertion of putting one foot in front of the other. The sound of her breathing filled her head. Usually when she ran, she had earbuds in, but she'd left her music back at the house. Instead Hana listened to her own gasping breaths synchronized with the sound of the pavement beneath her shoes and tried to lose herself in the pounding rhythm.

It'd been a while since she'd run. The past year it'd been just her and Isaac, and she couldn't leave him by himself. And even before then, she wasn't comfortable leaving him with Zeke. She'd missed the adrenaline rush that came from pushing herself physically. She knew she should take it easy, that she was pushing herself too hard, but she couldn't seem to decrease her pace. It was too intoxicating—this unthinking exertion. Her mind was filled with physical discomfort, leaving no room for anything else, and it was such a relief. Hana felt the stitch in her side, the sharp jab between the ribs that tempted her to slow down, to clutch her side, to give herself a break, but instead she pushed through it, welcoming the sharp pain as it snaked through her, shooting jabs of pain to her head, causing a dull headache to spread behind her eyes. Now her head was pounding in time with her feet. Her breaths, the thud of her footsteps, the pounding in her head. Gasp, thud, pound. Gasp, thud, pound. A perfect harmony of discomfort.

The morning was just beginning to lighten, and most of the surrounding homes were still dark, with some showing the beginning signs of life. The McCauleys lived in a sprawling neighborhood filled with tidy, middle-class homes set back far from the road and at a decent distance from one another, giving each house an ample yard. Occasionally, a dog announced her passing with indignant barks, and twice she passed commuters, but for the most part it was silent, still, and calm. Troy had already left for work, and everyone else was still asleep when she'd left. Hana figured she'd be back before Isaac woke up.

She'd spent most of the night tossing and turning, finally leaving the bedroom for the sofa in the living room, hoping the change in scenery would help her sleep. It hadn't. So she'd left the house early in the morning to run as fast and far as she could. All the prodding and poking about her past, it'd threatened that walled-off part of herself, the part that she'd been so diligent in secreting away, out of the light, out of sight—even of herself. She was trying desperately to prove the saying "out of sight; out of mind," and it'd been working—somewhat.

The mind itself was a tricky thing, though. There were different levels, all housing different feelings, different parts of the self. One level housed the superficial—it was a comfortable, unthinking plane of mindless distraction. The next level was where Hana spent most of her days—the functional, active, thinking part that allowed her to get dressed and make choices and conduct herself in all the socially acceptable ways so as to get herself to the end of the day when she could settle back into the mindless level. And then there was a third level, where all artifice was stripped away, and her nerves were laid bare and open. It was the level where secrets were hidden, where voices murmured, "You can't do this." "You're not enough." "You're too much." It was where her giant lived, walled off, large and lumbering. It was the quivering underside to everything else.

Hana found that if she kept moving in the other two spheres, kept her mind busy and occupied, she could outrun that third level. Except at night, when there was nothing to occupy the mind but sleep. It was then that the giant reared his head and said, "Welcome." And there was no climbing out of it. Nothing to do but war with it all night until finally morning came and she could climb back to the busy, functional level and pray that maybe the next night would be better, kinder.

It wasn't until the bright light of a Phillips 66 blazed into view that Hana realized she'd run straight out of the subdivision. She was just preparing to turn around when she saw the sign for a donut shop. *Donuts.* She slowed enough to shove her hand in her pocket. She probably had enough on her for a bag of donut holes. She'd buy Isaac donut holes and surprise him when he woke up. She ignored the handful of stares she elicited as she dodged around the gas pumps and up to the small shop next door. She left moments later with a small sack. It was the ultimate oxymoron—jogging with donuts. She let the thought make her smile for a moment as she broke into a fast sprint back through the gas station, entering the subdivision once more.

The pause in her run had allowed the old doubts to creep back. What would be waiting for them in Richmond? Would Zeke really leave her alone? Could she do this—raise Isaac on her own? Hana ran faster, the small white bag twisting in her hands. She just needed to get back to a fast pace, get her heart rate up again, so it crowded out all these thoughts. Unfortunately, she didn't know how to get back home. Hana ran blindly, her gaze trying to latch onto something familiar.

Had she passed that house with the yellow siding before? She didn't know. She hadn't noticed much of anything during her mad dash out of the subdivision. Surely that dog had been barking at her earlier; she must be going the right way.

Hana jogged through the neighborhood, going faster and faster as her anxiety increased. She hesitated at every side street, wondering if she should take it, and it was at one such street where she hesitated, her body turning slightly left while her feet pushed her forward, that she felt the split-second sensation of falling. The world shifted, and she felt weightless, as if she were being liberated from the earth. Only she wasn't, and her body knew this instinctively and hurried to correct itself. She twisted her body to catch herself, to stop the trajectory of a complete face-plant. And as she did so, she felt her left foot roll. She came to a stop and knelt on the ground groaning, her hands braced against the pavement, the bag of donut holes smashed between fist and ground. Her breath came quickly through gritted teeth as she turned to sit on the curb, hunching over to rest her head on her knee. The pain in her ankle was now masking all else as she sat and breathed through it.

There was no way she was making it home before Isaac woke up, not with this latest development. He'd probably be confused, waking up to find her gone. Kara would have to field that confusion, talk him through it. Thankfully, his breakfast was pretty easy to manage: two bananas sliced diagonally and chocolate milk. Kara knew to prepare it for him, right? She'd seen Hana do it enough times. Well, if she didn't, then Isaac would tell her—loudly. Hana grimaced as she examined her ankle. Would Kara know not to let Isaac go out back by himself? It was a constant fear, that Isaac would someday end up by a body of water by himself, get too close out of blind enthusiasm, fall in, and drown. Kara would know not to let him go outside unmonitored—unless Isaac woke up before her and just went outside to the back looking for turtles or to the front looking for her. Hana let this newest fear outweigh the pain, and she struggled to her feet. The pain was intense, but she pushed through it as she stumbled through the awakening neighborhood.

Kara was in the kitchen making breakfast when she heard the front door open. She looked up to see her sister standing disheveled and sweaty in the doorway, a crushed bag in her hand. "Hana, what on earth? Where have you been?"

"I went running and sprained my ankle." Hana leaned against the doorjamb and threw the bag onto the counter. "These are for Isaac. Where is he? Did he get his breakfast? He didn't go outside, did he?"

"Honey, come sit down!" Kara left what she was doing to run to her sister and ease her into a barstool by the kitchen island. "Isaac is fine. He's finishing his chocolate milk in the living room with the kids. That looks nasty." She grimaced at the swollen ankle. "You should have called me to come get you. I tried calling you. I was confused when Isaac came upstairs without you and said you were gone."

"I didn't have my phone." Hana leaned back in the seat and propped her ankle on another barstool.

"Let me get some ice." Kara dashed about the kitchen, her hands on autopilot as they found a plastic bag, filled it with ice from the freezer, and grabbed a dishtowel to wrap around the ice pack. Whenever Kara was around her sister, she always felt like she was in damage control mode. It had always been that way. Kara was the predictable sister and Hana was . . . well . . . predictability wasn't in her repertoire. Her choices had always seemed sporadic and unplanned, and as a result, she'd been the one to get most of the attention growing up—both good and bad. Unpredictable choices meant Hana got into more scrapes and required more scolding, but it also meant that Hana's life always seemed louder and more interesting, and that got more attention too.

Kara often felt dwarfed by her sister's personality. Hana was spontaneous, whereas Kara cared too much about retaining control. She supposed that was why Hana was prone to getting hurt—she went through life with her heart wide open, which made hurt inevitable. It was a messy, uncontrollable way to live one's life, but one that Kara had to admit she admired. Perhaps the chief reason Kara had disliked Zeke from the beginning was that Zeke unashamedly eclipsed Hana. The buoyant spontaneity she'd always loved and resented her sister for had been squelched by Zeke, who seemed all about receiving attention, no matter the cost.

"Do you want to tell me what happened?" Kara bent over Hana's leg and spent longer than necessary arranging the bag of ice around the swollen ankle.

"Happened? Nothing, really. I was running and pushed myself too hard. Thought I could do more than I could and hurt my ankle."

Kara gnawed her lip, unsatisfied. "Okay then." There was so much Hana wasn't telling her. Something had broken in her sister that now made her a mystery to Kara and that had increased the distance between them exponentially. She knew how her life must look to Hana—perfect and orderly. She knew she couldn't understand the depth of what Hana was going through, but sometimes she felt like Hana held that against her and used it as an excuse to hold back with her, which hardly seemed fair. "Well, next time you go for a run, maybe take your phone with you."

"I doubt I'll be running again anytime soon." Hana shifted her foot and winced.

Kara was about to return to breakfast preparations when Hana stopped her abruptly. "Hey, do you think . . . is it a good idea for me to get involved with VBS at your church?"

Where is this coming from? "Sure, why not?"

"It's just, Isaac isn't very familiar with church. I feel bad . . . we should have . . . I should have made more of an effort to raise him in church."

"Well, don't let that stop you now."

"I know, I just don't know how welcome he will be, or I will be."

Kara took a seat next to her sister at the island, sensing

that a larger conversation was happening. The eggs would just have to burn. "Well, I wouldn't let fear keep you away. I think it's a great idea for you all to get involved while you're here."

"Okay, I'll go to the meeting, then." Hana's voice was definitive, and she looked away.

The conversation was apparently closed. Kara stood again, trying hard to push back the frustration that rose in her. Hana did this so often lately—opened the door to deeper communication just a crack, only to shut it with a bang after she got what she wanted from the conversation. The truly frustrating part was that this closed-off tendency was something new in Hana. Her open, fun-loving sister had slowly become more and more withdrawn. Sure, some of it probably had to do with how preoccupied she'd had to be while learning how to raise Isaac, but Kara blamed it largely on Zeke.

She moved back to the stove and began scraping burnt pieces of egg off the frying pan. She listened to her children in the next room and, not for the first time, felt that sharp sense of relief for her family. It filled her with guilt to feel relieved that she wasn't in Hana's position. She didn't know why God chose to give such levels of hardship to some people while keeping it away from others. Of course, each family, each person, had their trials to bear, but it seemed some had especially more than others. Kara buried the guilty feeling in a smile as she entered the living room, breakfast—minus the eggs—in hand.

Hana watched Isaac eat the crushed donut holes, relishing his enthusiasm. They were sitting outside by the creek in the wretched heat. Hana would rather have stayed inside, but she knew how much Isaac loved the outdoors and so had decided to give him two of his favorite things: time spent by the water . . . with donuts.

She wasn't the only one who disliked the new climate. Isaac, ever the outdoor boy, had taken it hard that he could no longer run outside barefoot, as he was used to doing. The dry Oklahoma grass was filled with burrs, something he had learned the hard way. His calloused feet had seen more protection in the past month than in all his seven years of summers with no shoes.

"I want more," Isaac mumbled around a mouthful. Hana responded by holding out the bag. She smiled as Isaac reached a sticky hand inside and came out with no less than three donut holes.

"Okay, that's it after that." Hana laughed. Any more and he'd be bouncing off the walls. She glanced inside to see one lonely donut hole left and quickly popped it in her mouth and crumpled the bag. "See? No more!" she managed around the bite. "You ate them all!"

"I want to see." Isaac shoved a donut hole in his mouth and grabbed at the bag. Hana flattened it out again and opened it for Isaac to see for himself that there were indeed none left. Isaac nodded, as if he'd just proved a tricky theorem.

Hana leaned back in her chair, balancing her still swollen left ankle on her right knee so as to elevate it. She still couldn't believe she'd rolled it. Now she'd be hobbling around for who knows how long, looking even more pathetic than she already felt. Isaac let out a loud belch. "What do you say?" she reprimanded automatically.

"'Scuse me." The answer came quickly, robotically. And then he stuffed his mouth full once again.

Hana observed his profile. It was unnerving how much he looked like Zeke. Not only was he proving daily to have inherited his father's height, he'd also inherited the sharp jawline and sandy hair, the small focused eyes and large ears. Hana's chest ached to see it.

As she sat quietly next to her son, the summer stretched long before her, filled with moments defined by extremes: periods of high stress replete with meltdowns and verbal battles that left them both exhausted, or periods of intense quiet as she sat and observed her son doing something monotonous. Some parents probably looked forward to summers with their children, or so she imagined. They probably planned fun activities and vacations. Hana wished she was looking forward to the next two months, but in truth they appeared daunting. Isaac thrived on a schedule, which helped regulate him, so a summer defined by transition and upheaval was proving to be particularly hard on both of them.

When she'd first transitioned Isaac to public school a year ago, it'd been a challenge to entrust him to someone else, to believe they would have his best interests at heart. Not everyone who claimed to be an advocate for your child was indeed one—something Hana knew all too well. But over time they'd both adjusted, and now Hana found herself looking forward to the start of the new school year. Even though it would be hard to transition him to a new school that fall, Hana was also craving the regularity it would provide for them both—and the break it would give her. Guilt came on the heels of this thought, but she quieted it by turning to her son. "How did you like your donuts?"

"Good! Let's get some more." Isaac had finished his donuts and was staring at the empty bag.

"Not today, but maybe another day, okay?"

"Another day we will get more donuts. Maybe that will be today."

"No, not today."

"Then tomorrow."

"Probably not tomorrow either." Like most children, Isaac did well with concrete answers. He liked to know exactly what day and time you meant. "How about we make this a treat every Monday? Each Monday we will go get donut holes."

Isaac's face lit up. "Yes! Can it be Monday now?"

"That's not how it works, sweetie." The name slipped out before she could stop it.

"I'm not sweetie! I'm Isaac!"

"Yes, you're Isaac. Next week on Monday, we will go get more donuts, okay?"

Isaac grunted and turned away. Hana looked at the back of his head and for the zillionth time wondered exactly what went on in there. His questions weren't much different from other children's. He, like any other child, loved sweets and knew how to wear a parent down with questioning. But his questions *were* different. There was a centered focus and anxious edge to his questions. The need to know when, how, where was all-consuming. It was no mere pestering and wearing down to get his way—it was an insatiable need, like an itch that he couldn't reach and he needed her to scratch.

She followed the blog of a mother with two special needs children and remembered an especially helpful post comparing the author's son's mind to a laser. Most people have minds more like a scanner. We take in a bunch of different data at once and pick and choose what we want to focus on. The blogger's son, and Isaac, had minds more like a laser—directly focused on one thing at a time to the point of exclusion. Hana found this to be an apt description. When Isaac turned his focus on something, there was no getting it off that subject. Days, weeks, months could go by, and he would still be obsessing over something. This focus spilled into all of his life. He felt things instantly and intensely, and when he liked something, he absolutely loved it, and it was all he could talk about—for years. And when something devastating happened . . . well, that, too, took years of recovery.

Hana wiped some incriminating crumbs from her lap and let her eyes follow Isaac's to the creek. Still, she wondered what was going on moment by moment in his head. Zeke had never been able to do this—just sit with Isaac and interact with him on his turf and by his rules. She willed her thoughts to skip over Zeke, to push off him quickly, like a swimmer off the floor of the deep end, choosing to push toward the surface—toward air, toward life.

Pastor Schofield, now there was a man who seemed to intuitively understand how to interact with Isaac. She smiled at the thought of him with Isaac's hands in his beard. She thought of how Pastor's face lit up at the sight of her son.

It was such a gift to her to see someone genuinely like her son—not just deal with him, but to *like* him. With a start, she realized that Pastor was the closest thing to a friend Isaac had had in a long time. Who said friends have to be your own age? Sometimes friends come in all sorts of packages. Maybe even a stocky, bearded package. And suddenly Hana knew that whatever the personal cost and no matter the wagging tongues, Isaac needed to be at Hope with his new friend.

Hello, Button,

I heard your daddy crying today. I was in our closet putting laundry away, and he came in and sat on our bed and started crying, big, deep sobs. It scared me, Button. I'd never heard him cry like this before. It was just these deep gasps that sounded like someone was tearing them out of him, literally ripping them out of his chest.

I wish I could say that I went to him, that I put my arms around him and held him. But I didn't. I stood frozen in our closet, clutching one of his dress shirts— just standing there with his shirt in my hands as he cried and cried. Even after he left, I just stood there.

Oh, Button. I don't know what's happening to us, to our family. I feel like we are so tightly wound that we will break at any moment. It's like we are all holding our breath, waiting for something. And I think your daddy just let go, just for a moment.

I wish I could be stronger for him and for you.

XO

Mommy

12

The phone rang first thing Monday morning, five minutes into Matt's first cup of coffee. It startled him, and he grabbed at the phone, answering in a rush. "Hello, this is Hope Lutheran Church, Pastor Schofield speaking."

"Pastor, hi, how are you?" a smooth, feminine voice replied.

"Hello, Julie." Matt leaned both elbows on his desk and began rubbing his temple with his left hand. He needed to finish his coffee or he'd get a headache. "What can I do for you?"

"I'm wondering if I could stop by this morning to speak with you about something."

"Oh, um . . . " Matt shoved papers off his desk to look at the calendar beneath. It was filled with chicken-scratch memos. "Sure, I'm here most of today. When would you—"

"I can be there in twenty."

"Minutes?"

Julie laughed brightly. "Of course minutes. Not hours! Is that okay?"

"Oh, uh, sure. I don't see why not."

"Wonderful! See you soon!"

Matt hung up and took a large gulp of coffee, not caring if he burnt his tongue. Julie was perplexing. She volunteered in just about every capacity at church, so much so that she had been given a key to the building. She was young and vibrant and beautiful, which, in and of itself, wasn't necessarily perplexing, but she was also teeming with tension, which made her hard to read. She was a focused and pointed individual, arriving in their congregation like a fresh breeze two years ago and then promptly attaching herself to his side. She was at every church event, volunteering, always helpful. In his years of ministry, he'd found that there were usually three types of church volunteers: those who served out of a grateful heart and desire to praise God and give back to Him out of their talents; those who used church service as a way to earn favor with God; and finally those who used busyness as a way to escape something else. He wasn't sure which, if any, category Julie fit.

Matt finished his coffee and cleared off a seat for Julie just as he heard a knock at the door accompanied by a verbalized, "Knock, knock."

Why did people say "Knock, knock" if they were actually knocking? Matt had never understood that. It was like narrating your actions, which was completely unnecessary. The same people didn't go around saying "step, step" as they walked or "chew, chew" when they ate. Matt smiled and gestured toward the freshly cleared chair. "Come on in. How are you doing?"

"Doing well, thank you." Julie entered with a paper sack that she set on his desk. "Thought you might like a croissant." She sat, crossed her legs, and leaned toward him as he took a seat behind his desk.

"Thank you, that was thoughtful of you." She was always doing such things for him, as if she was head of a pastor appreciation committee that he knew nothing about. He opened the bag and pulled out a chocolate-filled croissant. "Care to join?" He raised it in her direction.

"Oh no, it's all yours." She was looking as beautiful as ever in her crisp blue uniform, the no-nonsense lines of the light blue shirt and dark blue skirt accentuating her natural air of efficiency. He realized she was on her way to work. "Thank you again for the treat. You're probably short on time, so how can I help you?"

"Yes, I can't stay long, but I wanted to touch base with you before our VBS meeting tonight."

Ah yes, she was heading up that meeting. He should have guessed this meeting was about the later one. Matt took a large bite of the croissant. It was warm and gooey.

"It's come to my attention that Kara McCauley's sister would like to volunteer."

Matt had been lost in contemplation of all things sweet and chocolaty but at Julie's words quickly looked up. "What about Hana?" He spoke around the bite in his mouth.

"It's just I'm concerned about her working with our children if we don't know much about her."

Matt set down the croissant, wiped his hands on a napkin, and cleared his throat of the crumbs.

"You have . . . a little bit . . . right . . . " Julie gestured to his face with a smile.

Matt quickly wiped at his beard. He felt silly now, cramming his mouth full of pastry. "What, exactly, are you concerned about, Julie?"

"Really, her past is not my business, and I wouldn't think twice about this except that it has to do with our children. I don't know that we as a congregation should be accepting just anyone to work with our kids."

"Well, she's family of one of our members."

"Yes, but what do we really know about her? I'm just concerned."

"Here's the way I view it." Matt dumped the rest of the croissant back in the paper sack. "She's family to the McCauleys, here for the summer, and expressing a desire to be a part of this church community. Why should we close the doors on her?"

"I'm not suggesting we close the doors on her." She

laughed and swatted her hand in a what-a-silly-thought gesture. "I think it's great that she's here with her son. Of course we want people to worship here and be fed the truth. What I'm saying is, should she really be volunteering with our children?"

"I'm sure a large part of her desire to volunteer with VBS is so she can help with Isaac."

"And that's another thing. Regina was telling me how resistant Hana was to having Isaac in her class. I get the sense that she doesn't trust people here to work with her son. She should be able to trust us to care for her son in VBS."

"Along those same lines, shouldn't we let her be present to help her own son? I think it's natural for her to want to be present to help her son transition into a new setting. She doesn't know us; Isaac doesn't know us. Let's welcome them both by showing some understanding." He'd spoken with a more authoritative tone than he'd intended. He observed Julie's closed features and tried to do some damage control. "Julie, I appreciate your passion for our VBS program and your commitment to our kids. Let me assure you that she'll be treated like every other volunteer. We'll be doing a background check. I'm sure everything will be fine."

"Okay, I understand what you're saying. As long as you feel comfortable with it then." She smiled at him, but it seemed tight and constrained, not the free, open smile she'd entered with.

"Thanks again for this." He gestured to the paper sack.

"You're welcome." She stood and flashed him another smile. "I guess I'll see you tonight, then."

"Yes, tonight. God's blessings on your day." He watched her leave and then sat back thoughtfully. Could this be what Hana had sensed the other day? Perhaps she'd been right— there were some people who didn't feel comfortable with her volunteering. It was confusing to him, really. Was it fear of the unknown that made people suspicious? Hana didn't fall into an easily understood category. He would admit that. He knew all too well how those who fell outside the norm were oftentimes marginalized. So is that what made her suspect? It was human nature to be open and welcoming to those who were similar to you—much harder to extend the same to those who were dissimilar, unfamiliar, and whose needs felt out of your depth. He rubbed a hand over his face. Perhaps that was it. Sometimes the deeper the need, the more the church resisted out of a fear of failure. Or, on the flip side, the more they tried and overcompensated.

He glanced at a wall clock. It was still early morning but not too early for a phone call. He picked up the phone and dialed. "Hi, Kara, this is Pastor. Is Hana there? . . . Oh, no, no. Please don't interrupt her if she's busy with Isaac. Just pass along a message . . . Yes, thanks. Just tell her I can meet with her anytime today before the meeting tonight. She can ring me at the office, or you have my cell, right? . . . Good. Okay, thanks." He hung up and rested his chin on his fist. They were about finished with their study of Colossians. Maybe a new topical study was in order. He usually preached exegetically and often in accordance with the Church Year, but he had been known to occasionally take tangents into the realm of the topical. And if others shared Julie's hesitation over Hana, then maybe it was time he did so once again.

Hana hobbled into Hope. She was thirty minutes early for the VBS meeting and was glad no one was around to witness her wobbling progression down the hallway to Pastor's office. Some over-the-counter pain meds and a compression bandage had helped tremendously, but her ankle was still swollen and hard to walk on. She tried to straighten as she reached the office door. It was opened a crack. She leaned in and knocked. Pastor was standing by his bookshelves with several volumes tucked in the crook of his arm. It was unclear whether he was shelving them or had just plucked them for use. Regardless, it was an appropriate stance for him. Hana felt a rush of warmth at the sight of him. There was something wonderfully safe and peaceful about this man. Like he was an especially comfortable pair of jeans that just made you happy every time you put them on. "Am I interrupting?"

"Not at all!" Pastor turned to greet her, his already broad face widening further in a smile, his lips disappearing into his beard. He set the books down on his desk and gestured toward a chair.

Hana willed herself to walk normally, but two steps in and she had to resort to a hobble.

"Are you okay?" Pastor was by her side in an instant, his large hand cupping her elbow.

"It's silly, really." Hana accepted his help into a seat. "I twisted my ankle running this morning. I was just pushing myself too hard."

"I'm so sorry; you should have told me. I could have come to you."

"No, it's fine." Hana waved her hand as if shooing a fly.

"Look, Hana . . . " Pastor leaned his elbows onto his desk, his steepled fingers poised in the air between them. "I want you to know that you're welcome—here at Hope and in the VBS program. I know you're worried about acceptance, but please don't be."

Hana leaned back in her seat and studied his earnest face. "I appreciate you saying that. It's just . . . I don't feel comfortable just throwing Isaac in by himself. He's been through so much change so quickly, and I think it'd be a good idea for me to be with him in his class."

"And I understand that."

"Which isn't to say I don't trust the other volunteers to care for him," Hana jumped in quickly, realizing she was touching upon their conversation on trust from last week.

"It's just you don't know them, and they don't know you, and VBS is an intensive week. I get it; I do."

Hana sighed deeply. "Thank you." She should feel satisfied, but she still felt antsy and unable to articulate why.

Pastor seemed to sense something unspoken in her. "Anything else on your mind that you want to talk about?"

"Well, I've been thinking a lot about what you said the

other day, and it's been encouraging—it has—but I still feel
. . . empty. I wish I could *feel* differently, you know? Like the
feelings are lagging behind me, and it's becoming annoying."

To her surprise, Pastor laughed. "Ah yes. Our feelings.
They either seem to be jumping way too far ahead of us, and
we're scrambling to keep up and regain control, or we're
dragging them along behind like a piece of baggage. Thank
God that our faith does not depend on our feelings."

"What do you mean?"

"Well, feelings are uncertain creatures; they shift and they
change constantly. Jesus certainly had them. He was fully
man, after all. This is why we see Him weeping at Lazarus's
grave, weeping over Jerusalem, enjoying the company of
beloved children, reclining at ease with His disciples. He
certainly felt things, both high and low, and felt them deeply—but our Lord never allowed feelings to compromise His
purpose. When the two aligned, well, that was fine and good,
but if they didn't, His Father's purpose always prevailed. We
see this quite poignantly in the Garden of Gethsemane when
the Lord is so conflicted in His spirit over the death that
awaits Him that He literally sweats blood. I've always found
this picture of Christ particularly compelling. His humanity is
just so evident here. Everything in Him did not want to meet
the bloody death ahead of Him. In fact, He begs the Father to
remove the cup from Him, but what does He ultimately fall
back on? Thy will be done. He is *feeling* dread, but He is *doing* His purpose regardless. In this way, He sets an example
for us. Feelings are not an enemy, but they are not the final
word either."

Hana had been listening quietly, observing his earnest
features come alive as he talked. She'd seen this before—
when he got going on a topic, he lost himself. Oh, he was still
talking to you, but he was also talking to himself. He leaned
forward, just like he did in the pulpit, and his voice became
more even and paced. You didn't want to interrupt him when
he was like this. The urge to just listen was overwhelming, as
if something in his voice invited one's attention and then kept

it. There was a pause, and so Hana filled it. "So, you're saying not to worry if my feelings don't catch up?"

He smiled at her then, his eyes crinkling in the corners. "Bingo. Also, I remember you saying before that you felt like you were learning to walk again. Well, remember when learning to walk, it's important not to push yourself too much. You must be patient with yourself while also trusting that you will get there."

"I guess that's true. Isaac walked much later than other kids, but I remember how he concentrated while he was learning and how frustrated he'd get when he fell."

"Yes, same idea here." He paused, and she watched something somber pass over his face. "Now, I don't know the details of what you've been through, and neither do I need to know." His voice caught. This was another thing she'd observed. When he spoke from the depths of his own feelings, his mannerism changed. He was less collected, more tentative, as if testing each board beneath his foot, tapping each one before taking a step. "The past is something that should be voluntarily shared and not extracted." He paused again—tap, tap—and then continued, "But I would be amiss if I didn't also give you words of counsel, should that be okay with you?"

It was a question, not a demand. She appreciated that he was waiting to be invited into her life rather than just barging in. She found herself nodding in agreement.

Pastor surprised her by gesturing to her injury. "What happened there—pushing yourself to the point of physical injury—that can happen spiritually as well. I know we talked about this a little the other day, but I want to reiterate that you don't have to worry about your feelings catching up and try to fix it by being in church more or doing more, somehow *being* more. Sometimes people equate these things with faith itself. They turn what is a work in the heart to a work of the hands, thinking if they try harder they will draw closer to God. Now, I am in no way suggesting that is what you are doing or experiencing, but I want to encourage you that as you are making this transition with Isaac to focus on the heart and not the hands. You don't have to feel guilty for being away from church. You don't have to play catch-up. You don't have to earn back God's favor. He who began a good work in you is faithful to complete it, and you need not worry about losing that good work."

Hana could sense the heart behind his words. She felt the tension in her body recede as she tentatively shared, "I think I'm finally beginning to understand that better. I'm finally beginning to realize I don't have to make up for lost time or something." She laughed shakily.

Pastor smiled at her, no condemnation in his eyes. "By all means, we welcome you and Isaac to the church, to VBS. We want you here, but more important, I want you to rest in the knowledge that you don't have to clock in on some divine punch clock to get God's attention."

Hana smiled at the comparison. "Thank you, that helps more than you know. I just, I wish . . . " she fumbled with how to express her concern. "I want Isaac to be welcomed, too, you know? And sometimes I feel like people are, oh I don't know, looking at him like he's some sort of project. Does that make any sense?"

Pastor had leaned back in his seat, his expression shrouded in thought. "Yes, that absolutely makes sense. When it comes to ministering to those with special needs, it is first and foremost a heart issue. Before jumping to procedures and strategy, it is first a question of how do we see the vulnerable? As a problem to solve? Or as a person to love?"

"I've never heard someone put it that way, but yes!" Hana leaned forward eagerly.

"We are blessed with some very loving Christians here at Hope, but like anywhere, there are some who may not know how to minister to Isaac. All I can say is to be patient with people."

"I'm just so thankful that Isaac has found a friend in you," Hana said. "Thank you for your encouragement." The emotion in the room was heavy. Hana tried to lighten it by pointing to her foot and saying, "And I'll try not to sprain my spiritual ankle."

Pastor laughed, his eyes brightening. "There you go. That's all I ask."

Julie collated the handouts in the fellowship hall, one eye on the door. She'd lingered outside Pastor's office before heading down the hall. She'd been able to make out a female voice inside but hadn't been able to see who it was since the desk was against the far-right wall, and the door, even though ajar, had still been blocking her view. Although it'd been tempting, she hadn't been about to stick her head around the door and announce her presence, so instead she'd resigned herself to waiting in the fellowship hall. When Pastor entered with Hana, Julie's jaw tightened. She should have known that's who was in his office. Worse yet, Pastor had his hand on Hana's arm. Julie observed them quietly, lips pursed. Hana was clearly favoring her left foot. Julie wondered if it was even hurt or if it was just a ploy to gain Pastor's sympathies. Her heart clenched at the negative thought. It was something her mother would have entertained—this idea that women should resort to any measure to secure a man—and she'd see anyone's actions, however innocent, through a negative lens. Julie had promised herself she wouldn't be like that, like her, but here she was, assuming that the hobbling woman before her was faking an injury as a way to one-up her in some sort of twisted competition. Julie bowed her head and focused on the papers in front of her. When had she decided such thoughts were okay?

Others joined them in the fellowship hall, and Julie turned her attention to them, steadfastly ignoring Hana and Pastor, who, of course, had decided to sit down near her. If she couldn't think gracious thoughts, she'd try not to think anything at all. When everyone was present, Julie opened the meeting. "Welcome, everyone! Thank you, first of all, for giving up an evening to meet with us tonight and, second, for your service to our children. Before we get to the meeting itself, Pastor, would you lead us in prayer?"

As Pastor's familiar, deep voice filled the room, Julie bowed her head and tried hard to focus on his words. The group was murmuring "Amen" and beginning to stir before Julie realized the prayer was over. She quickly looked up, hoping it'd appeared that she was especially fervent in prayer that night and not that she'd spaced out.

"Thank you, Pastor. So far we have thirty children signed up for VBS, up from last year, so . . . " She led in applause. "Of course, we'll be leaving registration open leading up to the event, so please, get the word out to your family, neighbors, and friends. As you know, the theme this year is 'God's Word Is a Lamp to Our Feet.' So the focus is on darkness and light. Here's an opening video to introduce the theme." Julie hit play on the remote and stood in the back as the short clip played. She watched as everyone took in the video, her gaze snagging on the pair just in front of her.

Even after years of association with Pastor, Julie didn't have the rapport that he apparently shared with Hana. Why? "You're not trying hard enough," was her mother's catchall, and for years Julie had engaged in questionable behavior as a way to "try harder." It wasn't until recently that she'd repented and realized that advice was erroneous and her implementation of it in direct contrast to God's Word. She supposed that's why this newest disappointment hurt so deeply. She'd felt she was on the right path this time. She was interested in a pastor, for crying out loud! She was engaging in God-honoring activities! But she still couldn't get it right.

With a start, Julie realized that the video had stopped playing, and people were beginning to fidget in their seats and turn their heads to find her. She bustled back to the front of the room. "So I have a sign-up sheet I'd like to pass around. Please mark which classroom you'd like to volunteer in or if you would prefer a different role. If you feel so led to be a craft leader or games leader, please indicate that on the sheet as well." She started the form on its way around the room and then turned to the handouts, which she'd sorted into folders. "This is for all of you to take home and look over. Please take one and pass it on. Most of it you can just look over on your own time, but some of it we'll go over now." As Julie went over the safety procedures, she noticed Hana open her folder and rifle through the papers with a frown. "The only thing I'll need back from you is the pink sheet: the background check authorization form. I'll go ahead and collect those from you all tonight. Any questions?"

She fielded a few questions, all the while aware of Hana, who was looking from the stack of papers back to her with a distraught expression on her face. A few people began handing the forms back in. Julie continued answering questions as she collected them, her attention split between the forms, the questions, and Hana. She shuffled the forms into a neat stack. "Okay, was that everyone's form?" A few more trickled in, and then Julie found herself facing Hana, who still had her form clutched in her hands. "Yes, Hana?" Julie paused in front of her, eyebrows raised.

"I-uh-I . . . " she looked lost and conflicted.

"Is there a problem with the form, Hana?" Julie prodded, watching as Hana's words stuck in her throat.

"No," Hana answered and slapped the form down on the table, quickly signing it and handing it to Julie without meeting her eyes.

"Okay, then, unless there are any other questions, I think we're done for the night." Julie stared down at Hana's rushed signature. The form had obviously made her uneasy. *What are you trying to hide, Hana Howard?*

Hana had insisted she could make it out to her car just fine, but Pastor had insisted more loudly that he would accompany her. She could still feel his strong hand on her arm, supporting and guiding her. She'd worried she'd feel pathetic hobbling around, but instead she felt valued as he guided her. He'd lingered by her car, asking after Isaac, making small talk, but all the while her mind was on fire.

A background check? She hadn't thought of that. Would a background check show what happened last year? She hadn't done anything that would come up in a background check, but what about the other stuff? Would all that come up?

She couldn't shake the panicked feeling as Julie stood in front of her. Her face innocent and open, politely waiting on her, obviously wondering why she was hesitating. She had sat there while everyone else signed unthinkingly and turned their forms in while she sat frozen in fear. She couldn't very well refuse, not in front of everyone. So she had signed and prayed nothing would come of it. *It wouldn't, right?*

Now Pastor was gone, and with him the warm feeling of comfort he brought. She was left with her own worries and doubts. She tried shoving them aside to focus on the words of encouragement and counsel he'd given her. It was true—she'd been running headlong into church hoping she could outrun the feelings of inadequacy and guilt. If she kept up this frenzied pace, she'd end up as she had that morning—crumpled in pain on the curb. She didn't need to try so hard—there was such relief in that thought. Relief, also, in the thought that her feelings would catch up eventually and that in the meantime, they weren't an indicator of what was *true*.

But as Hana drove home, her most fervent prayers were over her past and that it would stay where it was and not come to haunt her at this church or taint her or Isaac's friendship with a certain stocky, bearded, thoughtful man.

Hello, Button,

On especially rough days, I try to remember how thankful I am that you are what's considered "moderate functioning." It's easy to lose sight of this. In your behavioral therapy class, there's a boy who is completely nonverbal. He just doesn't speak. I look at his mom, and I realize that even though to an observer we may be the same, we're living two different realities, and I really cannot understand her situation.

It's humbling and challenging to realize how simultaneously alone and connected we all are in this struggle. There are support groups and therapies and other parents who are working through this too, but really, at the end of the day, we—all of us—are our own people. You, my sweet Button, are uniquely you. I am thankful you can talk to me, even as I mourn that it's not more than it is. Such a strange, mixed-up feeling. To be thankful and to mourn all in one breath.

I think your daddy is struggling to get to the thankful part. I can't judge him for that. But I do mourn for him, that he can't seem to get to the good—he's too caught up in the hard. I wish I could mourn with him, but there is an invisible wall between us. Like we are exhibits at a zoo, looking at the world and each other through glass.

But what we have in common is you, and we love you. This is what gets me through the day. You are my sweet boy—for better, for worse, for always.

XO

Mommy

13

The day dawned in pieces, the sun slowly casting off the dark as the earth reformed into a landscape, and its inhabitants slowly reappeared to meet a fresh start. Hana's morning, however, had been a loud one. Pastor had called Tuesday night to say he couldn't make their usual fishing outing on Wednesday. A congregant was in the hospital after an unexpected complication during surgery, and he needed to visit with the family. Isaac had already been in bed, so Hana had waited to tell him in the morning, and he'd taken it hard.

He didn't understand why Pastor couldn't be there, didn't understand that sometimes things come up last minute. Thankfully, a compromise had been reached with Hana agreeing he could still go as long as he stayed with one of his cousins, which meant no pond. It was a hard compromise for Isaac to take, and he spent the car ride over to the Madisons' bursting out with random, loud objections to the situation. In the end, he was forced to accompany Clem since Alex had stayed at home, and Charlie was too young for babysitting duty.

They pulled up to the Madisons', but before leaving the car, Hana twisted in her seat to stare Isaac down. "You need to stay with Clem, do you hear me? She's in charge."

Isaac grunted and turned away from her. Hana reached into the back to put a hand on his leg. "Look me in the eye, Isaac." He reluctantly turned to her but kept his eyes downcast. "If Clem tells me that you've misbehaved, then you will lose privileges. There will be no more fishing with Pastor for a while."

"No!"

"I don't want that either. So listen to your cousin and stay with her, okay?"

"Okay!"

When Isaac was upset, everything was uttered in exclamation marks, as if punctuating each word could change the distressing circumstances.

"Okay, that's what I want to hear." Hana turned to Clem. "I'll start with Sam and then send her out to you, okay?"

Clem nodded and took Isaac by the hand, leading him to the barn, while Hana and Charlie entered the house.

"Want to pet the goats, Isaac?" Clem dragged her cousin behind her.

"No! I want Pastor!"

"Well, Pastor isn't here this week."

"Will he come back next time?"

"I don't know. Probably."

"Say yes!"

"Yes, he will."

"And then we will go to the pond again."

"Yeah, I'm sure if he's here next week, he'll take you to the pond."

"Let's go to the pond now."

"I don't think your mom wants you going that far today. Besides we have to wait for Sam. She's meeting us here after her lesson." They'd reached the barn at this point, and Isaac wrenched his hand out of hers to sit on the ground in a huff. Clem squatted next to a stall that housed goats, clicked her tongue, and held out a hand. "Here, pretty girl." A black-and-white goat came trotting up, weaving its head up and down as it searched for food in Clem's hand. She laughed. "Come pet it, Isaac." She held the goat still and gestured to Isaac, who slowly scooted over to her and reached out a hand to pet the spiky head.

If she were honest with herself, Clem had been disappointed when she'd found out she'd be on Isaac duty. Suddenly something fun had been turned into something challenging. The silver lining, though, had been the fact that Alex had decided to stay home. Sam insisted she didn't like Alex, but Clem could tell otherwise. It was like Clem just disappeared whenever Alex was around. And then afterward that's all Sam wanted to talk about. Alex this. Alex that. Honestly, it was disgusting and annoying. Thankfully, she would have Sam all to herself today. Well, Isaac would be tagging along, but at least she didn't have to worry about losing Sam to Isaac.

"Here, I brought some carrots from home." Clem reached into her pocket and pulled out a plastic bag filled with carrot slices. "Hold your hand like this." She opened her palm flat, face up. Isaac held out his hand, face down. "No, like this." Clem turned his hand over and put a carrot piece in it. "Make sure you keep your fingers flat or she'll think your fingers are food and eat them."

Isaac's eyes grew big, and he flattened his hand so hard that the piece nearly fell off.

"No, silly, just like this." Clem relaxed his fingers a bit and then watched as Isaac held out the carrot to the goat, who eagerly nibbled it up.

Isaac let out a squeal and jerked his arm back. "It tickles!"

"I know, right? Their lips are so soft."

"Again! I want to do it again!"

Clem gave him another piece and then another. More goats joined them at the gate, until Isaac had quite a following. Clem set the bag next to him, so he could help himself and then moved farther into the barn. The light was streaming through some broken slats, and small dust motes were visible in the air. Clem had always thought of herself as a city girl. At least, that's what she'd been used to up until now. But out here on her best friend's farm, surrounded by all the rustic charm, Clem could imagine herself staying here forever. The sun made patterns on the barn floor, casting speckles of light across a weathered barrel that housed feed. There was a beautiful, bright red watering can next to the barrel, completing the rustic effect. Clem whipped out her phone. This would make an awesome picture. She knelt, angling her phone to capture the barrel, watering can, and the streams of light hitting it. Gorgeous. Clem straightened and posted it to Instagram with the hashtag "nofilter." It was a great picture, just the way it was.

Laughter from the other end of the barn reached her, and Clem looked up to see Isaac sitting cross-legged in front of the gate with the carrots in his lap. He had a fistful of carrots in front of the goats, who were stretching their heads as far as they could through the gate, straining to get at the goodies. Isaac was twisting away, as if anticipating their ticklish tongues. His whole body writhed in joy as he twisted away from them, his face scrunched and happy. Clem grinned and snapped several pictures. She flipped through them, finding the perfect one. Isaac was facing her, his head scrunched into his shoulders, a gritted smile plastered all over his face, eyes squinty as the goats reached toward him with eager lips. Clem uploaded it to Instagram and put a sepia filter on it that made it look antique and included the hashtag "pictureperfect."

"Hey, Isaac, want to see Sam's horse? He'd probably like some carrots too." Isaac bounded to his feet and followed her to Sublime's stall. As anticipated, Sublime was only too happy to accept the carrots. Clem was stroking the horse's soft neck when the loud ding of an incoming message reached her ears. She looked at her phone and saw she'd received a Facebook message. She opened it quickly and stopped in surprise when she saw that it was from her uncle Zeke.

"Hi, beautiful! Love your pics. Isaac and Aunt Hana are with you? That's awesome! Where are you all at?"

Clem frowned at the message. She'd forgotten that she was Facebook friends with her uncle. Or ex-uncle. She didn't know what happened with him and Aunt Hana, but she'd always liked Uncle Zeke. He was big and tall and handsome and had always seemed nice, always giving them treats when they visited. She couldn't remember the last time he'd contacted her, but her Instagram account was connected to Facebook, and he must have seen the picture of Isaac that way. He must miss Isaac and Aunt Hana. Hadn't Aunt Hana said she missed him too?

Clem typed back: "Hi, Uncle Zeke! Yup, they're staying with us for a while. We're at a friend's farm. Isaac loves the goats."

She saw that Uncle Zeke was typing back and waited until his response appeared.

"Neat! Send me more pics when you have a chance. He's really grown."

Clem snapped a picture of Isaac petting Sublime and sent it.

"Wow, horses too! This must be some farm you're at."

"Yeah, it's my best friend's farm."

"Where did you say this farm was?"

"Not far from where we live—" Clem began typing back but was interrupted by Sam bear-hugging her from behind. Clem giggled and nearly dropped her phone, turning to hug her friend.

"I see Isaac made friends with Sublime. Hey, where's Alex? Didn't he come with you today?"

Clem bit her lip and frowned. It was always Alex. Why couldn't Sam just leave it alone? "No, he stayed home today. So, can we take Sublime out for a ride?"

Sam looked disappointed but cheered at the mention of riding. "Sure!"

And then it was busy preparations to ride and busy keeping an eye on Isaac as they took turns riding and busy meeting everyone back at the house and busy loading up the car and busy unloading and talking about their morning, and Clem completely forgot about the unanswered question and her half-formed response waiting in cyberspace.

＊＊＊

Matt woke up in a cold sweat, heart thudding. He sat up and stared around his semi-dark bedroom, blinking rapidly until objects formed. There was the footboard of the bed, there was his armoire, there was his chair with yesterday's clothes draped over the back. He was in his room, and it was still the middle of the night. He sighed and leaned back in his pillows. Like most of his dreams, this one was quickly fading upon waking, but he could still feel the terror. He closed his eyes and revisited the dream before it slipped away completely.

He'd been fishing in the mountains, standing next to a teeming creek when something had snagged on his line. He'd pulled and pulled until finally he'd dragged a small cage out of the water, and in that cage was Rocky, upside down, dead. He'd sat by the side of the creek and cried over Rocky. Isaac was going to be so upset! Then a shadowy figure loomed from the trees. "Give Rocky to me." The voice was deep, but he couldn't make out the face.

"Who are you?" he'd called.

"Give him to me," the voice boomed. It was a terrifying voice. It was the voice of God on Sinai. It demanded obedience. Suddenly Rocky's cage was as hot as lava, and Matt dropped it, yelping in pain. Only it wasn't Rocky inside the cage anymore; it was Elliott, and he was sopping wet. He'd tried to open the cage then, tried to pry the bars open, tried to break the lock, anything to get Elliott out.

"Hurry!" Elliott cried to him. "I want out of here!" He could speak! Elliott could speak! Matt tugged at the bars, but they wouldn't budge. He'd hit the cage with his fists and screamed. It'd bounced away from him and back into the creek, taking Elliott with it.

"No!" One loud wail and then he was gone; he was back at Hope, standing in the pulpit staring out over an empty sanctuary—except for the small figure in the front row. Isaac. Holding a dead Rocky in his hands. He looked up at Matt with such hatred in his eyes that Matt recoiled as if he'd been struck.

"Why did you kill Rocky?" He tried to explain that he hadn't, but no words would come out. He tried to move to Isaac, to comfort him, but he was rooted to the spot, his hands tied to the pulpit.

"Why did you kill him?" Isaac had been replaced by a full-grown man with black eyes and long arms. It was the same voice from the creek, and Matt instinctively knew it was Zeke.

"I didn't kill anyone!" Matt shouted. "What do you want from me?" He tugged and tugged but couldn't get his legs to move. And then blessedly he had woken.

Matt concentrated on breathing deeply. "Lord, remove this hellish dream from me," he prayed out loud, filling the room with his supplication, replacing the darkness with light. "In the name of Jesus, remove this dream from me." The edges of his dream clawed at him, but Matt steadfastly refused them entrance. "Take every thought captive," he quoted. "Take every thought captive." He turned his face into his pillow. Such a horrifying feeling to see Elliott's and Isaac's small faces wreathed in grief and pain. And Zeke—he'd been an oppressive presence throughout. For the first time, Matt let himself wonder and speculate about Zeke unchecked. What exactly was his past with Hana like? And was he waiting in the wings somewhere?

Matt felt a shiver of fear and dread slither down his spine. Were Hana and Isaac *safe?*

He shook his head. It was just a dream. A horrible dream, and he'd take it to the Lord, repeatedly, as many times as was needed.

Hello, Button,

I had the scare of my life yesterday. I woke up from a nap to find you and your daddy gone. He hadn't told me he was taking you anywhere, and I had no idea where you were. I called your daddy, but he didn't answer. All afternoon and into the evening. I had no idea where you all were, and no way to get ahold of you. I almost called the police, but then finally that evening you both came home in one piece. Your daddy had you all decked out in a sports jersey. He'd taken you to a ball game. I must be going crazy. He said he told me about it weeks ago, but I would have remembered.

You were a mess, sweetie. You were fussy and crying and hot and sweaty, and I could tell you'd had a terrible time. Your daddy said it went fine, but how could it? You hate enclosed spaces and sitting still. There's no way you could have made it through a whole ball game without some sort of meltdown, but your daddy wouldn't tell me, and of course you can't tell me yourself. He says he told me about this. Am I going crazy that I don't remember? Or maybe your daddy is going crazy and just thinks he told me. Either way, I'm afraid one of us is losing it.

I'm so sorry, baby. I didn't handle it very well. We try to keep fights away from you, but I just lost it. I couldn't stop screaming at him, which only made you more upset, so then it was both of us screaming—you and me. And then your daddy joined in, and it was a horrible mess. I tried to calm down when I saw how upset it was making you. I tried to tell your daddy to watch his language, but do you know what he said? He told me, "What does it matter—the kid doesn't understand a word we're saying anyway!" He claimed he can just say whatever he wants to and it doesn't matter. What a horrible thing to say. And I think you do know what we're saying. You pick up on more than he gives you credit for. But he wouldn't calm down, and finally I took you in the car and we just drove. For an hour we drove around, and then we went home. And your daddy had locked himself in our bedroom, so you and I spent the night together in your room.

I'm sorry, baby. I'm sorry you had to witness that. I'm sorry you have parents who are coming apart at the seams.

He didn't tell me, Button; he didn't tell me where he was taking you, whatever he may say otherwise. I was scared I would never see you again. You're everything, Button, everything that matters, and I never want to feel like that again.

XO

Mommy

14

It was Saturday, and Hana sat down to look over the form Lynn had given her. She'd had a hard time locating it, finally finding it at the bottom of her purse, creased and crumpled from neglect. She sat at the kitchen table with the form spread out in front of her and a glass of sweet tea nearby.

Kara was stoically opposed to air-conditioning. Even here, where the heat was nearly unbearable, she'd opened every window of the house and employed an army of fans rather than turn on the air-conditioning. "I can't believe you; it's over a hundred degrees out!"

"But it's a *dry* heat, Hana. No humidity!" Kara had said, as if this made everything okay. "All that's needed is to increase air flow, and the fans do that just fine."

So Hana sat in a pool of sweat at the dining room table, pen in hand. The first few questions were easy enough: name, age, emergency contact. But then they turned personal. "Kara, did you have to fill out this ridiculous form?"

"What form?" Kara called from the laundry room.

"The form from that Lynn lady at church."

"Oh yeah." Kara walked into the room, folding a pair of Alex's gym shorts. "I filled one out for each child."

"It's just so ridiculous."

"It's just . . . Lynn, Hana. And it's just a form. What's the big deal?"

"It's not so much the form per se. I mean, I'm used to filling out forms. It's just, I don't know . . . Lynn keeps reminding me about it, like it's all she sees when she sees Isaac, a blank form that needs filling out, a series of check-boxes and fill-in-the-blanks. Like he's not even a real person, just something to be categorized before she even tries to understand him."

"I think you're reading into it a little, Hana. Lynn just operates like that. She likes all her *t*'s crossed and *i*'s dotted."

"In other words, she's a control freak."

"Hana." Kara uttered her name softly, but there was an unquestionable reprimand behind it.

"What?" Hana whipped her eyes up to meet her sister's conflicted gaze.

"Why do you have to be so judgmental sometimes?"

"What?" Hana couldn't believe her ears. "You're calling *me* judgmental?"

"Sorry, I don't want to pick a fight."

"Well, you kind of did."

"You're just so quick to assume the worst of people sometimes."

"Did it ever occur to you that's because I've seen the worst of people over and over?" Hana snapped before she could stop herself.

"Not everyone is out to make your life harder than it already is."

"Than it already is? I really don't need your pity."

"I'm not . . . you're being really defensive right now."

"That's because you attacked me out of nowhere, Kara. You can't just accuse someone and expect them *not* to be defensive."

"Okay, just forget I said anything." Kara turned and left.

Hana chewed her lip, finally grabbing the form and following Kara into the laundry room. Kara was bent over grabbing items from the dryer. Hana watched her arched figure in silence for a moment before launching back in. "Things have felt . . . off since Isaac and I arrived. If you have something to say to me, just say it."

"Why do you have to do that?" Kara straightened but didn't turn around.

"Do what?"

"Make things a big deal. There's nothing off between us."

"Really? It's felt that way to me. We don't . . . we don't talk like we used to."

"We haven't lived beneath the same roof since we were kids. Perhaps it's just that, Hana. Not everything has to be a huge deal."

"Oh, like I always make things a big deal? Is that what you're saying? I overreact all the time?"

"Like you're overreacting now? Kind of, yes."

Hana clenched her jaw. Perhaps the most infuriating part of this conversation was the fact that Kara wasn't even looking at her, but was instead methodically matching socks. "I don't think I'm overreacting. I think people like Lynn are obnoxious." Hana slapped the form down on top of the washer. "And I think this form is stupid. It's just a way for her to feel more efficient and in control. It's not helping Isaac or me."

"You automatically think everyone is against you, Hana, especially when it comes to Isaac."

"That's not true."

"Well, it sure feels like it. Sometimes people are genuinely trying to help, you know?"

"Look, I'm not saying that people don't have good intentions."

"Just poor execution, is that it?"

"You don't know what it's like."

"Exactly, I don't." Kara finally turned and faced her, Clem's purple tween bra suspended between them. "So would you please stop holding that against me?"

"I'm not holding anything against you!" Hana's throat tightened. How did they end up having this conversation?

"It feels like you are sometimes. Like anyone who isn't living your experience is cast into this subpar class of ignorant, misguided people who can't do anything right."

"That is *really* unfair." Hana's throat was so tight, she had to fight to get the words out. "Just because someone is living an experience doesn't mean they know how to handle it. You should have figured that out by now." Her voice broke.

"Yes, I know." Kara sighed, Clem's bra still clutched in her hands. "And on the flip side of that, just because someone hasn't lived an experience doesn't mean they can't help or understand or at least try to."

"Don't you think I know that? Do you know how long I've been the recipient of that help? My whole life has been one of getting help from other people. It's exhausting."

"I imagine it is." Kara finally released the bra, smoothing it out and folding it.

Hana watched her sister quietly for a moment. She didn't want to admit it, but there was some truth to what Kara had said. Hana had a hard time believing people were genuine. She hadn't always been this defensive and suspicious. It'd developed over the years and compounded in the last year. With the realization came a little bit of release. She looked at her sister and willed herself to breathe deeply, encouraging some of the tension to leave her, before replying. "Can we just start over, please?"

Kara finally turned around, her expression closed. "Are you about to do one of your dumb do-over stunts?"

"I wasn't, but now that you've mentioned it . . . " Hana began theatrically backing out of the room.

"Oh, come on, Hana. We're adults."

"Erp, eep, erp . . . " Hana made mechanical noises as she mimicked rewinding herself right out the door.

"Oh, stop it, Hana!" But Kara said it with a laugh.

Hana walked back in. "Hi, Kara, I'd like to discuss this well-intentioned but ridiculous form with you without starting World War III. Do you think we can do that?"

Kara laughed and slapped her with a sock. "There's my sister. I miss this side of you."

Hana leaned a hip against the washer. "I miss it too."

"And the form *is* a little ridiculous," Kara conceded as she raised pinched fingers. "Just a little bit."

"Thank you!" Hana turned and began helping Kara pair socks. The silence felt like a truce, and Hana didn't want to break it. Finally she turned to her sister. "You're a little right, you know. I guess I do make everything a big deal lately, but it's only because everything *has* been a big deal so far. Like I'm so wound up I can't figure out how to regain a sense of normal."

"Yes, I can see that. And you're still in an in-between place. Once you get settled in your new home and start your new job, maybe then things will start to even out for you."

"Maybe." They continued folding in silence for a while.

"You know, you do seem the most yourself when you're interacting with Pastor Schofield."

Hana blushed without knowing quite why. "He's one of the rare people who doesn't have to try to be understanding. He just is. And Isaac already loves him so much."

"And maybe Isaac isn't the only one?"

"What do you mean?"

Kara frowned as if in thought. "Only that you seem incredibly happy around him, and I've never seen him so attentive to anyone. I mean, his job *is* to minister to people, but still, he seems to go above and beyond for you and Isaac."

"He's a pastor, Kara."

"So?"

"So, he is completely out of the league of someone like me."

"So you *have* thought about him in that way?"

"No!" Hana glanced wildly from the pair of socks in her hand to the laundry basket, to the hamper, and back to the socks. "No!" she sputtered again.

"The lady doth protest too much, methinks."

"Don't go quoting Shakespeare to me." Hana rolled her eyes. "I won't deny that he's an attractive man, but if you're sensing anything at all, it's just the relief of having someone befriend Isaac."

"Uh-huh, okay. Whatever you say."

Silence descended upon them once more. Was Kara right? Did Hana like the big-hearted, bearded Oklahoman pastor as more than just a friend for Isaac? She pushed the thought aside. It didn't matter because she was leaving soon, and, more important, there was no way he would look at her as anything other than a person in need for him to minister to. Best to not even allow herself to go there. "I'm sorry if I come across as judgmental to you, Sis," she said softly.

"It's okay."

"No, it's not. It's just . . . " she struggled to find the right words. "It's hard not to feel like it's Isaac and me against the world. As a parent, you have to advocate for your child, right? But with Isaac, it's almost like I have to speak for him too. Like he really has no one else in the world but me. All the decisions, both big and small, are mine to make, seemingly indefinitely. And as much as people may want to help him, to understand him, ultimately I'm the one who will always be the most invested in him, who will understand him the most, and it's a heavy twenty-four-seven responsibility. And I guess it's hard sometimes, to see people who don't have that weight. It's hard not to envy them or feel bitter against them, when you know, you *know*, they haven't done anything wrong. Nothing about your situation is their fault, and you wouldn't wish your situation on them. It's just you get so tired of being so different and so alone and so . . . so messy. I wish my life wasn't so messy." The tightness in Hana's throat had returned.

"Oh, honey." Kara looked her in the eye. "What you're saying makes sense. From my side of things, I can tell you that it's hard being so close to someone but unable to fully enter into their pain or their experience. It's like you want to, but you don't know how to, and you're afraid that any attempt you make will somehow be the wrong one because you don't truly know what they're going through, and it makes you feel helpless. So sometimes people overcompensate." Kara pointed to the half-filled-out form. "Or they don't even try or they don't even *want* to try. Not everyone does have good intentions, and those rotten apples can ruin the barrel, so to speak. But don't let those who try and fail make you wary of all who do try."

Hana sighed and nudged her sister. "You surprise me sometimes with your wisdom."

"Gee, thanks." It was Kara's turn to roll her eyes. They finished folding the laundry together, and as Kara settled the basket on her hip, she turned to Hana. "So one last thing, and then I promise, we can be done with all the heavy talk. I know it's only been a year since Zeke, but don't think you're unworthy or undesirable. If God has someone He wants to place in your life romantically, be open to it, okay? Can you promise me you'll at least be open to it?"

"I promise to try," Hana said. "I can only promise to try." She thought of Pastor Schofield, his hazel eyes brightening in joy at the sight of her and Isaac. The way Isaac felt so comfortable around him. Why did he have to be a pastor? There was no way he would be interested in her, and he shouldn't be. But maybe there would be someone for her down the road. Just maybe.

Hello, Button,

Things haven't been the same between me and your daddy since our screaming match. Now it's as if your daddy wants nothing to do with you, and it breaks my heart. I confronted him about it, and he said, "I can't do anything right when it comes to Isaac, so better I do nothing at all." I feel horrible, like it's my fault. I never meant to push the two of you apart, but that's how he's making me feel—like it's my fault that the two of you are the way you are. Like I broke your relationship.

I want you to have good memories of your daddy, but these days I'm wondering if there's anything good to be had. I know that sounds horrible, but I feel like all I do is try to build bridges between all of us, and all your daddy does is tear them down and then blame the wreckage on me. He's coming home later and later from work. Most times we eat dinner without him, and he arrives barely in time to say good night to you. I don't know how to fix things when your daddy is so angry. My only consolation is that you seem unaware of it all, and I try to keep it that way as much as possible.

I've long ago decided that you will never read these letters. And yet, I write to you anyway because—I don't know—it makes me feel closer to you, to speak directly to you like this on paper.

XO

Mommy

15

I'd like to try something a little different this summer." Matt looked out over the congregation, his eyes latching on to familiar faces. "Now that we're finished with our sermon series on Colossians, I'd like to start a new series on 'The Practices of Love.' As a lot of you may know, 1 Corinthians 13 is often referred to as 'The Love Chapter,' and rightly so. But I think there's a misconception of what we mean when we talk about love. This is the passage most often read at weddings because, I suppose, it's seen as a charge. Two people are making a vow before God in marriage, and so we read The Love Chapter. But the love discussed here by the apostle Paul is much broader than the love usually thought about at weddings. It affects every area of life and, indeed, is at the core of how we ought to live as Christians. Without understanding the fundamental value God places on Christian love, the rest is meaningless, and we will live a fruitless Christian life. So I'd like this to be the first of eight weeks that we'll spend discussing 'The Practices of Love.' What is the apostle Paul getting at here in The Love Chapter? And how can we practically apply this to the Christian life?"

Matt glanced down at his notes before continuing. When he glanced back up, his eyes snagged on Hana and Isaac, sitting in the front row as usual. Rocky was sitting in his cage on Isaac's lap. At the sight of Rocky, Matt's voice caught, and he paused for a moment to clear his throat and take a sip of water. He'd kept the nightmare at bay this week, but it'd required constant surrendering to God. Seeing Rocky in church again brought it all back. Hana was looking at him with an open, expectant face. He allowed himself to get lost in her face for just a moment, and as he did so he felt the world slowly reorient and shift back into place. He sensed, too, God's guidance. These messages that God had placed on his heart—he needed to hear them himself, to be reminded of the truth of this passage of Scripture. And he knew the people of Hope needed to hear them too. He prayed for softened hearts.

Hana left Isaac with Pastor and scanned the narthex for Lynn. It'd been a convicting and uplifting message, and Hana couldn't wait to hear the others in the series. The first message, "Love Is Patient," had especially struck home. Routinely interacting with others out of impatience for their weaknesses and shortcomings was a form of pride because you saw yourself as being above such weakness. Now, as Hana sought out Lynn, the fortuitous timing of the message didn't escape her. She'd been impatient with Lynn and her form, finding it foolish and Lynn overeager and misguided. She'd nursed this impatience from a moral high ground without pausing to consider that her own view of the matter wasn't necessarily the "right" and only view, or that Lynn was on her own spiritual journey, and God was dealing with all His children in different ways and on different timelines. Who was she to operate out of a place of annoyance and impatience when God had been so patient with her?

Hana spotted Lynn by the visitor's center and made a beeline for her. "Lynn, I have that form you asked me to fill out." Hana withdrew the crumpled paper from her purse and handed it to the younger woman.

"Oh good!" Lynn's face brightened as she took it. "I'll make sure Regina gets a copy too."

Hana thought of offering a critique of the form. It seemed odd to her that each child that walked through the door was expected to fill out a questionnaire about pet peeves, food allergies, family history, vaccinations, and more. Like the children were being cataloged for future reference. But she decided it did no one any good to offer criticism, so instead she decided she could best serve Lynn by offering patience, just like Pastor had mentioned in the message. She hoped that she'd be able to find such a solid pastor in her new home.

Richmond, the thought filled her with alarm. She was just beginning to feel at home here, and even though she'd always known this was a temporary stop, she felt sad about the prospect of leaving. Even if she did find a solid church in Richmond with a great preacher, it wouldn't be Matthew Schofield; it wouldn't be the man who had so quickly and deeply embedded himself in her and Isaac's hearts.

Hana was jolted from her thoughts by a gentle hand on her shoulder. Charlotte was at her side. "Where's your shadow?" Hana asked with a grin. Charlotte pointed across the narthex to where Ruthie was holding Charlie's hand and chattering his ear off. Charlie had a look of long-suffering patience on his face, perfectly embodying Pastor's message from that morning. Hana laughed, "Oh, I should have guessed."

"So you know how you wrote me a blank check a while back to help me in any way you could for our church picnic?" Charlotte grinned expectantly at Hana with raised eyebrows as if to say, "You said it, I noted it, so don't you think about backing out!"

"Yes, yes, I did say that, didn't I?" Hana grinned back. "Is this you cashing in?"

"Yes, ma'am. Picnic is this Saturday, and I already feel neck deep in preparations."

"What day this week would be good for me to stop by?"

"Well, I know you'll have all the kiddos with you when you come Wednesday, so how about the day after—Thursday?

My good friend Pam Meyer is coming that day to help too, so all three of us can knock some of the work out. I don't think you've met Pam yet, but you'll love her."

"Sure! I'll double-check with Kara, but I think that will be fine."

"Have I mentioned that you're a gem?"

"Maybe once or twice." Hana laughed. She watched as Charlotte crossed the narthex to extricate Charlie from Ruthie's grasp. She was thankful to have found such a friend in Charlotte, and she was eager to spend time with her apart from tutoring her children and their brief exchanges on Sundays.

Pam brought her two young daughters, Margo and Lucy, with her on Thursday, and the two quickly joined ranks with Ruthie, running to the playroom amidst a cacophony of girlish squeals. "Thanks for having the girls over," Pam told Charlotte as they all three headed into the kitchen.

"Thank *you* for bringing them! Ruthie loves to play with them. If they weren't here, she'd probably insist on 'helping' us in the kitchen, and her kind of help isn't the kind I need right now."

"Oh, I understand!"

Hana listened to the two women talking and felt a sharp pang of jealousy. She'd often wondered what it'd be like to have a daughter. She'd broached the subject once with Zeke—the possibility of trying for another. It'd taken them years of frustration before Isaac arrived, which alone had taken an emotional toll. That, coupled with Isaac's needs, had been enough for Zeke to make his mind up decisively and quickly. No more children.

"Thanks for coming today, ladies. I thought today we could knock out some of the pies for Saturday, if that's okay with you. We have people bringing a bunch of food, of course, but traditionally I supply the pies."

"She's kind of famous for them," Pam leaned over and

fake-whispered to Hana. Pam wasn't much taller than Hana, plump and with curly, short blond hair; she had an engaging and unassuming manner.

"Strawberry rhubarb, chocolate chip, apple . . . " Charlotte started ticking off on her fingers all the pies that needed to be made.

"Goodness! I'm glad you called us in. I can't imagine doing all that on your own," Hana laughed. "I'm not the best cook in the world, but I follow instructions really, really well. So you tell me what to do, and I'll do it. Oh, and I'm also good with a knife, so I can peel apples for you."

"Praise the Lord, we have an apple peeler on our hands!" Pam lifted a hand in thanksgiving. "I can't peel anything for the life of me. I've nearly lost a finger or two trying in the past and I swore, never again."

The women's laughter filled the kitchen as they settled into their various roles: Hana in one corner with a bag of apples and a knife, Pam in the other with instructions to churn out crusts ASAP, and Charlotte in another, ready to roll out the pie crust dough when it was ready, chopping rhubarb in the meantime.

"So Hana, I'm glad to finally meet you, although I have met your son on several occasions. He just loves shaking everyone's hand with Pastor."

"Wait, he's been shaking hands?" Hana stopped, an apple peel curling from her fingers.

"Oh yes, I think Pastor was the one who encouraged him to start shaking everyone's hand with him. So now everyone who leaves shakes Pastor's hand, says hi to Rocky, and then shakes Isaac's hand. They're really quite the team, Pastor and your son."

She'd had very little success in teaching Isaac to shake hands. Clara, even, had observed his hesitancy and instituted the alternative fist bump. "I'm just surprised is all," she managed to squeak out. "I've noticed incremental changes in Isaac ever since coming here and interacting with Pastor. It's encouraging."

"Well, I don't mind telling you, I've noticed the same. Not in your son, mind you," Pam was quick to add. "I don't know him well enough for that, but in Pastor. You and Isaac seem to have unlocked a different part of his personality or something. He's really seemed to come alive. That sounds dramatic, doesn't it?" She laughed. "I guess I mean that he just seems different, better." She leaned toward Charlotte and gave her a meaningful nod as if asking for affirmation.

"I agree." Charlotte shot Hana a grin. "It's nice to see all around."

Hana felt the blush spreading across her face and turned away slightly in an attempt to hide it. Thankfully, the conversation continued in a different direction, flowing easily. Hana had been afraid she'd feel like a third wheel, but Pam was so easygoing and inclusive that she felt like a part of the group, even when Pam and Charlotte began talking about the difficulties of girl drama.

"Everything is just *such* a big deal," Pam lamented.

"Uh-huh. Every. Little. Thing."

"Were we like that as girls?" Pam shot them both imploring looks. "Seriously, were we?"

"Probably," Charlotte sighed. "Although at the time we thought we were simply being reasonable, and it was everyone else who was crazy."

"Or as Clem likes to say, 'cray cray,'" Hana jumped in. "Apparently that's a thing now—means crazy?"

"I think it means super crazy, like beyond crazy, second-level crazy." Pam laughed. "My girls are a little young to pick up the lingo, but believe me they are already acting cray cray."

The three women laughed, and Hana couldn't help but relish in the comparison of three little girls in the next room playing while the three women in the kitchen had their grown-up version of cray cray going on. It was fun and new, this easy banter.

The pies slowly came together, the women producing in assembly-line efficiency—rolling dough, mixing filling, and crimping edges, all the while talking and sharing. Hana found herself offering stories of Isaac, fun stories, stories too easily buried by heavier things.

"He's always been so inquisitive and observant, not of emotions—he doesn't really pick up on emotions that well—but mechanically observant. Like he will observe me operating something and then do it himself. When he was three, he locked me out of the house. He figured out how to lock all the doors, the ones with the little button that you push or the little knob you turn. I was outside getting the mail, and he went around in the house and locked every single door. We didn't have a spare key outside, so I had to call the fire department to come open the door. I was crying and banging on the windows, couldn't see him anywhere. When I finally made it back inside, where was the little stinker? He had climbed onto the counter, retrieved a box of cookies, gone into the master bath, and locked himself inside. He'd eaten most of the box by the time I got to him."

Pam was looking at her with mouth agape. "Now that, my friend, is calculated planning."

"Isn't it?" Hana laughed, oddly proud of her son in that moment. "Isaac definitely knows what he wants."

"And apparently will stop at nothing to get it." Pam raised an eyebrow. "Thank goodness my girls aren't quite that creative. Their escapades aren't exactly premeditated, more like chaotic uprisings."

"Like the time when they got into your nail polish . . . " Charlotte let out a half snort, half bark.

"Oh yes, so get this. We're getting ready for church, and my girls will *not* leave me alone. They want to play with my makeup, they want me to braid their hair, they just won't give me a moment's rest. So I do what any sensible parent would do and lock myself in the bathroom. You know, like Isaac did, except I wasn't stuffing my face with illicit cookies but was just trying to get myself ready for church. I mean, is it too much to ask? Anyway, I hear hysterical laughing on the other side of the door—never a good sign, never!—open the door, and what do I see? They've gotten into my bedside drawer, where my nail polish is, and they've thrown those suckers like Fourth of July bang snaps. Pop, pop, pop all over the bedroom."

"No!"

"Oh yes. Good-bye expensive Teal Lagoon, farewell my favorite Polyester Pink, hello two hours of cleaning." Pam shook her head sorrowfully, leaning toward Hana conspiratorially. "By the way, water does *not* remove nail polish. I tried dumping the girls in the bath because, you know, of course it was *all* over them too. I mean *all over them and pretty soon all over the bathtub. I mean this was a growing, legitimate mess.* The water just made the nail polish all gooey and goopy, so in the end, I had to douse them in more toxic chemicals to get it off. Nail polish remover bath it was!"

"Oh my goodness!"

"Yes indeed," Pam sighed mournfully. "It was a minor blessing, I suppose, that they didn't ingest any. Looking back, I probably should have been more grateful for that. But at the time, oh baby, at the time I was furious!"

"And your poor floor . . . " Charlotte prompted. Clearly she had heard the story before, and clearly it was a favorite.

"Ah yes, and my poor carpet is now teal and pink. And it's staying that way indefinitely cause mama ain't got the funds to replace it."

Hana laughed and couldn't stop. She giggled until she got the hiccups and her stomach hurt. Pam looked at her with wide eyes. "You going to blow a gasket over there?" She poured Hana a cup of water, which Hana took but didn't drink because she physically couldn't. She doubled over and guffawed so loudly she belched. This embarrassed her so much she instantly stopped, hand over mouth, hiccups still escaping through her fingers. The other two stood in surprise at this impromptu display, and at the belch and subsequent horrified expression, both let out unhindered laughs of their own. Charlotte's laugh was loud and barking, Pam's was loose and trilling. At the sight of the other two for going all decorum and giving in to uncontrolled laughter, Hana uncovered her mouth, let go of the embarrassment, and joined right in.

The three were all wiping at their eyes and letting out small, trailing gasps and "Oh my's" when the three little girls entered, hovering in the doorway with worried expressions on their faces. "Mommy, are you okay?" Ruthie asked uncertainly. The girls were clearly used to being the loudest in the house, and the rowdy display before them didn't appear to compute.

"Y-yes, we're fine, dear. We're just having a good time."

The girls lingered suspiciously. "Seriously, we're fine, girls," Pam affirmed. "Scoot along and play. We're busy, uh, baking." She grabbed at the nearest bowl, which was full of eggshells, and blindly stirred, ignoring the cracking shell noise from within.

Margo, Pam's oldest, seemed satisfied and nodded to the other two as if to say, "Come on, let's get out of this joint." And the three scampered off.

"Did you see their faces?" Charlotte squealed, leaning against the counter, arm draped over Pam's back.

Pam turned and silently raised the bowl with its crushed shells. "I'm . . . stirring . . . eggshells!" she gasped, tears welling in her eyes.

Hana took the wobbling bowl from her, and all three resumed laughing, passing the tissues between them and trying to be quieter so as not to bring the girls back in.

When the hilarity finally wore off and the women were able to focus enough to handle knives once again, they finished their baking with a newfound familiarity and ease . . . and the occasional chuckle. *This is how friendships are forged,* Hana thought. *From laughing together like you're cray cray.*

They finished off eight pies and left them cooling on the counters as they entered the playroom to track down the girls. All three were clustered around Ruthie's dollhouse and were busily chatting.

"Time to go, girls!" Pam called out. A chorus of "Noooo's" greeted her.

"But we just started a new game," Margo whined.

"Can they stay for a sleepover, Mommy? Please?" Ruthie ran up to Charlotte, hugging her knees in supplication.

At the trigger word, "sleepover," several enthusiastic voices called out, "Ooo yes, a sleepover! Please, Mommy? Please? I will be good forever and love you forever!"

Pam and Charlotte exchanged weary glances. "You know what, a sleepover is a great idea for another night. We'll talk about it," Charlotte gestured to herself and Pam, "and we'll come up with a day for you all to have a sleepover. How does that sound?"

"But why not now?"

"Sorry, girls, not tonight. Please thank Miss Charlotte for having you over." Pam turned both girls to Charlotte, a firm hand on each shoulder. Both stopped whining long enough to chime a dutiful, "Thank you, Miss Charlotte," before crumbling back to dismay. Pam began shepherding them to the door.

"Ruthie, don't you want to hug your friends good-bye?" Charlotte urged her youngest. To everyone's surprise, Ruthie burst into tears—not fussy, pouting tears but genuine, distraught tears—and ran from the room. "Oh dear," Charlotte sighed and turned to give Pam a hug. "I better go find her. Thanks for coming, Pam, and for your help." She leaned over and gave each girl a kiss. "Love you little ladies, and I'll see you soon." She then turned to Hana and whispered, "I'll be right back."

Hana followed Pam to the door. She was sad to see their time come to an end. Pam was clearly a hugger, and Hana soon found herself ensconced in a powerful bear hug. "So good to know you, dear," Pam whispered in her ear. "I had a lovely time, and you are a lovely person."

Hana didn't know what to say. Between the two of them, Pam had the personality that sparkled, the authentic gusto and good humor that drew you in. And yet she had called

Hana lovely. "Right back at you," Hana managed around a lump in her throat. She waved from the door as Pam left and then turned back to the quiet house. Charlotte had hinted there was a little more to be done after the baking, and Hana had a bit more time before she'd told Kara she'd be home. She entered the kitchen and began washing the remaining dishes, waiting for Charlotte to come back with Ruthie.

She was rinsing the last dish before she realized just how much time had passed. Surely Charlotte should have been back by now. Hana dried her hands and moved into the playroom, listening for Charlotte. She heard the television on in the living room and followed the sound to find Ruthie, Zach, and Tommy piled on the couch watching a show. Ruthie had her thumb in her mouth and upon Hana's entrance quickly jerked it out of her mouth and stuck it behind her back, looking at her with guilty eyes. Hana grinned but felt the worry grow louder in her mind. "Hey, sweetie, where's your mommy?"

Ruthie just gave her a blank look and shrugged her shoulders.

"Tommy, Zach, do you know where your mom is?"

"I think she's upstairs somewhere," Zach offered, his eyes never leaving the screen, a bag of chips rustling in his hands.

Hana frowned and turned the corner to stand at the foot of the stairs. She felt like just going up would be intruding, but it seemed rude to yell for Charlotte. Odder still that Charlotte was nowhere to be seen when Ruthie clearly had been found. Hana started up the steps, calling Charlotte's name as she neared the top. There was no reply. Hana could see the boys' room straight ahead with bunk beds and a cowboy theme. The rooms were in a U-shape around the stairs. Hana peered to the right and saw what was most likely Sam's room since the closed door was plastered with horse posters. She peered to the left and saw an open bedroom door, which must be Ruthie's because she could see a pink bedspread from where she stood. Had Charlotte found Ruthie in her room and then stayed behind for some reason? Hana moved toward the bedroom, passing a closed door on her right. She was just preparing to call for Charlotte again when a muffled sob reached her from the closed door. She turned away from Ruthie's room to stare at what must be the master bedroom. She hesitated, listening. Yes, there was definitely crying coming from inside. Hana's heart beat rapidly. What should she do? It'd be so much easier if she knew Charlotte better. If they had years of friendship behind them, she wouldn't think twice of just moving about the house like it was her own, of opening this door and going inside and encountering whatever was to be found with open arms of comfort. But she wasn't an old friend. She was brand spanking new, and she didn't know if her presence would be welcome or not. She fluttered by the door, like a bird jumping anxiously on its perch, and she found a prayer for wisdom on her lips without even thinking about it. "Lord, show me what to do." It came out of her easily, naturally, earnestly, and she found that her hand was on the doorknob and she was turning it and entering, and she was at peace with it.

Charlotte was perched on the edge of her bed, heels resting on the bedframe, forehead on her knees, a box of tissues clutched in her hands. Hana felt her heart constrict with compassion. She didn't overthink it; she just went to her and sat beside her and put a hand on her arm. "Charlotte, are you okay? What's the matter?"

"Oh, Hana." Charlotte turned red-rimmed eyes to her. "I'm so sorry. I was trying to pull myself together before coming down, but I just couldn't. I'm sorry to leave you like that. I'm sorry—"

"Shh, no, don't worry about it." Hana rubbed her back. "Do you want to tell me what's wrong?"

"I just . . . " Charlotte sighed shakily and blew her nose. "I came upstairs to find Ruthie. She was in her room, and she was just so *upset.* She was sobbing, Hana, and saying she never wanted Margo and Lucy to leave because she doesn't feel lonely when they're here."

Hana grimaced. There was nothing like encountering your

child's unhappiness head-on to start any parent weeping.

"I've told you before how Ruthie is my girly girl. How I try to make special time just for her. The truth is, she *is* alone a lot, partly because Sam is so much older and involved in so many things, partly because she has two rowdy brothers who are very close in age, and partly because I homeschool, and my attention is so split between all of them. I feel so guilty sometimes, like she's not getting enough."

Hana continued to rub Charlotte's back. She knew that feeling, albeit in a different context, the feeling that you weren't enough for your child.

"There's something that not many people know about me, but I feel like I can tell you?"

It was a question, and Hana answered it with, "Only if you want to. I will gladly listen if you want me to."

"You're very kind, thank you." Charlotte patted Hana's knee and sniffed. "We wanted more children, you know. There's a gap of five years between Tommy and Ruthie, and I had three miscarriages in those years. And then . . . two more after Ruthie."

"Oh, Charlotte, I'm so sorry." Hana felt tears clog her throat. Charlotte was facing her own giant, one that Hana couldn't imagine wrestling with. She'd never experienced a miscarriage herself. Years of infertility, yes, but she couldn't imagine having a child within you and then suddenly not. And five times? It would be devastating.

"I was so angry with God for years, and the worst part was that I felt like I was being so selfish. I mean, I have four beautiful children, and I should just be happy with that. Some people never have any, and no matter how many you have, children are a blessing, and I should just accept what God gives, but then I would think of all the beautiful little lives that I will never know on earth, and it still just breaks my heart." Charlotte was staring at the wall, the tears dripping off her chin. "And then I see Ruthie with those little girls and how much she wants a sister, how much she seems to *need* a sister, and I don't understand why. It's one thing for me to suffer, for Daniel to suffer, but why Ruthie? Three of the five losses were very early, but two were later, and they were both girls." Charlotte turned a stricken face to her. "Why, Hana? Ruthie's sisters. Why?" She leaned against Hana's shoulder, and Hana put her other arm around her. Charlotte was so much taller than her, and her weight threatened to knock Hana off the bed, but she braced herself and held on tightly to her sobbing friend.

She'd asked that question herself. *Why? Why?* It was a throbbing question, a hurting, deep question. *Lord, what do I say?* Sometimes there was nothing to say, and so she just sat quietly and made soothing noises of reassurance and held her friend for as long as she needed to be held.

When Charlotte finally raised her head, Hana gave her another tissue from the near-empty box on the bed. "Thank you, Hana, you're so kind to listen to me. I'm sorry for unloading on you."

"Please don't apologize. Sometimes you need to let go of the hurt a bit by sharing it with someone else." Hana swiped at her own tears and continued hesitantly. "I can't relate to your exact experience, but I know . . . I know what it's like to live with a hurt so big inside you that all of your life just seems to function around it." She let out a sigh like she was a deflating balloon. "Like it's this giant inside you that you're trying to contain, and no one really understands and you can't really explain it to them so you don't really even want to try."

"Yes!" Charlotte turned to her with bright eyes. "Yes, that's it exactly."

"I don't really have any answers." Hana gave her a shaky smile. "But there's something I'm just now beginning to realize, and it's oddly helpful in its own way. For a while, I was so focused on my own pain that I stopped thinking about anything else. I forgot that I'm not the only hurting person in the world. I don't know . . . it's not that knowing there's more pain out there should make you feel better; that sounds sadistic." Hana felt like what she was saying was slipping away, and she didn't know how to rein it in, tie up the loose threads into something meaningful. "I guess what I'm trying to say is that the more I let myself be open to others, to acknowledge their experiences, the less alone I feel." She was talking too much. She should just go back to hugging and holding and shushing. You couldn't go wrong with guttural comforting noises. But Charlotte was nodding and seemed to appreciate what she was saying.

"I see what you mean. Pain is really isolating, and I think that's part of the pain itself. It's easy to feel targeted by God. Why me and not her?"

"Yes, definitely!" It was Hana's turn to agree enthusiastically. "The comparison game is horrible, and you always lose."

"Right, for years I couldn't look a pregnant woman in the face. I kept thinking, why can she have a healthy pregnancy, and I can't? I was thinking about other people but in a toxic way."

"Rather than understanding that they may be going through something completely different but no less painful."

"Exactly!"

They sighed simultaneously and sat side by side on the bed. "When I say I've just been learning this, I literally mean I have *just* been learning this." Hana grinned. "I'm not speaking with any authority here, just so you know."

Charlotte smiled at her. "Yes, I realize that. But it's been helpful, truly." She squeezed Hana's hand.

Unspoken between them was pain like the giant that Hana had mentioned earlier. She sensed the unasked question in Charlotte but knew Charlotte wasn't expecting her to say anything more. And Hana wasn't prepared to say anything more. Sharing could be cathartic, yes, but Hana didn't want to open Pandora's box in the middle of Charlotte's hurt. She didn't want to sabotage the moment that way, and so they sat in silence and understanding, and they let that be enough.

Hello, Button,

Last night your daddy didn't come home. He just didn't come home. We ate dinner, the two of us, as usual, and then you played in the living room while I paced by the front windows.

I've been spiteful; I have. I've acted like your daddy's presence means nothing to either of us, like what does it matter if he's home by five or home by eight? I've refused to call him, to act like it matters one way or the other. Because I don't want him to see how much it hurts.

I usually give you a bath at eight but forgot. You came rambling in at eight thirty, all sleepy eyed and confused and holding Rocky's cage. You were hungry, grumpy, and tired, but you just looked up at me and asked, "Where's Daddy?"

So I broke down and called. It went straight to voice-mail, like his phone had died or he'd turned it off. I left a message and got you ready for bed. I expected him to call back; I really did. But an hour later, after you were all squeaky clean and in your blue-striped footed pajamas with a snack in your belly and your teeth all brushed, he still wasn't home, and he still hadn't called.

I told you Daddy had important work to take care of and would come home while you slept. I called him again and again, and each time it went straight to voicemail. I couldn't bring myself to sleep alone, Button, and you're so cute in your footie pajamas and smell so good after a bath. I finally snuck into your room at midnight, and you and I slept all snuggled and warm.

I was going to call the police in the morning. I was beginning to worry. What if something had happened to him? It'd almost been twenty-four hours since I'd heard from him, and don't they say it's considered a missing person case after twenty-four hours? Or is it forty-eight hours? Anyway, I woke up ready to call the police, but then I saw our kitchen. Cabinets left open, some dishes on the counter—someone had clearly come and gone.

I don't understand it, Button. Why would he act like this? What was he doing? It's so eerie to feel like your daddy is a ghost in this house, coming and going who knows when. I'm going to have to say something. I know I am, but I'm terrified. We can't seem to have a healthy conversation anymore, and I don't know how to approach him with this—what to say or how to act.

I just stood in the middle of the kitchen and closed my eyes and tried to go back to that feeling of comfort when I slid into your bed last night, and it was just you and me and the smell of soapy lavender.

XO

Mommy

16

The day of the church picnic arrived, hot and resplendent. The church folks slapped on layers of sunscreen; covered their heads with cowboy hats and ball caps; loaded their trucks, vans, and cars with hot slow cookers, steaming casserole dishes, and chilled salads; hollered for their kids to "Get a move on!"; and trundled up the Madisons' long, dusty drive, parking their trucks, vans, and cars behind the carport, along the lane, or anywhere else there was room.

The Madisons had pulled out picnic tables, bales of hay, barrels, and lawn furniture—anything that could seat a few sweaty bodies. There were twinkly lights strung here and there, draping from the barn to the corral fence, suspended between fence posts and light poles, giving the area a festive glow. Four long tables were placed end to end by the corral, and on these tables women had draped brightly checkered tablecloths with sporadic cheerful vases of sprouting wildflowers framed in baby's breath. As people arrived, the tables filled up with steaming dishes.

Always a highly anticipated part of the picnic was the chili cook-off. The chili pots received their own table, and six judges had been preselected and were already cleansing their palates in anticipation of the event. Kara had hemmed and hawed but had finally decided to enter a chili, pulling out Memaw's tattered recipe card. Hana had helped her make it and stolen a few bites.

"Cinnamon, that's the secret." She'd licked her lips and sighed with satisfaction. "Takes me right back to Memaw's kitchen."

"Remember how Papaw would always douse it in ketchup? Made Memaw so angry!" Kara had laughed.

"How can you taste the intricacies of my dish when you mask it with that stuff?" Hana had pantomimed, causing Kara to laugh even harder.

The air had been lighter between them since their talk the other day, something Hana was infinitely grateful for. Life was uncertain enough without feeling at odds with your only sister.

She'd explained in great depth to Isaac that even though they would be at the Madisons' and even though Pastor would be there too, they were there to socialize with everyone and not to go to the pond. Isaac had poked and prodded and tried to find a loophole or compromise. Hana had finally said that Wednesdays were "pond day," and since this was Saturday, they couldn't go to the pond. Isaac had always inherently grasped the concept of a "rule," even when he didn't understand the reasoning behind it. Hana had successfully navigated many a conversation by rephrasing things into rules, a language Isaac could comprehend. She tried to use this technique sparingly, however, because Isaac had an elephant's memory when it came to rules and would hold Hana to every single one.

If Isaac couldn't see the pond that day, then maybe he could bring Rocky? Hana had put her foot down—absolutely not. She'd tried to explain it was for Rocky's own good. "It's going to be busy and crowded, Isaac. I don't want you to lose Rocky or even worse, someone opens his cage and he gets loose."

Isaac's eyes had grown wide at the thought. "And then maybe he would go to the pond and I wouldn't be able to find him again."

"Yes, maybe." Hana had nodded solemnly. "I would feel much better if Rocky stayed home, safe and sound. That way you can have fun feeding the goats, playing with your cousins, and eating without worrying if Rocky will escape. And hey, I just had an idea! I'm sure people will be bringing all sorts of salads, so maybe you could collect some juicy lettuce to bring home to him as a snack tonight."

And so Isaac was solo that day. Hana was proud of how well he was managing it, how quickly he'd understood that leaving Rocky at home was what was best for him. Hana had seen him place Rocky's needs before his own time and again, and she felt a small burst of pride each time.

When the Howard and McCauley clans arrived, Charlotte was in full hostess mode, directing and welcoming people. She hustled over to Kara and gave her a squeeze around the brimming Crock-Pot before turning and enveloping Hana in a hug, quick but sweet, whispering in her ear, "So glad to see you." Kara and Hana joined the other ladies at the tables, while Troy sought out Daniel to give him a hand with a couple of picnic benches. Isaac was entrusted to his cousins and had run off with them and some of the other children to the barn.

Hana was finally recognizing more and more people. There was Pam and her family, Ruthie glued to Margo's and Lucy's sides. Clara and her fiancé, Tim, were setting up a drink station, replete with sweet iced tea and lemonade. Lynn was bouncing Amelia on her hip, part of a small cluster of young women with small children. There were many people she didn't know, but there were many she did, and it was a nice feeling. As her eyes flitted across the gathering, she caught sight of a handsome, dark-haired man in dark-wash jeans, boots, and a nice button-down navy shirt. He gave off a rugged yet approachable vibe, and he was looking right at her and grinning. She found herself blushing and looking away quickly. Goodness, she hadn't expected this! She dared another glance to find him not only looking at her but walking her way. Flustered, she fiddled with several utensils on the table, not sure where to look. The man stopped across from her, and Hana was infinitely grateful for the table separating them. She made herself look him in the eye, and when she did the realization of his identity finally swept over her, leaving her even more flustered than before.

"P-pastor!" she spluttered. "Good to see you. You look . . . different, nice, good. Uh, it's good to see you." She watched a slow smile spread across his face, and yes, there was not just one but two dimples, just as she'd imagined.

He wasn't sure why he'd done it, really. It was an impulse, and he rarely gave in to impulses, but Matt had woken up the morning of the picnic and thought ahead to the event and how hot it was going to be, and he'd thought, *I should shave it off.*

He'd had the beard for years. It was thick and full, and he'd always been careful to keep it neat and trimmed. But when his black hair had started to turn gray, it'd started in his beard. Just a few hairs at first that he'd plucked diligently every morning, and then streaks, and he'd resignedly retired the tweezers and accepted his new look. The gray had started young, which shouldn't have been a surprise since his father had had an entirely gray head of hair by the age of forty-five. It'd bothered Matt at first that he had such prominent gray in his beard at just thirty-five, but then he'd chastised himself—it was silly vanity—and he'd not thought much about it since. Now he was forty-two, and his thick, black hair was still that, thick and black, all but for the beard, which was still stubbornly streaked with gray.

What had he looked like without his beard? Younger, he supposed, younger and probably more attractive. Matt had stood in front of the mirror that morning, electric razor at the ready, thoughtfully appraising himself. Why not?

He'd nearly clogged the sink. It'd looked like an animal had crawled into it and died, curling up in a sad gray and black mass. He'd scooped it out, removing the stopper in the sink to get all the wads of hair out and into the trash instead. Note to self, removing large quantities of hair from one's face should be done over a trash can and not the sink. And then he'd appraised himself again and slapped on aftershave and winced at the unfamiliar tingling sensation. Yes, he definitely looked younger—perhaps *too* young? Also, he hadn't realized how tan he was until the bare bottom half of his face gleamed back at him, pale in comparison to the upper half. Perhaps he should have thought this through a bit more. Ah well, no second-guessing now; the deed was done. He'd dressed with care, appraising himself yet again afterward. When was the last time he'd looked at himself this much in the mirror? Probably never. So why start now? He left the question unanswered until he reached the Madisons'. He was standing by the corral talking to Spencer Douglas about his knee replacement surgery and casually looked over to see *her*, the answer dawning in his brain.

She was arranging food on one of the tables, her light brown hair pulled back in a ponytail with loose strands that got in her way. He watched as she swiped at her hair with the back of a hand and grinned as he saw some of her hair sticking to her lips. She was wearing something unfamiliar to him, a style he hadn't seen people wearing down here. A denim dress that wasn't really a dress but wasn't a shirt either. Whatever it was, she wore it beautifully, and he found himself staring with an alarming rush of self-awareness coursing through him. And then she'd looked up and found him watching and looked away quickly as if embarrassed. Didn't she recognize him?

Poor Spencer Douglas was saying something, but Matt wasn't listening. Where were his manners? "I'm sorry, Spence; I'll be right back." He watched her face as he crossed the yard and could tell that she was aware of him but trying not to show that she was aware of him, and then he was standing across the table from her, and she was finally looking at him, and it was as if she was seeing him for the first time, and she was blushing and fumbling her words and pulling the strands of hair out of her mouth, and she was utterly gorgeous and endearing.

"I almost didn't recognize you." Hana laughed nervously.

"Aw, I don't look that different, do I?" Pastor said with a grin, as if egging her on.

"It looks nice; you look nice." Hana stopped abruptly. She'd already said that—too much.

"Well, thank you. You look nice today too."

Hana tucked a strand behind her ear and glanced down at her sheath dress. "Thanks."

"Where's Isaac?"

"In the barn with the rest of the kids."

Pastor looked like he was going to say more, but Daniel Madison approached and put a hand on his arm. "We're ready to start eating, Pastor. Would you please say the blessing?"

Hana watched as Pastor nodded to her and let Daniel lead him toward the middle of the yard. Daniel stuck his thumb and forefinger in his mouth and let out a shrill whistle, gaining everyone's attention. "All right, listen up, folks! My wife and I want to thank y'all for coming out and braving the heat today." There was a rowdy cheer as several people raised their glasses in affirmation. "Pastor is going to say grace for us, then everyone dig on in. Judges, you should already have partaken of all the chilis and be in the midst of consultation over the winner." Daniel raised his eyebrows and pointed a finger at a few people. There were several chuckles. "So we can be expecting the announcement by the end of the meal. Where's last year's winner? Aw, thar she is! Come on forward, Marlene." A petite older woman came forward, and Daniel placed a large hand on her shoulder. "Now as y'all know, a winner can't enter the followin' year, so Miss Marlene is on a hiatus, so to speak, but just maybe we can expect more of her famous rattlesnake chili next year. I guess that'll depend on whether Mikey's willing to brave the hunt again next year, huh? So we'll all be praying for Mikey—his bravery and safety being whatcha call paramount." A smattering of laughter sounded at this. He leaned down to give Marlene a peck on the cheek, and everyone laughed as she shooed him away. "Now I know y'all are hungry, so without further fuss, Pastor?" Daniel stepped aside as Pastor came forward and lifted his hands.

"Let's pray together." The men took off their hats, and everyone bowed their heads. Some of the women had gathered the children from the barn, and Hana could just make out Isaac standing in the back next to Alex. Silence fell upon the group as Pastor raised his voice. "Dear Father, thank You for blessing us with a beautiful day and with each other. May we come together as Your church, our family, and uplift and enjoy one another today. Thank You for the food we are about to enjoy and for the hands that prepared it. Bless this food for its benefit to our bodies. We pray this in Jesus' name. Amen."

There was a ripple of amens, and then people were forming lines, and children were gathered close, and people were already staking out and claiming seats. Hana found Isaac with Clem, and got in line with him. "Did you have fun in the barn, Isaac?"

"Where's Pastor?" Isaac said as he heaped lettuce on his plate to bring home to Rocky.

"I'm not sure right now." Hana scanned the area for Pastor but couldn't see him. "I'm sure we'll find him later." Hana piled their plates high and then joined Kara and the rest of the family at a picnic table.

The food was delicious, and Isaac enjoyed eating the meat out of the chilis, as well as the mac 'n' cheese. The winner of the cook-off was announced. Kara had come in third place, Lynn second, and someone named Elizabeth came in first. "That's Ron Edwards' wife. He's one of our elders," Kara leaned over to inform Hana. She sounded like she was disappointed and trying to mask it.

"Hey, third's not bad." Hana patted her sister's hand.

Elizabeth was given a gift basket containing a cookbook, wooden spoon, spatula, and a bunch of chili peppers. "Yes, but third doesn't get a prize." Hana just rolled her eyes at her sister.

As people finished eating, they began breaking into the desserts, and slices of Charlotte's pies began materializing at tables along with big, juicy slices of watermelon. Pretty soon, someone had started a watermelon seed spitting contest. A gathering formed by the barn as people took huge, dripping bites of watermelon; chewed around the seeds, collecting them in their cheeks; and then took aim at a fence post to see who could hit it. As people pinged their seeds off the post, shouts arose, and the contestants were urged to step farther and farther back until only two people remained in the running, both looking slightly unwell from all the watermelon but both still gamely biting off chunks of the fruit and dutifully spitting out the seeds, faces red with exertion. Hana was watching and laughing at the sight when someone placed a warm hand on her shoulder. She turned to find Pastor's dimpled face smiling into hers.

"Clara and Tim want to get a game of cornhole toss going. You game?"

"Oh, ah, sure." Hana looked around for Isaac.

"Alex took him to get pie," Troy jumped in. "He'll be fine. You go have fun," he said with a glimmer in his eye.

Hana felt like a teenager just granted permission to go spend time with a *boy*. She tried to walk casually with Pastor but found herself wondering at the proper distance to stand from him. Was she too close? too far? Was she laughing at what he said too much? not enough? She was smiling normally, right? This big smile that hurt her cheeks was normal, wasn't it? They approached Clara and Tim, who were arguing over the proper distance for the cornholes. Clara greeted her with a smile and, before Hana could suggest guys against girls, piped up, "So how about couple against couple?" Hana froze and glanced awkwardly at the others. No one else blinked an eye.

"Sure!" Pastor accepted the beanbags and gestured for Hana to take her place at one end of the game. "You take that side, and I take the other?"

"Uh, sure." As they played, Hana couldn't help but observe the playful vibe between Clara and Tim. Engaged to be married in three months, they were in that special in-between time that can seem endless in the moment but is so fleeting and precious in retrospect. Hana felt a lump form in her throat as she recalled being in that in-between time with Zeke, when he used to make her laugh all the time. How he'd go out of his way to please her, and how she found herself constantly thinking of him and wanting to please him back.

It was slightly awkward being the other "couple" to the real couple in front of them. Hana found herself verbally sparring with Pastor, jumping into the spirit of the game and urging him on, loudly cheering his successes and moaning over his misses. And he was the same with her, openly happy to be with her. They played best out of five, with Hana and Pastor pulling through for the win at the end. Hana cheered unchecked. She pointed at Clara with a triumphant laugh and ran to meet Pastor in the middle, high-fiving him with a whoop. He was laughing at her, shaking his head in merriment. It wasn't until she'd quieted that she realized he'd snagged her fingers in the high five and her hand was still dangling from his.

"I guess you beat us fair and square." Tim walked up with Clara.

"That's right, we did." Hana laughed, but this time self-consciously, pulling her hand from Pastor's and smoothing the front of her dress. The four of them walked back to the picnic table, Hana keeping a little more distance between herself and Pastor. They reached the table to find Isaac, Troy, and Alex eating dessert. Hana guessed Isaac was already on his second piece of pie. He glanced up as Hana and Pastor approached, and that's when it happened.

In retrospect, Hana felt like she should have expected it. She knew how much change could upset Isaac, how much he loved Pastor exactly the way he was. But no, she'd remind herself any time she was tempted to be hard on herself, it's impossible to be able to predict every trigger. Still, she felt as if she should have known, should have given Isaac a heads-up.

When Isaac looked up, his expression froze in shock and confusion. His fork was suspended between plate and mouth, cherry filling dribbling from it. "Who's that?" He said it quickly, urgently, almost as one word, "Whosat?"

Hana wasn't sure who he was referring to until Pastor smiled and answered, "It's me, Isaac. It's Pastor."

Isaac dropped his fork and shook his head, turning to Hana for confirmation. "No, not Pastor. No, Pastor has hair." His hands fluttered near his own face, whether to indicate where the hair should have been or just out of anxiety, Hana wasn't sure. "Whosat?" This time directed to Hana.

"This really is Pastor, Isaac." Hana said it calmly, but her heart sank. Everyone else was still smiling, probably thinking how cute it was to see a young boy confused by a haircut, not knowing it went beyond confusion for Isaac, and this was the tip of the iceberg. Maybe she could defuse things, just maybe. "You're right, Pastor used to have a beard. But do you know how you sometimes get a haircut? Well, people who have beards can get their beards cut. Sometimes they even cut them off completely, like Pastor did. But it's still him, Isaac."

"No, no, Pastor has hair. I want to touch it!" Isaac was getting panicky. Hana knew he was in genuine distress, wondering what happened to Pastor.

"It didn't hurt me, Isaac. And it will grow back eventually. Here, do you want to touch—"

"No!" Isaac was standing and thumping his chest, his eyes wide and fixed on the ground, steadfastly avoiding Pastor's face. "No! Pastor has hair. I want to touch it. Where's Pastor?"

Clara and Tim stood by with worried expressions on their faces. Alex tried reaching out to his cousin, but Isaac jerked away. Troy had stood and come to Isaac's other side, while Hana continued to talk to him. "Isaac, please calm down. I know you're scared and confused right now, but—" Hana reached out to take his arm, and Isaac screamed and jerked it away, beginning to moan and rock.

Hana glanced up to see people frozen in painful silence. Those in the food line closest to the scene were idly shoving food around, as if pretending to be engrossed in choosing just the right amount of bean casserole to slop onto their plates. People at nearby picnic tables were diligently looking the other way. It was the equivalent of a car crash, but because it involved people and not vehicles, people who were known but not very well known, the reaction was embarrassed avoidance coupled with morbid fascination.

"I'm sorry, Isaac." Pastor was standing in front of them, his brow furrowed, his voice tight with distress. "If I had known how much it would upset you, I'd never have—"

"Go away!" Isaac jumped back as Pastor moved forward. "I want Pastor."

Hana knew this wasn't going to get better with everyone else around. Isaac needed to go somewhere quiet, where he could fall apart and Hana could help put him back together, away from everyone else—the well-intentioned worry emanating from Tim and Clara, the strained avoidance from people sitting at the tables nearby—best to get away from it all. She felt a gentle hand on her back and turned to see Charlotte. "Would you mind if I take Isaac inside?" Hana's voice was tight.

"Not at all, whatever you need."

"Isaac, let's go inside for a bit, okay, honey?" She *still* did it. Even after all the years of experience with Isaac, endearments still managed to slip out. The "honey" coupled with her tugging him toward the house sent Isaac over the edge.

He screamed and tugged his arm out of her grasp. Hana reached for him again, this time taking him firmly by the shoulders and pushing him toward the house. Isaac bucked and lashed out, his fist smashing into Hana's face. She groaned and dropped his shoulders to put a hand to her nose. Her vision blurred, and when it cleared she could see her hand come away from her face red with blood. Troy was by their side in an instant, trying to take over for her. He put a firm arm around Isaac's shoulders and steered him toward the house. Hana tried to join them and grabbed Isaac's arm, but Isaac bucked and kicked, catching her in the shins, and in that moment a fresh truth became painfully obvious to her, one that shook her to the core. Isaac was nearly her size now, and she could no longer make him do anything he didn't want to do. She might still be stronger, but his volatile movements were slowly and surely beginning to go beyond her control. She stopped then, stopped trying and let Troy, who was much bigger than them both, take over. Isaac was digging in his heels, and Troy was doing his best to use the least amount of force with him but finally had to bear-hug Isaac and carry him into the house.

"Hana," Pastor said her name in a broken voice. She turned and found him standing at her side, his face shocked and saddened, his hands reaching toward her. "Your face—"

"I'm fine. Just . . . it'll be fine." Hana wiped at her bloody nose with one hand and brushed Pastor's outstretched arm away with the other as she pushed past him toward the house. When he tried to follow, she turned. "Please . . . just don't." His expression—it was as if she'd slapped him. She turned and found that those who'd formerly been avoiding her had finally let their morbid curiosity outweigh their embarrassment and were full on gawking at her. Some looked away when she caught their eye as she dashed after her son and into the house.

Hana sat at the kitchen table tilting her head back and pinching the bridge of her nose. Charlotte stood at her side, quietly offering tissues. Troy had taken Isaac all the way upstairs and into one of the bedrooms, where his wails could still be faintly heard drifting down the stairs. Kara burst into the kitchen and gritted her teeth when she saw Hana. "Oh, honey . . . I'm so sorry. Where's Troy?"

"Upstairs." Hana straightened her head and sniffed a few times. The bleeding seemed to have stopped, but her nose was still tender, and her voice sounded muffled, like she had a cold. "Can you go check on them? Please. I don't feel up to dealing with Isaac right now. I'll be up there as soon as I can, but can you please just go check on them?"

"Yes, of course." Kara squeezed her hand and hurried upstairs.

Charlotte sighed and sat at the table. Hana stared straight ahead. Her face felt numb, mirroring the state of her insides. "He's never done that before."

"I don't think it was intentional." Charlotte rested a hand on her arm. "I saw it happen, and it really looked like he was just flailing and it happened. I don't think he intentionally did it at all."

"Yes, but . . . he's only seven, Charlotte. What happens when he gets older, stronger? What if he ever *does* hit me intentionally? What then?"

"I don't think it does any good to worry about the what-ifs now."

"He's on medication now, and he's seeing a behavioral therapist. Or, he was back in Ohio. He will be again when we get to Richmond. I just, I just don't want to have to put him on something that will change him, that will make him so drugged up that he . . . I don't want to lose my boy." Hana leaned forward until her head touched the table and let Charlotte stroke her back.

"Oh, honey, you're letting your mind jump way ahead of you. No need to go there right now."

Charlotte continued to stroke her back while Hana rested her head on the table, eyes dry, mind whirling. She needed to get hold of herself and go upstairs to talk to Isaac. Worse than that, she'd need to eventually go back outside. She knew it wasn't Pastor's fault, and yet she felt a niggle of resentment. Why did he have to go and shave his beard? She was tired of seeing his strained, worried expression in the face of Isaac's meltdowns. She felt unreasonably irritated with him and just felt like going home, crawling into bed. She raised her head off the table. The longer she sat here, the more she'd push off the inevitable. "I guess I better go upstairs and talk to him."

"Okay, just let me know if you need anything."

"I will, thanks." Hana ascended the stairs, realizing for the first time that the sounds of wailing had stopped—a good sign. She heard Kara in Sam's bedroom and entered to find Kara and Troy sitting on the bed with Isaac between them. Isaac appeared to be exhausted and was leaning forward, arms drooping off the bed, head nearly touching his knees. Troy rose and met her at the door.

"Hana, I'm sorry, I didn't know what else to do."

"Please don't apologize. You did the only thing that could be done, and I appreciate your help."

"I kept holding him for a while. I was afraid he'd hurt himself with his lashing out. He was trying to claw his arms and I was just worried, so I held him and restricted his arms until he cried it out. Then after, he seemed to want me to keep holding him."

"Yes, sometimes pressure helps. The pressure is comforting to him, so you did exactly right."

"Are you okay?"

"Me? I'm fine." Hana gestured to her nose. "Nothing broken; I'm fine."

Kara joined them at the door, all three speaking in whispers as if visiting a sleeping patient. "I tried talking to him about what bothered him, about Pastor. He didn't want to talk, but at least it didn't seem to upset him further, so I guess that's good?"

"Thank you to both of you." Hana felt tears form and blinked them away. "I really appreciate it." She watched them leave and then turned to her son, sitting next to him on the bed. He didn't look up and didn't complain when she began scratching his back. He'd always loved back scratches. A mixture of emotions sprang forward, filling the numb void with a cacophony of feeling. Resentment—at having been embarrassed in front of so many people. Fear—of having to go through this again with Isaac, of having unknowingly crossed some border with no going back. Anger—at Isaac, at Pastor, at herself. Guilt—over all of the above.

"Isaac, we need to talk about what happened just now, okay?" He was spent, and so was she, but Hana continued, praying for the right words. "You need to understand two things. First, I love you very much, I always will, and I know you love me too. And second, because we love each other so very much, we will *never* hurt one another. Kicking and hitting, biting or clawing, we won't do these things to each other because we love each other. Does that make sense?" Her controlled tone was slipping the longer she talked, until she was fairly gasping the words.

"I want you to know that I will never *ever* hurt you, and I want you to try to do the same for me because we love each other, okay?" She was crying now. She'd kept it together, but now that she was addressing something she never thought she'd have to address, she came undone. She knew Isaac was listening but also knew not to expect a response. She gulped deep breaths to calm herself, and as she did so, Isaac leaned into her, his head resting against her knee. She placed a careful hand on his head and continued to stroke his back. "Okay, Isaac? Okay?" She continued to say it, "Okay?" Saying it hard enough for the both of them.

She was thankful she'd driven separately, so she could leave with Isaac without disrupting Kara, Troy, and the kids. She'd set the television to a nature program and left Isaac in front of it with a cup of water and strict instructions to stay put. Now she peered out the windows to the picnic beyond and tried to find her car. There it was, parallel parked along the driveway, but not too sandwiched. She'd be able to wiggle out without having to ask anyone to move their car. For a moment, she considered just leaving, just ducking out the front door, which was rarely used, avoiding the side yard and all its festivities, and hightailing it down the drive to her car. She could probably manage it without being noticed. But no, that'd be rude to just leave. She should at least inform Kara that she was going and thank Charlotte for hosting. She scanned the yard for Kara and Charlotte, hoping they were together and she could just make a dash to them and be done with it. No such luck. Kara wasn't in sight, and Charlotte was by the chicken pen, just right of the barn, talking with a group of women.

Hana left through the front door, trotted down the steps, and made her way circuitously to the chicken pen, dodging parked cars, trying to avoid nomadic groups of people, some setting up lawn games, others toting food from one place to another.

"Hana! Hold on, Hana!"

She was in the final stretch of open ground between a cluster of tables and the chicken coop, literally the only exposed part of her winding path, when her name was called and she was caught, pinned as surely as an insect on a collector's board. Hana whipped around to see Regina with a stack of dirty plates hustling in her direction. She'd left a group of women, who hesitantly began following her, a tentative swarm moving in Hana's direction. Hana pretended not to see her, even though she'd jumped at her name being called, but Regina would have none of it.

"Wait up, Hana!" She arrived out of breath at Hana's side, thrusting the stack of dishes into the hands of one of the women trailing her. "Oh, I'm glad I caught you." She placed a wrinkled hand on Hana's arm. "My dear, I saw what happened with your Isaac, and I'm so sorry."

It wasn't the lead Hana had expected, and she stood for a moment, mouth opening and closing.

"That couldn't have been easy for you, dear. Not easy at all." Regina patted her arm gently. Hana let herself meet the older woman's eyes. They appeared to hold genuine concern.

"Thank you," she managed around the lump in her throat. She'd found herself instinctively avoiding Regina, but perhaps that had been rash and unfair on her part. "Thank you, it wasn't easy."

"And how is he doing now, dear?" The other women had finally caught up and stood at a slight distance, a part of the conversation but not a part of it. Not quite fully committed so they could slip away, if need be, without appearing rude.

"Much better, thank you. He just needed some space and time to process."

"Yes, of course, of course." Regina linked her arm through Hana's, her voice dropping into a tone reserved for confidential conversations, her demeanor giving off the vibe that they were just peas in a pod, the two of them, talking about mutual stuff that only they could possibly understand. "Oh, my dear, I feel for you." Regina sighed and squeezed Hana's arm. "You'll want to think ahead to when Isaac hits puberty."

Hana's heart sank. Why couldn't Regina have just left it at a brief compassionate word? There was no need to say more, and Hana certainly didn't need advice at the moment.

"My sister's autistic grandson just turned fifteen, and the other day . . . " She broke off as if overcome with emotion. "I got a call from Marge, my sister, panicked, asking for prayer because Damien, her grandson, well, he's just changed during puberty—completely. He's suddenly belligerent and . . . physical, and he lashed out and threw Janet, that's his mother, Marge's daughter, onto the ground. Actually broke a rib!"

Hana glanced at the other women in the group. Was anyone else hearing this? Regina was speaking to all of Hana's darkest worries and fears, but instead of panic, she could only feel disbelief. She longed to speak up for herself, to say something authoritative that would shut the other woman down, but she couldn't get anything intelligible to come out, and instead found herself mumbling incoherently. "I don't . . . what . . . why?"

"Oh, I'm sorry." Regina stopped and turned to Hana, looking mortified at potentially being misunderstood. "I'm bringing this up because even though Isaac is so young, it's something to consider and plan for, you know, in case."

Hana shook her head and stepped away. "No . . . no . . . I don't want . . . not helpful."

Regina must have misunderstood what Hana meant by "not helpful," seeming to choose to interpret it as "unclear." "I only meant, dear, that maybe you should consider some self-defense classes. That's why I brought it up."

"What are you . . . what are you saying?" Hana stared at her in confusion.

"It's been my experience that boys like Isaac can grow more and more . . . physical as they get older. And given how he was today, you may want to consider self-defense classes."

Anger pushed through the fog in Hana's mind, causing her words to finally form into full sentences. "So that I can what? Put my son in a choke hold?"

Regina squinted her eyes as if trying to read Hana, her lips forming a thin, tight line. "I'm just trying to be helpful, dear. I *do* have some experience, you know."

"No, I don't think you have the experience you think you do." Hana was not a confrontational person, but having found herself with one foot on the path, she began tumbling forward, headlong, her breathing becoming ragged as the adrenaline took over even as her mind screamed at her, *What are you doing?* "I don't want to hear this right now. I don't. Please stop. It's not helping."

Some of the other women in the group were looking at her with sympathy, some with chagrin, while others simply stared at the ground. Regina's expression had closed off, her eyelids lowered, face hardened. Hana had no doubt she would say more if given the chance, so she left; she turned and fled from the group of women. Charlotte was no longer by the chicken pen, and Hana found herself plowing straight for the barn with no true destination. Instead of stopping to reassess, however, Hana just plunged forward, into the barn, leaving the happy sounds outside.

The barn was empty but for a few children, who were playing hide-and-seek. Hana stood gasping next to the goats. A little girl stopped short in front of her, staring. "I'm sorry, sweetie . . . could you, I just need some space. Could you . . . just take your friends someplace else . . . just for a little bit?"

The girl nodded, wide-eyed, and a few minutes later Hana had the barn to herself. She sat down hard on a nearby barrel and placed her head in her hands, her mind whirling. It wasn't just her mind. In fact, the room itself was spinning, and she was dangerously lightheaded. Hana willed her breathing to slow as she placed her head between her knees. She needed to get more air into her lungs; she needed the barn to stop spinning. Because the last thing she needed was to be discovered passed out. She was so focused on breathing that she missed the sound of the barn door creaking open, the sound of steps approaching, the soft sound of a throat clearing. It wasn't until she felt a hand on her back that Hana realized she wasn't alone.

Hana's frightened eyes were the first thing she'd noticed. She'd been standing near the corral with a full plate of food, having gotten to the picnic late, when she'd seen Hana sprinting across the lawn, leaving a small group of women behind her. Hana had looked so determinedly scared that it'd taken her by surprise. She'd watched as Hana had entered the barn and, a moment later, a few kids ran out. What on earth? She didn't really want to talk to Hana, but she found herself walking the short distance to the barn anyway. She'd just take a peek.

Hana was sitting with her head between her knees, gulping in air as if she was drowning. And that's when she'd felt it—full-fledged concern, bubbling up in her unbidden. She'd crossed the space between them and stood silently over Hana, finally placing her free hand on Hana's arched back, watching as her head whipped up, her frightened eyes flickering in recognition. Her tone startled as she choked out, "Julie?"

This was absolutely the last thing she needed right now— the very last thing. Julie was standing over her with a plate of food and a concerned expression.

"I'm sorry; I saw you run in here, and you seemed really upset. I just got here a moment ago." She gestured ruefully with her full plate of food. "If you want to be alone, I understand." She half turned, as if she expected Hana to boot her out and was preemptively following orders.

"No, you can stay," Hana surprised herself by saying.

Julie's expression was equally surprised as she leaned against a nearby rail without saying a word, offering some of her food to Hana, who shook her head. Silence reigned over them for a moment before Hana broke it. She felt the need to vent to someone, anyone apparently, even this woman. "So you missed my son's outburst." Julie just raised an eyebrow as if to say, "Go on." So Hana did, telling her every detail. When she'd finished, she glanced at Julie, not sure what to expect from her.

Julie was chewing and spoke around a bite of food, "Wait, so you mean to tell me, Pastor shaved his beard? Off completely?" She swallowed. "That's crazy. I never thought I'd see the day!" She shook her head in surprise and took another bite.

Hana just stared at her, surprised that she'd focused on that part of the story. And then she laughed and couldn't stop. Julie joined in, choking on her food, which made them laugh harder until a coughing fit finally forced Julie to stop.

"So is that why you ran in here?" Julie said, coughing a few more times.

"No," Hana sighed and balled her hands into fists. "It's what happened afterward." She didn't want to be angry, bitter, and spiteful, and she tried to tell the story without embellishment, but the anger crept in anyway. Julie continued to eat, chewing slowly, her eyes never leaving Hana. When she'd finished, Hana paused for breath and waited. Why had she told this woman everything? Was it just because she wanted to talk badly of Regina, or maybe did she sense that Julie was actually listening?

Julie sighed at the end of the story and placed her nearly empty plate on the ground and made to sit on the barrel with Hana. The barrel was much too small, but Hana scooted over, and they both sat scrunched together, half hanging off and leaning one toward the other to keep their balance. Julie sighed again and stared into a far dusty corner. "Well," she finally said. "That's kind of horrible, isn't it? I'm so sorry."

Hana sighed also and said, "Yes, yes it is."

Silence fell over them, and Hana dared a glance in Julie's direction. Flawlessly beautiful as usual, her manicured eyebrows, usually sitting high and arched, were scrunched in thought and sympathy. There was a smear of barbecue sauce in the corner of her mouth, which made Hana smile. The barbecue sauce, combined with the concern, made this woman authentic. Hana thought back to her hurtful words in the restroom, the assumptions and gossip, the hostility. She held that memory up to this moment like a sheet of transparency film and wondered at the layers she now saw. The sting of Regina's words still lingered in Hana's mind, but now she found herself strangely pleased next to this woman whom she'd formerly avoided. People, she realized once again, were surprising. Sometimes that ended in tragedy. And sometimes that ended in hope.

Part III

Love

Hello, Button,

Well, it didn't go well. I didn't think it would, but I didn't think it'd go quite so badly. I suppose I was too antagonistic in my approach. At least that's what he said. I instantly put him on his guard and made him defensive—as if that empties him of any fault afterwards.

I asked your daddy why, why is he staying away from us, why is he coming and going like he doesn't even have a family? And you know what he said? He said it was because he didn't—have a family. He said, how can we be a family when I'm constantly leaving him out, shoving him aside as if he doesn't matter. Basically it's my fault. He says I try so hard with you that I stop trying after that. Like he doesn't matter, our marriage doesn't matter, nothing matters but you. He says I've "claimed you" as "mine," as if I'm the only one capable of meeting your needs. Like I've formed a family of two, me and you, and I've left him out.

After the shouting match and when he'd left, yet again, I tried to take a step back to take his words seriously, to examine things from his point of view to see if maybe, just maybe, he has a point. And do you know what I discovered? No—absolutely not! He is not correct, not in the slightest. I'm not blameless—no one is, but I'm certainly not the only person at fault here, and I certainly have not been doing what he says I've been doing.

He says I've "stopped trying" when it comes to anything else but you. But he's the one who hasn't tried at all! Does he honestly believe I want to be alone in this? I've had to be alone in it! If I've "claimed you," it's because he hasn't. And how does he expect us to spend time on our marriage if he won't engage in co-parenting you?

God gave you to us. For whatever reason, He placed you in this family, and I will never apologize for being your parent.

XO

Mommy

17

Noisy chaos—if Hana had to describe VBS in two words, it would be noisy chaos. To be fair, she should really say joyful, noisy chaos, for the kids were all excited to be there, and their enthusiasm rubbed off on all involved. Each morning began with an opening prayer and devotion from Pastor, after which children were dismissed into their respective classrooms for crafts, games, snacks, and story time.

All the crafts and games were tied to the theme of "God's Word Is a Lamp to Our Feet." One day they played some well-supervised flashlight tag. Another day the teachers set up a path and instructed children to follow it with the lights out. The kids all laughed when the lights came on and instead of staying on the path, they'd wandered into random parts of the room. The second try with a flashlight ended in a 100 percent success rate. For crafts, the children were given black construction paper and white crayons and told to draw pictures of light in the darkness. They made paper lanterns one day and another day made open Bible ornaments to take home.

Hana volunteered with Isaac's first grade class. It was touch and go at first. Isaac was still avoiding Pastor and didn't understand that Pastor was still Pastor, even without the beard. Isaac's avoidance mirrored her own because ever since the picnic, Hana had found it hard to get back to the easy place she and Pastor had enjoyed before. She'd been happy and carefree with him at the picnic, relishing in his attentions and allowing herself to flirt—just a tiny little bit. It was embarrassing to admit now, and that embarrassment was part of the reason for her avoidance, but not all of it. For if she were honest with herself, she was irrationally irritated with him for shaving that beard. Why did he have to go and do that for no good reason? And then stand there like a fish out of water, mouth opening and closing in dying horror at the sight of Isaac's unfolding meltdown. He was such a wonderful man; she knew that, but she felt like she and Isaac were somehow always devastating him, leaving him flopping on the bank, like one of his own catches, eyes agog, mouth a perpetual "O," silently screaming, "What's happening? What's happening?"

So the times of morning devotion, when Pastor spoke to all the kids at once, were the hardest times, for both Hana and Isaac. They sat in the back of the sanctuary together, and Hana scratched Isaac's back and kept reassuring him it was Pastor, and somehow they both managed to make it through.

Isaac's favorite part of the day, besides snacks, was the story time, which surprised Hana. She had to push him into trying the games, and she or someone else always had to help him finish his crafts, but when it came to story time, he sat in rapt attention as Elizabeth Edwards stood in front of the group and, with many exciting hand gestures and with a voice made for storytelling, told of people in dark places who followed the light of God's truth. People from the Bible: Daniel, Noah, and Joseph, as well as people from history: Corrie ten Boom, Jim Elliot, and modern-day martyrs. Hana found herself listening just as eagerly as the children.

As the director of the program, Julie was everywhere at once, checking on each classroom multiple times and filling in as needed. She closed each day with songs in the sanctuary. Isaac especially enjoyed "This Little Light of Mine," and although he didn't sing the lyrics, he would energetically participate in the hand motions, holding his "light" out along with everyone else, covering it with his hand, and—his absolute favorite part—yelling "No!" as loud as he could when it was suggested he hide the light under a bushel.

Being allowed to volunteer in Isaac's classroom gave Hana both encouragement and peace of mind. She was there to provide stability and familiarity for Isaac, and support should something go awry, but she was also able to observe how others came alongside him and helped, supported, and encouraged. Midweek she found herself being able to actually sit back and relax, to focus on the other kids a little more. Elizabeth, especially, had taken to Isaac, and he was her biggest fan during story time. The two gravitated toward each other throughout VBS, and Elizabeth quickly learned the ins and outs of what Isaac did and did not enjoy.

Lemonade, for example, was Isaac's favorite drink, and Elizabeth enjoyed being the first to the snack table, loudly proclaiming, "Let me see here, what would Isaac like to drink? Milk? Water? Orange juice?"

Isaac would squeal "No" at each suggestion, finally unable to stand it any longer and shouting, "You know! Lemonade!"

"Hmm, yes, I guess I do know that." And then she'd pull a prepped and ready glass from behind her back, delivered with a wink.

Clara was volunteering in another classroom but would give Isaac fist bumps whenever they passed in the hallway. These small instances piled up to make Hana feel more and more at ease. It helped tremendously that Regina wasn't volunteering in the program. Still, some of the women who had been privy to Regina's exchange with Hana were present at VBS, and none of them mentioned anything to Hana. She brought this up to Julie midweek.

"Something you have to understand about Regina—she's like the grandmother of the church—the grandmother who can say whatever she wants, if you know what I mean. She's had some of the elders as her Sunday School students. She's been a part of this congregation for so long, that she's given a certain amount of . . . um . . . grace. People don't usually call her out on anything."

"I can understand not wanting to call her out on something," Hana vented. "But that shouldn't keep them from, oh, I don't know, apologizing to me on her behalf."

She realized she sounded like a petulant child, but Julie had been gracious in her response. "Honestly, I've found that sometimes you do yourself more harm by waiting for an apology than if you just accept that you may not get one and move on."

"I guess that's forgiveness."

"Something like that." Julie had grinned. "I feel for you; I do. Regina, she's a lot like my mother." She'd grimaced at this. "She's often sharp and liberal with her tongue, and even though she may be well intentioned, she feels the need to interject on every little thing. Oh, and she's always right. It's hard to love someone who is never wrong and always has an opinion."

"Yes, exactly!"

"Take it from someone who's had experience holding on to bitterness," Julie had leaned in close. "Hate is too heavy to carry, so don't. Even if someone never seeks forgiveness, give it. For your sake, give it freely."

This was what had surprised Hana the most about the week, more than Isaac's adjustment, more than the way some of the students had chosen to sit by him and to help him with his crafts, more than the many gestures both big and small—it was the amazing turn of events that was Julie's friendship. Their relationship had shifted from cool distrust to confidants so quickly that it was almost unsettling. At first, she didn't know what to do with the rapid transformation, but then she just gave in and decided to go with it. She'd been wrong in her judgments before, and she was happy to be wrong about Julie.

It was difficult to see Hana every day. Even though Julie had come to genuinely respect and like her, it was difficult. The coolness between Pastor and Hana had helped . . . initially. The first day when she'd noticed it, her heart had soared. Maybe what she'd been observing between them was something casual or, better yet, completely imagined, but by the end of the day that happy possibility had been shattered.

Seeing Pastor and Hana at odds with one another was like seeing Johnny Cash without his June, like sucking the harmony out of a song. The void just solidified the rightness of the original. Anyone could see it, and instead of making Julie resentful toward Hana, it just saddened her because it meant she'd hit another dead end, another disappointment.

Julie started her Mini Cooper and pulled out of the church parking lot. After seeing Hana at a vulnerable point and hearing how she'd been the brunt of a misguided tongue, something Julie could certainly relate to, she'd done some soul-searching. She'd realized that she'd latched on to Hana as competition and had reacted to her from that standpoint alone. She'd masked her "concern" over Hana with lofty-sounding phrases, even in her own mind, convincing herself that she was only concerned about the welfare of the church, when, in reality, it'd been concern only about herself.

Forgiveness and disappointment—it seemed like she was constantly waffling between those two responses. The more she knew Hana, the more she liked her, and the more she regretted her earlier, envy-driven thoughts. She had to seek God's forgiveness and, in turn, forgive herself. And disappointment—her mother had made sure she'd felt like one, and she'd striven her whole life to be "good enough" in order to outrun that feeling of inadequacy. But she was thirty-six and unmarried, and her mother made sure she understood how completely unacceptable that was. Now Julie had to admit that the hurtful words had infiltrated her thinking more than she'd realized. She'd let fear of disappointment and failure dictate her behavior for far too long.

Julie felt like she was seeing things clearly for the first time in a while. Hana hadn't "taken" Pastor away from her. She'd never "had" him to begin with. She'd just built up something in her mind to combat her mother. It was uncomfortable seeing yourself so bare. She wondered if that was the only way growth happened—from a place of emptiness, when you were finally honest enough to realize you couldn't live life on your own strength, couldn't achieve results by your own effort. Self-reliance was completely counter to the dependent Christian life. This thought was both humbling and such a very great relief.

Usually VBS was a time of joy for Matt. Young hearts were the most receptive to the truth of God's Word, and Matt never tired of seeing children, from both inside and outside the church, being spiritually fed daily and having fun in the process. He counted it a privilege to lead in prayer and devotion each morning, to deliver the Gospel to them, and he usually spent the remainder of the day checking in on the various classrooms. But this time was different.

The distance between him and Hana and Isaac was palpable. Isaac could barely look at him, and Matt couldn't stand knowing that he'd needlessly distressed the boy. He'd been comparing Isaac with Elliott for so long that he'd foolishly attributed the quirks of the one with the other. How could he have lost sight of the fact that Isaac was his own unique person and not a copy of Elliott? How demeaning to Isaac and how sloppy and careless of him. Elliott hadn't taken much stock in people's appearances. Your hair could be purple and spiky for all he'd care. Matt should have known that for Isaac, his identity as Pastor was wrapped up in very tangible things, such as his beard. Isaac was much more aware of his senses than Elliott. How something appeared and felt was of utmost importance to Isaac. And yet Matt had blithely overlooked it out of vanity.

He'd already decided to let the beard grow back out. An experiment in personal appearance wasn't worth upsetting someone else so deeply. Matt's hair grew quickly, and by mid-VBS the stubble was there full force. The Lord had a funny way about Him sometimes. Matt had woken up, looked in the mirror, and smiled grimly. It was growing back all right—completely gray.

Matt had apologized to Hana the day after the picnic, and she'd graciously accepted, saying of course it wasn't his fault, of course he couldn't have known how Isaac would take it, she herself hadn't known, so how could he? She'd been gracious—but things were not the same, for not only was Isaac not looking at him, Hana, too, had put up a barrier. He felt it every time their eyes met throughout the week of VBS. Whereas before there was connection and openness, now there was a wall. He felt it. It was clear that she felt it. And he hated it.

How to close the distance between them? He kept coming back to one idea, one compelling and terrifying thought: Tell her. Tell her all about himself, his past. Tell her what he hadn't told anyone, not his parents and not even his sister. Tell her about Elliott. Maybe then he could apologize again from a place of vulnerability—and then maybe she'd listen.

Now it was the day before the closing program, and Matt was making his rounds to the various classrooms. He stopped outside the first-grade classroom and peeked through the window in the door. Elizabeth was telling a story, her voice smooth and mesmerizing. She was standing at the front of the classroom with hands outstretched, pacing back and forth and every once in a while pointing excitedly into the audience. From the children's response, she was asking questions they were enthusiastically answering. Matt smiled and let his eyes wander to pick out Isaac. He was surprised to find him, not in the back, but at the very front, sitting cross-legged, arms akimbo, mouth wide open as he listened. *Wonderful.* He wanted to burst into the room and scoop the boy up in his arms. He longed to see that eager little face looking into his and hear the inquisitive "Pastor?" as Isaac asked him random question after random question.

Matt's gaze shifted to where Hana sat in the middle of the group, a little girl snuggled into her side. She was absentmindedly stroking the girl's hair, running her fingers through it, working out any tangles. She was also watching Elizabeth and laughed out loud along with the children. A lump rose in his throat. There was horrible pain in this beautifully strong woman's past. Seeing her and Isaac in his congregation safe and happy was immensely satisfying, and yet he worried. Would it stay this way for them? Would they remain safe and happy, or would trouble follow them? Matt gazed at Hana's face and felt his hands clench into fists. It was unnerving to feel so much for someone but to not know if that person was in danger, to not know how or if to ask.

Matt willed his hands to relax, willed his anxious thoughts to still. He focused only on the happiness he saw before him. It was good to see and yet, somehow, also filled him with a sharp pang of dissatisfaction. He realized that he'd become accustomed to being that source of joy for them. He'd delighted to see Isaac's face light up upon his arrival, took immense satisfaction from Hana thanking him. He'd seen the three of them as a unit, a team, and, therefore, he'd become interconnected with their happiness at Hope. With pain, he realized he'd let it become a source of pride. How wily the devil was! That something wholesome and good was corrupted by pride.

Matt turned away from the door and placed his hands behind his bowed head. *Lord Jesus, forgive me, wretched man that I am. Forgive me for letting pride creep into this area of my life. I should never be the source of joy for anyone. You are the only source of true joy, and if I'm not pointing people to You, then I'm not fulfilling my calling. Tear out any root of pride in my life.* He found himself walking in the direction of his office. Once there he closed the door and continued praying, asking for forgiveness and for reconciliation with two very important people in his life.

Hello, Button,

I'm scared, and I'm trying not to be. Ever since my confrontation with your daddy, his attitude has changed. Before he was just distant, like he couldn't be bothered and didn't care. But now . . . I don't know how to describe it. It gives me goose bumps to see the way he looks at us now. The emptiness of before has filled with anger. Instead of looking right through us, it's like he's looking into us and doesn't like what he sees. Before it was like the house was our domain—you and me—and he was just a sporadic boarder. But now, it's like we're intruding on his territory and he resents it. He's home more, and it's not a good thing; it's not like I wanted. He's home but angry and silent and watching us all the time.

I'm scared and I don't know why. I'm not sure what I'm expecting from him. I think maybe that's the problem. He seems unpredictable. At least before I knew what to expect from him. Now I have no idea.

I've started sleeping in your bed every night. You had the sniffles for a while, and I told him I was staying in your room in case you needed me. But then you got better, and I just stayed in your room and he didn't ask any questions. I feel better, safer this way. I'm trying to take a page from your book and find joy in the little things throughout our day. I'm trying. Maybe it will help drown out this fear—this loud, relentless fear.

XO

Mommy

18

Hope was packed the night of the VBS closing program. It was a Friday night, and most family members were in attendance. Each class had a display table in the narthex, showcasing their crafts from the week. As families arrived, they stopped at their children's tables and ooed and ahhed over the brightly festooned displays with their glittery and sticker-filled crafts. And then it was into the sanctuary where the program would unfold.

Hana sat up front with all the children and other volunteers. She twisted in her seat to see where Troy and Kara sat. Charlie was squirming in his seat with the rest of the kindergarten class, Isaac and his first-grade class weren't much calmer, and Alex and Clem were sitting with the classes they'd volunteered in during the week. Julie opened the evening by welcoming the families, and then Pastor led with prayer. Each class took its turn lining up in front of the congregation and singing a song. When it was Isaac's turn, he followed his class to the front and stood on the steps facing the wrong direction. As the music started, Elizabeth rushed up and turned him forward, which he must have mistaken for her wanting him off the stage since he followed her back down the steps. Elizabeth tried to lead him back to his spot, but he kept following her when she tried to leave, so finally, halfway through the song, she gave up and stood with him on the steps, red faced and towering over the first graders as they collectively fumbled through the hand motions. Hana grinned. A few weeks ago, she would have felt the need to jump in, come to the rescue, apologize, try to "fix things." Now she was able to smile and relax, knowing that Elizabeth had things under control and that Isaac's faux pas was met with smiles.

The program closed with one final song during which the children from all the classrooms flooded the space and sang "This Little Light of Mine." Somehow Isaac managed to be standing on the top step in front of the lectern, forming a row of one. Hana tried to get his attention to motion him to step down with the rest of the group, but he was oblivious, too focused on holding up his "light," and, at the appropriate time, belting out "No!" along with the rest of the children, his "No" filled with more gusto and held much longer than the others. Hana grinned and covered her mouth, casting her eyes to where Pastor sat in the pew before her. She caught herself and looked away abruptly. It was instinctual, this desire to share her proud parental moments with him. She wanted to lean over happily to him and whisper, "See, look how well he's doing! Just look!" She shook with the desire of it, not fully realizing until that moment how much she missed him. Instead she swallowed the happy whisper, letting it stick in her throat like a half-chewed bite. She looked at his profile— he was grinning and staring at the kids, eyes shining, hands poised to applaud. His returning beard hadn't escaped her notice. She'd noticed it early in the week, and it was clear that he wasn't shaving it this time, that it was back to stay. And it was completely gray. Seeing this had taken the edge off her irritation. She knew he continued to feel badly about shaving it, and seeing him stoically growing that beard out again had made her stomach go soft. He looked even more dignified now than ever.

The children finished their song, and Pastor led in enthusiastic applause, rising to his feet. Hana turned her attention back to Isaac, who was applauding along with everyone else. He never passed up an opportunity to make noise. When the music was finished, Pastor thanked everyone for coming, thanked the volunteers again, and closed with a benediction.

A time of refreshment followed, during which people congregated in the fellowship hall, where a slideshow presentation with pictures of the past week played on repeat.

"It looks like Isaac really enjoyed himself." Kara leaned toward Hana and motioned to the slideshow, which showed a picture of Isaac's classroom during game time. A young girl was trying to tag Isaac, who was caught with a clenched jaw expression as he tried to run away.

"Well, that particular picture is less Isaac participating and more him trying to escape." She laughed. "But you're right; he really did have an excellent time this week. And Elizabeth, she's just so good with him, Kara!"

"Yes, I noticed that. It makes sense to me, though. She's actually a retired librarian, and I know she ran many a children's program for the library."

"That would explain her mad storytelling skills."

"Yes, yes it does." Kara laughed and then stopped abruptly as her eyes snagged on something. She lowered her voice. "Regina at ten o'clock."

Hana turned rigidly just enough to see Regina at the refreshment table before turning back to Kara. "Ugh, I haven't seen her since . . . you know."

"I know," Kara sighed. Hana had told her all about the infamous event, and Kara had suggested bringing the grievance to Pastor. Hana had declined, partly because she didn't want to discuss anything with Pastor at the moment. "You're just going to have to give it time, Hana. And really, you're not staying here, so you won't have to deal with her forever. It's just finding a way to let it go."

"Yes, somehow." Hana heard a booming laugh behind her and turned to see Pastor sitting a few tables away with Julie.

The achy feeling from earlier returned full force. She didn't like this distance between them, but she didn't know how to close the gap.

Toward the end of the evening, the McCauley family began gathering their children to leave. Hana waved good-bye to Julie and met the rest of the family in the narthex. They were just exiting to the parking lot when Hana heard her name called. She turned to see Pastor with the front door open, slightly out of breath, face urgent. Hana felt a nervous jolt go through her as she approached him. "Hana, thank goodness I caught you." He was indeed out of breath, as if he'd sprinted all the way from the fellowship hall. "I need . . . I really want to talk to you about something tonight if that's okay. I know it's late, and you've got Isaac, but I just need to talk to you."

Hana stared at him in surprise. Why the sudden urgency? She glanced at her phone. It was already seven-thirty, the light was fading, and most everyone had left.

"I'm sorry to stop you like this and make it sound like some sort of emergency. This could wait for another day. I was just hoping I could talk to you now, if that's possible."

She met his eyes and was surprised to see nervousness there. "Okay," she found herself saying. "Okay, just a second." She turned and jogged to Kara, asking her if she could take Isaac home, that she'd follow later, ignoring the outright question in her sister's face. She watched as Isaac climbed into the SUV with the rest of the kids, and the McCauleys drove off. She turned to find Pastor directly behind her and jumped. "Are you okay?" Her confusion bled into uneasiness as she saw the expression on his face.

"Yes, I'm okay. Maybe we could go somewhere to talk?"

"Do you need to lock up the church?"

"Ron is here; he can do it." He already had his keys in his hand and was unlocking his blue Subaru, the car chirping cheerfully.

"Um, okay." Hana frowned as he opened the door of the passenger side for her, but she slid in without asking any more questions.

He took her to Braum's, an ice cream and burger place that Hana had yet to try. The drive was all of five minutes, but they spent it in stilted silence, Hana hardly daring to breathe. He'd treated her with the utmost decorum, opening the door for her, buying her a small cup of ice cream and getting one himself even though they'd both just eaten at church. They took their cups outside to the small patio with concrete picnic tables. Dusk was settling, and the crickets were out. The patio was next to the drive-through, so the dusk was punctuated both by the hissing neon Braum's sign and by the headlights of cars pulling past them, their occupants clutching bags of greasy burgers or dripping ice cream cones.

Hana sat stiffly on the concrete bench and stabbed at the mound of cookie dough ice cream with her small plastic spoon. The bench was uncomfortable and was snagging unpleasantly at her thin skirt. She kept shifting and inwardly cringing at how her skirt stuck to the bench. A car pulled into the drive-through, momentarily blinding her. She squinted and shifted down the bench so that she wasn't directly facing the drive-through. Her skirt twisted around her thighs as most of the material stayed put in her original spot. She peeled it off the bench and arranged it more comfortably around her legs, finally glancing at Pastor. He looked just as uncomfortable as she felt.

Now that they were settled and alone, he hesitated as if reluctant to say what was on his mind. She decided to help him with a prompt. "Was there something you wanted to talk to me about?"

His hands were in his lap, and he was staring at his cup of rocky road like it was an unusual object someone had just randomly plopped in front of him. At her prompt, his eyes jerked up to meet hers. They were wide and vulnerable and made her feel like she was on the edge of something—a cliff perhaps. Not exactly a pleasant feeling.

"Yes, I apologize for the rush and secrecy. I just needed to talk with you tonight, and I appreciate you making the time." He placed folded hands on the table. "I feel like ever since the picnic, there's been strain between us. I don't know quite why, but I do want to make it right."

Hana swallowed hard and felt guilt wiggle its way to the surface. "About that . . . I feel badly because you didn't do anything wrong. I think I was just . . . strangely upset about that beard, about how it affected Isaac, even though, like I said, I know it's not your fault. And goodness—you certainly don't have to consult me or Isaac before making grooming decisions!" She tried to laugh, tried to break the heaviness of the moment with levity. She used to do that a lot before Zeke, before levity became something so foreign she didn't know how to employ it anymore. "It's irrational and ridiculous, and I don't want you feeling like you have to apologize for something that isn't your fault." She watched as his eyes flickered and a smile began to form on his face. "And really, if you want to keep it off, please do. Please don't let Isaac dictate what you do with your own face." She tried laughing again, but it sounded forced, and she was beginning to sound like a broken record. She really should stop talking, but he still wasn't saying anything, just looking at her with those steady hazel eyes. It unnerved her and made her keep going, in an effort to fill the silence, to ease whatever emotion was hanging between them. "Although, it was sweet of you to start growing it back." She paused because that had come out in an intimate tone that surprised and embarrassed her. "I mean, assuming you're doing that for Isaac. It's a nice gesture." She delicately avoided mentioning the color change in the beard, but he jumped in.

"I think I'll keep the beard." He stroked it thoughtfully. "You know, as penance."

She glanced up at him sharply to find him grinning. "Oh, you're being silly." She slapped his hand from across the table, and he laughed.

"Maybe, but I shaved it off out of vanity, and that's not a good reason to do anything."

She raised an eyebrow at him. "Vanity?"

"You know, vanity: the quality of being vain; caring an inordinate amount about one's appearance; pomposity; self-conceit; self—"

"Okay, okay, I get it." Hana laughed, cutting him off. "I can't imagine you ever being vain." He just smiled at her without saying anything, and Hana found herself blushing for reasons she couldn't pinpoint. She took a bite of half-melted ice cream in an attempt to collect herself.

Pastor finally picked up his spoon and began stirring the contents of his cup. "So I wanted to clear the air between us, and I wanted to begin by sharing something personal with you, by way of an explanation of sorts and just . . . because I feel like I need to. I want to."

Hana quickly swallowed the overly large bite in her mouth, which gave her a brain freeze. She powered through it to choke out, "Please don't feel like you *have* to. Like you owe it to me or something."

"I don't have to, but I want to." He glanced up at her again. "It's a big part of who I am. If you're . . . okay with hearing it. I don't want to impose on you."

"No, no, not at all." Hana didn't know what to think. Pastor was the last person she would expect to have something big to share, something big and secret. She definitely knew how that felt, and she found herself appraising him in a new light. Apparently he knew how that felt too. "Please, if it'll make you feel better, please share."

He was stirring and stirring his cup of ice cream like it was a small pot of soup. "It's a large part of why I felt—I feel—so connected to Isaac. I think I might have mentioned when we first met that I knew a child with autism when I was just a boy."

Hana squinted as she thought back to that first meeting. "Yes, yes, I do remember you saying that."

"His name was Elliott." He'd stopped stirring and sat with his hands clasped around the cup of soupy ice cream, his eyes finally finding hers. "And he was my brother."

Matt sat on the hard, concrete bench and tried to keep his hands from shaking. He gripped the cup tightly and made himself maintain eye contact with the concerned woman across from him. "Elliott was two years younger than me. Our sister was a lot older and busy with her friends and activities, so it was just the two of us growing up." He felt a lump forming in his throat and tried to swallow past it. "Back then there wasn't the awareness or resources there are now. It became clear early on that Elliott was what they called 'simple.' He was a lot less functioning than Isaac. He was mostly nonverbal. My parents didn't know what to do with him. There was no aid, no diagnosis, no therapy, no real understanding." His hands were shaking, despite his best efforts, so Matt shoved them out of sight beneath the table. "My parents weren't bad parents. They just didn't make the effort with Elliott. He was, in their minds, their stupid, helpless son—a burden and an embarrassment. Rebecca, my sister, didn't have time for him either. I grew up looking out for him. We were only two years apart, but it was like he was my child, my responsibility. When the bullies mocked him until he cried, I was there to yell at them and throw rocks until they ran away. I was there to hold him, console him. I didn't have many friends because Elliott was always with me, and no one wanted to spend time with him." He paused as he noticed tears on Hana's cheeks. The sight made him swallow uncomfortably. "I'm telling you this because I want you to understand . . . to understand my heart in all this." She was nodding at him, encouraging him to continue.

"It was a full-time job, being Elliott's brother. I think as a young child it was just a part of who I was, and I could never remember a time when it was different. It wasn't until I was older that I began to battle heavily with resentment. I was jealous of other people's lives. They looked so easy to me. I was angry with my parents because they saw me as their 'solution,' as if because I was taking care of Elliott, they didn't have to. And then that resentment turned onto Elliott. I began resenting him for things he absolutely couldn't help. I began separating myself from him. There were days . . . " He stopped abruptly to collect himself and try again. "There were days when Elliott wouldn't eat because I wasn't . . . I wasn't there to feed him."

"Oh, Matt . . . " She was reaching across the table, seeking out his hand. And he gave it to her, holding on tightly, noticing the use of his first name and how right it sounded on her lips.

"I think I reached my lowest point as a junior in high school. I was an awkward kid, and I blamed all of my problems on Elliott, every single one. It was Elliott's fault that I was never invited to anything, his fault that I never had a girlfriend. I even blamed bad grades on him. Everything was Elliott's fault." He took a deep breath before continuing. It was time to share the guilt and shame that had shadowed Matt most of his life. "I remember lying in bed one night, and I was just angry, at God, at myself, everyone. And one thought kept running through my head. I wished that Elliott had never been born. I created a whole alternative life for myself—one in which Elliott didn't exist. I fantasized about how perfect this life would be and went into great detail over all the things I could do and be and have and enjoy if not for Elliott. I wished it so hard that it felt like a prayer, even though I didn't have a relationship with God and didn't know the first thing about Him really, or about prayer." He sighed deeply, remembering Elliott as a child, happy to be with his brother by the lake, choosing to keep that image of him in mind rather than the image of neglect he'd later become.

"A week later, Elliott was dead. He just didn't wake up one morning. It was heart failure, and an autopsy showed that he had a congenital heart defect that we had known nothing about." Matt stared at their clasped hands on the hard concrete table and felt the tears slip down his cheeks. "And I blamed myself every day for years and years. I believed with all my heart that I had killed my brother."

"Matt, no—"

"It wasn't until years after I came to faith that I finally recognized that I was forgiven, but a day doesn't go by when I don't see his face and feel the guilt threaten me again." The tears had subsided. He let go of her hand to wipe at his face with a thin restaurant napkin. Ironically his beard had trapped most of the tears, which meant his shiny cheekbones were the only things betraying him. "I share this with you because I want you to know my heart in relation to your son. Maybe you feel like you and Isaac are burdening me? You are not. Maybe you feel like the recipient of pity? I assure you that is not the case. Seeing Isaac and how loving you are with him, it provides me with so much joy, more than you can know. And seeing Isaac in pain, distressed . . . and to be the cause of that distress, however tangentially, feels unbearable to me because it brings me back to Elliott and to all those old feelings, of fundamentally letting him down."

There, he'd said it. He hadn't thought past just getting this off his chest. Now, as he sat numbly on the bench feeling vulnerable in ways he'd never felt before, he didn't have long to wonder "What next?" because Hana was standing and coming over to him. She was sitting next to him, putting her arm around his back, and leaning her head on his shoulder. He was a short man, and he wasn't used to many women being shorter than he was. Hana's head found his shoulder easily and rested there comfortably, her arm stretched across his back, her hand barely reaching his other shoulder. He wasn't used to being on the receiving end of compassion and comfort. He was usually the one giving it out. His heart calmed and settled at her touch. His hand rested on her knee as they sat there in silence.

Cars were still driving by, their headlights piercing the darkness. Both Hana's and Matt's faces were swathed in a neon pink glow from the Braum's sign. Finally, she turned her face to him and looked him in the eye. "Thank you for sharing your heart with me tonight. Thank you."

He squeezed her knee. "Thank you for listening." They sat

with their former rapport restored, and he debated whether or not to ask her more about herself and her past, finally deciding that now was not the time. He didn't want her thinking he'd shared intimate details about himself only so she would return the favor. Most definitely not the message he wanted to send. And so he didn't pry into her life and didn't offer her any more of his own. He would wonder afterward if he'd been even bolder that night, if he'd gathered her into his arms and jumped headlong into her pain, offering her even more of his heart right then and there, if she would have stayed, if it would have made a difference. But he didn't.

Clem sat in the third row seat of her parents' SUV and munched on some trail mix she'd brought from church. Her parents were passionately discussing something in the front, her mother's insistent "What do you think he wants?" threading its way to where Clem lounged in the back seat. Charlie and Isaac sat in the middle seat, Charlie happily chattering Isaac's ear off. Alex sat moodily next to her, arms crossed and staring out the window. She wasn't sure what his problem was, but it might have something to do with Sam spending the evening talking to Luke Schroeder. Whatever. He'd just have to get over it.

She popped her earbuds in and flipped through her playlists until she settled on one, then opened up her pictures to go through the ones she'd taken that evening to see if any were Instagram worthy. She scrolled through pictures of kids standing by their craft tables in the narthex, standing clustered on the sanctuary steps, eating in the fellowship hall. Most of the sanctuary ones were from too far away. The ones where she'd zoomed in were too blurry to be usable. She found one of Charlie proudly showing off his crafts in the narthex. It was kind of cute, so she posted it along with a selfie of her and Sam making duck faces. Ooo, Luke was in the background of that one, photobombing it with a goofy expression—even better. Alex would be so mad! If he ever saw it, that is. Her serious, stuffy older brother was hardly ever online. Clem went through the rest of the photos quickly, already receiving likes on the duck face photo. Here was a cute one of Aunt Hana and Isaac. They were standing with plates of food in the fellowship hall, and she'd made them stop and smile for her. It was the only close-up she had of them, so she posted that one too.

They arrived home, and Alex huffed off to his room while Charlie begged his mother for a snack.

"A snack? Goodness, child, we just came from an entire smorgasbord of snacks!"

"I'm starving. I'm *so* hungry, Mom."

"How about a banana?"

"No, I'm not hungry for that."

"An apple?"

"No. Hey, how about a cookie?" he said as if the idea was inspired and had just come to him.

"How about not? It's a piece of fruit or nothing else, young man."

Clem left the kitchen and Charlie's loud protestations, walked past her dad, who was taking Isaac to get ready for bed, and made her way to her room, where she flopped on her bed and began browsing Facebook. Her friends from Michigan, where they'd lived before Altus, were already commenting all over her picture with Sam and Luke. "Who's the hottie?" Sophie asked, and Clem was immensely grateful she wasn't friends with Luke on Facebook; otherwise this would be so embarrassing. She hummed to her music, kicking her feet in the air and finishing off her trail mix.

"Clem, honey? Clem!" She glanced up to see her mother in the doorway, hand on hip.

Clem removed an earbud. "Yeah, what?"

"How about 'Yes, Mother?' instead?"

"Yes, Mother?" Clem rolled her eyes.

"And without the eye roll, please. Is that too much to ask?"

"Yes, Mother?" Clem stared straight into her eyes and worked hard to control her tone. Otherwise she'd hear, "Don't take that tone with me, young lady. Let's try this again," and they'd be here all night.

"You've been on that all evening, and it's time to get ready for bed." Her mother gestured to the phone and held out her hand as if asking for the device.

"No, Mom, please! I'm almost done. It's just . . . I'm talking with Sophie, and she's been away at camp, and I haven't heard from her in a while. She'll think I'm ignoring her if I don't finish the conversation." She used her best friend's name from Michigan, knowing it would make her mom feel guilty and bad for moving so often and separating her children from their friends. And it was sort of true—Sophie had gone to camp . . . last month. And she was talking with Clem. She'd asked who the hottie was in the photo. That counted as a conversation.

Just as she expected, her mother sighed and ran a hand over her face. "Well, okay. Tell Sophie hi from me, but please finish up with that and turn it off so you can get ready for bed and get some sleep. Remember what we said when we gave you the phone. You need to be responsible with it."

"Yes, I know. I will be. Thanks, Mom." Her mother closed the door, and Clem put the earbud back in and answered Sophie. "It's this guy, Luke. Sam and I hang out with him all the time." It was sort of true. If by "hang out" you mean, "see from a distance each week at church."

A half hour later, Clem heard her mom's footsteps in the hall and quickly shoved the phone beneath the sheets and began changing into her pajamas. But the footsteps passed, so she slowed down as she finished. She left the phone hidden as she made her way to the bathroom to wash her face and brush her teeth. When she returned, she hopped into bed and grabbed a book from her nightstand, flicking on her lamp and sliding her phone in front of the pages. A little while later, her mother knocked on the door and peeked in. Clem glanced up over the edge of the book.

"All ready for bed, sweetie?" At Clem's affirmative, her mother blew her a kiss. "Okay, don't stay up too late." She smiled and nodded toward the book, turning off the overhead light and leaving the door open a crack behind her.

Clem turned back to her phone. She'd begun an actual text conversation with Sophie, who wanted more details about this Luke she hung out with all the time. A few minutes passed, and then Clem heard the ding of an incoming Facebook message.

"Hi, beautiful! I just love your latest pics, especially of Aunt Hana and Isaac."

It was Uncle Zeke. Clem felt a jolt of surprise. She'd forgotten about him. "Oh hey, Uncle Zeke. Thanks!"

"You all have a church event tonight? Looks fun!"

"Yup, it was for VBS."

"Did Isaac have a good time?"

"Yeah, I think he did."

"Oh good! Hey, is that Hope Lutheran Church you guys are at? I think I see that in the pic of your aunt and cousin."

Clem frowned and opened the picture. Aunt Hana and Isaac were standing by the refreshment table in the fellowship hall, and the slideshow was playing in the background. The picture was of a group of kids posing outside, right by the sign displaying "Hope Lutheran Church." Her uncle was really observant. Clem hadn't even noticed that. "Yup, that's where we go to church."

"Cool. How do you guys like it there? Much different than Michigan, right?"

"Oh yeah, totally different! But I guess it's okay."

"Remind me where you all are again?"

"Oklahoma."

There was a long pause, during which Clem could see the icon showing that her uncle was typing a reply and then stopping and then typing again. She frowned, beginning to feel slightly uneasy. Why was he asking *her* all these questions? Why not ask Aunt Hana? Finally a reply came.

"Gotcha. Hope Lutheran Church in Altus, Oklahoma. Wow, that is totally different from Michigan, isn't it? Must be super hot there."

"Yeah, it's hot. We don't really get snow." Clem chewed her lip and then wrote, "Hey, are you thinking of coming to visit or something?"

There was another long pause, no indication that he was typing. Had he left? "Uncle Zeke? Are you coming to visit? Is everything better with you and Aunt Hana?"

"Sorry, beautiful, I'm here. Yes, things are much better. Thank you for asking! And maybe, maybe I'll come visit. But don't tell anyone cause I want it to be a surprise, okay? Only you can know so that you can help me make it a surprise. Deal?"

Clem sat back, smug. So that's it. He was trying to surprise everyone and wanted her in on it. "Yeah, okay, cool."

"Got to go, okay, beautiful? Did I ever tell you that you're my favorite niece?"

"I'm your *only* niece, silly."

"Oh yeah, but still my favorite!"

Clem smiled and clicked on his name, opening his page. He didn't have much information on there and hadn't posted anything in a long time. She scrolled through some past pictures. He was so handsome. She remembered being scared of him when she was younger because he was so tall, but now that only added to his appeal. And she was his favorite!

Clem heard footsteps coming down the hall and hurriedly turned off her lamp and slid lower in the sheets, squeezing her eyes shut and hiding her phone beneath the covers. She heard the steps pause outside her door and didn't dare look, just in case someone was peeking in on her. Finally she heard the steps fade away and opened her eyes with a sigh. She thought about her uncle Zeke's message and wondered when he would come and how surprised everyone would be. Thoughts of her handsome uncle, however, receded as she thought of the handsome Luke. She hadn't given it much thought before, but she guessed he was a "hottie," like Sophie had said. Sam liked him, and Clem liked that it wasn't Alex that she liked, so she guessed she was okay with this Luke guy, as long as he didn't infringe on her and Sam's friendship.

Clem finally drifted off to sleep and dreamt of her uncle dressed as a cowboy arriving in town on Sublime. She was hiding behind a bush with Luke, and they both jumped out in front of a startled Aunt Hana, yelling, "Surprise!" The expression on her face when she realized what was going on was hysterical.

Hello, Button,

Your daddy has begun taking a renewed interest in you—not me, certainly, but you. He watches me like he's challenging me to just try and stop him. I think he's absolutely convinced himself that we're on opposing sides, that I'm somehow fundamentally against him, and it just breaks my heart. How did this happen? I don't know how we got here, and I don't know what I can do to fix it. How do you try to repair things with someone who is convinced you are the enemy?

So like I said, he's around more, and he's spending time with you and taking you to do things—all without me. I'm not invited, not included, and he just looks at me as if to say, "What are you going to do about it?" I don't like it when he takes you places without me. It reminds me of the time when he took you to the ball game and didn't tell me, and I had no idea where you were for a whole day. It's hard to explain—I feel like one day he'll take you somewhere and just never come back, just leave me in this house by myself. I keep telling myself it's ridiculous to be so scared. He's your father, after all! I remember how happy he was when you were born, and all the small, sweet moments after, when he'd bathe you and make you laugh by blowing raspberries on your bare belly. Or how he'd insist on buying you something every time we went out, even if it was just a piece of chocolate. Those sweet moments, they got fewer and fewer as you got older, but they are still there and he is still your daddy, and I feel guilty for feeling so terrified when you're with him.

But I'm scared, honey. I'm scared he's going to take you away from me. And then I wonder if that's how he felt before this—like I was taking you away from him. And then I get confused. It's just all so confusing, and it shouldn't be, should it? It shouldn't be like this with a family, right?

XO

Mommy

19

Kara was brimming with questions the next day, as Hana suspected she would be. "What did he want, Hana? What did he say?" She'd barely walked into the kitchen before the barrage of questions hit her. It was Saturday morning, and the kids were all asleep. Troy was in the kitchen with a mug of coffee and his tablet, most likely skimming the news, and Kara was at the counter, hand on hip, eyes agog.

Hana groaned and shuffled toward the coffeepot. "Can this wait until I've at least had my first cup?"

"Um, absolutely not." Kara sidestepped so that she was standing in front of the pot.

"I'm not talking until I've had coffee." Hana raised an eyebrow. "We can stand here all day if you like."

Kara sighed and stepped aside. "Fine, but talk as you pour."

Hana grabbed a mug from the cabinet and poured a healthy serving, stirring in just a dab of cream and sugar. As much as she appreciated her sister's interest, and as much as she'd enjoyed their renewed closeness lately, Hana wasn't about to tell her the specifics. Matt had disclosed those details in confidence, and she wasn't about to violate that. She grinned as she stirred her coffee. She'd begun thinking of him as Matt. She had seen past the pastor last night and to the heart of the man, and even though he was still Pastor, he was now Matt in her mind.

"You're smiling. That's a good thing, right? Why are you smiling?" Kara peered into her face, hip against the counter, hands cradling her own freshly poured mug of coffee.

"Nothing, it's just . . . he just wanted to clear the air between us, given what happened at the picnic. You know, sweep away any remaining tension between us." Kara was still looking at her expectantly, clearly unsatisfied with this reply. She needed to tell her sister something, or she'd be on her all day. Hana decided to tell her a portion of the truth. It wasn't everything, but it was pretty big and fresh and surprising. She took a bracing sip of coffee. "And . . . you may have been right."

"Of course I was," Kara replied quickly and then paused. "About what, exactly?"

Hana laughed and shot a glance at Troy before leaning forward and whispering, "You know, about . . . me appreciating Pastor as more than just a friend for Isaac."

"Ah *ha!*" Kara yelped, nearly sloshing her coffee everywhere in her enthusiasm.

Troy glanced up and cast a suspicious eye in the sisters' direction before returning to his coffee.

"Keep your voice down, would you?" Hana blushed.

Kara dragged her into the living room and sat her down on the couch, plopping down next to her. "I *knew* it!"

"If I knew you were going to be *this* obnoxious and big-headed, I wouldn't have told you." Hana rolled her eyes.

"Whatever." Kara swatted at her. "Seriously, Hana, he is such a kind and genuine man, and I know he really does care for you and Isaac."

"You don't have to convince me." Hana couldn't look her sister in the eye.

"So what changed? Did he declare his feelings for you?"

"Now you're just being melodramatic! No, nothing like that. We just had a heart-to-heart, and I realized afterward exactly what you just said—that he's one of the most caring and genuine people I know."

"Ooo, I'm so glad!" Kara squealed.

"Don't go getting all giddy on me." Hana sobered as the next thought took hold of her. "I'm moving in just a few weeks. That hasn't changed."

They sat in silence for a moment. "Well, that's true." Kara said slowly, thoughtfully.

"I just, I don't know why God would put Matt—Pastor—into our lives if it was just going to be so temporary."

"I'm definitely familiar with temporary," Kara said. "The military life is kind of defined by temporary. Just when you put down roots and allow yourself to make friends, you find yourself torn away yet again. It's not always the duration that matters, though. God puts people into our lives for a reason, and sometimes the impact can be deep, even if it's brief."

"Yes, but what if I don't want it to be brief?"

Kara sighed deeply. "I don't have an answer for that one, honey."

They sat and sipped in silence. Hana had awoken that morning with this thrilling new knowledge settled deep in her chest, as sure and certain as her heartbeat. She was falling for Pastor Matt Schofield. It was a relief to stop fighting it, to stop denying it, to finally acknowledge and just accept it. On the heels of that heady knowledge, however, was the logical impracticality of their relationship. She was leaving. He was staying. The freshly launched emotion would not be silenced, though, even by cold logic. It rose in her chest and filled her head, hovering and beating at her brain all throughout the day, refusing to be silenced or quieted by reality. It was like a persistent moth, beating its wings against the window, striving to get to the light.

That unrelenting, fluttery feeling lasted all throughout the day, even when the kids woke up, and the early morning peace was shattered; even during the long hour drive to Central Mall in Lawton to go back-to-school shopping; even while forcing Isaac to try on outfit after outfit or listening to

Clem complain that they weren't visiting any stores *she* liked; even during the brief and complaint-free lunch while everyone scarfed down Chick-fil-A; even during the tedious hour drive home; even during the evening fashion show, when all the children (minus Isaac, who adamantly refused to try on one more piece of clothing) modeled their new clothes for a wise Troy, who had stayed home from the expedition; even when all the children were finally in bed, and the sisters ended the day as they'd begun it, sitting relaxed on the couch, this time with wine glasses instead of coffee mugs.

Throughout the whole, tiring day, that fluttery feeling persisted. It beat against her chest and stole her breath at the oddest moments, leaving her dizzy, and not in the usual panicky way, but in a new and exciting way. It accompanied her all throughout the evening and wouldn't be silenced. For the first time in a long time, Hana fell asleep with a smile on her face.

The feeling didn't go away until the sharp, unnatural ringing of the telephone at three in the morning shocked it away, the cold tone—so typical during the day—sounding shrill and frightening throughout the house, jolting everyone out of their beds and ripping that fluttery, happy feeling straight out of Hana's chest.

"He was trying to go to the bathroom by himself and slipped and fell." Kara, Troy, and Hana sat huddled at the dining room table, having already assured the children everything was going to be okay and putting them all back to their respective beds.

"Broken hip," Hana whispered, dropping her face into her hands as the reality sunk in. "And a heart attack on the way to the hospital."

Troy rubbed Kara's back as she began to cry. Their father had been living comfortably in an assisted-living facility in Richmond for years, and even though he had trouble getting around, had never had any serious health concerns.

The prognosis didn't look good, and the urgency over the phone had been clear.

Hana felt the tears well up in her eyes as she watched her sister cry. She reached out a hand and grasped her sister's arm. "Kara, we have to go."

"Yes," Kara's voice was wobbly, muffled from having her face planted in the crook of her arm. "The sooner the better."

Hana didn't get any more sleep that night, and come morning she could tell that neither had Kara. Both opted to stay home from church, as there was now a trip to plan and pack for. Troy took the children to church as the sisters began the unexpected work of preparing to leave as soon as possible.

If Pastor Matthew Schofield looked particularly happy that Sunday morning, only a few noticed and commented on it. He stood at the church's entrance, greeting all who entered with smiles and a handshake. As for his part, he felt like a completely new man. After the emotional heaviness of Friday night had come a bursting buoyancy unlike anything he'd experienced. Perhaps it was from having shared his heart so fully, things he had never given words to before. Or perhaps it had to do with the renewed closeness between Hana and himself, and not just renewed but enlarged and enhanced. They'd both sensed it while parting ways on Friday, and Matt had let the joy of it carry him all throughout the next day.

He had felt guilty for his attraction to Hana, but now he realized that part of that guilt was a default response he'd learned years ago. He'd felt guilt anytime he had desired or pursued a relationship because it made him feel like he was shirking responsibility—the responsibility of Elliott when he was younger, the responsibility of schoolwork, and eventually the responsibility of his pastoral duties as an adult. But God was the author of marriage. He looked with approval on the intimate bond between husband and wife. He'd observed and felt a pang of longing over the marriages of his colleagues many times over the years. There was no shame, no guilt in acknowledging that such a relationship was a good gift from God. And so he had consciously let go of the guilt, had prayed and given it over to the Lord. And what was left behind was peace and a buoyancy so light he felt like he needed to be tethered to a pole to stay put.

Matt recognized the McCauley SUV as it entered the lot, and his grin widened. As the family walked up, he extended a hand to Troy and to all the children, pausing when he came to Isaac. The boy was still largely aloof, and Matt didn't want to aggravate him by coming across too strong. Isaac surprised him, however, by initiating the conversation. "I brought Rocky." He lifted the cage.

"Yes, I see that. I'm glad to see him, and to see you." Matt put out a hand, and was immensely pleased when Isaac took it. "Where are Hana and Kara?" Matt turned to Troy.

To his surprise, Troy's expression was serious. He stepped aside to let others pass them, drawing Matt with him and saying in a low voice, "We got a call in the middle of the night. Their father fell and broke a hip and then suffered a heart attack on the way to the hospital. It's not looking so good."

Matt's heart grew heavy as he realized the pain the sisters were experiencing at that moment. "Troy, I'm so sorry to hear it."

"They're at home now, planning their trip back home to be with their dad."

"Yes, certainly. If there's anything I can do . . . "

"Thanks, Pastor, your prayers are appreciated. And if you could include them in the prayers during the service, we would appreciate it."

Matt nodded. "Of course." He watched Troy usher the kids inside, his heart getting heavier by the second. He was saddened for the family but also saddened that Hana was leaving so abruptly, so soon. And there was still so much he wanted to say. He breathed a prayer of healing and strength for the family and their loved one, refocusing his attention to where it needed to be, pushing aside the other pain, the pain of missing Hana.

It was Sunday afternoon, and Matt found himself at home digesting both the sub sandwich he'd consumed for lunch and the news he'd received that morning. He'd been praying for Kara and Hana's father and the family on and off all morning, shifting his concern and focus to the family every time he was tempted to feel sad for himself. But now, in the privacy of home, he let those feelings creep back up with all their numerous implications.

What did this mean, exactly, for Hana and Isaac? He knew they were leaving in a few weeks anyway to live in Richmond, where a new home, school, and job awaited them. The more he thought about it, the more it seemed unlikely that they would bother coming back to Altus, just to turn around and return to Richmond again. By midafternoon, he'd convinced himself that he would never see Hana and Isaac again. Just like that—gone. He should have said more to Isaac at church, offered a hug, even though he doubted it'd be received. He couldn't bear the idea of not seeing the boy again . . . or his mother.

Finally he picked up the phone and called the McCauley number. Troy picked up on the second ring. "Pastor, good to hear from you."

"I was wondering if I might speak with Kara, let her know that we're praying for her."

He waited as Troy called for his wife. Silence, and then a breathy, "Hello?"

"Hello, Kara. Troy told me this morning about your father, and I'm calling to let you know I've been praying all morning and will continue to keep you and your family in my prayers. Perhaps Troy told you that your church family prayed for all of you this morning as well."

"Yes, thank you so much, Pastor. We appreciate it. It came as such a shock."

"I'm sure." He wanted to ask after Hana but the words wouldn't come. Again, the old war between desire and duty reared its head like twining vines, confusing him at each intersection.

"Pastor would you . . . would you like to talk with Hana?" Something about Kara's tone made him snap to attention. It was almost like she had read his thoughts . . . and approved.

He found himself fumbling a reply, blushing furiously. "Oh, sure, um, I mean, yes, if she's there, if it's no trouble, sure." Was that a soft laugh he heard? He instantly stopped talking, as it was probably only further incriminating him, and waited nervously for Hana to pick up the phone.

"Pastor, Matt, hi."

Was this the first time he'd spoken with her over the phone? Her voice was just as beautiful this way as in person, soft and kind. He was furiously smiling at the use of his first name. "Hana, hi. Listen, I'm so sorry to hear about your father."

"Yes, it was so sudden and unexpected."

"I'm so sorry," Matt repeated, wishing he could think of something better to say. It's not like he wasn't in this position all the time, offering comfort and support to loved ones facing the potential loss of a family member. He'd just never been in this position with Hana.

"Matt, I . . . Kara and I have been going over our plans. We want to go be with Dad, the sooner the better."

"Yes, I understand."

"So we'll be flying out tomorrow morning . . . with Isaac."

Tomorrow morning—so soon—of course so soon. They needed to be with their father. "Yes, that's probably for the best. Has Isaac flown before?"

"A couple of times, yes, and it's not something he enjoys."

"Enclosed space, sitting for a long period of time. It's hard on anyone."

"Especially since he can't have Rocky with him."

"Oh dear, yes. I imagine Rocky will be traveling via cargo."

"Exactly, and it's hard for Isaac to understand why he can't have him with him."

There was a short silence between them, which Matt filled with an understanding grunt of sympathy.

"Matt . . . " her voice nearly a whisper. "I—I don't think we'll be coming back."

Matt swallowed past the lump in his throat. "I wondered about that. Seeing as you're moving there anyway. Where will you stay?" He tried to keep his tone light, even, measured, tried not to show that his heart was being squeezed with emotion, so tight he could hardly get words to come out.

"We have a cousin there who will put us up until the rental house is ready. Kara will come back, I guess whenever it makes sense. I mean, she'll need to come back anyway to bring my car to me. I'm just hoping it won't also be in order to plan a funeral." Her voice broke, and he could tell she was trying to stave off tears.

Matt felt his heart squeeze for a different reason. How selfish to sit here in a panic over losing this beautiful woman when she was in the throes of personal crisis! She was possibly facing the death of a parent, her last remaining parent at that. It was something that Matt blessedly knew nothing about. He thought of his own parents back in Idaho and tried to imagine what it would be like to get that call in the middle of the night. "Hana, I'm so sorry." He needed to come up with a different phrase. "Can I pray with you right now?"

He heard a sniffle through the phone line and then a quiet, "Yes."

And so he prayed, bringing their requests before the throne of grace with boldness. He prayed for what they desired—a return of health for Hana's father—but he also prayed for strength to accept whatever God's will might be for the situation. He prayed for Isaac to be comforted on the flight and not too anxious over Rocky or the confined quarters. He prayed for the new job and housing situation and for all the unknowns in Hana's future. He prayed for peace and guidance, all the while knowing he needed those exact same things.

When he finished, he heard another sniffle. "Amen. Thank you." There was a pause and then a broken, "Oh, I'm going to just *miss* you so much."

Matt didn't think he could trust his voice to reply. He coughed once, twice, started a reply, and then abruptly stopped as his voice broke. He kept clearing his throat until he could form a response. "I'll miss you too, Hana, you and Isaac." He didn't want to push, but he also didn't want them to leave without a chance to say good-bye. "Listen, I don't want to impose, but would it be okay if I, would you mind if—"

"Yes, please, can you come over? Tonight? Isaac will want to get a chance to say good-bye, and tomorrow will just be too hectic."

Matt sighed with relief. "Oh, thank you, good. Just let me know what time. I don't want to be in the way."

He paused as Hana shouted to her sister, "Kara, Matt's coming over for dinner, okay?"

"Oh, no, no, I don't need to come for dinner . . . "

"We're ordering pizza, nothing fancy. Hold on . . . " He heard muffled voices. "Okay, yes, just come whenever you're able. We're planning on ordering around six."

"Oh, okay, if you're sure."

"Absolutely sure."

Matt got off the phone feeling like the room was tilting. It was all happening so fast. One second he was pouring out his heart to this woman; the next she was leaving suddenly, unexpectedly, and now he was looking ahead to a whole evening spent together. He was half looking forward to it, half dreading it, because as much as he longed to see Hana and Isaac, to say good-bye, he also didn't quite know what to say or how to act. It was like the beginning and death of something all in one weekend, and Matt was unsure how to cherish and mourn something with such a short lifespan.

Hello, Button,

I finally broke down and talked to your aunt Kara about everything. Mainly I think I was looking for her to laugh at me and tell me how crazy I'm being. I need someone to tell me that I'm too much in my head, over-thinking things and worrying too much. But instead she just exploded on me! She launched into how your daddy was never good enough for me, how I'm not myself around him, and that she's always been worried and uncomfortable with his temper. His temper? Certainly he has a short fuse now, but he wasn't always like that. I tried to remind her of how great he was, how funny and spontaneous and outgoing and amazing he was, but she just didn't want to see past her image of him as an "angry man."

She didn't make me feel better, Button; she made me even more nervous. I wanted her to blow off my worries, but instead she just blew them up to such monumental proportions that I got angry and hung up on her. She called and called, finally leaving me a message. I didn't want to listen to it, but of course I did. I couldn't help it. She was apologetic and crying, begging me not to isolate myself, to talk to her, to let her know if I ever felt unsafe. She's making me feel like a victim, and I hate it. Just because your daddy doesn't fit her particular mold, she thinks he's no good. She's always been like that. If things aren't done her way or someone isn't up to her standards, then they're no good. And of course she has the perfect husband and perfect family. It's just so infuriating, and it's not what I needed, not at all. I'm just so frustrated, and I don't know who to turn to.

XO

Mommy

20

Everyone was gathered around the McCauley's dining room table with paper plates filled with large slices of pizza. Matt had noticed a definite uptick in mood once the pizza was passed around. "They're all worried about their grandpa," Kara had told him earlier. "They're worried, but they also don't have a super close relationship with my dad. We've just traveled so much, and he's been unable to travel. We try to visit him when we can, but it's been more sporadic than I'd like, and I think Clem and Alex are feeling a little guilty for not being *more* distraught by the news, if that makes sense." The kids chattered nonstop during the meal, seeming to momentarily forget that this was a farewell dinner and that their aunt and cousin would be leaving in the morning.

Matt couldn't forget. He drank in the sight of Isaac's face smeared with grease. "Pizza is one food he doesn't have stipulations on," Hana had told him with a grin. "It seems that with just about any other food, he wants five things changed before he'll consume it, but give him pepperoni pizza, and he's happy as can be." Matt made a mental note: Isaac loves turtles, bodies of water, donuts, facial hair, and pepperoni pizza. But then stopped himself when he realized with a sad abruptness that he would no longer be seeing Isaac. He filed the note away anyway, slowly, reluctantly. He noted as well how Hana was more at ease with her sister than when she'd first arrived. He wouldn't have really noticed it if he hadn't already been highly in tune to everything Hana related. But there was an easiness between the sisters that hadn't been there before, and it made him happy to see it. They'd need each other to lean on during this time.

The conversation flowed freely with so many people present to contribute and so many of them eager children. Matt enjoyed the chatter but wondered at his ability to miss Hana and Isaac so much while they were still in the room with him.

After dinner, Isaac was eager to go out back and look for turtles in the creek, and Kara was eager that Hana and Matt have time to themselves. "Why don't you two take Isaac outside?" She tried to keep her tone offhanded.

"Are you sure? I can stay and help with cleanup." Hana gave her a pointed look, appearing not to buy Kara's nonchalance for a moment.

"What cleanup? We had pizza on paper plates. I think we can manage." She grinned and shooed them out the door, watching as Isaac ran doggedly to the creek, Hana and Matt taking their time behind him. Her heart ached for her sister. It was odd, really, Hana and Pastor meeting at such a brief, transitional time in Hana's life. It made Kara wonder why. Why now? If it was meant to be, then how? She was lost in contemplation, when her youngest bumped into her on his way out the door. "Hey, slow down there, buckaroo." She grabbed at the back of his shirt, catching him before he made it past her. "Where do you think you're going?"

"Um, *outside*." Charlie looked up at her with a frown, as if to say, "Isn't it rather obvious, Mother?"

"Let's stay inside for now, okay?"

"But why? Isaac's outside, and I want to go play with him."

There was really no way to delicately put Kara's reasons into words. She finally settled on, "Well, honey, I think it'd be nice for Aunt Hana and Isaac to spend a little time with Pastor to say good-bye. He's become their good friend."

"But I'm Isaac's cousin," Charlie pouted.

"And you'll have the rest of tonight and some of tomorrow morning to be with him. I promise."

Somewhat pacified, Charlie scurried off and Kara turned around to find her husband staring at her suspiciously from the kitchen. "Don't think I can't see what you're doing."

"Whatever do you mean, Troy McCauley?"

He just squinted at her and shook his head in mock disgust. "Shameless. You're absolutely shameless."

Kara grabbed at a dishcloth on the table and made menacing strides to her still-smirking husband. "Come here, you, and I'll show you shameless."

"I wish I had been able to say good-bye to some of the people at Hope." Hana avoided looking at Matt, instead using the excuse of her son to keep her eyes averted from the man at her side. They stood, shoulder to shoulder, facing the creek and Isaac's squatted form. "I'll really miss Charlotte . . . and Julie."

"Julie?" Matt turned to her in surprise. "I didn't realize the two of you had become friends."

Hana laughed at his surprise. "Yes, well, it was sort of a last-minute friendship, so to speak. Surprised me as well. You know how some people you don't peg as becoming your friend and others," she turned, finally, to look him in the eye, "like you, you know right away will be a friend." Seeing the look on his face, she turned away again quickly to avoid the rush of feeling. "Julie didn't strike me as a friend at first, but I think God used that to show me that I, just as much as anyone else, can be wrong about first impressions."

"That's an interesting take on it, a good perspective."

"I think my perspective has been challenged in many ways while here. I think I'd let myself forget a lot of things I once knew. It's easy to let life get in the way of remembering, you know?" Hana glanced at Matt. His gaze was directed toward Isaac, studious and pained. The beard was conspicuously full and gray and, in her opinion, looking even better than before. With a sudden stab, she realized she wished she'd told him—she wished she'd told him everything, every last shameful, sad, humiliating detail of her life. She should have just torn down the wall and invited him to confront the giant with her. He would have done it. She knew he would have; he was that kind of man. After he had shared so openly with her the other night, she'd considered it; for a brief moment she'd held the idea of telling him everything in the palm of her hand, weighing and assessing it, finally putting it down, deciding that she had time to tell him later. She didn't want to use his pain, his story, as a launching pad for her own—as if she was one-upping him on the emotional scars they carried. But now it looked as if she wouldn't have time after all. To tell him now would feel rushed and awkward, and then she'd be gone and that'd be how he'd remember her—as the sad and broken woman who'd visited his church for one lonely summer. No, it was too late. And maybe it was better this way, better that he didn't know. She jumped as she realized she'd been staring at him none too subtly and that he'd picked up on it and was politely trying not to show that he'd noticed, his gaze still pointed to Isaac, his mouth twitching. Hana looked away abruptly, embarrassed.

"I thought maybe you'd be missing some of the new friends you made," Matt spoke up, reverting back to their earlier conversation. "So I brought you a church directory, that and a couple other things. If you wouldn't mind waiting, I'll be right back."

She nodded, surprised. He was back in a few minutes with a bag. "Here's the directory." He handed her a small booklet. "Names, addresses, email. That way you can stay in touch, and you can send me your contact info once you're settled in, and I can make that available to people, if you'd like that."

Hana nodded, not trusting her voice, hoping he saw the appreciation in her eyes.

"And then I brought you and Isaac a couple of presents." He must have seen the shock on her face, for he quickly jumped in, "Nothing big, just a little something. I just wanted to, I don't know, just give you something as a parting gift." He pulled out a beautiful, hand-carved wooden cross and held it out to her. "For your new home."

Hana cradled the cross in her hands. It was maybe seven or eight inches in length and very ornate, with intricate spirals spreading out from the center. "It's absolutely gorgeous. Have I—I think I've seen this before?"

"Probably. It's actually from my office. I got it on a mission trip to Ecuador years ago, and it's been hanging in my office ever since."

"Oh Matt, I can't let you give me this, especially since it's something of meaning to you." She held it out to him.

"But that's exactly why I want you to have it." He gently pushed it back toward her. "I can't think of a better home for it than yours. It's been a beautiful reminder of God's grace and love for me, so I hope it can be the same for you."

Hana looked down at the gift, again diverting her gaze to something other than Matt's earnest hazel eyes. A warm sensation spread throughout her body, and not from the waning sun. To know that it'd been in his office for years and now would be in her home—it was like having a piece of him. "Thank you. This is such a generous gift, and I'll cherish it." She made herself look him in the eye.

"You say you've gained a fresh perspective while staying here." She watched Matt stare at the cross as if he hadn't seen it every day for years. "Well, I've gained one, too, since knowing you and Isaac. You say God has reminded you of things you'd forgotten. He's reminded me as well, especially of His love. His grace, mercy, and forgiveness—they all stem from His deep and abiding love for us. Everything begins and ends with His love, which is why it's so important for His children to imitate it." He cleared his throat and pulled something else out of the bag. "I have something for Isaac too."

Hana moved toward her son, using the opportunity to swipe at her eyes. She hadn't expected to cry, and she didn't want to, not in front of him, not knowing he'd be compelled to reach out to comfort her. She didn't think she could handle that level of care without completely losing it.

"Isaac, Pastor has a gift for you." Hana watched her son's face light up with interest.

"What is it?"

Matt had followed her to the edge of the creek and was squatting next to Isaac, holding out a small wrapped package. "It's something for you and for Rocky."

Hana watched Matt watch Isaac open the gift. Her son's eagerness was perfectly mirrored in Matt's face. The wrapping off, Isaac held up two small identical figurines. Each was a beautiful rock with two turtles nestled on top. "You see, one is for you, and one is for Rocky, for the plane ride." Matt pointed to one figurine. "You can put this one in Rocky's cage, and then you can keep this one with you. Your mom told me how you don't like flying. I don't blame you at all. I don't like it either. So I thought this way, you and Rocky could be connected. When you're on the plane, and you're missing Rocky, you can just look at this figurine and know that Rocky is looking at the exact same one."

"Will Rocky know that I have one too?"

"Yes, I'm sure he will know because you can explain it to him, right? When you put this one in his cage, you can show him yours. I'm sure he'll be missing you just as much as you miss him."

"And then, maybe, maybe this will make him not feel lonely?"

"Right, this way he won't feel sad without you."

"I don't like it when he's alone. I don't want him to be alone. I want him to be with me."

"And this will remind Rocky that you are thinking of him, and the two of you will see each other again really soon."

Isaac appeared to be digesting this, finally nodding and putting the figurines on the ground next to him. "Okay."

"Isaac, tell Pastor thank you. This was a very sweet and thoughtful gift."

"Thank you," Isaac mumbled, looking at the creek.

"You're welcome." Matt straightened.

"I'm sorry for the lackluster thank you. He really does appreciate it. The fact that he was asking questions about it shows how interested he is. Seriously, he does appreciate it, and so do I. It's such a thoughtful gift. I wish we'd gotten you something. I wish—"

"It's okay, Hana, it's okay." Matt held up his hand as if to stem her overcompensating thank-yous. "You've been busy. And I'm not offended. I know Isaac appreciates the gift. I really do. And of course you didn't have to get me anything. Your friendship has been all the gift I needed."

Hana let out a long and shaky sigh. "Well, I could say the same for you. Your friendship has done us both so much good. It's been the biggest unexpected gift." She hadn't thought she'd be able to handle a comforting gesture from Matt, but when he reached an arm around her shoulders, she found herself leaning into his side, laying her head on his shoulder, and accepting the embrace with thankfulness. It didn't feel like pity; it didn't feel like weakness—it felt like strength; it felt like wholeness and healing. It was a mutual uplifting of spirits.

Most of the family was in the living room watching a movie, except for her mom, who was in her room packing. Clem made her way to the kitchen for a drink of water. Her mom had always been a compulsively anxious packer. No matter how prepared, she was always trying to be more prepared, to double- and triple-check everything. It was one of the things that drove her kids nuts. There were only so many times you could answer "Did you pack your toothbrush?" before you just snapped. Seriously, given how often they'd moved, you'd think her mom would be used to packing by now. But no, right after dinner, she'd nervously declined the movie, saying, "I'm just going to make sure I have everything I need for tomorrow." Which prompted not a few eye rolls.

They'd picked a guy movie, of course, so Clem was only half watching and didn't mind missing a few minutes of an endless action-fighting scene to grab a glass of water. She was filling her cup at the sink when she caught sight of her aunt Hana with Pastor. The kitchen opened to the dining room, so she had a direct view out the sliding glass door leading to the back. She frowned and moved closer to the door. Pastor had his arm around Aunt Hana, and they were standing side by side, her head on his shoulder. They looked very comfortable together, and it surprised Clem, who hadn't given much thought to Pastor as anything other than the stocky, loud man she listened to once a week. But here he looked like Aunt Hana's husband, the way he was standing there with his arm around her. And there was Isaac, trolling the creek for turtles. Seriously, they looked like a family, which was weird, because Aunt Hana and Isaac hadn't known Pastor that long. Clem was frowning, and her teeth were clenched. It was confusing to see her aunt like this. Was Pastor going to be her new uncle now or something? And what would Uncle Zeke think about that? He had said things were much better now between him and Aunt Hana. Did he know about Pastor? Why would Aunt Hana do this to him? She didn't want a new uncle. She didn't understand what was wrong with Uncle Zeke, why Aunt Hana and her mom were so mad at him all the time and wouldn't talk about him, like he'd never even been a part of the family or something.

Clem set down her glass of water and whipped out her phone. She snapped a picture of her aunt Hana with Pastor and angrily opened Facebook. It wasn't fair to Uncle Zeke. He probably didn't even know about Pastor, and it wasn't fair. Hastily, before she could rethink it, Clem sent the photo to Uncle Zeke in a private message and then stared angrily at the screen, waiting for a reply. Several minutes went by and nothing. Clem sat down hard at the dining room table and glared out the door. Five minutes, ten, and no reply.

Aunt Hana and Pastor looked like they were getting ready to come inside. Quickly Clem jumped to her feet and dashed back through the kitchen and down the hall to her room, slamming the door behind her. Five more minutes and then the ding of an incoming message. Clem looked eagerly at her phone.

"Hey, beautiful! Who is that with your aunt Hana? I'm so confused. Is she seeing someone?"

Just as she thought—he was surprised and hurt, just like she was. He was typing again, and his next words drove straight to her heart.

"Please just tell me what's going on. I miss your aunt Hana and Isaac so much. Please tell me who this man is and what's going on."

So Clem told him.

Hello, Button,

Does God hear us if we're only talking to Him out of desperation? What does it say about me that I'm only turning to Him now, when I feel like I have no other option? I'm sure He doesn't appreciate this. I know I wouldn't. I'd probably tell me to get lost. I'd ask me where I'd been all these years. I certainly wouldn't listen, wouldn't answer, wouldn't help.

But I'm trying anyway. We used to be on a first-name basis, me and God. My parents took me to church every Sunday, and I grew up knowing I could come to God as I'd go to my own father. I think I took this for granted, didn't fully understand the privilege I had. I don't know how we fell out of touch, God and I, but we did. It happened gradually but surely. That's the problem; not talking to God is as much a habit as talking to Him is. And pretty soon you just stop and don't even worry about it. That sounds so bad, and it is so bad.

But here I am, praying again. I literally locked myself in the bathroom last night and ran the water in the tub and sat on the toilet and cried out to Him. I want to believe He is truly like a father—someone who will always love you no matter what and will always welcome you back. I think that's how it's supposed to be, or at least, that's what I remember being told, but at the end of the day, He's GOD. He deserves more from me, and look what I'm giving Him. How can He not just close His ears and heart to me? I'm praying hard for Him to listen and to help. I'm praying hard for the both of us.

XO

Mommy

21

Strange how you don't fully appreciate someone until they're gone. Matt sent out a prayer-chain request for Kara and Hana's father, and instantly the calls and emails came back, asking for updates and more info. Matt wished Hana could see the reactions to her and Isaac's departure. Elizabeth had been among the first to call.

"I thought I had a few more weeks with that sweet boy." Her voice was wobbly over the phone; whether from age or emotion, it was hard to tell. "It pains me I didn't get a chance to say good-bye."

"I was just getting to really know her!" Pam confided in him that Wednesday. "We'd spent some time together at Charlotte's, and I really liked her. You don't meet that many people that you just instantly like, you know? And she was one of them." Yes, Matt knew exactly what she meant.

"She called me the morning she left to let me know." Charlotte had collapsed in his office, close to tears. "She wanted to apologize for cutting our tutoring sessions short. Can you imagine? To be going through what she's going through and to be worried and apologizing to me? She was like that, wasn't she? Always thinking of other people. Oh, I'm going to miss her so much! She was so kind, so sweet." Matt had nodded and agreed and offered tissues.

He'd paid special attention to Julie's reaction after learning that Hana was going to especially miss her. Julie hadn't come up to him as others had, but appeared distant and troubled, and Charlotte had mentioned she'd come across her crying in the bathroom and was convinced it was because of Hana.

It was astounding how many people had formed connections to Hana and Isaac during their short time there. The weeks went by, and Pastor was continually confronted with fresh reminders. During his premarital counseling with Clara and Tim, he'd learned how much Clara was missing Isaac. "He was such a cool kid. He knew everything there was to know about turtles, and he didn't mind telling you exactly what was on his mind. It's just not the same with him gone."

In speaking with Lynn, it sounded as if she'd missed out on a challenge as she claimed, "He was beginning to fit right on in. I made sure all of his teachers were well versed in his likes and dislikes, the particulars of his condition, the need for extra care and attention. I made it my personal mission to make sure everyone was well informed on what he needed, and he did so well at VBS! I think it was good for the other kids, too, you know? Good to have that diversity for them to learn compassion and understanding." Matt couldn't tell if Lynn truly missed Isaac or just missed the idea of him, but either way, the distress was evident in her voice.

Regina had remained oddly aloof on the whole matter. She usually never missed a chance to put in her two cents on anything. But then he'd heard her not so subtle voice informing a group of women that it was a shame Hana had left when she did, as she was in dire need of help. Matt had frowned at that, not quite understanding the intent behind the words. Hana had indeed been someone in need of help, as were they all. And he liked to think she'd found that help, that God had used him and all the people at Hope in some constructive way in her life.

Matt continued his "Practices of Love" sermon series, finding fresh meaning in it after his creek-side conversation with Hana before she left. It was amazing how God took an ancient truth and applied it new and fresh to your heart right when you needed it most. Truly the Word of God is powerful and sharp and alive! The emphasis on love and the need for it at the center of the Christian life became more and more impressed upon Matt's heart. He thought about the times he'd spoken without love as the motivation. Yes, such speech was simply "a noisy gong or a clanging cymbal." Even faith powerful enough to move mountains was considered as nothing without love. Good works done without the motivation of love had no eternal reward or merit. What was faith without love? What was hope without love? And this is why the apostle Paul could confidently say that out of all these, love was the greatest, for love was the precursor, the foundation, to all the rest.

Matt poured himself into the sermon series with renewed vigor in the weeks ahead, even as he continued to receive and process everyone's reactions to Hana and Isaac's sudden departure. It was hard to handle everyone's bereavement when he was battling his own sense of loss. Reminders of Hana and Isaac were everywhere. He had stopped fishing because it reminded him too sharply of his time spent with Isaac. The boy's small, intense face as he kept a lookout for turtles would rise unexpectedly in Matt's mind, and he'd have to stop and work hard to push it back. At church was no better, for people had become accustomed to greeting Isaac and Rocky, along with Pastor, after the service. He took several weeks of repeated tongue-in-cheek remarks about his handshake not being the same without a turtle to look forward to. Some of the smaller children repeatedly asked him where Rocky was. Isaac had been a hit with the younger crowd and had let them pet Rocky and ask him questions. Strange how you didn't fully realize the impact someone had until they were gone.

When he was in the pulpit, he found his eyes straying automatically to the first pew. It wasn't the same without Hana and Isaac there, but especially Hana. He didn't realize how much he'd come to rely on her rapt focus. He'd glanced at her for encouragement and strength a lot, apparently, for now, with her gone, he found himself strangely bereft during the service. She was everywhere at church, in the sanctuary, in the fellowship hall, in his office. He tried to turn each thought of her into a prayer. He wished he could be more like Paul with the Philippians and thank God at every remembrance of Hana, but instead he found himself battling a deep sense of sadness and loss.

He'd heard from Hana shortly after they left. Her father was stabilized and in the hospital for a while longer, but it looked like he would recover. In the meantime, they remained at a cousin's home until moving into their rental in another few weeks. She asked him to share her email address with the church, and he'd given it to the people who'd asked for it. He'd emailed her a few times, knowing she was receiving messages from others as well. She'd sent him a picture of Isaac and Rocky, and he'd printed it and kept it on his desk and smiled every time he saw it.

Significant and insignificant days often dawn the same way. The day Elliott died, Matt had woken from a bizarre dream involving kangaroos chasing him across a college campus. He'd woken up with a start on that chilly morning, and he'd taken a longer shower than usual, reluctant to leave the steamy spray. So he'd been running behind, chugging his usual Mountain Dew as he got dressed. His mother had yelled at him to stop lollygagging and to get his brother ready for the day. He'd entered Elliott's room, shouting for him to get up already, and that's when he'd made the discovery.

And the day had started out with a kangaroo dream and a longer-than-usual hot shower.

The day Jesus became Lord of his life, Matt woke up nervous about a social studies exam. He'd stayed up too late the night before and didn't feel fully prepared, even after hours of study. He'd been so nervous, in fact, that he'd thrown up his breakfast burrito. He'd been going to a Bible study with his friend for a couple of weeks, and that night he went again. The test, he felt, had gone poorly, and he'd confided to the group how stressed he was about school, even though his grades were decent. They'd listened and understood and were supportive.

When he heard the Gospel that night, it was like his heart was open in a way it hadn't been before, like he was hearing it for the first time. It was water to parched ground, and he'd soaked it up.

And the day had started out with pretest jitters and a regurgitated burrito.

Our days are tricky things. They mask themselves, and so one day brings nothing more startling than your favorite show being suddenly canceled, and the next your world is turned upside down.

That morning Matt went through the drive-through at Mc-Donald's and bought himself a coffee, something he normally didn't do, but he was out of coffee at home. He'd picked up a breakfast sandwich while he was at it, instantly regretting it upon consumption, as it stuck in the pit of his stomach like clay. By the time he got to church, he'd developed heartburn from the sandwich, and the coffee only aggravated it. Once in his office, he popped a few antacid tablets from the bottle he kept in his drawer and waited for his symptoms to subside.

The bell signaling a visitor sounded late morning. Their church secretary wasn't in that day, so Matt made the trip out to the narthex. There was a tall man standing outside, pacing back and forth impatiently. Hope wasn't exactly at a major crossroads and usually didn't get many unsolicited visitors. Matt typically didn't even keep the door locked. It wasn't until Will Parker, a retired police officer, came on the board the previous year and insisted they follow more safety procedures that he'd begun locking the door.

"May I help you?" Matt unlocked and opened the door, observing the man closely for signs of danger.

At the sound of his voice, the man turned toward him abruptly. He was very tall, by anyone's standards, and well-muscled. His eyes were a piercing blue. "You're the pastor, right?"

"That's correct. May I help you?" Matt repeated his question. The man didn't look dangerous, just agitated. His eyes roamed over Matt quickly and then jerked away.

"Yeah, if you have a minute. I need some advice. I'm new in the area and don't know many people. I got your information from the phone book."

"Oh, um, sure. Come on in." Matt opened the door wider, letting his visitor enter before him. The man had a plausible story. If Matt was pastoring a church in a more populated area, he imagined he'd have this type of encounter quite frequently. "We can talk in my office, if you like. Right this way." Matt gestured for the man to follow him. There was something slightly familiar about the man, although Matt was certain he'd never seen him before. The visitor's vivid eyes swept the church as if taking everything in at a single glance. His stride was long and powerful, and he was obviously restraining it to match Matt's much shorter one. Matt felt an unreasonable surge of irritation at this realization. The man's hair was sandy and shaggy. For the life of him, Matt couldn't understand why he was familiar.

Matt typically allowed people first entrance into his office, a force of habit, as if he were the doorman bidding them welcome. But this time, Matt unthinkingly entered first, eager to be behind his desk and put some space between him and the unusual visitor. He turned around to find the man looming in the doorway, filling the frame. For the first time, Matt felt a surge of unease. The man's presence suddenly felt imposing. "Please, take a seat." Matt gestured toward a chair, but the man ignored him, choosing instead to take two purposeful steps inside and plant himself squarely in the middle of the office.

"You're Pastor Matthew Schofield." A statement.

"Yes, that's correct."

"I recognize you from the photo." He took another step forward and lifted a large hand to point a finger at Matt's face. "I'm here to tell you to stay away from my wife and kid."

The next few minutes were a blur, and yet in retrospect Matt would remember every moment with precision. First came the jolting realization that this man was familiar because he had Isaac's hair, his chin, his cheekbones—because he was Isaac's *father.* Matt stood there, numb with the knowledge, staring at the man before him with the finger pointed at his face. Somewhere between the front door and the office, the man had transformed from agitated to furious. "Zeke." The name slipped out before he had time to consider his approach. "You're Zeke Howard."

"Yes, and I don't like you getting close to my family. You need to back off."

Matt blinked rapidly, his mind spinning, disoriented. He should have insisted on knowing Hana's background. He had next to nothing to go on here, and he felt the disadvantage keenly. "Does Hana know you're here?"

"That doesn't matter. What matters is that you're in between me and my family."

"Wait, I'm confused here. Please, sit down and let's talk about this."

"I'm not sitting."

"Fine, suit yourself." Matt was half crouching in order to sit but stood again. "Look, I don't know anything about you. All I know is that you're Hana's ex-husband and Isaac's father."

"Yes, I'm his father. Not you, me." Zeke pointed at his chest. The fury in his face was obvious.

"I don't know where you got the impression that I'm in between you and your family . . . " He broke off midsentence as he saw Zeke's gaze shift from him to his desk. His heart dropped as Zeke grabbed the picture of Isaac and Rocky off the desk, staring at it intently before shoving it in Matt's face, waving it like proof.

"Yeah, so tell me again how you're not putting yourself between me and my family." Isaac's face danced in front of

Matt's own, erratically, helplessly. "Tell me again. You have his picture on your desk." Zeke stopped and glared at the picture. "In a *frame*. So yeah, I don't really believe anything coming from you."

Matt paused and tried to slow his breathing before replying. He decided to ignore the picture, choosing instead to focus on the facts. "It's my understanding that you are divorced from Hana, so I'm sorry, but I just don't see how I've come in between anything when you are no longer together."

"Technically, yes, we're not together, but that doesn't give you the right to take them away from me."

Matt felt a flicker of recognition. The man appeared to be delusional. Probably in his mind, he was still married to Hana, still one big happy family. It was hard to speak past someone's delusions. "Forgive me, but I was under the impression that there was a significant life event or reason why Hana left with Isaac."

"What gives you the right to say that?" Zeke yelled, slamming the picture of Isaac hard onto the desk. The glass in the frame shattered and numerous glittering shards skittered across the surface, some falling on the floor at Matt's feet.

Matt took a step back and tried to keep his voice even and calm. "You standing here yelling at me, accusing me in my office, and destroying my property gives me the right." There was blood on his desk. Zeke had sliced his hand on the broken frame, and now there was glass mingled with blood all over his desk.

"It was a misunderstanding, all a misunderstanding, and Hana completely overreacted." Zeke waved a bloody hand in the air, oblivious to his wound and the mess he'd made. "I tried to explain that to her afterward, but she wouldn't listen. Every time I tried to show her she was wrong, that I cared, it was like she used it against me."

"You should know that I have no idea what you're talking about. I don't know the details of what happened between you and Hana."

"I find that hard to believe." Zeke smirked, his face turning ugly. "I bet she just couldn't wait to bad-mouth me. She has her own way of twisting the truth and making you feel like the bad guy. She's so good at playing the poor victim, even when you're trying with all your strength to show her otherwise. It's sickening, really."

Matt felt the first real surge of anger. The disgust and loathing in Zeke's voice was evident. How could he stand there insisting he wanted his family back and in the next breath talk with such hatred in his voice? It made no sense. "Please don't talk about Hana in that way. She deserves to be respected, and I find your tone very disrespectful." It was the first instance of an outright rebuke from Matt, and Zeke responded by swearing at him and knocking over a chair with a long sweep of his arm.

"Who are you to tell me what to say or not to say about my own wife? You Bible-thumping idiots think you know everything, don't you? Don't you?" He drew closer to Matt, kicking at the overturned chair as he came right up to the desk and bent over it. His tone turned soft, secretive, and somehow that was worse, more frightening. "You don't know Hana like I do, so don't act otherwise. You know nothing when it comes to her. I'm sure she painted herself in the best light possible. She's always done that. She can do no wrong, and everyone else can do no right."

Matt's breathing had accelerated upon Zeke's advancement. He was close enough now that Matt could see the veins standing out in his forehead, his neck. Matt tried to keep his voice steady. "There's no need for you to address me like that. I don't think I'm the best person for you to be working out these issues with. I'm asking you to leave. Clearly you need help that I can't give."

"What is *that* supposed to mean?" Zeke's voice rose in pitch as he thumped Matt's desk with a fist for emphasis, further injuring himself as more glass became embedded in his hand. "You think I'm crazy," he hissed in pain.

"Maybe you are, maybe you aren't, but you have to admit that the way you're acting right now isn't very rational or reasonable."

Matt watched as Zeke's face turned red. "Look, I don't have time to waste on you. You think you know me—fine. You preachers think you can psychoanalyze anyone with two legs—whatever. It's pathetic. I don't care about you or this church. I only came here as a pit stop to let you know to back off. Hana has a husband. Isaac has a father. They don't need you. They don't want you. So stop trying to steal my family."

"What do you mean a pit stop?"

"You haven't put in all the years of hard work I have. You haven't had to put up with Hana's hysterical paranoia, her obsession with Isaac, her complete neurosis. You haven't had to deal with Isaac's twenty-four-seven tantrums. You think you can just pop in and take what I've earned, what's *mine*." Zeke's voice broke, and he cradled his injured hand with a miserable expression on his face.

Matt breathed deeply, trying to steady the panic rising in his chest. It wasn't fear for himself but the realization that this man was completely volatile and unstable, that he had implied he was moving on from here to somewhere else. To where? To find Hana? There was now no doubt in his mind that Hana, and possibly Isaac, had experienced some sort of violence from this man, and the thought sickened him. Reason wouldn't work with Zeke. He needed to defuse the situation and find out what Zeke was up to. "You're right." He raised his hands, palms outward. "You're absolutely right. You have years of experience with Hana and Isaac that I just don't have."

Zeke glared at him and shifted from foot to foot as if he didn't know what to do with all the pent-up anger.

A soft answer turns away wrath. Matt could see the truth of this unfolding before him. "I'm sorry if I inadvertently caused you pain. My exposure to Hana and Isaac has, admittedly, been limited, but in that time, they have struck me as wonderful people, people we should all consider ourselves fortunate to know. I acted as a friend and pastor to them while they were here, and for that I won't apologize."

"*Were* here. Are they not here anymore?"

"Hana and Isaac?"

"Of course, Hana and Isaac!"

"Is that why you're here? To find them?"

"It's none of your business. Just answer the question. Are they here or not? Where did they go?"

Zeke was looking for them. Matt felt wave after wave of fear sweep over him. "I don't know where they're currently at." And it was true, at this exact moment, he didn't know where Hana and Isaac were. He wasn't about to give this angry man their contact info.

"I think you're hiding something." Zeke was breathing hard and pacing now. "But they're not here, right, so I guess it doesn't matter. He doesn't matter."

Matt watched Zeke pace and tried to keep his features smooth and calm. The man appeared to be talking to himself, figuring out his next move.

"Kara and Troy, they never liked me, especially Kara. They're not going to tell me a thing."

"Do Kara and Troy know you're here?"

"Shut up. I'm not talking to you."

"Then perhaps you should leave," Matt suggested quietly.

"You'd like that, wouldn't you?" Again, that sneer. It was uncanny the way his face could shift from one emotion to another like he was changing shirts. Matt imagined Hana and Isaac in the presence of this man, and the image made him sick and filled him with dread. "Whatever. I said what I came to say." Zeke stopped pacing and faced him again. "Stay away from my family. I don't care if they're not here anymore. You're not to see them or contact them. They're not your pet project or flock to heal or whatever goes through you pastors' twisted minds. Whatever you thought you were doing with them, stop. It's over."

"I think you should go now." Matt watched the perfectly chiseled, dynamic, and powerful man sputter in front of him. The anger for this man would come later, but for now Matt could only feel a numbing fear for the people he'd come to love.

"I'm done here." Zeke turned abruptly, kicking viciously at the overturned chair again and cursing under his breath before striding to the door. He exited and slammed the door shut behind him with so much force that it knocked a picture off the wall.

Matt stood stunned and silent in his wake. He heard the distant sound of the front door closing. Numbly he left his office and made his way to the front just in time to see Zeke's car peeling out of the parking lot. Matt made sure the door was locked and then went back to his office, mechanically. He shut the door, picked up the fallen picture and overturned, abused chair and sat down woodenly behind his desk. Zeke had taken Isaac's picture with him, and all that was left was broken glass and smears of blood. A horrible trade-off. Matt felt as if Zeke had physically assaulted and dragged the boy from the room.

He needed to call the McCauleys. Would Zeke go there? Was the family in danger from him? He hadn't appeared to be carrying a weapon, but maybe he was. Maybe it was in his car. It hadn't sounded like he was going to bother with the McCauleys, especially since Hana and Isaac were no longer there. Would he find them? Would he hurt them?

He was calling Ted Brannon before he realized what he was doing. As the Chief of Police and longtime member of Hope picked up, Matt found he could hardly speak. Was this his reaction to emergencies? No fight or flight, just frozen shock? A lot of help he was. Matt finally found his tongue and described the incident, the man himself, and the vehicle he'd seen leaving the lot. He only wished he'd gotten the license plate number. Ted assured him a vehicle would be dispatched to the McCauley residence.

Matt got off the phone and, with a cry, slid off his office chair and onto the floor, narrowly missing the shards of glass in the carpet. His heart heavy with fear and grief, he prostrated himself and placed his hands on the back of his head. "Abba! Father!" He cried into the carpet. *"Elohim shomri!* Protect them!"

He stayed on the floor, crying out to the Lord until there was no voice left in him. He needed to think clearly and act. That much was apparent. The hateful picture Zeke had painted of this beautiful family, mother and son, was nothing like the one he knew. By condemning them, Zeke had only condemned himself. That they were in danger from this man was abundantly clear to Matt. And something else was clear as well. He needed to be with them. He needed to know what had happened and to warn them. But the action started here on the floor at the feet of a merciful God.

And to think, the day had started with McDonald's coffee and heartburn.

Hello, Button,

I've gotten back into the habit of prayer, and it fills me with so much peace. I found my old Bible and started reading it at night in your room when you're asleep. It's like this beautiful secret that is all my own. It makes me feel understood and not so alone.

But then I got careless and left my Bible out, and your daddy found it. He came charging into the kitchen, waving it at me, asking me what it was. I was snarky with my reply, which I know aggravated him. I shouldn't have done it, but I just snapped, "What does it look like? An aquarium? It's a Bible." I guess I was asking for what happened next. He just curled my Bible up in his hands and said some nasty things. He accused me of trying to be better than him, of trying to turn you against him. He said I had a "holier-than-thou" attitude that was like poison to the family. I tried to reason with him, tried to remind him of how we used to go to church together, how he used to care about the Book he was mauling in his hands. He said he'd never cared, that he'd only pretended because it'd been so important to me.

And in that moment, I wondered if Kara had been right all along, and it just broke my heart. I think my heart has been breaking off in slow, painful bits for a while now, but this completely shattered it. I just started crying and couldn't stop, and he accused me of being melodramatic and turning this against him. I begged him to give me my Bible back, but he wouldn't, and he left, and I haven't seen it since. I've been scared to get a new one. So now I don't even have this bit of comfort anymore.

But I did find a chunky board book Bible buried in the bottom of your toy chest, so now I read that with you at night before bed. I hope and pray that your daddy doesn't find out. We read one of the short stories together, and then you go to sleep and I keep staring at it—pictures of a cartoon Jesus. And I don't feel peace anymore. I feel empty.

XO

Mommy

22

The call came at lunch, the voice on the other end barely hanging on to the edge of calm. "Kara, Pastor here. Is everyone okay over there?"

"Yes, why? Why wouldn't we be? Pastor, is everything okay?" Kara took the handset into the living room. She'd been back for around a week, leaving Hana and Isaac with their cousin and their father, still in the hospital but stable. Hana and Isaac were in their new home now, their father was still doing well, and she'd finally felt a level of peace and calm return. But now her pulse skyrocketed at the unmistakable alarm in Pastor's voice.

"Oh, thank the Lord. Zeke was here, Kara. He was here just a moment ago."

"What?"

"He was here, and he was angry, and he accused me of stealing his family."

"What on earth? How did he . . . but he doesn't know where we live or that Hana or Isaac were . . . how . . . " Kara felt the panic lurch in her chest. It didn't seem possible.

"I don't know what has been communicated to him, but he very clearly knew that Hana and Isaac had been here staying with you, and he knew that they had befriended me and had become a part of the church family. He saw our friendship as a threat to him."

"Oh Pastor, I'm so sorry. Was he violent?"

"Not really. Just gave me a good tongue-lashing, but it's your family and Hana and Isaac I'm worried about. I called Ted, and he's dispatching a car to your place."

At his words, Kara jumped into action. She charged to the front door, opened it, scanned the front yard, then closed and locked the door. "Zeke's not here, hasn't been here, I don't think." The police car wasn't there either; she prayed it arrived soon. What if Zeke *had* been there though? Observing them before going to the church? Kara's breath came faster as she sprinted to the back door and locked it, then to the basement to check the door there. "I'm locking the doors, just in case."

"I'm so sorry, Kara. I feel like this is somehow my fault."

"How could it be your fault? I just don't understand how he knew where to find us and that Hana and Isaac were here. But what really confuses me is how he knew about you at all, enough to come to you and confront you. It's baffling. I should be the one apologizing to you."

"Not at all. I'm not worried about me." There was a strained pause. "Someone needs to tell Hana."

"Yes, yes, absolutely. She needs to know. I don't see how he could know where she is now, but if he found out where she was once, he could do it again. I'll call—"

"I'm in the process of booking a last-minute flight to Richmond International Airport. I'm going out there. Can you give me their new address? Hana only gave me her email."

"What? Why? Are you sure?"

There was another strained pause. "Kara, I have to. I have to see them and know they're okay."

The tone of his voice told her everything she needed to know. He loved Hana and Isaac. It was as if someone had come in and threatened his family. He needed to go be with them, just as Troy would need to be with her if someone was threatening her and the kids. "Okay," she said gently. "Okay, hold on." She dashed to the kitchen and rummaged around in the messy notebook she kept on the counter, finally locating the scrap of paper with Hana's new address and reading it off to Pastor. "You'll be careful, right? Make sure he's not monitoring you or something. The last thing we want is for you to lead him straight to her."

"Yes, yes, of course."

"Pastor, I feel like we owe you an explanation. You've been dragged into family drama, and I'm so sorry for that. Did Hana tell you about Zeke?"

"No, not much." Pastor sighed heavily over the line. "I won't lie; I was curious. I wondered, but I didn't want to pry." He seemed to anticipate what she was going to say next, for he jumped in quickly, "And you don't owe me anything. Everything I need to know I'll hear from Hana directly. It's enough for me to know that she might be in danger from this man."

"Okay, if you're sure." Kara felt relief at the thought that her sister would soon be reunited with Pastor, that he'd be there, and she wouldn't be alone.

After getting off the phone, Kara went back and double-checked all the doors, then the windows, just in case. "What are you doing, Mom?" Charlie came wandering into the room, a quizzical expression on his face. He'd recently started calling her "Mom" instead of "Mommy," a sign of him growing up, trying to be older, trying to shed what he saw as the telling habits of youth. The use of the new name sent Kara over the edge. She stifled a sob and swiped at her eyes before turning around. "Nothing, baby, just making sure all the windows are closed. We, ah, might get rain later today."

"Huh, okay." Pacified, Charlie left the room.

Kara went back to the living room and picked up the phone to call Troy, realizing at the last minute that he was flying that afternoon and would be unreachable. Instead she sat and gnawed at her lip, finally reaching out and grabbing her laptop, a horrible suspicion arising in her mind. She opened her passwords document and located the social media passwords for Alex and Clem. Alex only had a Facebook account, so she started with him, logging on and searching through his posts, his messages. He was rarely on there, apparently, for posts were few and far between and all harmless. Next, she moved to Clem, who had numerous accounts. She opened Instagram, knowing it was Clem's favorite. She saw some pictures of Isaac, but nothing that indicated Zeke had been monitoring her. Was Zeke on Instagram? Did he even know what it was? She moved to Facebook next. Why couldn't Clem be more like Alex, thoughtful and responsible with social media usage? Instead, Clem appeared to live on Facebook. Kara felt the familiar mother guilt raise its ugly head. When she was Clem's age, she was interested only in hanging out at the mall with her friends, buying makeup, and going to the movies. Now, there was this whole online community that allowed teen girls to portray whatever persona they wanted, to be whoever they wanted. She knew Clem was on her phone a lot, but this was just over the top. Kara made a mental note to speak with Troy about some serious media limitation. Her gaze caught on a photo of Clem and Sam with Luke Schroeder in the background, and she frowned as she saw the comments. Was she into boys at Clem's age? Surely not. Surely that had come later. It appeared that Clem had posted her Instagram photos to Facebook. There were the ones of Isaac, and one of both Isaac and Hana, but again, no comments or indication that Zeke had seen them. And then Kara opened Clem's messages, and her eyes grew round, her heart stopping in her throat and then thudding painfully hard as she read message after message. She was finding it difficult to breathe, to move. And the mother guilt was no longer a small and pesky murmur but a wildly roaring monster that would not be tamed.

Kara had debriefed Troy as soon as he'd walked through the door, the presence of a squad car outside their home raising plenty of questions. Troy's horror and guilt mirrored her own, and now here they were, standing together, a united front outside their preteen daughter's bedroom door. Charlie was in bed, and Alex was in his room, and now was the moment for a dreaded sit-down talk with their daughter. They looked at each other, as if to draw strength and comfort before entering battle, their eyes belying their fear and dread. Kara took a deep breath and knocked on the door before cracking it open. Clem was propped up in bed, her eyes wide with surprise, her hands shoved beneath the covers.

"Can we talk to you, sweetie? Your dad and I?"

"Uh, sure." Clem sat up fully as they entered, meeting Kara's eyes suspiciously.

"And we know you're hiding your phone under there, so no need to pretend," Troy added.

Clem rolled her eyes and drew her phone out, tossing it on the bedspread. "What did you want to talk about? I'm sorry about the phone, okay? I know you want me to turn it off at night."

"That's not really why we're here. Although, that is something we need to discuss." Kara sat on the bed next to her daughter and looked up at her husband, who stood, arms crossed, by the bed. "And soon, but we're here about something else."

"Clem, honey, your mom found something on your Facebook account that was concerning."

Kara shot her husband a look that said, "That's *not* how we were going to start," but the damage had been done.

"Hey, wait, you were on my account? That's not cool."

"Now, Clem, you know the deal we had. You can have these accounts as long as we also have access to them. We agreed."

"Yeah, but you should at least *tell* me if you're going to be hacking my account."

"No one hacked . . . " Kara started and then stopped, shooting her husband a withering look for landing them so instantly in the hot seat. "Clementine, that's not the point. You're missing the point. Let's skip over the fact that I was on there. We can come back to that later. And let's focus instead on what I found on there."

"You've been talking to Zeke, Hana's former husband, haven't you?" Troy jumped in again. Kara knew he was managing his guilt and worry by masking it in a severe authoritarian voice.

"Or rather, *he's* been talking to *you,* hasn't he, sweetie?" Kara followed quickly. "I saw the messages he sent you, and how you told him things about Hana and Isaac." She swallowed past the lump in her throat. "And what you said about Pastor."

She'd never seen the particular emotion that she saw now on her daughter's face—a mixture of fear, worry, distrust, and confusion. It broke her heart to see it. "Yeah, so? He's my uncle. What does it matter?" Her tone was guarded, defensive.

"He *used* to be your uncle," Troy clarified. "You needed to come straight to us when he contacted you, straight to us, Clementine."

At her father's tone, Clem's angry guard crumbled, and Kara saw the little girl in her again, longing for her daddy's approval.

"I-I don't understand the big deal. I mean, Isaac's his kid, right?" Her tone had slipped into a whine that Kara knew was concealing tears. She saw all at once and with clarity the line that her daughter walked—a girl trying to be a woman too soon. Kara was the mother, and she should be the one to help usher her daughter over that line. If she didn't, her little girl would stumble over it, pushed headlong by the world. She placed one hand on her daughter's bent knee and covered her own face with the other. "Mom?" Clem asked hesitantly, obviously not expecting her reaction.

Kara had avoided telling her children what happened with Zeke because she'd convinced herself that they were too young, didn't need to know, a decision she now realized was a mistake. Troy had apparently softened at the sight of Clem's confusion, and was now crouching by the bed. "We're not mad, honey. You didn't understand, and that's why we're here now."

Kara looked up and wiped her eyes. "I know you have a few good memories of your uncle Zeke. I can see how confusing it'd be to have him contact you. I should have been more honest with you." She swallowed hard and looked at Troy for support.

"Sometimes people can get really angry, Clem, so angry that they stop acting like themselves," Troy said softly. "You know how Charlie gets when he's having a tantrum?"

Clem had calmed down and was listening closely. "Yeah, he gets crazy."

"Some people don't know how to handle that feeling," Kara said. "They bottle it up sometimes and it just builds, or sometimes they just let it all out and it explodes. Does that make sense?"

"I guess." Clem shrugged. "I feel like that sometimes."

"Yes, sometimes," Troy said. "But some people feel like that all of the time, and when they feel like that, they don't act very nice."

"Like Charlie having a tantrum?" Clem asked.

"In a way, yes," Kara stroked her daughter's red hair, sad that she had to have this conversation, sad that the world and the people in it were so broken. She tried to be fair with her next words, tried not to let the old prejudices and the anger tint her words. "Uncle Zeke could be nice sometimes, but he was also very angry a lot of the time. We don't want him knowing where Aunt Hana and Isaac are because he hurt them, sweetie. He was very mean to them and hurt them, and they aren't safe with him anymore." Kara made herself continue, made herself say what she should have said sooner, every last detail, and she watched as her daughter's face broke open, and her own heart along with it.

One of the first things Hana had done was to hang the cross Matt had given her right inside the front door. That way, every time she and Isaac entered their new home, they'd be reminded—both of him and of the God who loved them, who had always loved them, even in their darkest moments.

Hana had been sad to see Kara go back home. Their time together had been intense and sweet as they'd grieved together, prayed together, and then rejoiced together when their father had pulled through. He'd taken one look at them and said, "Why the long faces, Flossie and Freddie?" His pet names for them, based on his love of the Bobbsey Twins, a love his daughters hadn't inherited but put up with benevolently, the names which now brought great bursts of joy springing to the sisters' faces.

He'd doted on Isaac, delighting in his grandson's interests, claiming he got his love of nature from him. Hana felt a rush of healing fill her as she observed her father watching Isaac with loving eyes. They'd made the right move, coming here to be close to him. Especially after the close call, the sisters both realized how short time could be, and whereas Kara hadn't come right out and said it, Hana knew she was relieved that she'd be close to their father.

Hana had seen another side to her sister over the last few weeks that'd given her a fresh perspective. Over the years, Kara had taken on a perfect glow in Hana's mind. With each thing that fell apart in Hana's life, she'd pinpointed something shiny and perfect in Kara's, until Hana had built up a wall so tall, she'd been unable to truly see her sister. But while living with her and now facing their father's illness together, Hana had realized that her sister could be vulnerable and fearful too, and her worries manifested themselves with certain compulsive habits. She'd checked their luggage sixteen times before they'd left. She'd been jumpier than Isaac on the plane, and she'd insisted on cleaning their cousin's house as a show of appreciation for them staying there—even going so far as to wipe down the windows and vacuum beneath furniture. Her sister, it seemed, was a real person after all.

The night before Kara had left, Hana had confessed to her. "I feel like I owe you an apology. I haven't been a great sister.

I chose to see you a certain way, and I told myself you had no problems because they weren't the problems I had, so I resented you. I felt like you always had your act together, and it made me feel so small. I'm sorry I let that get in the way of our relationship. I'm sorry I stopped seeing you, *really* seeing you. I'm sorry!"

And Kara had laughed. "Oh Hana, for years I was hard on myself because I felt like I *couldn't* keep my act together. You had your hands full with Isaac, and you were such a good mom to him, and then Zeke—you didn't have the support I had, and I spent a lot of time beating myself up for not being a better wife and mother when I saw you giving all you had day in and day out. On top of that, I gave you an endlessly hard time about Zeke—I always did, and I'm sorry."

"But I closed my ears to anything you had to say, even if it was the truth."

"But I didn't really speak truth in love. I just wanted to be right."

And so it had continued, with each sister one-upping the other in how low they could make themselves until they were finally forced to declare a draw. And now Kara was gone, and it was just Hana and Isaac in their new home.

Isaac missed having a creek right out back but was happy when Hana found a nearby park with a pond where they could go turtle watching. The rental house was small but met their needs and was located in a quiet older subdivision. Hana foresaw peaceful evenings spent exploring their neighborhood and taking trips to the park. She looked forward to helping Isaac decorate his room and spruce up Rocky's large aquarium. And then there'd be evenings spent with her father. She'd be able to do that more now that they were so close.

School loomed around the corner, but Hana found that she wasn't even anxious about it. She and Isaac—they'd been on quite the roller coaster, and they'd get through this too. She'd settle down to her new classes and workload, and Isaac would settle into his new school, and it would be okay.

When Hana focused on the future, she felt satisfied if not completely happy. She'd left happy back at Hope. The messages came flooding in, and she felt her throat tighten up with each one. Elizabeth sent Isaac a funny e-card with a turtle on the front. Charlotte had sent a warm email with messages from each child in the family. And Julie had surprised her with a phone call, saying sometimes she traveled for work and had been sent to Richmond in the past, and maybe she'd be able to stop by for a visit if that happened in the future.

Isaac usually didn't ask after people, but it didn't surprise Hana in the least when, a few days into their stay, he looked up suddenly as if he'd misplaced his keys and said in a confused voice, "Where's Pastor?"

"He lives in Oklahoma, remember?"

"Oh," Isaac's face fell, even though Hana had already had this conversation with him multiple times. "But he would like the pond where we go."

"Yes, he definitely would. Pastor really enjoyed being outside, just like you, and he liked being by the water, just like you."

"Maybe he will come here, and we can show him."

Hana swallowed with difficulty. She didn't want to get his hopes up, but she couldn't bring herself to verbalize the truth—that visits were unlikely, that time with their new friend was over. "Maybe."

"Or we can go there and go to the pond again, the one with all the turtles."

He was referring to the Madisons' pond. They had yet to see any turtles at the new pond, so it was not up to the standards of the Madison pond, not yet. "Maybe," Hana replied weakly.

She missed the people of Hope, and especially Matt, with a ferocity that surprised her. It'd been years since she'd been able to easily connect with people, so the fact that she had, in so short a time, connected with so many at Hope surprised her. But nothing had surprised her as much as Matt. He'd been a friend when they'd needed one most. He'd shown them God's love when she'd been in doubt, and as a result she knew herself to be stronger now than she'd been before. The shiny new Bible she'd bought at the Altus Wal-Mart was quickly on its way to becoming thoroughly thumbed and marked. Matt had directed her to the church website, where he posted all his sermons, and she'd listened every Sunday as he'd continued in his "Practices of Love" series. Isaac listened too, the sound of Pastor's voice drawing him into the room, and then he'd ask, "I want to see Pastor. Where is he?" And it tore at Hana's heart.

She knew she'd need to find a church in their new community, but the thought filled her with dread because it wouldn't be the same, couldn't be the same. There could only be one Matthew Schofield.

It was a Tuesday morning, the Tuesday before school started, and Isaac was begging Hana to let him play outside. The house had come with a rope swing hung from the large maple out front, and Isaac dearly loved to swing. "Okay, but you need to stay in the front yard, okay? No straying anywhere else." Hana walked out to the front porch with him. "Remember the border? No farther than that tree over there and the mailbox over there, got it?"

"Yes, yes," Isaac breathed out, eager to be done with the lecture.

"Okay, I'll be right inside if you need anything." Hana went into the kitchen and opened the window facing the front yard so that she could monitor him.

A half hour went past, and Hana had finished doing the dishes and made her way to the living room, when a shout outside startled her. It sounded like Isaac. The shout came again. She couldn't tell if it was a happy or a scared shout, and her heart clenched in her chest as she rushed to the nearest window. There was a man out front, and he had his arms around Isaac. Hana let out a yelp and dashed to the door. It wasn't— It couldn't be— Hana whipped the front door open to see Isaac struggling out of the embrace. She was so panicked her vision was blurring. She blinked rapidly, trying to see her son clearly. "Isaac!" Hana's voice was sharp and shrill as she dashed into the yard. She expected her son to collapse in tears, to scream and cover his head, sights she had never wanted to see again. But instead he turned an excited face to her, finally free, running to her with a burst of energy.

"It's Pastor!"

"What?" Hana stopped abruptly, all the adrenaline seeping out of her body at once, leaving her weak. The man was standing and turning toward her. He was stocky and broad shouldered and had a full gray beard. He turned the most beautiful hazel eyes she'd ever seen in her direction, seeming to pierce her with one look. She sat clumsily on the front step, numb and still blinking furiously. She couldn't be seeing this correctly. "What?" She repeated, even though she was now staring the man in the face.

He was by her side quickly, taking her hand and helping her to stand, folding her in his arms. She fit perfectly against him, her head at just the right height. She began to shake uncontrollably. He was shushing her and squeezing her hard. With a rush, the adrenaline came back and fueled anger. He'd given her such a fright! What was he doing sneaking into town like this? She pushed against his chest, elated and angry all at once, wanting to hug and hit him at the same time. She pushed him back, ready to unleash her tongue, but stopped when she saw his face. He was crying and smiling, and when he spoke, his voice was uneven, and his words chilled her. "You're all right. God be praised, you're all right."

Hello, Button,

I see things so clearly now. I've been walking around in a fog, unfocused and confused. But no longer.

Yesterday, all the loose pieces were shaken together, and I don't know how I ever doubted what I need to do. I'm just ashamed that it's taken me this long to realize it, that it's taken THIS to make it happen.

I don't know where God was in all of this. I don't know how we got to this point. I don't know a lot of things.

But this one thing I know.

I will never, ever, ever let anyone hurt you.

Never again.

XO

Mommy

23

Isaac was babbling nonstop with joy. "I told you Pastor would come! There's a pond we found. It's not as good as the other one, but you'll like it. We should go now and see it." Isaac was pushing his way between her and Matt, eagerly straining forward to get Matt's attention.

"We can take Pastor to see the pond later," Hana said gently. They were inside by now. "Why don't you see if Pastor wants anything to drink."

"Okay." Isaac waited.

"You ask him yourself, Isaac."

"Okay, do you want anything to drink?"

"I'm fine, but thank you for asking, Isaac."

They were acting casually, as if Matt flying halfway across the country and just showing up on their doorstep unannounced was a completely normal thing. "Isaac, Pastor and I need to talk. You can have some extra TV time just this once while I talk to Pastor, okay?"

"Okay!" Isaac dashed out of the room as if eager to take Hana up on her promise before she changed her mind.

"I'll be right back." Hana followed her son into the living room and put on a show for him before returning to the kitchen. Matt was standing looking out the open window. He turned when he heard her approach.

"I know this is bizarre, and I'm sorry for surprising you. I got your address from Kara. I hope you don't mind."

Hana poured herself a glass of water. She needed something to occupy her hands, anything, and something to occupy her mouth, for she didn't know what to say. She gulped convulsively at her water as she waited for Matt to explain himself.

"It's just that I received an unexpected visit yesterday that prompted this trip." He approached her and touched her elbow gently. "Maybe you should sit down."

Hana frowned but took a seat at the kitchen table. She watched, concerned, as Matt paced before her, as he ran a large hand through his hair and made soft, indecisive sounds. Finally, he sat at the table with her and looked her intently in the face. "Zeke came to see me at my office yesterday."

One sentence and it stole all the breath out of her body. Matt was continuing to speak, but she was having trouble focusing. "I heard from Kara that he had been contacting Clem on Facebook and found out that way that you'd been staying with them. That, and our, uh, relationship, which he clearly perceived as a threat."

Hana took in a shuddering gulp of air. "Did he hurt you?"

"No, no, not at all," Matt reached across the table and put a steadying hand on her arm. "He warned me to stay away from you. Apparently Clem sent Zeke pictures of us in their backyard, and I guess from that he got it into his head that I'm his rival. After meeting him, I doubt he needed much encouragement to see me that way. He's under some sort of impression—"

"That he and I are still a family. Yes, I know." Hana let out her breath, her hands shaking.

"What really scared me, though, was that he clearly wanted to find you and Isaac. He thought you were still with Kara, and he wanted to know where you'd gone."

"Did he bother Kara? The kids?"

"No, please don't worry about that. Kara hasn't seen or heard from him, and the police are watching their house, just to be safe. Kara assures me that Clem didn't communicate the location of your new home, so that's a relief."

Hana bowed her head until her forehead nearly touched the table. First Vicky and now Kara and her family—how many more people would have to worry about Zeke because of her? And Matt—she wanted to know the details of how Zeke had conducted himself toward Matt, and at the same time she absolutely didn't want to know. It would only make her even more sick to her stomach. People she loved were being put in a position of fear and anxiety . . . because of her. "Matt, I'm so sorry you got pulled into the middle of all this. I'm so sorry."

"Don't apologize. You didn't do anything wrong."

"You came all this way to tell me?"

"I wanted to warn you and to make sure . . . I needed to know you were both okay."

Something in his tone caused Hana to glance up sharply. He sounded broken, deeply distressed. She could see the concern etched on his face, and it sent a warm jolt through her. He still had a hand on her arm, and she placed her own over his, giving it a squeeze. "We're okay, truly. And I imagine, I hope and pray, we remain that way."

It was Matt's turn to look at the table in anguished silence. Finally, he returned his gaze to hers. "Hana, what happened with you and Zeke? I want to respect your privacy, but this man has involved me in something I know nothing about, and I—I feel like I need to know."

Hana sighed deeply. She knew he was right and that it was time. "Yes, you do. I agree, and actually, I've been wanting to tell you for a while. It's just, the timing was never quite right. How do you share something so big?" Matt just squeezed her arm. Hana took a steadying drink of water and breathed a prayer for the right words. There was a reason she'd built a wall around this part of herself. It was to keep the giant of her past contained, manageable. The wall gave her a sense of stability and possibility. If she could keep the ugliness separate, maybe she could have a future after all. To talk openly about the past was to demolish the wall and expose the giant it contained; it was a place of vulnerability she wasn't sure she was ready to visit. But sitting here, looking across the table at Matt, she knew she needed to try.

"When I met Zeke in college, he was a charming and passionate guy." Facts, she'd start with facts, simple and true. As if she was talking about the weather. "He had a very loud and vibrant personality, the kind that dominated a room and demanded to be noticed. He was in marketing with a minor in theater." She let out an abrupt laugh.

"What? What's funny?" Matt looked confused.

"Oh, I just realized something. Toward the end, Zeke constantly accused me of being melodramatic, but *he's* the one who studied theater." She chuckled again, her practiced stoicism momentarily compromised by misplaced humor. "Sorry, that's beside the point." She coughed and collected herself. The weight of the moment was making her giddy. She schooled herself back to emotionless.

"Kara never liked him, but I chalked that up to her being jealous. She'd had bad luck with guys, and I just dismissed her dislike as jealousy. Anyway, I was much quieter than Zeke and was surprised when he, who could have his pick of girls, picked me. I let it go completely to my head. And I won't lie and say we didn't have our good times because we did. Zeke was always outgoing, always funny, and I was always grateful to be the recipient of his attention. We struggled to have kids; that was the first test of our marriage, but the biggest test was when we finally did have a child, Isaac." Hana paused to self-congratulate herself. She was doing pretty well so far. Her voice was even; her mind blank. Keep this up, and she might be able to get through this conversation in one piece after all.

"Isaac was diagnosed with autism when he was around two. I think back to that time often because that seemed to be the turning point. Zeke was used to being the center of attention, and suddenly he wasn't. Isaac and his needs became an all-consuming part of our relationship. And I think—people just react differently to disappointment, to grief, you know? I coped by pouring myself into it—into the diagnosis, I mean—as a way to understand and handle it. But Zeke, he sort of—hardened. He drew into himself, which wasn't typical for him, and he wouldn't talk much to me, didn't seem to want to treat Isaac any differently because of the diagnosis. It was like he saw the diagnosis as something optional. Like because he didn't want to deal with it, he wouldn't or didn't have to. Our marriage became very different, lonelier, as we worked through things in our different ways." Hana stopped to take a drink of water. She could sense the giant stirring behind the wall, shaking off sleep in a preparatory gesture that made her uneasy.

"You have to understand that this explanation is coming years after the fact. In the moment, I was hurt and confused and felt like Zeke didn't want to be Isaac's father anymore. It's hard to see things clearly or understand them in the middle of something. Our marriage just continued to fall apart, and Zeke became distant and agitated and then abruptly smothering and controlling. It was confusing and terrifying for us."

"Like he was flipping switches on and off in himself."

"Yes, exactly. It became impossible to know what he was thinking or what he would do."

"I noticed that in our brief meeting."

"We'd become so isolated and alone that we'd stopped seeing our friends, doing things together. Stopped going to church. I later found out that Zeke had only ever gone to pacify me. Our marriage was slowly being torn apart piece by piece. I felt separated from God, from my family, from myself even. I've thought back and searched for signs for what happened at the end. And there were warning signs, but I just didn't see them as such. I was too confused and alone."

"And you feel guilty about that now."

"Yes," Hana squeezed his hand, which was still on her arm. "You know how that feels, the guilt. Anyway, Zeke became very unpredictable, especially with Isaac. I should have listened to my instinct but didn't. Kara would tell you that I was used to making excuses for him at that point, that he was emotionally abusive, which was part of the reason why I didn't see things clearly. And maybe that's true. I don't know, and I don't know if that matters now. But I reached a breaking point when he turned violent, when . . . " Hana breathed deeply, willing her hands and voice not to shake. She hadn't gone through the particulars of this since court. Matt was steadying her with his eyes, giving her the time she needed to collect herself, but she couldn't seem to draw comfort from him. He was too separate from the tension she was experiencing. The shifting giant was awake now, the wall shuddering in anticipation of being breached, and it was becoming nearly impossible to keep her emotions in check.

"It was just a normal day," she choked out. "Zeke had started coming home at random times and without notifying us, and he was home early that day. I needed to make a grocery run." Anger wiggled through and made a lunge at the wall, battering against it, weakening it, causing Hana to spit out the next words. "I should have taken Isaac with me. I should have— But he was having a bad day, and I didn't want to deal with him at the store. Zeke told me to go, that he'd stay home with Isaac. It made me uneasy, but I agreed. Why did I agree? I left Isaac with him. I normally didn't leave Isaac alone with him. I mean, sometimes Zeke just took him places without telling me, but I usually never knowingly left Isaac alone with him. That should have been a sign—that I didn't feel comfortable leaving our son alone with him—right?"

"Stop blaming yourself," Matt said reassuringly. "That will lead nowhere, trust me."

Matt's words sounded distant, as ineffectual as a bird battering against a window. They couldn't reach her anymore. Hana tried shoving Anger down, tried to keep it from destroying the wall. The giant was pacing now, hungry for freedom.

"Against my better judgment, I left Isaac with him and went to the store. When I came back home, I heard horrible screaming coming from the living room." Hana closed her eyes. Panic had joined Anger, and now the two of them were systematically attacking the wall with joint effort. She could feel it, despite her best efforts, that first gut-wrenching twist of panic when she'd heard the sound of her son in pain. And then on its heels—Disbelief. It joined the other two, Anger and Panic, but instead of actively helping with the destruction, it stood by in agonized silence, observing and fueling the efforts by its supportive presence.

"I can't even describe it, how it sounded, how I felt." She wasn't breathing. The effort from trying to restrain Anger and Panic was paralyzing. "I ran inside to find Zeke . . . he was hitting Isaac, hard, and shaking him so violently, I thought he'd snap his neck." Fear, a close cousin of Panic, joined in the demolition efforts. The wall was crumbling, and there was nothing she could do. The giant was visible from behind the wall now, and she had no choice but to face him head on.

"Isaac was making noises I'd never heard before, like the screams were literally being shaken from him." Gone was her control. Her voice shook with all the emotions she'd tried to keep at bay. As if from a great distance, Hana heard Matt suck in his breath. Was his hand still on her arm? She supposed it was, although she couldn't feel it any longer. She was with the giant, and he was filling her sight, her senses.

"Zeke was swearing at him, screaming for him to 'Knock it off.' I just stood there in shock. I couldn't believe what I was seeing. You don't ever expect—someone you used to trust, love—you don't . . . " Hana was staring into Matt's face without seeing him, but at the sound of choking her gaze refocused, and she saw how her words were destroying him. He appeared to be physically choking down sobs. She would have comforted him had she had the emotional energy. As it was, she watched him struggle as she continued talking, her voice wobbling with the effort.

"I'd noticed bruises on Isaac before that day, but I had thought they'd been self-inflicted. Back then, Isaac's chest pounding and hair pulling were worse, and it wasn't uncommon for him to hit himself so hard I was surprised he didn't leave bruises. So when I did see bruises, that's where my mind went, not to . . . " Hana swallowed hard. The wall was down completely, and the giant stood mocking her with his enormity. *And you thought you could keep me contained,* his grin said. *I will never go away. I cannot be contained. I am who you are. Now and always.* Anger, Panic, Fear, Disbelief—they stood on the rubble, flag planted in ownership, claiming the territory as theirs. She bowed her head in acceptance. "I should have known. I should have pieced it together sooner." Guilt, the clincher, now entered, larger than all the rest, and took hold of the planted flag.

"No, please don't make this your fault, Hana," Pastor said, his voice shaking.

Now that the wall was down, the giant exposed, the emotions victorious, Hana realized she was numb. It was easier, after all, to stop fighting it, to accept it and with it the numbness. "When it finally registered what I was seeing, I screamed at Zeke to stop. I tried to pull him off Isaac, and he just turned on me." Now that the wall was down, Hana shifted her gaze outward and watched the emotions pass over Matt's face. What she would say next would devastate him further. She didn't want him to view her as broken. Didn't want to be cast as a sad person, but he deserved to know—everything. And she *was* broken, so why pretend otherwise?

"He turned on me and grabbed me by the throat and slammed me against the wall before I knew what was happening." She was right. She watched the devastation break over Matt's face. She closed her eyes to keep from seeing it, but as a result, the terror of the past filled her completely. The feel of Zeke's hands squeezing her, hands that had once touched her tenderly, now clutching in hate and anger. The strength behind those fingers, the inflexibility, the shooting pain of it, and underneath it all the sheer shock.

"You saw Zeke. He's so tall and I'm, well, really short." She laughed, a humorless, barking laugh that instantly died. "It was a running joke that someone so tall and someone so short would end up together. He used to call me his precious midget. We'd make jokes about it. Kara thought it was derogatory, hated it. I used to love that nickname though. I thought it was cute." There were two faces in her mind—the open, laughing, glorious face of her husband and the closed, twisted, angry face of the man he'd become. She ached at the sight of those faces side by side.

"So when he grabbed me and held me against the wall, I just dangled there. I could see Isaac on the couch. He was throwing himself around, like he was still in pain, and he was screaming so loudly I thought surely the neighbors would hear him, would call the police. Then I couldn't see him anymore. I was blacking out, and the only thing I could think of was that I would be leaving him—again. I couldn't leave Isaac again. I couldn't leave him with this man." Hana slumped in her chair and stared out the kitchen window before closing her eyes and facing the giant. *Is this what you wanted?* she confronted him. *It wasn't enough to destroy me once? You want to do it again? And again? Well, here I am.* She paused, and in the silence she could hear Matt breathing hard, a pained, panting noise. "I could see the surprise in Zeke's face," she continued. "I don't think he meant to do what he did; I know he didn't mean to, but then he didn't stop. He just held me there until I eventually blacked out."

"Oh, Hana," Matt mumbled. The choking sounds were back, and then they loosened and he was weeping, and even this couldn't fully reach through the numbness, which was slowly spreading throughout her body.

"When I came to, Zeke was gone, but he hadn't taken Isaac. That's what I noticed first—that Isaac was still with me. I was just so thankful—that Isaac was still there. But he was in really bad shape. He'd pulled big chunks of hair out, scratched himself; he was bleeding everywhere." She turned suddenly to Matt and focused on his eyes. They were red rimmed and sad. "I didn't know Zeke was capable of that. I didn't know."

"You don't have to convince me," Matt said gently. "Trust me, I know how much you love Isaac. You are a good mother."

His voice broke, and his eyes jerked away from hers. "What did you do afterward?"

"I got us out of there as quickly as possible. I filed for divorce." It was over; the worst of it was over. Matt knew about her now. The wall was down, and the giant that was her past was out. Could she construct the wall again? Maybe with more time.

"I tried to rebuild a life for Isaac, but Zeke wouldn't leave us alone. I got a job, put Isaac in school, got an apartment, tried to establish something, just Isaac and me, but I couldn't do it—not in the same city as Zeke." Now that Matt knew the worst, knew just how broken she was, Hana found that she was physically exhausted. Without realizing it, she'd slipped her arm out from under his hand. She sat slumped in her chair, cup of water forgotten, hands limp in her lap.

"He was everywhere. I told him to stay away. He didn't have custody of Isaac. He was supposed to leave us alone, but he'd wait on our front step for us to get home and confront us in the middle of the apartment complex in front of the neighbors. He was so apologetic. He didn't mean to hurt us. He loved us. But when I resisted him and wouldn't let him see Isaac, he turned nasty again and would start yelling at me and cussing me out." The giant was prodding at her, trying to get a rise, but she just looked at him wearily, as if to say, *You've done your worst. I have nothing left in me.*

"And then one day he waited outside Isaac's school and convinced Isaac to get in his car. When I couldn't find Isaac, I contacted the police, and they issued an Amber Alert. I didn't know where he was for a full day. It was hell, worse than when I walked in on Zeke hurting him. I didn't know if Isaac was alive or dead. I didn't know . . . " Panic, Fear, Anger, Disbelief, and Guilt took hold of their flag and prodded her, succeeding where the giant had failed. She found she could still feel something, even in her numb state. She felt the tears on her cheeks before realizing that she was crying.

"You're afraid of it happening again. You're afraid Zeke will take him again."

"Yes," she gasped. "It's my worst nightmare."

Matt scooted his chair closer to hers and put a steady hand on her back.

"I took out a restraining order and left soon after that. A friend helped me get the job here in Richmond, and Kara let me stay with her over the summer. And I guess you know the rest."

She watched as Matt slumped forward in his seat, his hand still on her back, the other covering his eyes. "Hana, I'm so sorry."

What must he think of her, now that he'd seen who she really was? "Does this change anything? How you see me, us?"

"What on earth do you mean?"

"I feel . . . shame when I think of what Zeke did, what I *let* happen. How weak I was, am."

"Weak?" Matt let out a laugh. "Hana, believe me, I do *not* think you're weak." Hana watched as his eyes shifted away from her abruptly. Seeing his averted expression, how deeply he cared, she felt a small flicker fighting to chase away the numbness. "You are probably the strongest woman I've ever met."

This was something Hana hadn't anticipated. She looked away too, embarrassed, and shook her head. "I don't feel strong. Most days I feel like I'm barely getting by."

"Well, you haven't been given much of a choice, have you?" Hana looked sharply at him. "I mean, you had no choice but to be strong—for Isaac. You have to be strong for him."

"Yes," Hana said softly. She hadn't thought of it quite that way before. She struggled with the giant, so he wouldn't have to.

"Doesn't give you much freedom to process or fall apart if need be, does it?"

"No," she whispered. "It doesn't." Again, that flicker confronting the numbness.

"I call that incredibly strong and brave—managing as best you can the responsibility God has given you in the worst possible circumstances."

Oh, how she wanted to believe him. She tucked his words far away from the giant's reach and promised herself to revisit them—soon, when she could think more clearly.

"Hana, thank you." Matt's hand was still on her back. With the other, he reached for her hand and held it firmly in his own. "You once thanked me for sharing my heart with you, and now I want to thank you for sharing something so personal and painful. You shouldn't feel alone with this."

Hana studied his eyes and knew he was sincere. She found herself staring into their depths, wanting to draw strength from them but feeling a slight pull of resistance. "Why are you here?" The question slipped out with no thought or planning. It hung between them, their expressions both surprised as they faced it.

"What do you mean?" Matt answered softly.

"I-I know you wanted to warn me, to tell me of what happened. But why not just call? Why come all this way?"

Matt slid his hand off her back and cleared his throat. He dropped her hand and thrummed the table with his fingertips, eventually standing as if the agitation in his body was too much to be contained in a sitting position. She watched him pace her small kitchen, the sound of Isaac's television show filtering into the room, making an odd cartoon backdrop to Matt's jerky movements. "Why are you here, Matt?" She repeated softly. She needed to hear him say it.

"Because—" He started and stopped abruptly, finally turning to face her. "Because I realized something when Zeke confronted me. He accused me of stealing his family. He told me to stay away from you. He basically told me to take a hike and find my own family. I had a picture of Isaac—that picture you sent me? I printed it and framed it." He laughed abruptly. "I put it on my desk. He took it, took the picture. On the flight over, I realized how it must have looked to him—me with Isaac's picture on my desk, Clem sending him a picture of us together, you and me. I realized how it must have looked, and then I realized maybe he wasn't completely wrong."

"What are you saying? What do you mean?" But even as

Hana asked, she knew.

"I'm saying that Zeke had it somewhat right—I think of you and Isaac . . . the two of you . . . " His expression jumped between her and the living room, where the faint sounds of cartoons could still be heard. Finally, he turned to her with pleading eyes. "You both—you're my family."

"Oh, Matt . . . " Hana closed her eyes. He'd said it, and now she wished he hadn't because she didn't know how to feel, how to respond. On the one hand, she was thrilled that such a caring man felt so deeply for her and Isaac. It was a beautiful, strange twist of events that she could never have anticipated. But on the other hand, it was a bit too much, too soon. She was just learning what it meant to be a family, she and Isaac. She didn't think she could add another person to that equation just yet.

"It took a crazy man yelling it at me to realize it," Matt laughed. "But it's true." The humor left his voice, and his tone turned tender. "When he came in the room so angry and so obviously unstable, I can't even begin to tell you the fear that just filled me. At the thought of him finding you two, the thought of what must have happened to you. My imagination just went wild, and I couldn't rest, couldn't breathe, until, until . . . "

"Until you knew we were safe."

"Yes."

"And a phone call wouldn't do because—"

"Because what's your reaction when the people you love are threatened, in danger?"

The word *love* stuck out like a blaring sign, but Hana skipped over it for the moment. She knew the answer all too well. "You need to be with them."

"You need to be with them, to see them, to know for a fact that they're safe, to be a part of that safety, to *know* that your family . . . " He broke off, his voice wavering, finally managing to whisper, "To know that your family is *safe*." He turned from her, whether out of embarrassment or just too much emotion she wasn't sure.

Hana looked at his averted profile and tried to feel—something. It was such poor timing. She was emotionally spent, still achingly numb from the wall being torn down, from the giant still lumbering around in her, bumping against the walls, knocking things over, grinning at her with that winking certainty. She was too empty and too full to respond.

Theoretically, she knew she should be happy, overjoyed even. Here was this honorable, loving man, whom Isaac clearly adored, and who, if she were being completely honest, had occupied her mind almost constantly since she'd known him—this wonderful man declaring his feelings, and all she could do was sit and stare at his averted face and open and close her mouth and will the right words to come, the right emotions to surface.

"I shouldn't have said anything," Matt turned even farther away from her. "You've shared something big with me, and what do I do? I burden you with this." He sighed, and she watched his shoulders slump. "I'm sorry, Hana. I should have called. I shouldn't have surprised you like this, just jumped right in uninvited. You've been so open and kind with me, and I shouldn't have—"

"You were just being open and kind in return." Hana finally found her voice. She saw him visibly pause in his self-tirade, and it surprised her to see how much her words affected him. She felt the power keenly and shook with it. "I started this conversation by asking you a question, and you were being open and honest with me, and I appreciate that; I do."

He finally turned to her, his eyes hesitant. "I haven't overstepped? I don't know . . . spooked you maybe?"

"No." She smiled at his word choice. "You can't scare me away that easily." But he could. He kind of had. And she felt her smile wilt with the realization.

He smiled too, his eyes turning hopeful, and again Hana felt the power she held over him in this conversation. He was waiting for her to say more, to respond to the content of what he'd just said, and he deserved a thoughtful response, something that Hana felt incapable of at that moment. She made herself look him in the eye. His words were a bright and beautiful flicker, but it wasn't enough to really break through the numbness she felt. "Matt, I can't even begin to tell you how immensely thankful I am for you. From the beginning, you have been a friend and advocate for Isaac, when he needed a male role model the most, I might add." She couldn't feel the emotion behind what she was saying, but she knew the truth of the words. She prayed that God would help her communicate truth even if she couldn't feel it in the moment. "And I would be lying if I said I haven't thought of you as more than a pastor, more than a friend." Again, that beautiful blossoming in his face; it was achingly sweet, but she knew it wouldn't last, couldn't last, because she couldn't fully give him what he'd just given her. "You're dear to us, you are." There it was, written on his face—he finally sensed the "but," his features freezing, the budding hope abruptly aborted. "It's just, Isaac needs stability right now. And my dad. We're about to start school, Isaac is settling in, and I have a new job, and we need to be—"

"You need to focus on healing, focus on you and Isaac and establishing your home, your routine, being with your dad."

She sighed shakily. "Yes."

He was nodding slowly, sadly. "The timing isn't ideal." He shot her a look, further realization dawning on his face by degrees. "And perhaps the feelings aren't quite mutual."

"I wouldn't say that." Hana jumped in quickly but stopped just as abruptly, as she recalled the feeling he'd displayed in his voice, the certainty with which he'd called them his family. The man had boarded a plane with no hesitation, taking off at a moment's notice to be with them. It was a level of love and commitment that she felt unworthy of and that she was surprised he felt. She didn't know how to let him in as fully as he'd seemed to let her and Isaac in. Was he her family? Would she drop everything, no questions asked, and go to him?

He seemed to find his answer in her silence. She watched as he turned away from her again. She swallowed painfully past a lump in her throat and gave him a moment before rising to stand hesitantly behind him. She stared at his back, aching to put her arms around him. But that wouldn't be fair. Instead she placed a soft hand between his shoulder blades. "Thank you for coming. Thank you for checking on us, for caring so much for us."

He turned to her, his face quiet, and she sensed that whatever emotions he was struggling with had been buried deep. "I'm just glad you're okay." He reached a hand to her and she gave him hers willingly. "And you'll stay that way, right? You'll be okay?"

"I'm sure we will be. He might think to come back here, seeing as it's my hometown, but I haven't been back here in years, so it's not an obvious place for him to check."

"Even though your dad is here?"

"There's always that possibility, but he can't come near us without endangering himself. The moment he violates that restraining order, he's in deep trouble."

"He didn't seem to care about that."

"Matt, I think you're just going to have to leave us in God's hands." Hana gave him a lopsided smile, her heart aching. If he truly thought of them as family, this was going to be a hard challenge for him to meet. She could see the tension playing across his face, the desire to keep them safe, the knowledge that their lives, however intersected, had indeed separated, and finally the understanding that he couldn't force them together, no matter how much he wanted it.

"Yes, yes, you're right." He looked down at their clasped hands. "Please stay in touch, won't you?"

"Yes, of course," Hana answered softly.

"Isaac won't be too upset, will he, that I'm not staying? Not seeing his new pond?"

"You're welcome to stay," Hana said quickly, already missing him, the anticipation of him not being there hurting and breaking through the numbness with sharp clarity.

"Thanks, but I really should get back."

"Of course." Hana nodded. She was being selfish now,

expecting him to stay and what? Visit with them after she'd so obviously not given him the desired response? "I'd better go get Isaac then. He'd stay in front of the television all day if I let him."

"As would most kids, I'm sure." He smiled, but there was so much pain in the smile that Hana had to look away. "I'll come with you."

Together they entered the living room, where Isaac was slouched on the couch. "Isaac, Pastor is leaving, so let's turn this off and say good-bye." Hana expected a fight, but Isaac let her turn the television off without complaint.

"But you haven't seen our new pond."

"I'm sorry, young man. I wish I could have seen it, but I need to get back home."

"But Rocky hasn't seen you yet!" Isaac wailed.

"I do want to see Rocky." Matt looked at her, asking for approval. She nodded, a lump in her throat, and followed them down the short hallway to Isaac's room.

Now that they were in a permanent home, they'd gotten out Rocky's huge aquarium, the one with all the works. Hana stood in the doorway and watched with a sad smile as Isaac excitedly pointed out all the features. "He likes to spend time on this rock here, and he eats his meals over here. At night, this light comes on. It makes him feel safe. He spends a lot of time in the water, usually half in and half out." On and on the stream of description went.

Matt crouched in front of the aquarium and made all the right sounds of approval. "Hi there, Rocky, my old pal." The figurine he'd given to Isaac and Rocky was standing in the center of the aquarium. Hana saw the moment he noticed it, for his face lit up.

"He keeps the other one by his bed," she managed to say, gesturing to the nightstand. In fact, having the figurine by his bed had helped lessen the need for Isaac to have Rocky sleep right next to him. Instead, most nights she peeked in to see both turtle and boy fast asleep next to their respective figurines. She wanted to tell Matt, wanted to share how even this small gift had been profound, but she couldn't form the words and instead watched Matt swipe at his eyes before turning again to Rocky.

"Did you know that everyone misses you at church, Rocky?"

"Really?" Isaac squeaked out.

"Oh, yes, Rocky made quite the impression while he was there. People don't want to shake my hand anymore. They just ask me where Rocky is."

Hana had never seen such a clear expression of pride on Isaac's face. He nodded slowly, as if what Pastor had said made perfect sense. "Yes, Rocky is an exceptional turtle."

Matt turned to her in an unguarded moment of levity and mouthed "exceptional?" with such a wide grin that it hurt to see it. Hana laughed out loud and then perversely began to cry, ducking her head in time so Matt didn't see it. He'd turned back to Isaac and was telling him of all the kids who had asked after Rocky.

Hana stepped into the hall and took a deep breath. What was wrong with her? She wanted to run back in and beg Matt to stay with them or conversely to promise that she and Isaac would come back with him, that somehow it would work out, that he was their family too, but it was too much, too soon, and she knew she couldn't uproot Isaac again. She knew, too, that she had an obligation to Isaac that outweighed all else. If Zeke had recently been in Altus, then she shouldn't be there. She needed to stay where she was, needed to give Isaac safety and stability.

"Everything okay out here?" Matt and Isaac were leaving the room.

"Yes." Hana smiled shakily. The time had come for them to say good-bye—again. They moved to the living room, and Hana watched as Matt noticed the cross he'd given her. Pain and longing flitted across his face and were quickly extinguished. Hana felt the tears threaten again.

"Let's go to the pond now," Isaac said loudly, and, as if expecting resistance, quickly countered with, "If not today, then we can go tomorrow."

"Isaac, we told you, Pastor is leaving now. He won't be here tomorrow."

"But I want him to see the pond."

"I know, honey, but . . . "

"I'm not honey!"

"Isaac, listen." Matt was crouching in front of him. "I really want to see the pond, but I don't have time. How about you take a picture of it and send it to me? And then I'll go to the Madison pond, and I'll take pictures of any turtles I see there and send them to you, okay?"

That piqued Isaac's interest. "Okay, but make sure you take pictures of every turtle you see."

"Yes, I will."

"And maybe . . . maybe even if there aren't any turtles that you can see. Maybe still take a picture and send it to me."

"Are you sure?"

"Yes, because maybe, maybe there will be turtles, and you just won't be able to see them. I'm very good at seeing turtles," Isaac said seriously.

"You are a very good turtle spotter, indeed," Matt answered. "And it wouldn't surprise me if you could find a turtle that I missed, so I'll send you a picture of the pond each time I'm out there, okay? And if you see a turtle I missed, then you let me know, okay? I could take lessons from you; you're so observant."

"Yes, I am," Isaac agreed. "It's okay, if you can't see them like I can. I'll help you find them."

"Thank you, Isaac. I appreciate it. Can I—?" Matt stopped abruptly. The even, serious tone he'd been using while conversing about turtles evaporated. "I know you don't like to be hugged, but could I—could I hug you good-bye, Isaac? Please?"

Isaac frowned, as if wondering why Pastor would choose to ruin a perfectly good turtle moment. "No, I don't like hugs."

"Yes, yes, okay." Hana watched as Matt battled with his emotions. She didn't want him to leave and simultaneously wanted him to go as quickly as possible, so she could properly fall apart. "That's okay," he was saying. "I understand. How about a good-bye handshake, then? Like we used to do at church?"

"Okay." Isaac submitted to his hand being shaken but squirmed it out of Matt's hand when he held on too long and instead thrust his hand deep into Pastor's beard.

Hana sensed Matt's emotional control slipping as he let out a shaky laugh. "Good-bye, Isaac. I'll miss you. I'll be thinking of and praying for you, that you do well in school and that you find lots of new turtles in your new pond."

"Yes, and I'll send you their pictures!"

Matt stood, freeing his beard from Isaac's hand, and ruffled Isaac's hair, causing him to yelp and duck. "Hey, don't do that!"

Hana knew Matt was struggling with the desire to show more affection than Isaac would allow. She knew the feeling all too well. He was turning to her now. "I'm sorry for springing this visit on you."

"Please stop apologizing. You're always welcome in our home, and I'll make sure Isaac's pictures get to you and yours to him."

"Thanks, and—don't be a stranger yourself, okay?" He was refusing to look her in the eye, choosing instead to focus on the cross behind her head. "Let me know how you're both doing. How you're adjusting."

"Yes, we'll stay in touch," Hana whispered past the lump in her throat.

He seemed to be restraining himself from hugging her, as he'd been forced to do with Isaac. She was just about to initiate the hug when he opened the door. "Good-bye, you two. Stay safe, stay well, and God bless you both." And then he was gone, and Hana had never known such emptiness.

Isaac was watching him leave from the big picture window in the living room. He was narrating Matt's actions. "He's getting in the car. He drives a blue car. He's backing out of the driveway. He's waving to me."

And then the last description, which sent a shot of pain through Hana and gave her permission to finally weep and wrestle unhindered with doubt and indecision:

"He's gone."

Hello, Button,

We are building a new life, you and me, and it's going to be beautiful and safe; I promise you. We're leaving the only home you've known, and I've been preparing you by telling you that we're going on an adventure. I said it's like your favorite show, Franklin the Turtle, *in your favorite episode, Franklin the Fearless, when he goes down Thrill Hill. Sometimes you have to do things that are scary, and that's okay. Sometimes new things, seemingly scary things, turn out to be fun and a great adventure! So we're going on an adventure together, like Franklin.*

We're going to go see your cousins and aunt and uncle in Oklahoma and from there to a new home near Papa. We don't know what these new places will bring or who we will meet. It's as scary as Thrill Hill, but we are fearless, you and me!

And who knows? Maybe we will make some fantastic friends. And maybe we will have a marvelous time. Maybe this will be the best adventure ever.

XO

Mommy

24

The first time he visited the pond without Isaac, he wept; he dropped his tackle box and rod and placed a hand over his eyes and wept. He kept seeing Hana's face when he'd told her they were his family—that frozen, suspended expression of an animal in a trap. How foolish he had been, how self-absorbed. If he could take it back, he would, but the words were out there, suspended between them, and her emails reflected that fact. She was polite and friendly, but now there was also caution, as if she'd trigger another impromptu plane flight should she say the wrong thing.

There'd been an email already waiting for him when he got home, a picture of Isaac's new pond with Isaac standing proudly beside it. He'd resisted the urge to print and frame it, to replace the one that had been stolen. "They are not your family," he told himself. The sooner he could accept that, the better off he'd be, and keeping framed pictures about wouldn't help anything.

There weren't any turtles out that day, but he took pictures of the pond anyway as promised. He made himself walk the length of the pond, taking pictures all along the way, weeping silently.

Hello, Button,

Well, we are here, and you are enjoying your cousins very much. I was worried you wouldn't transition, but I think you're having an easier time of it than I am! You've made a new friend, and what an unusual friend he is! You share a common interest of the outdoors, and he is perfectly happy to "talk turtle" with you. He lets you pet his beard and seems to enjoy hanging out with Rocky just as much as you do. I've just been scratching my head about it, but it goes to show that you never know where you'll find good friends. Sometimes they come in unusual, unexpected packages, and I think we just need to embrace them when we find them.

I've seen you broken, sweetie, and the image still haunts me. I know it always will. But now I feel like I get to see you put back together, piece by piece, and that is a beautiful thing!

XO

Mommy

It wasn't long before Hana and Isaac adopted a new routine that involved school, therapy, dinner, and walks in the park and visits with Papa. Isaac was in a bigger school with more resources and, as a result, received more one-on-one care, thriving because of it. Without Zeke constantly in their periphery, Hana could relax. The anxiety that had been plaguing her throughout the past year slowly subsided as things became less unknown and more settled and as Zeke became more and more a figure in the past. Isaac seemed to sense this new freedom, and as a result, his panic subsided. Hana wondered if living with Zeke as he had become more and more agitated and unpredictable had exacerbated Isaac's problems, for now, out from under that shadow, some of his symptoms eased. The hair pulling, the panic attacks, and chest pounding dwindled until they were the exception rather than the norm.

Having Isaac doing so well helped with Hana's well-being, which, in turn, fed back into Isaac's progress, creating a positive cycle that kept Hana up some nights, praying and weeping with gratitude. She was doing more of that now, calling out to God. She was able to freely pull out her Bible and read it and pause long enough to listen and receive without fear.

She'd continued listening to Matt's sermons for a while, Isaac joining her, continuing to be drawn by the sound of Pastor's voice. They sent emails to him weekly, exchanging pond and turtle pictures. At first, Matt had included a message for her first before moving on to one for Isaac, but gradually the messages to her became shorter and shorter until they were merely cursory in nature, a brief and friendly "hello" before moving on to the business of comparing ponds with Isaac. Hana tried not to read into it, tried not to let it hurt her, and then one day she opened an email and read "Hello, Isaac!" with no mention of her and no personal greeting. She'd cried that day, and called out to God to tell her why she cared so much and to ask Him to take the pain away.

So they stopped listening to Matt's messages because Hana couldn't bear to hear the sound of his voice. They found a church and began attending, but Hana's heart wasn't into it. Isaac asked about Pastor relentlessly after each service. "Why isn't Pastor here? Pastor would let me have Rocky. Why can't I bring Rocky here?" As painful as the questions were, it was nothing compared to the pain of when they stopped. One morning they came home from church and had made it halfway through the afternoon before Hana realized that Isaac hadn't mentioned Pastor once. She'd gone into her bedroom and cried, wondering at her capacity to hurt over this man.

Her days felt hollow, as if something essential had been sucked from them, and Hana was left searching for the marrow.

Almost a year went by, and the McCauleys were moved to a base in California. The West Coast—Hana knew how much her sister would love this move but ached when she realized she was nearly an entire country apart from her sister now. The distance had always been silencing before, but they'd been doing well with maintaining contact since Hana's stay with them. Their move meant Kara no longer had any information to siphon to Hana. When Matt had stopped sending her personal messages, Hana had resorted to asking Kara about him when her curiosity finally bested her. He was always "doing just fine" and "oh, you know, doing okay, I think."

"No!" Hana wanted to yell. "No, I want to know the details of his life. I need to know how he *is*." And she would gnaw, gnaw, gnaw in search of the marrow.

She'd asked Julie during a recent phone conversation if Pastor was happy. "Happy? I don't think he's unhappy. Seems about the same, really. Just kind of busy." Julie had surprised her with a phone call soon after their move, and a tradition had been formed. Every month they called and caught up with each other. Julie had recently been transferred to San Antonio, where she'd begun online dating. "I would have tried this long ago," she'd confided to Hana, "but my mom always says online dating is only for desperate and pathetic people, so I was just afraid of what she'd say if she found out I was doing it." But now she was seeing Brent, a "huge hunk of a cowboy who loves Jesus," to use Julie's words, and she couldn't be happier. "Yeah, I've honestly lost touch with Hope a bit and with Pastor. But he seemed fine to me last time I was there."

It wasn't enough, and Hana ground her teeth with the frustration of it. Charlotte wasn't much help either. "He's good, Hana. You know, teaching, preaching, writing, I think. Was published recently in some journal. I think he gave a guest lecture at a college too. His alma mater, I think."

It was more than she'd gotten from Kara and Julie combined, but it still wasn't enough. And so she would continue to gnaw, never satisfied.

Charlotte's emails were always the highlight of Hana's day when they arrived. "Hi, friend!" the typical, cheerful opening. Sam was showing in a regional competition with Sublime. The boys were learning woodworking with their father. And Ruthie? Well, Ruthie was loving on Natalie and Tiffany, one-year-old twins whom the Madisons had begun fostering. "She calls them her 'babies,'" Charlotte wrote, the joy emanating from her email. "She won't let them out of her sight and delights in helping me feed them, dress them, play with them. I've never seen her so happy." And Charlotte, Hana could tell, had never been so happy herself. "In answer to your question, Pastor seems to be doing well. He's started teaching a class at the local college on top of all his duties here, so I think he's keeping pretty busy," the message ended.

Hana sat staring at it, chewing her lower lip. Pastor indeed sounded busy but obviously wasn't too busy for Isaac, as the emails still arrived weekly. Even if he hadn't made it out to the Madisons' pond that week, he still emailed Isaac with an update on anything interesting he'd seen outdoors. "I was driving down the highway the other day and saw a dog on the side of the road that'd been injured by a porcupine. I called animal control and stayed near the dog until they came. Have you ever seen porcupine quills, Isaac? Man, oh man, you don't want to get messed up with those! The dog, by the way, was okay. He's going to be just fine."

Isaac had spent two weeks afterward reading up on porcupines and amazing Hana with facts. "Did you know? Did you know?" He'd run breathlessly into the room.

"Do I know what?" Hana would reply, laughing.

"Did you know that porcupines stamp their feet and rattle their quills to warn predators? And they even growl and hiss.

But they don't shoot out quills, despite popular belief."

"Despite popular belief, eh?" Hana laughed. Isaac had begun reading more broadly and quickly, consuming books at a surprising rate and often spouting off their exact language to Hana.

"Yes, so I bet the dog that Pastor saw was a predator, and the porcupine was just protecting itself."

"Yes, that does make sense." Hana tried to remain grateful that her son was enjoying an ongoing friendship with Matt, but she couldn't help but feel saddened and yes, even re-sentful. He'd said they were his family, right? Isaac *and* her? Then why was he not continuing a friendship with her? Why write her out and focus only on Isaac? She'd kept writing to him, and in depth too, even as his correspondence to her dwindled, but the day he left her out of his email was the day she'd stopped too. If he was only going to use her to correspond with Isaac, then she'd do the same. She'd send him Isaac's pictures and brief messages and no more. It was a fitful, petty reaction, and she'd spent many a day going back and forth on it. *Just write to him, Hana*, she'd counsel herself. *Just do it. Just ask him how he is.* But the longer the silence went on between them, the harder it was to break it.

Hello, Button,

I'm finally beginning to understand that sometimes bad things happen so good things can follow. I used to won-der how God could love us and let us hurt at the same time, but then I was reminded recently that because this world is broken, pain is inevitable and sometimes God allows it as a necessary part of His larger plan. In VBS I was reminded that God allowed His Son to go through great pain and darkness, so our lives might be filled with light. I'd never thought of it that way! I think I can understand just a little how God felt watching His Son suffer. It's something no parent should ever, ever have to experience. But to think that He did this willingly? So that I might know Him? I can barely imagine such love.

And I'm beginning to understand, too, what it means to be the recipient of that love. I mean, if I loved someone enough to let my son die for them, there's no way I'm ever going to stop loving that person! The price was too costly, that person too valuable to just throw them away. I can't stop being the recipient of His love—ever! No matter what I go through or what I do or have done, I am forever loved because something extremely valuable was given for me.

Something bad had to happen for something good to follow, and just because something bad happens to me doesn't mean I'm not extremely and forever loved.

XO

Mommy

"I haven't seen him since he parked outside our house." Vicky's voice was hushed. "Sorry, Brian is napping. Just got back from a business trip and he's jet-lagged. Let me take this outside." Hana waited while her cousin moved locations. "Okay, that's better. So I've been trying to keep tabs on him for you, but he hasn't been coming around here at all, which, you know, is good."

Hana had reached out to Vicky shortly after learning Zeke had gone in search of them. Through Vicky, she'd learned that Zeke had returned home and was at work again, and Vicky had promised to let her know should she learn of anything suspicious.

"He was gossiping about you to Carl," Vicky had said one time, referencing Zeke's brother. "Said some pretty nasty things about you and some pastor? Of course, it made its way to us because Carl knows Judy, and she does my hair. Honestly, though, I think Zeke isn't trying hard to hide anything. He can be pretty vocal, you know?"

Oh yes, she knew.

"As far as I can tell, he hasn't tried to find you all again. I did hear from Judy that he was asking after you during the Memorial Day picnic, probably testing the waters to see if you'd been in contact with any of his family. I'm like, why would you be in contact with any of *his* family? Anyway, it didn't sound serious to me, just sniffing around, you know? Certainly nothing like what he pulled in Oklahoma."

The reports became less and less frequent with less and less to tell. He'd posted a nasty comment on social media, had reached out to Vicky via phone but only once and then stopped. "I told him, 'Dude,' I said, 'Dude, you gotta stop this. I *will* turn you into the authorities.' I mean, I don't know if I technically could since he wasn't doing anything really, but still, I just said it really convincingly, you know? Like forcefully, and he must have bought it 'cause he didn't call again."

With each phone call from Vicky, the tension in Hana lessened. The picture was of a disgruntled man who wanted to air his grievances with anyone who would listen. And then the latest phone call: "Girl, I have something juicy. Apparently he's been seeing a co-worker for, like, four years! Like, romantically, if you know what I mean. Can you imagine? Well, I should say she's not really a co-worker. I guess she's the gal they get to come in and do maintenance on their printers. Don't guys normally do that job? Weird. Anyway, it's been going on for, like, four years. I'm guessing you didn't know?"

No, she hadn't, but the more she thought about it, the more it made sense. The sporadic nights when Zeke would be gone for long periods of time, sometimes overnight. Hana felt sick to her stomach and breathed a prayer of thankfulness to be out from under that roof, away from that time of fear, loneliness, and confusion.

"And my first thought is, like, how on earth is this woman still *with* him after he goes around blabbering about you and Isaac and searching for you and never leaving you alone after the divorce and all that. I mean seriously, come on!"

"Zeke can be very secretive when it suits him," Hana said quietly. Even now, years later, this new revelation could cause pain, knowing his betrayal ran even deeper than originally thought.

"I guess so, but the real news is that he's left with her—moved away. She got some money, I think, from a dead grandparent, and they're moving to Florida, of all places. Isn't that where people go to retire? Is Zeke even a beach guy? I didn't think he was. He doesn't seem like a beach guy."

So he was gone. He'd moved to Florida with his longtime girlfriend. Hana didn't know whether to rejoice or to be sick.

"Listen, I'm sorry if this is upsetting. I probably shouldn't have said it with such, uh, relish, you know? It's just, girl, I really think he's done messing with you guys. Like, he's moved on, literally, and good riddance is what I say."

Hana got off the phone and peeked in on Isaac. He was in his room, curled up on his bed with a bag of crackers for him and some lettuce for Rocky, which he was systematically shredding and feeding to him, his eyes glued to his latest nature book. *Thank You that we're safe. Thank You that Isaac is happy.* Hana's smile wobbled as she looked at her son. *And please let this newest hurt pass over me quickly because I don't have energy to live in past pain. I have too much to be thankful for.* She watched Isaac for a while longer. She knew he was happy, but was she?

Hello, Button,

You keep asking after him, your new friend—
Pastor. He came to visit us, you know, and he told
us that we are his family. I'm beginning to realize
that he may have been picking up on something
that I just missed. I think both you and he knew
it—we're a family—but silly me didn't know it
yet. You've never missed your daddy the way you
miss Pastor. It's like he's unlocked the part of you
that your daddy couldn't reach, and I'm seeing
new things in you because of it. Like how you
look forward to Pastor's emails and how you're
so alert for anything interesting to share with
him. It's been nearly two years, and even though
you stopped asking me for him, you still email
him every week, and he emails you, and I know
how much it means to you. I think he's part of
the reason you've begun reading so much. With
each new thing he writes to you, you pick up a
book and research it, so you can write back to him
knowledgeably. You're a happier, richer person for
knowing him and you know what? So am I.

I'm so upset, Button. I've ruined something
amazing. Why couldn't I just say it back? Why
has it taken me so long to know what you and
Pastor already knew? I'm happier than I've been
in years but also so miserable that I don't know
what to do. How can I be both at the same time?

XO

Mommy

The news came from Charlotte in a postscript to her email. "Oh, there've been some big changes at Hope lately. We've got a new pastor! Pastor Vernon Walker. He seems nice and has a lovely wife and three teenagers. Pastor Schofield accepted a position at James Madison University teaching religion. He gave a lovely good-bye from the pulpit, and there was also a note in the church's weekly newsletter. I'm forwarding it to you. You probably already know this, since I know you and Isaac stay in touch with him, but thought you'd like to see his letter. Of course we'll miss him. He was such a wonderful pastor and a good friend, but I know he'll be an excellent professor and make a great impact in his new position."

Hana opened the attached newsletter, instantly looking for a date and finding it in the footer. It was from over two months ago. He'd written to Isaac many times since then and had mentioned nothing of moving away from Hope and accepting a position somewhere else. Why had he not told them? At the very least, it'd matter to Isaac to know he would no longer be getting pictures of the Madisons' pond. Didn't they deserve to know that he'd up and moved? Hana felt her chest constrict as she read the letter Matt had written to Hope.

Dear brothers and sisters in Christ:
Grace, mercy, and peace to you in the name of our Lord, Jesus Christ.

After much prayer and thoughtful consideration, I have asked for and received a peaceful release from my call to serve at Hope as your pastor.

It has become increasingly clear to me that the Lord is leading me into a new role in His Church on earth. Therefore, I have accepted a position as professor of Biblical Studies at James Madison University in Harrisonburg, Virginia. As you all know, instruction and biblical training have always been at the heart of my ministry. My years at Hope have been filled with joy, warmth, and friendship. You've welcomed me into your homes and hearts, and I pray you have felt welcomed in return.

I ask that you consider my new role at James Madison not in the sense of leaving the ministry but as a continuation of it. My new mission field is a secular university where the hearts and minds of young people are being challenged and where many will either be pushed farther away from Christ or invited closer. College is such a crucial time in a young person's life. It was at a secular university that I, myself, became a Christian. Dear friends, I have felt a burden on my heart and a fire in my bones to be salt and light in this mission field, a field that represents a transitional and formative time in young people's lives.

I feel nothing but continuing love for all of you and will miss you dearly. I invite you to write to me and, if you're ever in the area, please stop by and visit.

I praise the Lord for you and for what He is doing through you here at Hope and in Altus and that you will continue in your fellowship with Him and with one another. I will keep you and your new pastor in my prayers, for as St. Paul said to the church at Philippi, "I thank my God in all my remembrance of you, always in every prayer of mine for you all making my prayer with joy, because of your partnership in the gospel." And I ask that you keep me in your prayers as well.

In Christ's love,
Matt

His contact information, including his new address, was listed at the end of the letter. Hana had stopped drawing breath upon learning of his new location—Harrisonburg, Virginia. She brought out her phone and opened her maps app, but her hands were trembling so much she could barely make her fingers type. She had to try three times before she correctly typed in Harrisonburg to Richmond, Virginia. A little over two hours—he was only a little over two hours away from her. She sat at the kitchen table shaking with the news. Two years had gone by since he'd sat across from her at this very table. She'd spilled her heart out to him, and then he'd done the same. But she'd met his open heart with a closed one, his words unable to penetrate and her mind unable to compute in the moment. She'd now spent two years computing it, more than long enough to let his words finally sink in and her heart, like receptive soil, to accept it. The more she'd healed, the more she'd found herself ready to embrace love—both God's and Matt's.

It was a Thursday. Hana looked at the calendar on her phone. The weekend ahead was wide open. The beginnings of a plan were forming in her mind. It was spontaneous, but once the thought took hold of her, it spread until she felt the rightness of it to her core, until she couldn't imagine doing anything else.

The trembling had stopped, and in its place was—what had Matt called it?—a fire in her bones. She sprinted down the hallway to her bedroom, pulled an old suitcase down from her closet, and lugged it back to Isaac's room, where she plopped it on the bed and unzipped it.

Isaac looked up abruptly from where he was lounging on his beanbag chair. He watched in silence as she began opening and closing his drawers, shoving clothes into the suitcase. The question finally came, "What are you doing?"

Hana didn't pause, didn't stop, didn't even look her son in the eye—just continued shoving clothes into the suitcase. Her hands were steady, but her heart had begun thudding hard in anticipation. "Packing. We're going on a trip."

The house was small and neat, part of a larger cultivated neighborhood with a mixture of one and two-story homes, old enough to be surrounded by tall trees but not old enough to be in need of constant maintenance. Hana glanced again at the address in her hand and back up to the cozy home in front of her. It was a one story with dormer windows, which made it look quaint and inviting. There was a sweetgum tree in the front, and their spiky balls crunched under Hana's tires as she parked along the side of the road.

"Is this it? Are we here?" Isaac spoke up from the back, where he sat holding Rocky's cage. It'd been a long two hours. Hana had thought telling Isaac that they were going to see Pastor would make the car ride go easier, but instead he'd been so excited that he'd spoken nearly nonstop since they'd left, asking every minute if they were almost there.

"Yes, this is it." Hana gazed up at the house. Adrenaline had taken her this far, but now that they were here, she felt it seep away, and she was left weak and uncertain, hands idle in her lap. She'd just jumped in the car and gone. It wasn't as dramatic as a last-minute flight, but still—it was pretty dramatic by her standards. *What if he doesn't want to see me?* That niggling worry that'd been nesting in her mind came rushing to the forefront. He wasn't expecting them. His car was in the driveway, so there was a good chance he was home, but would he be glad to see them?

The sound of the car door opening made Hana snap back to herself. "Isaac, what are you doing?"

Isaac looked at her as if she'd lost her mind. "Going to go see Pastor." Unspoken was the obvious, "It's why we came, right?"

He was right. It was why they'd come, and now wasn't the time to hesitate. Hana exited the car along with him, and together they crossed the gumball-riddled yard to the front door. Isaac reached up to open the door, and Hana stopped him just in time. "We can't just go on in, Isaac. Be patient." The trembling was back. Hana reached out and knocked on the wooden door then returned her hand to her side and hid it behind her skirt. There was no response. Maybe he wasn't home. What would they do if he wasn't? Hana reached out to knock again, but Isaac beat her to it and, instead of knocking, rang the doorbell over and over and over. "Isaac!" Hana hissed. "Once is enough." She was going to say more, but the sound of the door unlocking stopped her mid-chide.

The door opened, and Matt appeared. He was dressed in a pair of sweats and a T-shirt promoting a radio station. She'd never seen him so casual, and the sight made her already flushed face heat even more. He'd kept the beard, and it was still gray. It was trimmed close, and there were a few streaks of gray now in his black hair. His eyes were still a steady and brilliant hazel, and they were looking at her and Isaac in disbelief. She watched him blink rapidly, as if trying to make sense of what he was seeing. Isaac, however, wasted no time.

"Hi, Pastor! I brought Rocky with me." He held the cage aloft. "I saw a mouse the other day, and it was half eaten. I wanted to take a picture to send to you, but Mom wouldn't let me. She said it was gross." He brushed past Matt and into the house.

"Isaac!" Hana peered past Matt into the hallway beyond and then back up at Matt, who had turned from staring at Isaac's retreating figure to staring at her, his mouth open, his eyes a question mark.

"Come in, please . . . " He turned, so Hana could follow Isaac.

Hana found that she couldn't move. She stood where she was on the front step and stared up at the man before her and found she couldn't move, not until she'd said what she'd come to say. And now that it was time to say it, she found she didn't know how to start. Vaguely she thought she should pray for the right words now that the moment was here, but even that thought was buried beneath the painful thudding in her chest.

"I realized something." A blurted statement, not at all the beginning she'd silently rehearsed during the drive. "You came to visit us years ago, and you told me something beautiful and wonderful." She watched as Matt turned back to face her. The surprise had left his face and, in its place, an expression she couldn't quite pinpoint.

"You said that it'd taken a screaming, crazy man for you to realize something and that, when you did, it hit you suddenly and clearly."

Tenderness, that was the expression. His face had relaxed until he was almost smiling, and his eyes were so full of tenderness that she was finding it hard to look into them directly.

"Well, it wasn't so sudden for me. It came to me in pieces."

He was coming outside, joining her on the front step. He was taking her hand in his own.

"It took years of missing you for me to finally get it."

In the background, Isaac was still chattering, making himself completely at home. Hana squeezed Matt's hand and looked fully in his face.

"You are our family, Matt. You are our family."

He drew her closer, and she watched as the sun dawned, bright and clear and warm, all across his face.

Hello, Button,

When you were born, my soul latched on to you like a frightened thing. To love someone so completely—it was a new sensation, and I was terrified.

That fear grew as you got older. Would I mess you up? Was I doing enough? too much? I held on to you tightly and didn't know how to let go.

It's freeing to know that I can let go.

God loves you more than I ever could. He invites me to let go, to offer you—my Isaac, whom I love—as Abraham did his Isaac. To not hold anything back out of worry and fear but to come to Him with open hands, willing to give, ready to receive.

Not only do you have a heavenly Father who loves you, Button, but you've been given a new earthly father who loves you too.

I didn't think I could be happy again, not really. I felt like I would forever be chasing something just out of sight. Or rather—that something would always be chasing me. But just as I need to let go of you, I need to let myself go as well, to give myself over to the Father who loves me and to trust in His goodness. And He is good and gracious beyond all understanding!

The other day, we were all three at the park and had stopped at the pond. Your dad was trying to teach you how to skip stones, but we could both tell that you were unconvinced it was a skill worth learning. I was sitting on a bench and just watching the two of you— your dad squatting so intently by the water and you, standing tense and unsure by his side—and it just hit me. I was calm and relaxed because I wasn't grasping at you, taking you in my hands and turning you over and over like a worry stone. No, I was content knowing I could share you, that you are in God's hands and that He, in turn, has given you into your new dad's hands. I'm still learning what this means—we are a family. We hold and share each other, love each other. I'm still learning what love means. Day in and day out God impresses it on my heart, and I'm learning.

Well, I hate to say it, but you did not grasp the appeal of skipping rocks. You finally harrumphed noisily, shaking your head in disgust. "This is just frivolous!" You spouted off and went down the pond to go watch for turtles. Your dad and I couldn't stop laughing. Frivolous.

Your dad sat by my side, put his arm around me, and slipped the unskipped rock into my hand. "Seems a shame to let it go to waste."

We watched you look for turtles until sunset and then went to go get donuts, just like we'd promised you.

"You still have that rock?" your dad asked me as we trekked back to the car, his hand seeking mine and finding the stone still there.

I showed it to him, warm and round in my hand. I didn't want to part with it, to let it slip to the bottom of the pond unnoticed.

We got to the car, and you jumped inside and loudly told us to do the same, to "Hurry up!" You were rattling off a list of your favorite donuts as if debating which was best when we both slipped into our seats. "Powdered and cherry-filled. No, long john. No, chocolate glazed. No . . . "

"I think I'll keep it," I told your dad.

Not to worry it, mind you. Not to slip it repeatedly in and out of my fingers with anxious energy. No, just to keep it. On our dresser at home. To let it sit there and remind me.

"I think I'll keep it to remind me."

"Remind you of what?" your dad asked, squeezing my hand and smiling at me with his eyes. He really does have the most beautiful eyes.

"Oh, I don't know." We began driving to the donut store. You were still debating which donut you wanted to get. You're only allowed one, so it's kind of a big decision.

"I don't know." I squeezed your dad's hand. "Just . . . of everything."

XO

Mommy

ACKNOWLEDGMENTS

It takes a team to create a book, and I am profoundly thankful for the instrumental people God has placed in my life to make sure this story gets told. Peggy Kuethe, editor extraordinaire, your great care and talent shines through in all you do, and I'm so thankful for your encouragement and insights. To the whole team at Concordia Publishing House, you are pros. Thank you for all the tender care you've given and continue to give this book!

To the people who encourage me, both in writing and just in all of life—Lisa, Emily, Rich and Chris, Steve and Christy, Kendra, Lauren, Kristen, Mandy—life is sweeter and the road less rocky when you have such great people cheering you on! Amanda Lansche (aka AGL Creative), you are a rock star! Thank you for being an invaluable first reader and amazing friend. To my beautiful friend Betsy, who is a model of God's grace and strength in action—your love and support are priceless, and *you*, my dear, are priceless! And to My Lovelies: Jordan and Alicia. You girls seriously mean so much to me! You're a steady harbor in any storm, a continuous expression of God's undeserved love to me.

To my family at South County Bible Church, you are just that, my family. Thank you for loving, supporting, and encouraging me! George and Jackie, Dan and Karen, Clegguart and Jenny, Jess, Christina—your investment in my life is so appreciated! To my Kaufman family with love—Donna and Darris, Aaron, Carrie, Lillie, Jenna, Adam, and Desiree. Mom and Dad, for showing me what love in the trenches looks like, and Isaiah for showing me that love is not love unless it's unconditional. Thank you for lovingly coming alongside me as I explored these themes so close to our hearts and to my amazing mom, especially, for being a first reader and lending me honest insights so that this book could be as authentic as possible. And to the rest of my wonderful siblings—Michael, Laura, Efe, Anna, and Domenic—you all bring such joy to my life! To Grandma and Grandpa Mai, Tata, and in loving memory of Nana—some of my biggest fans and dearest people!

Andrew, my support system, my bedrock—thank you for exemplifying the fruit of the Spirit to me, for loving me, bringing joy, harboring peace in our home, showing patience and kindness when I'm impatient and unkind, promoting goodness and faithfulness as pillars for our family, modeling for your sons what it means to be gentle and humble of heart, and for living out the Christian life with dignity and self-control. I can't believe I have the privilege of building a marriage and a family with you! And to my two jewels: Tristan and Seth. Loving you has given me a glimpse into the heart of God our Father. If I can love you *this* much as such a broken and sinful person, how much must our Father love us in all His perfection? Which brings me to my Savior, the One who *loves me*. There can be nothing more extravagant and wonderful than this truth.

We are, all of us, a collection of experiences. I hope this story does justice to those who have had some of the experiences depicted here, and I pray that it spurs all of us on to love more deeply, more completely, and more simply. For we, after all, are the recipients of such love.

XO Heather